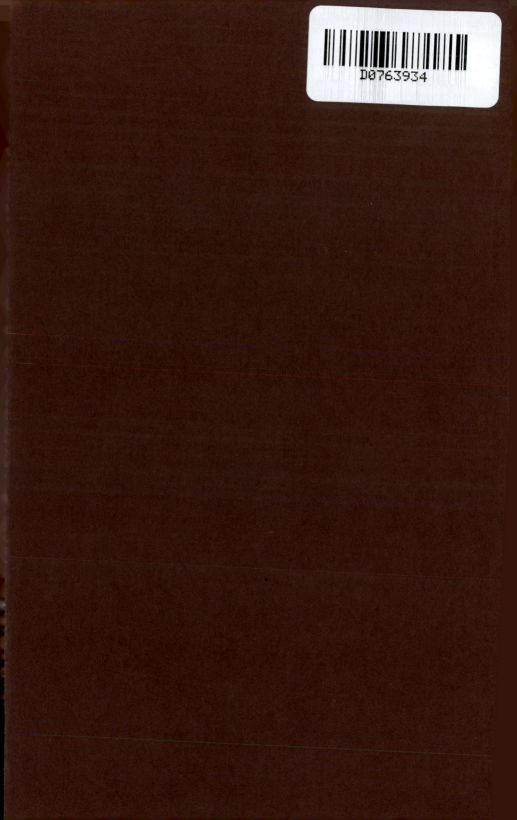

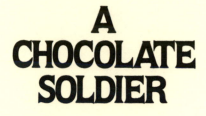

A
CHOCOLATE
SOLDIER

A CHOCOLATE SOLDIER

A NOVEL BY

CYRUS COLTER

THUNDER'S MOUTH PRESS

NEW YORK

Copyright © 1988 by Cyrus Colter

All rights reserved

Published in the United States by

THUNDER'S MOUTH PRESS,

93–99 Greene Street, New York, N.Y. 10012

Design by Loretta Li

Grateful acknowledgment is made to the

New York State Council on the Arts and

the National Endowment for the Arts

for financial assistance with

the publication of this work.

Portions of this book were previously

published by TriQuarterly.

Quotation on p. 278 from "Burnt Norton" in

Four Quartets, copyright 1943 by T.S. Eliot;

renewed 1971 by Esme Valerie Eliot.

Reprinted by permission of

Harcourt Brace Jovanovich, Inc.

First Edition

Library of Congress Cataloging-in-Publication Data

Colter, Cyrus.

A chocolate soldier : a novel / by Cyrus Colter.

p.   cm.

ISBN 0-938410-42-3 : $19.95.   ISBN 0-938410-49-0 (pbk.) : $9.95

I. Title.

PS3553.0477C5   1988

813'.54—dc19   87-25365

                     CIP

Manufactured in the United States of America

Distributed in the U.S.A. by:

CONSORTIUM BOOK SALES

213 E. 4th Street

St. Paul, Minnesota 55105

612-221-9035

TO IMOGENE

and from the early days—

IN GRATITUDE TO:

MICHAEL ANANIA

DAVID RAY

AND

MORTON WEISMAN

A CHOCOLATE SOLDIER

1

ONE THING I REMEMBER about that afternoon, almost as vividly as I remember the aristocratic old white woman we would encounter, was something as quixotic as the scorching rays of the sun. The temperature was possibly a hundred degrees. Across all these intervening years, I can still see Cager perspiring as he harangued me with an outstretched arm and splayed, gesticulating fingers. This, though, was but a minor display of his uniqueness—as seer, soothsayer, crystal gazer, but also chameleon. Sui generis, then, is probably the aptest expression to apply to him—even as murderer.

Murderer, you say.

Precisely. True, the ordinary murderer is by definition not all that unique. Hardly more so than, say, a sitting hen, a computer, a flat tire, or a pederast. But Cager was not ordinary. He was to kill, yes, but he somehow was not a killer. Rather he should be seen more as justifier, redresser, as a kind of visionary paragon installed here to put things aright. In these qualities lay the acid flavor of his differentness.

On this seemingly innocuous day in question the two of us were standing in the humid shade of that big old magnolia tree in the courthouse square, where we were waiting for the Jim Crow bus that went out by campus. "Rev," he said (this was his nickname for me as a divinity student), "do you ever get tired of being a boot? Don't it get you down sometimes?" "Boot" is what he called blacks, though the more proper term most of us used in those days was either "Negro" or "colored."

"Not particularly," I laughed. "Does it get you down? There's nothing we can do about it, anyhow."

"But would you if you could?" He was earnest, frowning.

I had to hesitate and think. He was always coming up with some baroque observation involving blacks. He had this fanatical, proprietary hang-up about them; angry with them one minute, tender, or fiercely protective of them, the next. "I guess I would if I could," I finally said. "At least that way get rid of some of the hassle."

He was adamant. "If you wanted to you could overnight. It's no big deal—not like if you was trying to be white. The only thing you got to do is *think* white. Huh?"

3

Early September, the harbinger, though on faith, of eventual relief from the heat, had finally come to this stifling town of Valhalla, Tennessee. Now Cager stood swabbing his brow with the heel of his hand, next glancing up at the courthouse clock, before turning to look across the street where, stripped to the waist, a labor gang of sweltering blacks was digging a ditch into which later the white engineers would lay a gas main. "See what I'm talking about?" he said, pointing. "*Tote* that bar, *lift* that bale," he mocked to me. "There we are, Rev. That's us, man. All the time thinking black instead of white. How long, oh Lord, how long?" He gave a theatrical sigh.

Long, tall, rangy, loose-jointed, with gigantic feet, a corrugated mahogany complexion, and fierce beetling brows, he slouched merely standing there on the edge of the sidewalk. But even if, as now, he was often a comical sight to watch, I always took him seriously. I admired him, looked up to him, actually, and had confidence in his crusty, perverse judgments, despite the fact we were almost the same age, in our very early twenties.

Suddenly he whispered—"Look out!" He was staring up the street. I saw it then. An elongated, gleaming, black Cadillac, a liveried black chauffeur at the wheel, was coming slowly down our side of Culpeper Street. In the backseat, alone, sat, like the queen mother of England, this white-haired, pink-jowled, patrician old woman staring straight ahead through fierce pince-nez. Cager's mouth was open. So was mine. "Lord, look here what's coming, will you?" he breathed. "That's what I'm talking about. You can tell she's been thinking right—by which I mean white—all her natural life. Ain't she?—you can see for yourself. Yeah, ruling the roost. I wonder who she *is*. Huh?"

The big sleek car was about even with us now. Cager was all but leaning over the curb into the street to get a better glimpse of the regal old matron. But, oblivious, she still stared straight ahead. Then occurred a kind of phenomenon. Suddenly something— fate?—seemed to startle, wake, her. She turned, as if against her will pulled by a magnet, and stared him full in the face. Their eyes met, then held, in a somehow strange, curious, frightened fixation, for just that one brief moment before the stately car moved on.

Ten minutes later, in the back of the bus headed out toward campus, Cager sat silently beside me. He sighed again, once. He sometimes had these brown studies, mute séances, so to speak, when it seemed life presented him as, say, a captive audience of one in some bleak cinema, with this great symbol, this giant

4

lighted, but vacant, movie screen looming up before him. Life, animation, had stopped; did not exist. No one of course can say what his thoughts were but to me at this moment he was a sort of Siddhartha of mystery, his mind almost a misnomer, yet somehow throbbing with its heavy premonitions.

2 ALMOST FROM THE BEGINNING my daughter Carol had been opposed to my going into all this . . . all this history, yes—I still hesitate to use the word. "Memoir" might be better. I must tell you, though, that my definition of history is somewhat singular. It is redeeming and unlike that of many would-be educated people. Even Carol, certainly educated (I have seen to that), has her own skewed definition lacking in many ways the sanction of history itself. That is why I think she so fears history, and of course its rigor, logic, and deterministic implications. I do not fear history (even that brand touted by Pascal). I revel in it. Indeed, from a certain standpoint, this account could be said to treat *why*.

But Carol. I, Meshach (biblical, and pronounced *Mee*-shack), her father and your narrator, have a great dependency on this girl . . . rather, on this most original young woman of sorrows. True, we quarrel, at times violently, yet we are very close, have been all her life. When I told her of my plan to undertake this task, the writing of this "history," she, although trying to hide the fact, was very upset. I feared she would go into one of her tantrums. "How can you *do* it, Father?" she said. "How can you go that far back . . . into . . ." She was distressfully twisting in her chair. The setting is White Plains, New York, where I have now, at long last, after so many peregrinations and crises, settled. On this springlike Saturday morning she and I were seated in my study situated, though almost concealed, just off the rostrum of this little church I— following my great debacle—now pastor. "Father, how can you summon the strength to go back into all that?" she said. She really, though, did not mean "the strength" but "the moral fortitude."

At first I ignored her. "How could I summon the strength *not* to do it?" I finally said, watching her. I thought for an instant I saw her hand trembling. Again it made me conscious of her fear of history. "Yes, I must do it," I said, "although it has in fact been a long time—over thirty-five years. Long before you were born. But I

5

remember it all." What an understatement! It was burnt on my brain. Suddenly I was seized by a kind of manic compulsion to justify the whole project, and ramifications, to her. I got out my keys, unlocked the bottom drawer in my desk, and took out this thick, handwritten-in-pencil, unfinished manuscript. She gasped. When I handed it to her she at once put it back on the desk, as if it were soiled, or illegal, or at least something very embarrassing.

It nettled me. "Look through it," I said. "It won't bite you." I then began giving her a quick summation of how I planned to go about revising, rearranging, refining, the document. Strangely, as I continued talking, I seemed to become oblivious of her presence there in my little book-lined church office. Rather, I began to relive what, so far, I had written. At once it filled me with emotion and I soon seemed no longer talking just to her but somehow to the whole world, actually, even to unborn generations. But what I was actually trying to do, I realize now, was justify not so much the project as my entire life, and justify it not to Carol, nor to posterity, but to myself. "Huh?"—as Cager, God rest his soul, would have punctuated it.

But now, to my surprise, Carol had reached for the manuscript and begun scanning a few pages. I started talking heedlessly then, almost preaching to her, about how, and why, I had begun this unlikely venture, this test of my sanity, what I planned to do on it next, and the fearful challenge the end of the narrative would surely present for me, who had personally participated in so much of the original action. Also, even before she had gotten through the first three or four pages, I wanted to explain to her certain other features of the writing, warn her of the possible difficulties of, for instance, my peculiar, untried manner of presenting certain pivotal episodes, but, above all—this was critical—to reassure her that at no place throughout the text had I become clinical. At this her eyes grew large as she watched me. Soon, though, she was busy again reading other parts of the manuscript and only occasionally lifted her eyes from the page to observe me as I talked without letup. Between the manuscript, then, and my own insistent blatherings she, I am sure, began to get some idea of the utter symbolism involved in the disaster she held in her hands.

So after three decades and more of retrospect—thus went the general drift of what both I and the manuscript were imparting to her—yes, of retrospect, indulged in by me after the facts from away here up North, I began to understand, on more than one level, that what had happened to those two predestined souls on

6

that sultry afternoon down in Valhalla, Tennessee, the highborn old woman and the highly agitated, confused, country black boy, human beings from virtually different planets, had been actually a case of mutual fates in collision. Carol had now placed the manuscript back on the desk and was finally listening to me in earnest, when shortly I was alarmed to see her begin, none too gently, pulling, tugging, at both her ears. She apparently was, for some unknown, unbelievable reason—I have never solved it—no longer able to hear me. So she went rummaging in her purse, took out a pair of sunglasses, and put them on—as if they were a hearing aid. Though temporary, it was a strange, unsettling occurrence, a contagion, really, for I now seemed somehow levitating in a different realm of communication which briefly enveloped me in what felt like some amorphous, exhilarating trance. Oh, Carol.

Yes, then, that collision to which I had been a moment before referring, of the two Valhalla fates, and the aftermath and proliferation, had now, if in a circuitous way, become the undoubted burden of my narrative, a labor, however, which it was my lot to undertake only because the uncut version of all that had taken place back then is, alas, mine alone. But by now Carol, quite serenely, had removed the sunglasses and, it appeared, was once again able to hear me, or so I imagined. She was afterward to sit there to the end and, hardly moving, scarcely breathing, hear me out as I went on to speak of my trials with the manuscript, yet of my hope for it, and how I had assumed this duty despite the fact that I make my living not by writing but by word-of-mouth communication, namely, expounding (the gospel), exhorting (sinners), counseling (the ingenuous), playing all-round shepherd to the flock. I am, then, yes (or was), a true cleric, a man of the cloth, schooled and ordained for it, which, though, here makes my task all the more tricky, precipitious, if not frankly unpromising. And for a host of reasons—both sacred and profane. Yet I persevere.

But also, to make matters certainly no easier, portions of the narrative are based on a complex and, I admit, occasionally apocryphal body of lore, for, no matter what thorny issues become here involved (and they are legion), I have throughout wanted to do the impossible, tell all, *everything,* yet at the same time hold certain things back. Of necessity, then, scenes are at times made speedily to shift, sometimes leaving, here and there, an event to dangle or an incident ruthlessly telescoped. And what you will also find quite evident is not only my florescent (preacherly) style of writing, but the unconventional, that is, nonlinear, way I have of

7

dealing out the episodes to you like a poker hand. None of this is deliberate but, alas, comes from ineptness and inexperience. It does, though, unfortunately, often produce page after page rife with ellipses, plus a pastiche or potpourri of ever-escalating incidents, piled one on top of another, all now and then punctuated, I hate to tell you, by my sad, guilt-ridden, rhetorical outbursts on far, far too many pages of this mangled score, ending finally in the inevitable elisions and erasures betokening my total rout. A holy mishmash. But so be it.

What at long last, then, will—it is hoped—find its way into fair copy derives from a rich, at times passionate, if occasionally melodramatic, variety of sources, some firsthand (from Cager himself), others second- or thirdhand, a few even pure hearsay. Moreover, though rarely, "essential" facts are, or seem, missing altogether, meaning, though again infrequently, that there may be deduced, or even imagined, portions of the account, all handily, even magnanimously, supplied by your fertile, inventive narrator himself.

It must, however, also be remembered that all this—my embarking on this pathless mission—was before I had come fully to know myself, as I actually was, and am. Yet am I really certain about this even to this day? I can only be sure that there exists an almost storied green envy, no matter that I have suppressed it, that I still feel about hero Cager's overly fulfilled, even if in the end tragic, selfhood. He is, yes, my rival. For our younger lives paralleled. This fact, as you will later understand, has impelled me to tell not only his story but, often in closely alternating segments, that of my sorry own as well. Is it not, then, an irony that the success or failure of this effort at chronicling "history" will, no matter what, depend on how clearly I see, and how faithfully I portray, the *hero*? Also—more important still—on how I refract in the white glare of *his* moral light? Yes, irony. But on this fragile axis rests the weight of the drama. Listen.

3 BEGINNINGS.

Two children, boy and girl, walking down this Virginia country road. "Did your mother and father look like you?" he said to her.

She almost stopped. "What do you mean?"

He did not know how to ask it any differently so he said nothing.

8

To the west a bleak winter sun crouched low in the haze and the ground was hard. They were heading home from the two-room Negro school and he, still thinking, tried it again. "Did your mother and father have light skin like you got?"

"My mother did . . . some."

Still puzzled—as was she—he picked up a piece of bark and hurled it far beyond the rotting rail fence.

"What're you trying to get it?" she said.

He observed her, but then, capable of no greater specification, he picked up some gravel off the road and let it filter through his fingers. "I dunno," he finally said.

He was in the sixth grade, she, the fifth. But what set her apart from him and the others was her color. She was whey-faced, almost white. ("Color, color, color!" said our gossipy old closet-radical professor, Moses Wardlow, himself quite black, to a few of us one Saturday afternoon sipping Cokes in his cluttered little house. "Why didn't God make us all the same hue, and with our other physical attributes similar, instead of ordaining all the *myriad tribes of men?*—white, black, brown, yellow, red, and so forth, and so forth! What a ghastly anomaly! Even one of our own campus sororities has fallen for it," he snickered behind his hand. "You know whom I'm talking about, all right." More snickers. "The Betas, of course. Of the twenty-or-so girls making up the roster of Beta Epsilon, only three can be said to be of really dark skin—ha, like my own! But, you see, that trio of sorors has other 'advantages' that offset—to a degree, that is—their unfortunate 'disability.' The father of Alene Farmer is a Memphis physician. Zoe Campbell is a straight-A student, bless her heart, but, besides" (snickers), "has pretty legs and 'nice' hair! Little Coralee Hines, of course, is none other than President Groomes's niece from Shreveport! *Awake,* Black—and I don't mean High Yellow— America! You have nothing to lose but your pigment complexes!") Now the two children were passing the shack of Muncie Henry who sharecropped for Judge Timothy Carr.

"Look!" she suddenly gasped. Behind the house they saw standing in Muncie's lopsided barn door his gaunt old white mule. It gawked at them, then, still gazing curiously but now woebegone, moved its long ears up and down, forward and back, as if somehow plaintively beckoning to them. "What *is* it?" she said. "It's scary!" The ghostlike critter, still propelling its ears, now emitted a feeble bray and started ambling toward them. "Let's go, Rollo!" she said, recoiling—as she addressed the young "Cager" (his later nick-

9

name). "It looks like a hant! It makes me feel bad, like when they slid Mama's coffin into the hearse!"

He grinned. "It ain't no hant. Ain't nothing but a mule. Lord, you city folks."

"Can a mule be *white*?" She was aghast.

He thought for a moment. "This one is, ain't it? But looks like it's going to the glue factory before long. Won't be white then."

Shuddering, Alma hurried on.

She was not a pretty child but her ways were feminine and shy most of the time and he liked that. It made him feel strong and protective. He also felt sorry for her. She had come all the way from Gadsden, Alabama, to the Virginia tidewater to live with an uncle and aunt because her mother had recently died. But the children at school, including himself, were mystified by her whiteness. Never had they seen a Negro person like her. It caused whisperings, even among some parents, who, though, knew better, knew the answer. Although he understood none of it he was angered by the whispers. They made him actually want to fight those at school who engaged in them.

He finally took the matter to his grandmother—"Granny"—his father's mother who lived with them. Granny gave her dry, sardonic cackle, saying, "Lord, boy, don't you know all colored folks ain't colored? Some're black, some're white, some're in between. But we was *all* black when they brought us here from Aficka." For a long time he thought about this; still he did not understand. But his affecting friendship with Alma continued. Vividly, he always remembered the following Easter (her last) and seeing her at the little rural church that Sunday. Although she looked thin, and paler still, he had never seen anyone so dressed up. Her uncle and aunt, trying to divert her mind from her illness and her loneliness for her mother, had taken her into Cook's Grove and bought her a whole new Easter outfit, complete with spring coat, little hat, dress, shoes, everything too, except the shoes, powder blue. Seeing her with the other children in front of the church he knew he liked her more than ever. He sat beside her during the service, then afterward walked her home. "You sure look nice," he said.

She smiled mischievously. "I know it." But her voice was thin and reedy, and once she coughed. "I like to look nice if I can," she said. "I know I'm not pretty, though. I'm too white." Again she coughed, hollowly, as a shadow passed over his heart.

But he could not forget what Granny had said, though only the ensuing years would bring him full comprehension. A font of

10

"old-timey" myths and lore, she was full of odd songs and sayings as well. "From birth to death we travels between the eternities," she said one day to him and his brothers and sisters. The crone then drew on her clay pipe and laughed, "Did you chirren hear that? Then don't forget it." Again neither he nor they had any idea of what she was talking about but, looking at each other, laughed with her. The old woman might then, though, turn grave, reflective, even testy. "You'all may be young now but just the same death's got a warrant out for you!" This always filled them with awe, especially when she followed it up by singing one of her old Judgment Day Songs:

Oh, see the little black train a-comin',
I know it's goin' to slack;
You can tell it by its slow rumblin',
Besides, it's all draped in black.

This old train is like a phaeton,
It has no whistle, no bell,
And if you find your station
You're either in heaven or hell.

Oh, see the little black train and engine,
And one small baggage car;
But you won't need no baggage
When you get to the judgment bar.

Rollo asked his father what Granny meant by all this queer talk and singing, but Amos Lee, limp in his chair before supper, bone-weary from his long day in the fields, only went on nodding until he had fallen asleep as the boy talked.

The family lived on a forty-five-acre piece of land that Amos sharecropped for Nathan Blatchford. Although he was not, Blatchford seemed as poor as his tenants, if one noticed only his ragged overalls, worn-out brogans, or the hole in his hat. But the tenants knew better and said he could also be mean and unreasonable, even for a white man. Yet he was confounding too, his behavior beyond predicting. His children, the boys *and* girls, sometimes visited and played with the Negro children, and Blatchford, but never his wife, liked attending the Negroes' little church almost as much as his own. One Sunday morning he became so aroused by the visiting preacher's loud sermon, the praying, moaning, humming, and singing, that he jumped up and began outshouting everybody—no mean feat, for Rollo's Granny, although a tiny woman, was herself a great shouter, and huge Emmy Beecher, a

11

childless widow, was known far and wide for the uproar, fist-swinging, and violence of her own shouting.

But that day Blatchford, a big man, outdid everybody. He was a spectacle. Members of the congregation ducked and dodged his rushing, stampeding, and bellowing more than they ever had Granny's or Emmy's. It was pandemonium and took five minutes to bring under control, leaving Blatchford panting and drenched in sweat but sated and momentarily humbled. Yet, a few days later, in a fit of arbitrary rage, he knocked one of his tenants down with his fists for a trifling infraction amounting to nothing. The following Sunday, however, he was back at the church as if nothing had happened.

"Sure, sure, wouldn't you know it?" someone in the congregation whispered.

Things got quiet. More whispering began then and soon everyone was looking up at the pulpit to the regular pastor, Reverend Minnifield, to see what, if anything, he would do, for as the minutes passed and the little church filled up they thought Minnifield might do what they themselves were afraid to do, namely ask Blatchford to leave. Rollo, by then a teenager, recalled to me years later how the beefy, red-faced landlord had sat there midway in the church, but off to himself, and stared up at the pulpit where uneasy Minnifield, himself a Blatchford tenant, was waiting to begin the service. But as time ticked on everyone was getting as upset at the pastor as at Blatchford. Then before anyone knew what was happening big Emmy Beecher was on her feet. She was frowning hard and, nostrils flaring, breathing hard, as if the time had come, her patience not only exhausted but outraged, for her herself to take charge. A hush fell over the church.

"Reverend Minnifield!" cried Emmy up at the pulpit. "We got business to take up 'fore you start preachin' here this mornin'!"

"Oh, no, now," somebody whispered. "Shhhh."

Everyone suspected, even knew, what was up—except Blatchford.

Nervous Minnifield half stood. ". . . What business, Sister Beecher?"

"Aw, Reverend Minnifield," said Emmy disgustedly, but pointing at Blatchford, "what do you mean 'What business?' He's the business!"—still pointing. "He ain't got no right to set foot in this church no more after what he done. You oughta tell him so, Reverend Minnifield!" She turned again to Blatchford, whose red face bore an incredulous, shocked expression. "Mr. Blatchford, the other day you beat up Cready Mott, a member of this church, somethin' awful, with your two fists, when he hadn't done nothin' 'cept keep your boar with his sows two or three days longer'n you told him he could. He can't even be here this mornin' on account of his face is swolled up like a punkin. But I see you's here, all right—just like you was one of our members. You got your nerve, Mr. Blatchford! You could be taken to court for what you done, only the judge wouldn't do nothin' to you, we all know that. But if you *do* think you're a member here, I'm for puttin' you out. I'm willin' to give you a church trial, all right, if Reverend Minnifield and the others here say so, or even if you say so, *sir,* then *out you go!*"

Everyone sat stunned. Emmy had gone *too* far, they thought now. There was not a sound, only the frantic fear in the air. This could mean bad, bad trouble, it was the general frightened consensus. You did not talk to a white man, much less the landlord of many of them, like that, somebody who could put you off his place, with no trouble or recourse, quick. Emmy's audacity had immobilized them. Even Blatchford sat with the stupefied look still on his face, until finally he spun around and glared at them all, especially his own tenants. The fear mounted. Nor was Minnifield saying anything, only fidgeting and moving his lips as if any moment he had meant to interrupt Emmy but had then thought better of it and done nothing. Suddenly then Blatchford stopped his truculent staring and rose. Head bent, chin rammed down on chest, fists clenched, he barreled out of the church.

Cager said that although eventually none of them lost their tenancies, within the month Emmy was dead. It was a stroke. She had been having sundown supper one hot August evening in Joe and Mamie Mims's backyard. Mamie had made a peach cobbler for dessert and Emmy was enjoying it despite the flies which Mamie kept shooing off with a willow branch. Soon Emmy, her eyes staring wildly off in space, began an incoherent babbling monologue. She thought she was talking to Mapes Beecher, her dead husband. Joe and Mamie, much disturbed, could tell she was out of her head. "Mapes," said Emmy, "I knowed what you was up to all the time. You wasn't fooling me none. I remember how cold it was—coldest winter since I was a girl. You was heating water for old Mr. Townley's bath, wasn't you? Lord, he was eighty-seven *then,* and you thought that was enough, didn't you? If he'd kept on he'd been ninety before long—ha, you didn't want that, no sir. Remember? Then when you was carrying that big thing of scalding water to the tub you slipped and fell. But old Mr. Townley got burned worse'n you did, 'cause he was naked. Or 'cause you aimed it at him, one. Shoot, *I* don't believe it was any accident, I don't care what you say. You hated that old white man and wanted to see him dead, or at least burnt bad. But he didn't die on you, did he?— not for another three years; ha, when he *was* ninety. Lived long enough to get his son's boy, Jasper, elected town marshal of Cook's Grove. That right? Then you tried to get Jasper when you couldn't get his daddy, Herman, didn't you—messed up the brakes on his Overland. But Herman got you first. Then sent the biggest ham I ever saw in my life for your wake. I don't lie, Mapes. Now Jasper's doin' right well. You probably know. His daughter, Emerald, married Judge Tim Carr's youngest boy. Blatchford damn near died. He hates the Carrs and all their works. But I don't get it—what's Jasper's children to him? Blatchford's got two daughters himself that'll be marrying age before long, but he wouldn't want one of 'em to marry a Carr. Ain't nobody figured that one out yet. But, you know, Mapes, you was after all the slickest one of all of 'em. You proved it and I give you credick. I missed you there for a while but got over it. Us folks ain't got no time to be spendin' on feelings. It's hang tough or go under. Always has been. So I made it a rule since you left to be hard, and keep my mind busy, and talk to Jesus. No, I don't miss you no more. That's the truth, Mapes, I swear 'fore God. Only thing I miss is we didn't have no kids. But I don't miss *you* none at all! . . . God bein' my judge, I don't!" She was crying now.

A week later, deep in a coma, her stertorous death rattles rocking the room, yet surrounded by friends and admirers, she passed. Cager said her funeral was the biggest that colored folks ever had in those parts. Blatchford read the Scripture lesson.

4

PARALLEL BEGINNINGS.

During my own, your narrator's, adolescence—down on the farm in Texas—I was always hungering (not hungry, but hungering), although I was perfectly innocent of any awareness of symptoms, or causes, or cures. I did not so much as understand that I had a soul. And, to be honest, I am not too clear on that whole subject today. My little mother, Maude, however, detecting my strange malaise, sought to relieve it by trying to *talk* me out of it, comfort me, telling me that in every boy's life there came such times of frustration and confusion—the "jimmies," she called them. I did not necessarily take to this, though, knowing she was away out of her depth, that she understood practically nothing about boys' lives, and, beyond any paradox, knew even less about mine. Her attempts, then, to help were for the most part unavailing. Bless her anyway.

We lived on this scratchy little farm—which, however, Maude owned—in the northeastern-most corner, or pocket, of the state. I could almost have sailed a shard of rock over into Arkansas. On the lovely summer morning in question, following a hard rain, I—then fifteen—was on my way into town. Maude had sent me into Sheets (Texas), population 4,100, to try to find a secondhand set of harness for this young plow horse she had just acquired in a somewhat ingenious trade. But I was driving our old sorrel mare, Pearl, hitched to a gravel bed, in to see about Mom's business. It may have been the odd way I felt, though, that had some bearing on my perverse reaction to all I saw around me. This despite the fact that it was a gorgeous bucolic scene right out of a Turner watercolor—everything wet, fresh, green, beautiful. But all to what purpose? I thought.

It had been raining on me and Pearl most of the way but it had stopped now. The sky had brightened and soon there came this great arching tutti-frutti rainbow across the heavens. The trees dripped water, the wood thrush and sparrow hawks were still heavy-winged, and even the millions of blades of grass glistened like a carpet of East Indian jewels. But it was that great arc of prismatic colors high above that stirred me—that is, until I realized I knew nothing about what caused it, or what, if anything, it meant. Super-religious little Maude always had one answer for everything—God. So I accepted this and thanked Him for whatever I happened to experience, including the "hungering" days and nights that so unceasingly plagued me. Today was no exception.

Now I could hear the wet creaking of Pearl's harness, watch the steam rising off her flanks and her all-too-visible ribs, and see the foam flecks flying back from the bit in her mouth. I knew I loved that old horse, although the more we fed her the bonier she got. She was almost as old as I, for it seemed I had known her from beginning memory. She whinnied now as, nearing town, we skirted the edge of Barker's Bluff and came out into, on either side, small, low mounds of clodded earth yielding a morass of wild grapevines fronting a clump of oaks. It somehow made me think of possum hunting.

When we got into the town square I pulled on the reins, whispered "Whoa" at Pearl, and soon had her hitched in front of my destination, Mr. Nellis's general store. I went in. The sudden shock then nearly made me reel. "*Oh!* . . . oh, Lord!" I breathed. It was *she!*—Mr. Nellis's daughter-in-law Cass, except for her two small children the only person in the place. Ah, what bad luck this was for me! I thought—not because Mr. Nellis wasn't there, but because *she was.* What a woman!—so terrific to look at; still under thirty, florid, busty, suntanned legs bare, her wild, tangled straw-colored hair in such profusion it almost hid her virile profile reminiscent of Julius Caesar's, all carried on a buxom, lascivious frame. She made the town's men drool. That was not all. She it was who had first aroused, jarred, my own fantasies and reveries, inflamed my sexual longings in a manner fit to make them oxidize and consume. Ah, but also fit to fill me with a chilling, deadly fear—of the rope and tree!

Now Cass, squatting between her two pawing little boys, looked up from the apples she was sorting, though not at me; at Pearl. "*Mee-*shack," she said in her Texas drawl, "why don't you'all feed that dern old nag? She's about to fall down."

"We feed her," I said, and smiled. But there was chaos inside me—the hungering. "I came in to see Mr. Nellis for my mother. Is he here?"

She emptied the pail of better apples into a bushel basket. "He's over in Cooper at the auction," she said. "I can take care of you."

Oh, there she went!—torturing me; it hit me, hurting like a sudden pang in the groin. Would that she had meant it differently! Oh, had she only known what utter truth she spoke—of her capability. How, too, could I have taken care of *her!* That was why she had always been—at this early time there had been no other—in my hot reveries, when at home alone in the barn I would "abuse" myself. I would fantasize about her yawning thighs, the tangled yellow pubic hair, her flailing red heels, as well as my own trembling young brown body in congress with her freckled white flesh, as I humped myself in Pearl's vacant stall and whispered prayers, prayers to Him both of thanks and for my yearned-for escape from this terrible hungering. My prayers of course went unanswered. I understood none of it. In those days I was a walking quandary. Psychologically, I itched.

16

Later, though, by age seventeen, I was slipping the few miles over into Ashdown, Arkansas, there to visit the colored whores (the "hightown fluzzies," they were called), who so loved to call me "Baby" and "Pig Meat" as they wrestled, grunted, and wallowed on top of me. Was it, though—come to think of it—really Ashdown? Or Sybaris, Arkansas? And I its sybaritic vassal with my foretold future already well laid out for me?

Aughhh!—how sordid, you say. How, you ask, can you claim these two so-clearly-different beginnings, yours and Cager's, "paralleled" each other? My reply is that the common, though absurdly ironic, thread entwining us was our hungering. His, though, was to be in furtherance of a mighty cause and was lofty, while mine, whose inauguration you have just witnessed, bespoke flesh, naked flesh, and was base. It is nonetheless my stubborn perversity in this narrative to insist on by some means sharing his spotlight. Like Banquo's ghost, it will not "down." Indeed, for me, it has now itself become one more variety of my hungering.

Let us, then, rename this phenomenon I have called parallelism and make it, more accurately, "the rivalry," though it was never such to him who was oblivious of all trivialities. So this farcically one-sided bond between us at least affirms the obvious, namely, that I as well as he would, so to speak, writhe in the fiery furnace. On this consult Daniel in your Bible. My given name, you will see (bestowed by little Maude), is not "Meshach" for nothing. Here, then, on the vaster canvas, despite all my self-pitying and bewailing of my failed aims and visions, larger truth is somehow never violated nor moral plausibility even strained. Remember, Cager was himself, as I have indicated, no royal-blooded scion. His role started as inconspicuously as mine. But soon, then, at an early stage his took off like the streaking meteor it was, leaving me, over this whole ensuing span of years, fairly rankling with an envy I have often, defensively, called "moral."

We were, however, in this connection (and in my defense), both born, yes, black and poor in the rural South. The South too is where we would ordinarily have drudged out the remainder of our lives. But something predestined—I do not know what else to call it—intervened. It portrayed, it fixed, us as we really were and would always be. I, Meshach Coriolanus ("Preacher") Barry (the imposing Roman middle name is of my own choosing at age nineteen in an attempt to offset my dear little mother's horrible

17

earlier choice of "Meshach"), was born in the extreme north-eastern corner, a mere niche, of, as I say, Texas, while my Olympian friend, Rollo Ezekiel ("Cager") Lee, was a by-product of the great effluvia of tidewater coastal plain known, in part, as the ("Old Dominion") state of Virginia—already introduced. Yet we somehow managed to escape these thwarting environments and in the midst of World War II get ourselves, he a year ahead of me, admitted to this small all-Negro college, Gladstone, in this town (small city) of Valhalla I have mentioned in southwestern Tennessee—only thirty-eight miles north of rampant Mississippi. Here it was, though, that, as we studied our books and went to classes, we tried to support ourselves by any manner of side employment, in any case meager, likely to come our way.

But I had arrived at Gladstone with the naive expectation of having myself transformed. I was to be molded, according to Maude's quiet but implacable specifications, into an educated, *God-fearing* preacher. She, in her soft but fanatical way, had, long before, all but decreed it. But my confidence wavered from day to day although I badly wanted her to succeed. Already, even at that early time, a boy near to being, psychologically, in extremis, I could only hope. Yet at times I seemed helpless, as if in the grip of some cold automation, which brought a sense of real doom, until somehow then a strange euphoria might descend over me, when, inexplicably, I would almost exult in my ignoble plight. At once this would shock me. Thankfully, Maude—may she be granted eternal rest—was not to survive to experience all the sequels.

Early on, though, she would have adored what she saw. I, her very strange and only child, would not just become a "preacher," or even a "minister of the gospel." Rather, I would go on to scale the ecclesiastical heights, as it were, transcend the lower and middling stations, the outposts, and eventually attain that high palmy eminence of the robed academic, that is, for a time (before, as I say, disaster struck), the chaplain of this small but extremely toney (white) eastern college, a *lecturing* "preacher," if you will, with four divinity degrees (though two *honoris causa*) plus, much earlier, a year and a half's graduate study at Yale.

But at Yale, strangely enough, I became more interested in reading literature than in studying the world's great religions. Although I would never have told my mother, I really craved to become some kind of heavy, polysyllabic, grand—yes, Miltonian—poet.

18

Hence loathèd Melancholy
Of Cerberus and blackest midnight born, etc.

And this is a fatal inclination I harbor to this day, which is doubtless already apparent to you in some of the prolix, studied, even (would-be) grandiloquent syntax of this writing. But it is also, and quite necessarily, because the sheer weight of Cager's dark spectral presence, which indeed survives, all but mandates it. Yet, too, as a saving grace, there are lighter, actually often hilarious, moments, the product of the hero's multiple misfires, the burlesques, his unwitting mad comedy of errors, all before tragedy moves in. Listen, yes.

5

Down in Virginia it was a scorching summer morning as Rollo, wielding a tough sapling stick, decapitated plants and flowers—morning glories, honeysuckle, hydrangeas, ferns—along the roadside as he walked, strolled, with the absentminded, playful-colt vigor, yet concentration, of any boy left to his own lonely devices for a time, though biding that time until, the journey over, he would find at his destination far more interesting things to do. Now suddenly he realized the flowers he was destroying were beautiful and at once he was contrite, laying off with the stick now and stopping the carnage, though knowing that by noon the July heat might well already have played havoc with these florae even if the Virginia crops, the Cherokee roses, the dogwood, et cetera, were all well past their burgeoning time and in sync with the country schools which had been out since May. These, though, were low-priority matters and his mind, along with his feet, moved on. He was on his way to pay an annual visit. Each summer he spent a week or ten days with his favorite aunt, Bernice Tidings, his mother's maiden sister, in Knightstown, county seat of adjoining Greenway County. Abruptly now his span of thought was broken by a rivulet of sweat trickling down his right temple. He removed the big floppy straw hat he wore, and in which in a paper napkin he carried a sandwich, in order to swab the perspiration from his brow with his shirtsleeve. The heat always seemed to him somehow to hit hardest on these backcountry roads where the heavy air, commixed with a broiling sun, pulsed and shimmered knee-high above the gravel, the weeds beyond the road, and even the drainage culverts underneath the gravel.

It was strange, though maybe not, that the heat always made him think of the Prestons. It *was*, however, always in the summertime when he encountered them. They were the Knightstown family, smug, casual, and fairly well-to-do, whom his Aunt Bernice worked for as live-in cook and maid-of-all-work. Except, though, when on the blazing country roads as he was now, the heat, or something vaguely resembling it, as, say, faint miasmata, seemed to him most stifling whenever he found himself in the Prestons' presence, an experience having such a constricting effect on him he was seldom if ever at ease. It was not that he was afraid of them, for they had not mistreated him, or that he was unduly awed by them, but only that somehow he was uneasy around them.

On he trudged in the heat, his stick now idle in his left hand while with his right he ate the sandwich. He would reach Knightstown in little more than an hour, unless sooner by getting a ride, and anticipated the happy prospect of seeing his aunt again though wondering what tomorrow, or even today, might bring with the Prestons, for suddenly again he had that strange feeling—a vague caution, a slight breathlessness, even a trace of awkwardness, though never quite fear. No matter, as always he rather sensed something in the air, did not understand it necessarily, but knew it was there. On arrival he was told by his happy Aunt Bernice that tomorrow they were all going to the fair—the Greenway County Fair! He wanted to be glad—he *was* glad—especially when Bernice described it so vividly and with such enthusiasm.

Next day, therefore, they were both up early and he helped her with her work. It was Saturday, and another sweltering day, when slightly past noontime the Preston family made ready to descend on this annual county extravaganza sprawled on the outskirts of town, there to see and hear the gaudy, outlandish sights, raucous sounds, all the color, activity, and hoopla, and then later attend a "speaking" in the big forum tent. The clan comprised Langhorne Preston, one of Knightstown's leading lawyers, his wife Isabella, the three Preston children, Matt, Dillie, and Warner—all the children except Warner slightly older than Rollo—then Bernice, obese, excitable, naive, also a worrier, and (his first time ever at a fair) Rollo. At 12:30 as he and Bernice waited out on the big back porch, which faced onto the garage, for the Prestons to emerge from the house, he, who had been so high-spirited and talkative

20

with his aunt all morning, had now retreated into a silent, moody meditation. Mere thought of the Prestons skewed his mind. Suddenly then they all appeared, as if on stage cue and in full pomp and pageantry, while he lowered his gaze and tried to keep his mind away. Finally he summoned the resolve to observe them— once.

Soon now the party, numbering seven, all piled into the lumbering old Packard and prepared to leave. Preston, a large man with a profuse head of russet hair and a cavalryman's handlebar mustaches, bent over the steering wheel and first peered down hard at the fuel gauge before starting the motor and driving off with his "family." The car, in the oppressive sun glare and heat, soon moved over the asphalt and scalding tar of Belmont Street and on out toward the fairground. Rollo and Bernice, she in the mandatory white uniform of the domestic, occupied the two jump seats in front of the Preston children and sat silently listening to Dillie's and Matt's aggressive prattle. But Warner sat, even as Rollo, stiff and glum.

Dillie, in age the middle Preston child, thirteen, blond, captious, headstrong, said to her brothers: "First *I'm* going on the Ferris wheel."

Matt, the oldest, responded. "Okay, but *my* money's going for baseballs."

Dillie laughed. "I know what for, too, Matt!"

Warner looked as confused as Rollo. "We've got baseballs at home," he said. "Why do you want to buy more out here?"

"Oh, stupid," Dillie said. "That's not what he means. He's not *buying* them. You weren't with us here last year, were you? You pay to use the balls to throw at the nigra man in the sideshow tent. He sticks his head out through the hole in the canvas curtain. It's a game but you can win real money. They call it 'Beaning the Blackie.'"

Rollo had frozen stiff as ice.

Warner gravely thought over what he had heard. "What if you hit him?" he finally said. "A baseball could kill him."

"Nobody's ever hit one of them yet," laughed Matt. "They're too good at ducking. Wow!—wait'll you see."

Warner pondered this, as Rollo, rigid, throat dry, heart pounding, sat staring straight ahead through the windshield.

Suddenly Langhorne Preston slammed on the brakes. They had just passed a farmer's makeshift Saturday fruit and vegetable stand and, on second thought, he backed up and stopped in front

21

of it. "Those are some good-looking peaches," he said to his wife. "Let's get some, maybe a crate, and put them in the trunk." He turned around—"Bernice, you can make some preserves."

"Sure thing, Mr. Preston," said Bernice.

Impatient Dillie made a face as her father got out and went over to the farmer. Bernice too climbed out and followed him and as he paid for a crate of the peaches she called to Rollo to come help her put them in the trunk of the car. He came readily enough, and as Preston went and unlocked the trunk Rollo and Bernice picked up the crate and started to the car. They were not halfway there when Rollo saw it—a huge black and bronze hairy tarantula, twice the size of a silver dollar, that had emerged from the peaches and was crawling up his bare arm. Grinding his teeth, he stared at it as he walked—just as Dillie saw it too.

"*Look*," she whispered to Matt, "there's a great big spider on his arm."

Rollo, now sweating from more than the heat, steeled himself with all the discipline of which he was capable and continued walking. The tarantula, now on the inside of his arm just below the elbow, stopped crawling.

Matt yelled, "Bernice, knock that spider off his arm!"

Bernice looked and, nearly fainting, dropped her end of the crate, crying out, "*Rollo!* Look! . . . Oh, my God!—don't you see that thing on your arm? That *spider?* Knock it off! . . . hit it! It'll bite you!"

Rollo finally set his end of the crate down, but, trembling, grimacing, still grinding his teeth, he instead held his arm out defiantly for all to see. Time seemed to stop.

It was Preston who now leaped forward, knocked the spider to the ground, and stomped it. He wheeled on Rollo then. "Are you *nuts?* Get in that car!" He threw the crate of peaches in the trunk himself, climbed under the wheel, and, muttering under his breath, drove off. They rode the rest of the way in a tense silence.

When at last they arrived in the fairground Preston told them they were all free to be on their own until just before two, when they would meet back where they were and go to the "speaking" over in the big tent where their U.S. senator, Honorable Cassius Boggs, was to deliver an address commemorating the sixty-ninth anniversary of the Battle of Gettysburg.

"Wow!" said Matt again. "I want to hear him. I'm going to be a senator myself someday."

"Let's hope so," said his father, "but it will take more than talk." Whereupon Preston took his wife off over in the direction of the refectory.

At once Matt wanted to go over to the "Bean the Blackie" sideshow tent. But Dillie insisted they first go ride the Ferris wheel. Matt and Warner finally trooped off behind her, Warner, though, unenthusiastically lagging.

After they had gone Bernice shook her head. "Lord, that Matt. Ain't he something? And talking about wanting to be a senator. You heard too what him and Dillie was saying about throwing them baseballs at that good-for-nothing guy. But, young man, *your* behavior ain't been anything to brag about. Rollo, why would you scare everybody half to death, especially me, letting that awful thing crawl up your arm like that? Or was you just showing off?"

He looked at her as if really wanting to find an answer but at last remained silent. Soon he asked if they could go get some popcorn. Despite the heat the fairground teemed with people roving among the sideshows, exhibitions, and concessions and listening to the shrill, bagpipelike tunes from the calliope and the shouts of sunburned hawkers. Rollo, walking at Bernice's side, was all eyes and ears. A bag of popcorn in his hands now, he next asked her if they could go see the livestock in the pens. She took him around to the barns located across from the racetrack entrance where they soon stood watching the sheep, hogs, cows, and horses. Before long his attention was monopolized by a great roan stallion snorting and rearing in its stall. His eyes riveted on the animal, Rollo stared in wonder at its huge genitals. To him they signified the strength and power of the whole earth. Somehow, though, they also confused him, made him uncomfortable, indeed self-conscious. Granny at home had tried to explain to him, with great patience and sympathy, that when it came to "private parts," her expression, the Lord had not always seen fit to treat all men, all males, alike. He had occasionally thought about this but had found it one more phenomenon in life, about the world around him, that he could not understand; at times things seemed so puzzling and complicated to him they made no semblance of sense. After what Granny had said, he had taken to studying his naked physical presence before the mirror. He also wondered why she, his mother and sisters as well, were always so anxious about him, and so kind, whenever Granny talked this way. Now in the fair barn he stood transfixed, gazing at the great beautiful nervous horse, until Bernice took him

23

away to go watch the baby chicks just hatched in the fancy incubator next door to the seed corn display.

It was then that they heard the shout go up—followed by a wild burst of cheering. "Oh, Lord," said Bernice, "there they go! Throwing them baseballs at that fool again. Let's get away from here, Rollo. It's a shame—*he's* a shame—to let them throw at him like that. It's a disgrace, to *us*, to self-respecting colored people. And you can bet Matt and Dillie are right there taking it all in, maybe throwing at him themselves. Come on, let's go back over to the racetrack and watch the horses run."

"No, no!" he said. "Let's go see. Maybe we can help the man."

"Help him!" Bernice cried. "Why, he don't want any help. They ain't *making* him do it, you know." But he had already veered off in the direction of the clamor. She ran after him. "Oh, Rollo, don't go over there. It'll make you ashamed. I was embarrassed in the car coming here just listening to Matt and Dillie talking and laughing about it. Wasn't you? Why would you want to go watch something like that? I tell you it's a disgrace! It's ugly! And everybody connected with it is ugly, too!"

"Why do they throw at him?" he asked excitedly over his shoulder.

"It's because it's ugly, that's why! It's dirty!" Panting, she was trying in vain to keep up with him. "But you do what you please. I ain't about to disgrace *my*self!"

An even greater distance separated them now. "You wait here, Aunt Bernice!" he cried. "I'll be right back! . . . I won't be long—I just want to see! I bet we can help him!" He was gone.

Soon, as he approached the commotion, he saw the big sign in front of the tent. BEAN THE BLACKIE! it proclaimed. A man standing beside it was shouting, "Step up, folks! Right this way! Get your fun right here! There're cash prizes, too, if you can hit him!"

Rollo came up behind the noisy throng now, just as it let out another shout, followed by still more raucous cheering. Soon he also saw at the head of the crowd a big man wearing a sailor straw hat, a baseball in his right hand, standing like a frustrated pitcher on the mound waiting for the batter he had so far been unable to get out all year to step in the box again.

"Curve him this time, Jake," someone called to him. "You'll never hit him with straight stuff." It was Jake's friend, Wilson, tall, gaunt, features withered and unshaven, pushing through toward him.

However, Jake, the thrower, sweating through his shirt, ignored both the advice and the adviser and still stood waiting.

Suddenly the target reappeared. At the other end of the rectangular tent, protruding from a twelve-inch-in-diameter hole in the canvas backdrop, the sweating black face loomed. Leering now, it cried out in a strange high falsetto voice, "Come on, white folks, try it agin! See ef you kin hit me! You'all been tryin' all day but ain't done it yet! You still cain't, neither! Come on, throw yoh little old white ball on up here! I'll ketch it in my mouth, my teeth, and *spit it out!*"

Jake wound up and, grunting, threw the ball with all his might, as another shout went up from the crowd. The smirking black face had not deigned to move although the speeding ball missed it by less than a foot.

"You see there, white folks!" cried the black target. "You'all caint hit me! I'm too smart for you! You ain't hit me yet, has you? Hah! Hah! Hah!"

Jake's friend, Wilson, had pushed through now. "Goddamn it," he said, "I told you to *curve* him."

"Get outa here, Wilson, and leave me alone." Jake was already gripping another ball.

"Here, gimme that," Wilson said, wrenching the ball from him. "Watch me tear his bur head off."

Jake, winded, sulking, at last stepped back.

Rollo, in his excitement hardly able to breathe, had eased his way still farther forward into the crowd where everyone was waiting for Wilson now to throw. But for the moment he and the black head as target only eyed each other. Rollo shivered from his nervousness; his heart felt in his throat.

Then with one quick violent southpaw motion Wilson let fly, hurling the ball underhand with the speed of lightning. The black man never saw it. Or else misjudged it. The ball, zooming, suddenly broke into him, connecting between the eyes and hurtling him back out of view, as the crowd in unison let out a great shocked gasp. "*Good God!*" somebody said.

Someone up front screamed then. It was Dillie. Soon she was hysterical and Matt, at her side, was trying with no success to calm her. Warner, on the other side of her, for a moment was speechless. Then he yelled at Matt— "*I told you!* I told you it could kill somebody!"

The sideshow proprietor and two other men had already run

25

back behind the canvas curtain to the black man. Soon the excited spectators were loudly conferring among themselves, speculating on the extent of the injury, waiting for some word.

A seedy farmer in overalls now laughed to those around him, "Jake and Wilson ere gone already, by golly. Vamoosed in a hurry, didn't they?" Rollo too had seen them hurriedly go—Wilson, with Jake at his heels. The man in overalls then said to the others, "Do you know who they was? No? Jake only pitched in the minors, but, Lord Amighty, Wilson was in the big leagues there for a while. Clay Wilson. Name ring a bell? He pitched for Connie Mack and the Philadelphia Athletics. Was knowed for his speed and control. That is, till the bottle got him."

The proprietor had reappeared from behind the backdrop now and had told someone to go up to the first-aid station and bring back a medic. Also to have them call for an ambulance. The Preston children were huddled together now, looking subdued and scared, ignoring the garrulous talk of the crowd where everyone had an opinion, dire or optimistic, about the black man's fate.

Suddenly then Rollo heard Bernice frantically calling to him from the midst of the milling crowd. When he had finally pushed through to her he found her terrified. "What on earth's happened?" she cried. "Why's everything stopped?" Then she saw the sick expression on his face. "What's the matter with you, Rollo?"

"They hit him." Sorrow weighted his voice.

"Oh, no! . . . I don't believe it! Oh, my God! But it's good enough for him—he had it coming."

He bristled, then stared hostilely at her. "He got hit *bad*! They've sent for help, maybe a doctor." He was in despair.

"Oh, my Lord! I told you not to come over here, Rollo! Now you see, don't you?" He was too shaken to reply.

Soon a man and woman, the woman in a white uniform not unlike Bernice's, arrived from the first-aid station and, the man carrying a stretcher, hurried back behind the canvas curtain. Instead of an ambulance a small pickup truck next arrived and maneuvered around the crowd, though only partially in behind the tent, as Rollo and Bernice could only stand there looking on. Very shortly then the black man was carried out, limp and seeming unconscious, a great swollen bloody knot on his forehead between the eyes, and placed in the rear of the little truck. But just as the vehicle was about to pull off, the crowd gasped again, as if witnessing a miracle, a resurrection. The black man had somehow aroused himself. Although feeble, reeling, his eyes dazed and wandering, he somehow pulled himself to his knees in the truck and, grasping the tailgate, again leered his insolence and definance at the crowd. "You white folks think you hurt me, eh?" he cried out in a high tremulous weakened voice. "Well, you's wrong! I'm tough, I am! You throw at me 'cause you want to kill me and *all* niggers—takin' yoh hate out on me and that way gettin' yoh kinky kicks! But it won't work—I'll still be around, white folks! I'm here to stay! You brought me here, didn't you? I'm the only one that didn't ask, and didn't *want,* to come! I smelt this wasn't no place for me! You *kidnapped me,* white folks, and put me on that ship! I'll never let you forget it, neither! So here I am—you see me, don't you? I'm here and I'll *be* here!—just as long as *you're* here—yeah, right here makin' trouble for you for a long, long time to come! You cain't kill us *all,* you know! We're way too many for you now. It's way too late. Yeah, we'll be right here—*I'll* be here—till you cain't tell us from the rest of you'all. But you won't be here, either, then—it'll be somebody else, somebody different, *and not white*! Hah! Hah! Hah! Suffer, then, white folks—oh, *suffer*! Yeah, I'll be right there in that very tent agin *tomorrow*!" The high, screechy voice was finally depleted.

The crowd was aghast at the insults. And at last furious. Some were soon muttering the direst threats against their defamer. Yet a few were merely surprised, or confused, and others disgruntled, though also unsure of themselves. In any event, by the time the little truck had taken him away most of them appeared greatly relieved, some of them even chuckling, or outright laughing, a few collapsing in laughter.

6 By SHORTLY AFTER TWO the members of the Preston entourage were in their seats in the fairground's sweltering big tent, as laconic old Nate White, Democratic party chairman of Greenway County, and the richest man in any three counties put together, rose to introduce to the large crowd the speaker of the day, their U.S. senator, Cassius Dexter Boggs. "It's a pleasure and an honah," old White said slowly in a frail voice, having recently turned eighty-two, "for me to bring you a man that has done as much as anybody I know for our state—puttickly this region and county. I have known him since he was a little shaver carryin' the

watah bucket out to us at harvestin'. His daddy and me and my brothers hunted coon and possum—and bobcat too—down in Putnam County over fifty years ago. I don't have to go into a long rigmarole about what he's done. You-all know it. He's a fighter. If you don't believe it ask the Yankee Republicans up in the Senate in Washington, they'll tell you. Today he's goin' to talk about the War of Sixty-one, and all we went through in that bad time. Folks, Senatah Boggs."

After the long applause had crested and ceased, Boggs, in his late fifties, slight of stature but with a head of hair like a lion's mane and the stentorian voice of a Baptist country preacher, distinguished in white linen suit and flowing black tie, he required only a half-dozen sentences to get to the meat of his great commemorative subject: "*Yes!* Gettysburg, my friends! It was the season of truth for the South! And Lee was its advance herald! Every southern schoolchild knows this. To be cast in this role was indeed Lee's fate. He did not seek it. He had been bred—he had been *created!*—for it by the Almighty! The greatest military leader West Point, or the nation, for that matter, South *or* North, had yet produced, it was his destiny thus to stand at the crossroads of a furious history!" Boggs paused now and stood dramatically surveying his perspiring, fanning audience, as if to let his words well settle before proceeding: "For at least two generations before 1861 the South and its institutions had been reviled and slandered, its dignity trampled on at will! It was to be Lee's mission to throw down the gauntlet to this tyranny!—if necessary, challenge it *vi et armis,* by force of arms!" His fist struck the lectern, triggering the salvoes of applause that now came up at him.

The Prestons, though not Bernice and Rollo, sat five rows from the front. Langhorne Preston's grandfather, a brevet colonel in the Army of Northern Virginia, had not been with Lee at Gettysburg but would have been had he not been killed, almost at Lee's side, the prior September at Antietam. Preston's eyes merely glowed but inwardly his emotions surged.

"So, my friends," said Boggs, "it was only by armed conflict, *by war,* that the South could ever hope to redress the grievous wrongs done it! Only by cannon, by musket ball—yes, by the bayonet's cold steel—were we ever to regain our honor!"

Bernice and Rollo, he still stunned and preoccupied by events of the past hour, their attendance to hear Boggs all but obligatory, sat listening back in the roped-off COLORED section, far in the rear of the tent.

28

"All of these resolves were personified in Lee!" cried Boggs. "Yet, his prospects were anything but bright sixty-nine years ago this week! His men, although steadfast and courageous as ever, were miserably short of all kinds of supplies. Food was especially scarce. Even horses were dropping dead for want of provender. Many of the men were also without shoes and their hardships and exhaustion from Lee's long forced marches showed not only in their bloody feet but in their hollow eyes and bony faces! Yes, my friends!—it was a dire time for the South sixty-nine years ago today! A *time of testing!*"

At this point an old man, frail, wizened, ancient, strange, his white beard reaching halfway down his sunken chest, entered on a cane and, accompanied by a tall slovenly woman half his age, perhaps a daughter, made his way slowly down the aisle toward the front. He looked in his mid-nineties and near death. Although his beard covered much of his chest it only partially concealed the assortment of military ribbons and medals worn on his faded Confederate tunic. At a snail's pace, of necessity, the bizarre couple continued down the center aisle, looking both right and left for seats as near the speaker as possible. Although a most mysterious pair, as if ghosts had suddenly appeared out of oblivion (no one there had ever seen either of them before), they were finally made room for far up front in the second row.

"But, ladies and gentlemen," the senator was saying, "it was Lee's faith in these very men, in their stamina and bravery, their still-high morale against all hardships, their devotion to *the cause,* that sustained him! Despite all its trials and burdens, the spirit of the Army of Northern Virginia was still as high as it had been at Seven Pines, at Second Manassas, Fredericksburg, or Chancellorsville! This was of course due to one fact and one fact alone: their confidence in their *leader!* A true son of Virginia, of the Old Dominion—*Robert Edward Lee!*" Heavy, prolonged applause.

Rollo, anxieties, worries, about the fortunes of the injured black man now finally forced to the back of his mind, sat listening intently to Boggs, his young guileless face prematurely drawn and engrossed, the body strained forward, the better to see and hear this amazing speaker and the history he expounded.

"Lee, my friends," said Boggs, "realized in the early summer of sixty-three that the Southern cause had reached the crisis stage. He knew the longer the conflict went on, the poorer were the South's chances. The industrial might of the North, its large population, the great material resources, were stark facts he could not ignore. He knew that something decisive must be done while there was yet time. He also knew what it must be. He must *invade the North!*" Riotous applause and whistles—a din.

Rollo, his whole musculature tense and tingling, eyes rapt and glowing like coals, leaned still farther forward, hardly knowing where he was now.

"Lee acted!" cried Boggs, mopping his florid brow. "In June of sixty-three he began his fateful move. As the Army of Northern Virginia marched up the Shenandoah Valley, the men, despite all the hardships and privations, were in the highest spirits ever. They knew what was in the making—history!—and they were eager and ready to take part in it! All the way up the Shenandoah they sang 'Maryland, My Maryland' as they marched, until on June seventeenth they had crossed the Potomac, and by the twenty-third were already approaching Chambersburg, *Pennsylvania!*" Loud hurrahs and more.

During the prolonged cheers and rebel yells the bearded old man in the second row had laboriously pulled himself to his feet, as Boggs helplessly paused. Frowning up at the orator he took from his tunic pocket a tiny red flag on a stick, a miniature Stars and Bars, and half turning to the audience, lifted it as high as his enfeebled arm would permit, for all to see. "*I was there!*" he cried hoarsely, fiercely, his raised hand trembling. He now turned and stared up at Boggs again. "I was there, suh!" he repeated. "My musket slung across my back, I marched with 'em—the Seventh Fusiliers! Sho, singin' 'Maryland, My Maryland,' but many a song of the Old Dominion, too! Lee was riding up and down the ranks on old Traveler and every once in a while waved to us. But he was deep in his own thoughts. He heard us singin', though, all right. But then again he *didn't.* He was too busy listenin' to *hisself!*" Everyone sat puzzled, but unamused.

Boggs, tapping his foot, was also unamused, though trying to make the best of the interruption. He smiled down at the old man, then out at the audience, saying loudly, "I believe we have here today a chapter in that history I have been describing, but history *personified,* in the flesh, thus more real than anything I could ever portray to you by mere words! Here, if I make no mistake, is one of the tiny handful of that revered band—our Confederate veterans!—of the great four-year struggle between the states, who still remain!" He beamed down at the old man—"Am I not right, sir?"

"You ere right, suh," said the other, though almost ignoring Boggs in turning back around to the audience. "Lee was there and

I was there!" he cried—"*I am a witness!*" Then clutching his tiny red Stars and Bars, he sat down again—as a man in shirtsleeves seated behind him tittered and, twirling his finger around his ear, whispered to his fanning wife, "Don't pay the old geezer no mind. He's either goofy or senile—maybe both, ha!"

But Boggs had resumed now: "My friends, we finally then see Lee at Gettysburg, a cozy little hamlet amidst gently rolling Pennsylvania hills. The Army of Northern Virginia had been drawn to it by reports that the town had a shoe factory. Ah, but it was here that fate would intervene. Lee's vanguard, north of town, accidentally—blindly—(because his cavalry commander, General Jeb Stuart, was not where he was supposed to be) ran directly into the pickets and outriders of some unidentified Union forces. But, lo and behold, those forces turned out to be none other than the great Army of the Potomac!—commanded by General George G. Meade! A hundred and fifteen thousand strong! And Lee with barely seventy-five thousand hungry, shoeless men! But what did he do? What, ladies and gentlemen, knowing him, would you expect him to have done? Why, *he struck!* He struck like lightning!—driving elements of the Federals back through Gettysburg and onto Cemetery Hill just south of town, where they sat the rest of the day licking their wounds. You see, it was always Lee on the *attack*—carrying the fight to the Yankee enemy. We all know what a quiet, cultured gentleman he was, from one of Virginia's oldest and most distinguished families—a true aristocrat of the old South. But he was also a cold-blooded and decisive man of action—a fearless *aggressor!*—who not once ever flinched from the bloody test of combat! Gettysburg was one more proof of this—*his Southern valor!*" Long, tumultuous applause and shouts.

Rollo, eyes burning now, body straining ever farther forward, not only to hear and to see but to feel, took a deep, deep breath, sighed, then sat trembling, as Boggs resumed.

"But, my friends, the position to which the Federals had been driven on Cemetery Hill gave Meade the opportunity, indeed, as it turned out, the luxury, of using it as a rallying point to consolidate, redeploy—to strengthen—his forces. And he made the most of it. He knew Lee well, knew his character and methods, for they had served together in the Mexican War as young officers; had even been friends. He knew Lee would strike again—and soon. He was right, of course. Next day, the second day of the battle, and, except possibly for Spotsylvania and Antietam, the bloodiest of the war, Lee attacked both the Federal left flank at Round Top and the

31

right on Cemetery Hill." But Boggs paused now and looked out over the audience with a histrionic countenance and heavy heart, finally saying, "Ah, but, my friends, he failed."

Rollo stiffened. He felt the shock but was still unbelieving. He swallowed now and turned his eyes aside, as if Lee's failure had occurred just then up on the platform beside Boggs.

"Sad to say," continued the senator, "the second day's attempt ended in a terrible and bloody stalemate." He now bowed his head to the audience's somber breathless silence. "Lee," he said, "knew now that the next, the third, day would decide it all, including the fortunes, already hanging in the balance, of the Confederacy itself." Boggs's arms dropped to his side in a dramatic gesture of helpless despair. "Accordingly, he ordered General James Longstreet, his second in command, to make ready on the morrow to attack the Union center, the Federals' other strong point, on Cemetery Ridge, to the south of Cemetery Hill. The desperate gamble was to be taken!"

The bearded old man in the second row had been watching the orator with piercing eyes of displeasure, almost scorn, and finally now outright rage.

"On the afternoon of July third, then," said perspiring Boggs, "the third and last day of the great engagement, after a prolonged and savage artillery preparation, Longstreet, under the dire, fateful circumstances gravely apprehensive and reluctant, sent General George Pickett, a vain, daring, almost foolhardy young man, and his division of Virginians—*Virginians*, my friends!—into the final, the predestined, assault! I declare to you what you must know already, that this was the South's most magnificent hour in all its history! Its most tragic, yes, yet its most glorious!"

Rollo's head, shoulders, and at last his whole torso, experienced electrification; he was dizzy then.

Continued Boggs now in his greatest height of passion: "As the ranks of the Confederates, muskets high, fixed bayonets gleaming in the broiling sun, scarlet battle flags flying, moved out, then up the slope of the ridge, young Pickett, still ever the dandy, dressed to the nines, his long ringlets of dark hair scented and pomaded, his bejeweled sword brandished high overhead, led the assault, turning and crying out to his men, '*Don't forget today that you are from old Virginia!*'" Stormy, prolonged, impassioned applause—pandemonium; most standing now, some crying. Langhorne Preston, surrounded by his loving family, cleared his throat once, then furtively, clumsily, swiped at his left eye to smear the tear already

32

slipping down into his handlebar mustaches. Rollo, limp, eyes glazed now, sat in a kind of numb frenetic inner trance.

In the thunderous din of applause, however, few had noticed that the bearded old man, the little red flag of Stars and Bars still in his hand, was on his feet again. He was not talking, not even attempting to talk, only standing there, his wrathful eyes ever on Boggs.

"But, fellow Virginians," said mournful Boggs, "before Pickett's famous charge had even reached the crest of the ridge, hundreds of his men were mowed down by the Federals' murderous musket and point-blank artillery fire! Yet they kept coming. But not half of them ever reached the top, and even those were so outnumbered and disordered that they were either killed outright or lay grievously, bloodily, wounded. It was tragedy! It was disaster! Before long, then, it was all over. The end. Yes, my friends, Lee had failed. So, therefore, had the Confederacy. We call it now 'The Lost Cause.'"

A pall had fallen over the audience. Utter silence. Some dolefully hung their heads. A fragile old woman near the rear of the tent pinched her red nose again with her wet handkerchief.

"Four thousand of our bravest, our finest," Boggs cried out in anguished lamentation, "died in the three-day hell of Gettysburg, with some twenty-five thousand more wounded, in Lee's valorous frontal assaults in the bloody carnage! Yet, it is that very struggle that we commemorate here today! We do it proudly in memory, in honor, of our imperishable heroes who, during those three frightful days in the very maw of hell, made the supreme sacrifice! Someone has said that Gettysburg was the high-water mark of the Southern Confederacy! That is a true statement, my friends! Yet, over a span of sixty-nine years, we have had the glory of it to celebrate, too! That is no unworthy privilege or purpose! It is our heritage! It is our *glory* also!" Yelling, thunderous applause, more tears.

The bearded old man, excited, vehement, his frail body quivering, still stood impatiently waiting, as if insisting to be formally recognized. But apparently Boggs, in his oratorical fervor, had not even seen him, for now Boggs, pounding the lectern again, cried out once more: "For in that glory we see, and celebrate, *ourselves!* It tells us everything about ourselves as a people! It is what the South stood, and stands, for! It is what makes us what we are today as Southerners! We cherish the motto: 'Blood, Valor, Sacrifice, Honor!' We did not cringe and submit as would a lessor nation or people! Our honor was at stake and we fought and died to uphold it!" He was shouting his words now, hoarsely. "*And may it be ever thus!*" Wildest cheering, handkerchief waving, huzzahs, earsplitting rebel yells, general chaotic tumult. The blood had rushed to Rollo's head rendering him faint; already he saw visions; he also felt a dizzy vicarious exultation he could not possibly have understood.

Again in the tumultuous ovation that Boggs's oratory had set off, the still-standing bearded old man had been forgotten. Yet, the miniature Stars and Bars ever in his palsied hand, he almost hovered over the assemblage as if indeed a ghostly witness, or both a disembodied warning and prophecy. He seemed now to summon all the strength left in his aged, withered body, now near death and dissolution, in this final gesture of vindication, not for himself but for comrades now sixty-nine years in dusty Pennsylvania graves. Somehow suddenly then, miraculously, all eyes, including Boggs's, seemed to have become fixed, riveted, on his little red flag. To all, time appeared to have ceased. Then Boggs, within a few sentences of finishing his speech, but now seeing the crowd's attention again preempted, at last lost his patience. He fixed his aged tormentor standing below him with an angry stare. However, the old man, defiant, embattled, magisterial, once more turned to the audience and for the first time his high, croaking voice carried to the very rear of the tent. "*I was there!*" he cried. "I was with young daredevil Pickett on the ridge and took a minnie ball in the shoulder and another in the neck to show for it! Hear *me* now! I was *there!* Longstreet, 'Old Pete,' we called him, was against the charge! It was hopeless! It was loony! Old Pete cried like a baby! He knowed it would be a slaughterhouse! Lee was a gentleman, sho! He was a butcher and a murderer, too!" The audience gasped. The old man's trembling right hand went up again, waving the little red Stars and Bars, as he uttered his frenzied valedictory: "*Rivers of Southern blood stain his hands forever!*"

With that, followed by the frowsy woman with him—the audience muttering confused, outraged imprecations—he began his slow departure, with his cane painfully making his way up the aisle toward the exit.

When it was all over and the somber but much edified crowd was filing out, Rollo, still in his dazed, bewildered state, let himself be led away by his aunt. It was next morning, then, that Bernice learned from servants up the street, and, her face long, eyes averted, told him, who had hardly slept at all the night before, that the black man who had been hit by the baseball would, contrary to his heated vows to the crowd yesterday, not be back at the "Bean the Blackie" tent today. Or rather, *she* would not be back. The hospital examination had revealed not a man but a woman. Her name was Lizzie, Lizzie something—Bernice could not remember. But that now Lizzie was dead.

7 Up North in Boston.

The sunlight flooding the courtroom hardly entered any longer in a straight beam. It rather seemed falling, a cataract plunging, through the vaulted windows, as the giant old wall clock hemmed and hawed and the dust motes kept filtering down. All the while the clerks and other functionaries, prior to His Honor's entry, hustled about like wretched little spiders, prattling about the fourth race at Aqueduct, or the judge's hemorrhoids, or the tabloid's baseball scores. Time was running fast for me too, your very much adult though hardly wiser narrator, the tension mounting, my heart beating ever faster, yet not entirely from trepidation, for there was also involved this strange admixture of exhilaration.

Think of it, this ritual was being staged for me, for my exquisite benefit. No, more accurately, for my undoing. Already, though, I was impressed by the awesome rite to come and the metaphoric laying on of hands. I fancied the imminent entrance of the specter of first Baron Jeffreys, British lord chancellor, who had hanged some three hundred-odd unluckies from the gibbet in the Bloody Assizes of 1685 following the duke of Monmouth's rebellion. The gavel rapped now and we all stood as thrice the cry of "Oyez" went out from old Casmir Pilsudski, chief bailiff, and, in an aura of august pomp and purple, the law, here verily embodied before our eyes, mounted to the bench. I could hardly bear it and, momentarily losing control, moved my gaze straight up, only there to behold the great grand friezes, their magisterial impersonality, yet bloodily turbulent history, hovering in the very air—Hammurabi, Justinian, Coke/Littleton, Napoleon, Marshall—while high over the judge's dais in scarlet and gold leaf cherubs blew trumpets from fleecy clouds or out of the black maw of Styx and the loftiest entablature of all read: WHERE JUSTICE IS INFIRM ITS TEMPLE IS NULL

I had not been at all surprised, however, when, prior to His Honor,

35

Carol had entered. There were still empty seats, which prompted her to pause and give play to her natural caution and fussiness before choosing a place midway the chamber and, having sat down, admantly kept her eyes away from me—I, her erstwhile dread but familiar hallucination. I wanted to get up and go over to her. I did not, though. Instead I furtively watched her, a slender sloe-eyed quadroon, gloomy bluish-black circles under her eyes, nails bitten to the quick—a ghost girl, like her mother Lisbeth. Except for age they could have been twins.

Our modern Judge Jeffreys, bourbon scarlet of face with jutting irascible jaw, his Brooks Brothers' buttoned-down shirt and silk repp tie visible above his black robe, was as usual today out of sorts. I trembled. The proceeding had already become ritually murky, the jury at this odd stage sequestered, the hustling clerks now seated and yawning. Old Pilsudski, liver spots at his temples and on the backs of both hands, eyed his awesome lord and master Jeffreys, then himself yawned. The lawyers were arguing the motion to dismiss, a tedious, boring exercise coming at the close of the government's (airtight) case and involving a surfeit of pettifogging, my own blustering lawyer in the very midst of it. But the young assistant U.S. attorney was a gentleman. Unlike my gauche counsel, he was courteous, even to the defendant, me.

Still I tried to catch my daughter looking at me. She had not, of her own choice, seen me in twenty months. Ah, Carol. But I could not. I wondered if, in response to my letter—my SOS—she had only this afternoon arrived in town. My spirits were already benumbed, however. I had acknowledged to myself with contrition that I was insufficiently moved when she had walked in. But—a trifling excuse—I had been at the moment busy glancing in the direction of the jury, then down at the jury list in my lawyer's lap, checking names against faces, though knowing the jury's eventual verdict, a foregone conclusion, would only spin off more of my faculties, dilate my tired, reddened pupils, and unravel still more threads off the bobbin of my mind. When I thought about all this I did finally begin to feel some emotion, that, for instance, Carol might, undoubtedly would, still be here when tomorrow or next day the verdict was read.

My counsel spieled on. But stubbornly I tried to ignore his posturing. Instead I began to look straight up again no matter that my poor contorted neck rebelled. Up, up, though, my gaze panned the azure plaster firmament. The grinning seraphs, their hoary paint flaking, hovered in flotation over the throne as the two processions of Tiepolo-like lawgiving monks, all in the foreground of a mass of dusty,

36

stucco-peeling tapestries, stretched beneath a canopy sheltering the huge diadem. I grew dizzy.

I was not much for courtrooms anyway. I had not been inside one, as I now reckon it, throughout these three decades and more—not since Cager's famous aborted Tennessee trial during the latter days of the war culminating in his gory, fiery immolation and martyrdom. The fateful question before that tribunal's jury, a far more dread issue than here, had also been a foregone conclusion. There the wild redneck special county prosecutor, one Barney Renfroe, in a yelling, raging, apoplectic performance, had kept brandishing before the jury the murder weapon (ironically, an aged relic of another war— "between the states"—a memento owned and cherished by the Old South unreconstructed [except for her final weeks] victim herself), this enormously long Confederate Enfield musket, its fixed bayonet (it had done the grisly work; no shot was fired) almost as long, and he, Renfroe, screaming to the jury about the old doyenne's pitiful blood, "her blood, blood, blood!" It made one's flesh crawl. But throughout Cager had sat there coldly, stoically, observing Renfroe before the jury, listening to his shrieking and bellowing, until, that is, the proceedings were suddenly, violently, interrupted and superseded by intrusion of stormier community forces.

I glanced at Carol again now. She was still quietly aloof, impervious. Growing up, she had been such a high-spirited, sweet child, while I had been a miscreant father. I, that first time, had visited her room one night when my wife Lisbeth was away at a sister's funeral. Dereliction and miscreancy can bring regrets, which beget guilt, foreshadowing, almost presciently, all these emotions I speak of which eventually, alike, engulf both heroines and heroes, dead or alive. It was, though, I believe, Lowry's sad, bedeviled consul who, while under the volcano, said: "Once a year even the dead live for one day."

8

AGAIN EARLY SOUTHERN SKIES.

Hot, quite still, exuding a stifling sulfurousness, and full of portent. But at its outer edges our town Valhalla is pastoral enough and serene, where sparse jasmine, azalea, and spiraca grace the scene while willows, live oaks, alder, and alluvial grit abound and cotton is king.

Today, however, I was in *the* presence. His—the hero's, one of nature's and the Almighty's most unique creations and archetypes. That is how I see him even to this day—at once a fierce, prodigious, and internalized youth, who, though, had the capability of a direct overtness which could please, exasperate, rile, charm, excite pity, as well as the wish to protect and shield him, or, on less felicitous occasions, cause you to want to do him bodily harm, the latter, however, a most inadvisable, if not unthinkable, undertaking. Cager indeed.

He and I, your two Cervantian characters, and for our Rocinante riding the hindquarters of this Jim Crow bus, sat silent, morose, jaded. My mind, ever wandering, was vaguely recalling that morning's Humanities 213 class. Old Moses Wardlow, our crypto-Marxist professor, lecturing, had said that somebody, I do not remember who, was a "modern-day Comte," or was it Fichte? He had bandied about other names as well, more familiar ones, that it was his wont to drop, about most of which, however, or their owners, some clown in the rear of the classroom—Slick Borders—chortled that old Wardlow knew absolutely nothing. But when Slick, his chair tilted hazardously back against the wall, then tittered over his own tomfoolery, Cager and I (looking for any pretext), in plain view of everyone, though stupidly tiptoeing, took off.

But by the same act we had, prospectively, cut Haley Barnes's two o'clock American history class. (For example, John C. Calhoun: "It is a great and dangerous error to suppose all people to be equally entitled to liberty. Rather, liberty is a reward reserved for the intelligent, the virtuous, the deserving, not a boon prodigally to be bestowed upon a transplanted people, bestial, ignorant, degraded, and from the darkest continent of all.") Our bus seat was directly over the rear axle and we were getting some hard jolts. We though were on our way across town to the Negro section to check out any daytime action in Ma Moody's place, the classy pub/dive by day and jumping Jehoshaphat cabaret by night. So much then for the great senator and vice president Calhoun on our Afric degradation.

Another jarring axle jolt! "Let's move up front," growled Cager.

"Are you crazy?" I laughed, glancing at the movable Jim Crow sign a few seats ahead.

We fell to musing again then. The hot fickle sky was saturated with an aureate light. The sun's high artwork, mottling and delicate, suffused the expansive crew-cut lawns, their pirouetting sprinklers, the manicured hedges, plus other profusions of fresh bright foliage, all trappings of these comely Caucasian environs which gave us both distinct feelings of jealousy and alienation. I was moreover sure, knowing him, that he, Cager ("Cage," some of us called him for short), would be reacting with an acerbity far outstripping even my own sense of blighted hopes. The sight would soon trigger one of his characteristic mean-and-evil moods when his speech might blurt from wet-flashing teeth and spatter you in the eye. I had not long to wait.

"Looka there," he said, pointing to the big new stucco house rising high beside its turquoise swimming pool. Acid irony skewed his voice tone. "You see, don't you?"—speaking in all the variations of a dangerous guttural bass-baritone as he again threw a hand off in the direction of the blue-lagoon pool. "Ever hear of Clausewitz? . . . Of course not," he hastened to answer himself— also grinding his teeth, which always set my nerves on edge—"If not," he said, "you got plenty company. Amongst *us*. We missed the boat. You know *that*, I bet. I'm not talking about the slavery boat, either. Which we *didn't* miss. We didn't have a Clausewitz, though, like the Germans had, did we? Or learn anything about the art, much less science, of warfare. *Huh?*" He was of course now getting excited. He pleaded, "You *know* we didn't, Rev! This Clausewitz was a German general, a Prussian, back in the early 1800s. I've studied him. He was a military professor on top of that. Wrote a book called *On War*. He said it's the people that make war, but first they gotta have *leaders*. You following me? Where're *our* leaders, huh?"

I laughed before I thought. "Sure, I'm following you," I said. "Is that what you want?—to be my leader?"

He frowned. "Don't make jokes. This is serious. The *people* make war if they got leaders. Oh, maybe at the beginning the diplomats will have to go through their routine, their lip service, but then the leaders take over—I mean *the military men*. Clausewitz laid it all out in that damn book. He showed the Krauts how to *wage war*, man. Preached the *iron fist*. You see what happened, don't you? They caught on *fast*. Hitler's liable to win this damn war yet, you watch. But it was Clausewitz that taught them how to fight, not Hitler. *Us*, though—oh, Lord. Where're we? Don't forget, in Haley Barnes's class, what old John C. Calhoun said about us. Or what the Supreme Court said in the Dred Scott case—that we didn't have any damn rights that anybody had to respect. Oh, Lord. We missed the boat, that's all." He heaved a heavy sigh. I did not laugh.

But now we had arrived. And the first thing we saw as we alighted from the bus in the Negro section of Valhalla was a commotion. It centered on this greasy scarecrow of a black man, a scruffy street hawker, tending his heavily laden stand, as he sought to fend off a cluster of juveniles bent on stealing him blind. His assortment of gaudy eye-catching gewgaws was, to say the least, arresting if not astonishing—neckties, fake jewelry, hair pomade, plastic birds, water pistols, more. He hailed us the moment he saw us—"Hold on, there, you two lords! . . . Come here and take a look." His mangy hands waved around at his myriad merchandise.

Cager in his dour dignity had paused. He observed the scarecrow. While I, his acolyte, stopped only just behind.

"Y'like any of these, Slim?" said the old vendor, ignoring me. He dangled a cheap wristwatch, then a yellow fountain pen, and finally a big vulgar glittery ring, before frowning Cager. "Or how 'bout this?" He held up a khaki necktie bearing in navy blue machine stitching a crude likeness of President FDR. "Commander-in-chief's lookin' for you, Slim," he said. "Your buddy here, too." He scratched, dug, into his sweaty armpit, adding, "I oughta know 'cause I'm a draft board spotter. I got *authority*, you bozos. See here?" He pulled a grimy paper from his shirt pocket, grinning maniacally. "I can almost tell neither one of you is registered to go help Uncle Sam. Whut? Why don't you say somethin'?"

Cager only gaped. So did I. Our sole purpose in life was beating the draft. Cager quickly turned on his heel to go. But then he wheeled and came back. "Let's see that," he said to the vendor and snatched the paper. But in the lightning-swift motion he knocked a large item off the vendor's stand to the ground.

"Oh, my Gawd!" cried the old man, sailing down to retrieve it. It was a black plastic horse at least ten or eleven inches high, its belly somehow grotesquely distended, and had bounced, then caromed, when it hit the sidewalk. "Oh, Nestor, my big prancer!" lamented the vendor, having now rescued his talisman. "Poor thing!" He began minutely examining it for damage.

A laughing boy in the crowd yelled over at him: "You just dropped something, Joshua!"

But vendor Joshua had now turned wrathfully on Cager—"Say, don't you see when he hit he coulda broke open and spilled everything *out?*" Cager by now, though, was busy studying the grimy paper he had snatched. "Okay, then, High Pockets," said Joshua, "start gettin' your things together. You're goin' to meet Uncle Sam. You too, Buster," he turned and said to me. "We're gonna be missin' you two pretty quick. The Uncle can make use of you, all right. Gimme your names and addresses." He pulled out a pencil.

Cager and I were, if anything, indecisive. We merely gawked.

Suddenly then, though, Joshua began fondling the black plastic horse again. "Oh, Nestor, I shoulda left you home," he said to the inert, inanimate object. "You ain't for sale, anyhow." He now opened what turned out to be a trapdoor in the toy's bulging belly, placed a hand underneath to catch whatever it was he expected to see come tumbling out, then winced before lurching madly when nothing came. "Whut the hell?" he said. He frantically shook the horse now. With the same result. He grew wide-eyed with fear, saying, "Whut's happened to 'em? Oh, where'd thay all go? I only left him in the draft board office overnight." He shook the toy now with a manic ferocity, before jiggling and joggling it against his ear to listen for any possible sound or commotion inside the great belly. All was futile. "White folks been messin' with us again," he said disgustedly, then forlornly. "They's the one that's pulled this trick. How you goin' to beat 'em? Ain't no way. They captured the soldiers and maybe killed the little rascals. Yeah, they're gone, ain't they? Oh, oh, Lord! . . ." He was inconsolable. "Gone! . . . ah."

Cager yelled it at the top of his lungs—"*What's gone?*"

Joshua seemed aghast at his ignorance—"Why, the little black soldiers that was stashed inside, that's whut's gone." He appeared crushed. "Brave soldiers they was, well-trained, 'cause they had a big job to do. We was dependin' on them to change things. Nestor was goin' to be taken into the enemy's camp, then the soldiers would all jump out, open up the gates, and let *us* in. You understand *that*, don't you? *We'd* take over then." But now he seemed to despair of everything. "Oh, hell, whut am I talkin' about? It's just a stunt—it's really a game, a crazy game you can play. That's why I sell a lot of these horses—but not Nestor. I say it's a game, but then again it *ain't.* There's more to it than that. Educated colored folks are the ones that got the idea together—much better than any of the rest of us could. They're mostly the customers that buy these horses like Nestor, that look like they're 'big,' in the family way, with mighty great things expected to come outa them. Yeah, educated colored folks pay money for 'em and take 'em home and

41

put 'em up on their mantelpieces—yeah, wishin' for a better day to come for us, almost prayin' to the little black soldiers to deliver 'em, although the Bible does tell us that we ought not be worshipin' graven images. It says that, I know it does, but, oh, hell. . . ." His face grew long.

"*Come on,*" Cager said to me. Soon we were walking down the street a block away. "What was that crazy nigger talking about?" he finally said.

"Beats me," I said. Strangely, though, I wanted to laugh. "I don't think he knew himself," I added.

"Weird cat. Yeah, yeah, crazy, man. Or else he knows something we don't." He lapsed into silence again.

I still somehow wanted to laugh, until, that is, I realized how silly it was of me to want to do that when I had no idea what this scruffy old character *had* in fact been talking about—if anything. There should, though, have been a name for the way I felt. It was not a feeling of foreboding or anything dramatic like that. It was more like a needling humorous curiosity, but maybe with a few tiny jagged edges. It was, though, burdened down with the mystery of Cager and his innocent dumbness, his high moral sappiness, but also with his gigantic, almost apostolic, vision. Maybe what I felt smacked of what they call, in one of my Gladstone religious textbooks, a divination—whatever that is—or, in a way, like the song "Lo, Hear the Gentle Lark" that I first remember from down in Texas. On that particular dark night (of the soul) I was sitting in our old privy in the midst of a violent thunderstorm. I was also trembling with fear of the snakes that sometimes took refuge or rendezvoused there. But it was here that, triumphantly, I overcame this prolonged bout with constipation. Pitifully straining and sighing against the cannonading black heavens outside, I at last chattered congratulations to myself and then, miraculously— the divination?—burst forth in the song of the lark. In a very profound sense this, possibly, was not unlike our (Cager's and my) strange encounter with the seedy scarecrow Joshua and his Trojan horse. This of course is speculation. Yet, even back then, it somehow seemed to me no trivial matter. I don't know why. I think, however, Cager, uneasily, felt the same way—that is, about the totality of our experience with all those demons riding Joshua's back, including his shibboleth, "educated colored folks." But, as I have just intimated, it bade Cager pause, for in what appeared a very wary, precautionary measure he changed our plans. We proceeded now—to use some of his Clausewitz military lingo—to do an elaborate "flanking maneuver" and, "bypassing" Ma Moody's dive (and, with it, all of Senator Calhoun's maledictions), we repaired to our friend Shorty George's greasy spoon restaurant, there to relax over a plate of red beans, rice and neckbones. We seemed—for the time being at least—to have given something or other the slip.

9

TIME (DECADES) AND EVENTS have at last brought your narrator to Pressman. It involves that mortifying period in my life when His Honor Judge Jeffreys, abetted by the jury, had for a time removed me from the larger society to Pressman's cold gray federal confines and to those daily encounters there with that most tormented and woebegone of human creatures—fellow-inmate Guy Bahr. Is it possible now that I once knew him?

I had predicted the jury's guilty finding based on the government's airtight case. And poor Carol had sat there in the courtroom watching as the "twelve good men and women true" filed in with the bad news. My silly offense had been the petty mishandling of federal educational funds, an infraction into which I had been suckered by this salacious-looking Antiguan woman, briefly an academic colleague, whom I had tried, without success, to seduce, only later to learn her true paramour was another woman. It had all, then, brought me to this semblance of a prison, this prosaic but minimum-security institution, where Bahr occasionally showed an interest in some of these already-alluded-to and other experiences (misadventures) of mine. But I would soon learn that, besides having a sour and mistrustful disposition, he was also at heart a frightened self-hater, as well as in other ways a most mercurial man. His enthusiasm for what I had to say ebbed as often as it flowed.

Yet this only made me more tenacious. I had this unslaked craving to talk about my guilt-ridden life. Somehow, I thought, I must externalize what inside seemed bent on eviscerating me. The pressure, if not soon vented, would destroy me. Consequently, those days and nights in the Pressman lounge, when for short periods Bahr would sit and listen, elated me no end, especially when, with great deliberation, almost gravity, he would pull out this tiny ruled note pad and pencil stub he always carried

43

around with him (an irony, for he had been a bank auditor, now defrocked) and begin taking notes. I thought this entirely proper, however, for I was convinced beyond doubt that I was saying something significant, if not momentous, for us both—even beyond the therapy I sought.

Yet, by his note-taking he may also have succumbed to this "epidemic" rife at Pressman. Almost everyone there was either writing his memoirs, à la Watergate, or, if not memorializing some knavish politician, at least penning a wooden novel about corporate life and the fine arts of defalcation (which could have been, in another setting, a real Bahr contribution), or some other roman à clef. There was certainly enough time. I had most of my sentence—a year and a day—yet to do and he had even a few months more than I.

But what I wanted more than anything was for him to understand his role as listener, its vital importance to me as well, for, as you might expect, it of course related to Cager—to my weird concept of our "rivalry." At times lately, though, when I would bring up the subject to Bahr—of the dramatic contrasts—he, to my disappointment, would show little or no interest, especially if I dwelt at any length on the sad but symbolic difference between the two involved lives, Cager's and my own, and what this all meant in moral terms. This thread seemed somehow always cropping up in whatever I told Bahr, though it was unavoidable because the phenomenon was constantly gnawing at me, forever on my mind. He must have recognized my paranoia but nevertheless appeared so aloof that I began to be suspicious. Did his seeming boredom equate with genuine disinterest? This was hard for me to believe. Or, more likely, was he thinking about his own wrecked life, possibly some shame of his own?—though, earlier on, I knew hardly anything about his private life, even if I suspected taint. Did, then, he wish to avoid, for himself, any more unpleasant promptings my constant talk might already have produced? These questions plagued me.

But on this particular evening in the Pressman lounge he and I were—rather *I* was—talking about, actually expatiating on, some of the crucial experiences in *my* life. Tonight, however, for some reason, he was unusually morose and uncooperative. "Barry," he finally interrupted me, "why is it you're always spilling your guts to me like this? I've never been able to figure it out."

It surprised and, secretly, offended me. Spilling my guts, as he put it, was what I had *not* been doing. I was most careful, very selective, about what I told him, for, while I did not necessarily dislike him—he had his own problems—I did not completely trust him, either. So now, cunningly, I smiled. "I notice, though, you try to write down in your little notebook there most of what I have to say." He did not remonstrate, only gave me a worried, hangdog look. He was very pale and washed-out looking, and, I suppose, his constantly upset nerves accounted for his ever-fidgety, cigarette-yellowed fingers; they twitched, were seldom still. "Does my talk bore you?" I asked.

He looked me furtively in the eye, and rather pitifully, I thought. "No," he said. "Sometimes, though, I don't think it helps me."

I wanted to ask him to explain but, unsure of his answer, I played it safe and kept quiet. But it was the first time he had ever so much as hinted he (too) was looking for help. He was a mystery, yet I somehow resented him. I was pretty sure he took the usual equivocal, if not jaundiced, view of most Afro-Americans and had had little contact with them. Why, then, you ask, hadn't he instead taken up with some of the other, white, Pressman inmates? Actually, despite the unevenness of our relationship, we had somehow become, though in a very unclear way, almost friends. Diffidently, he would come and, sort of without any purpose, hang around me, reminding one of how a random white person, a stranger traveling, say, and lost downtown in the big city, will walk past a dozen other whites until finding a Negro of whom to ask directions—preferring, of course, not to reveal his ignorance or other difficulty to a fellow white, though caring not a fig about what some black might think. This, I am inclined to believe, even if I may be wrong about it, had some application to Bahr.

Yet, tonight, no matter what, I somehow felt sorry for him as we sat there on Pressman's handsome, spare, Scandinavian settee though he and I were looking away from each other. He was clearly hurting about something—I had no idea what. Hell, though, I resentfully told myself, I have my own hurts. For there was always in attendance, lodged deep in my psyche, Cager's silent, brooding shade that I, by some means, eternally, it seemed, had to deal with. The "rivalry," yes. But suddenly, then, before ever realizing it, I had turned to Bahr, my face, I am sure, lit up, and said, "Say, stop sulking and let me tell you another Cager story."

Bahr groaned audibly.

"No fooling!" I said, smiling frantically. "It's a very funny story. All about Cager when he was a student at Gladstone College, down in Tennessee, during World War Two—about the guys in

45

the dorm one night, drinking cheap wine, laughing and raising hell, mercilessly razzing and poking fun at him, also telling all manner of wild jokes at his expense! And all, mind you, when Cager *was not there!* He was goofing off in town somewhere. I, though, supposedly his good friend, his buddy, right there listening to it all and never once lifting my voice to defend him, but laughing my head off right along with all the others. I'm ashamed of myself now and wish I could call back that rowdy night. But wouldn't you like to hear about it, *really?*" I was manic.

Bahr looked more trapped, miserable, than ever before.

My situation now had become exigent. My temples fairly throbbed with the power, the thrust, of this crazy, self-aggrandizing doctrine of mine, of my own manufacture—the "contrast," the "rivalry." I rushed on talking. "You *must* hear about it, Bahr—now, right now! You'll *collapse* laughing!" I felt some mad compulsion. Now, though, he was squirming, almost writhing, on the settee, he was that wretched. I could finally see how desperate he was to leave. Still it made me furious. "Well, go ahead and leave, then," I said. "I can see Cager holds no more interest for *you.*"

He sighed and looked away. "How did you come to know so much, Barry?" he said. "What you *don't* know, though, might just someday make a whole little pamphlet." Scornfully, then, he rose and left.

I therefore sat there and relived it all alone. Listen with me, in memory, to the utter cacophony:

"*Tell me, what gives?* What's come over General Cager?" It was Roscoe Lomax's mad, hoarse outcry, red jug wine souring his breath, at a typical Friday night bull session in the Gladstone men's dorm. "Did you ever in your life see any such change? He's different from last semester as night and day! Six months ago the campus bookworm, hipping syllabi assignments round the clock—no foolin'! Boning up on all of history's great *military* men! Attila! Genghis Khan! Cromwell! Marcus Garvey! Even the damn *Visigoths*, man! Getting himself together to go out and start his own war! Save the whole Negro race! He's a *race* man, you hear me? Putting a *a hundred divisions* of blacks in the field! Hey!"

"In the field is right!" somebody said. "*Cotton* field!"

An avalanche of hollering, stamping, and laughing ensued. Guiltily, as I say, I laughed right along with them.

"*Now* look at him!" cried Roscoe. "He's the campus clown! Won't crack a book! Won't do nothing! I say, *what gives?*" The surreptitious jug of dago red went around again.

"He's changed, all right, no question," said quiet Dred Scott Mullins, our giant cow-pasture fullback. "Hundred eighty degrees. Just like that." Snapping his fingers.

Roscoe returned. "Even Haley Barnes can't do nothing with him, much less anybody else on this faculty. No more midnight oil, books thrown under the bunk, and carrying on in town every night, like tonight. Cutting the fool to a fare-thee-well! Campus has been in an uproar ever since. The kids love it! And now—get *this*!—he's claiming he's Robert E. Lee's great-grandson!" Whoops, wild shouts, more stamping.

Dred Scott shook his head—"Yeah, you gotta admit it. Cage's wiring's faulty, his roof's leakin'. Ha, General Robert E. Lee. Lord, Lord—great white gentleman and slave master. Look out."

"Well, remember," somebody else said, "Cage's name *is* Lee."

"What're you talking about?" scoffed Roscoe. "There're a million Lees! But why's he pick out somebody like that of all people to identify with, that fought his ass off for four years to keep us in slavery? He could at least have come up with Grant or somebody. Didn't he even go downtown and put a wreath at Lee's statue in the courthouse square?" Hilarious groans, wails. "Man, he shoulda known this town's got some of the meanest, the wildest, crackers outside of Red Dot, Mississippi! Naturally, a bunch of 'em were sitting, lazing, around on the courthouse lawn that day, gabbing, whittling sticks, spitting tobacco juice. When they looked up and saw Cage lean that wreath down against Lee's statue, they couldn't believe what they were sittin' there lookin' right at in broad daylight! They damn near fainted, that is, before they went berserk! They made it hot for him then, I'll tell you! Ran him all the way back to campus! You coulda played whist on ole Cage's coattails!" Shouts and yells.

When the pandemonium had sufficiently subsided Roscoe resumed: "But it wasn't a month after that when he was right back downtown in another scrape. That was the march, you know!"

"Oh, what the hell," somebody said, "who don't know about that?"

"Never you mind," said Roscoe. "Just listen. Some crackers had shot into a Negro's house and the police hadn't done anything about it. So Cage rounds up a bunch of real street niggers, nails some placards to sticks, and leads a protest march, right downtown! That takes nerve, man—in *this* burg!—when you know before it's over those redneck gendarmes are going to be whipping some heads! Well, sure enough, no sooner had they got to Davis

47

and Main when the cops took out after them, cussing, kicking, swinging their nightsticks like crazy, and arrested the whole bunch, Cage getting the first bloodied head. But when they got them all over to the jail, he was raising so much hell they decided they'd fix him by putting him in a cell all by himself, then later on, like they do, work him over real good with their fists and billy clubs. But Cage, of course knowing all this, gets loose some way, whips both the cops messing with him, and locks *them* in the cell—the 'cage'—they'd been trying to put *him* in!" Whoops and howls of laughter and handclapping. "Then somehow or other— Lord only knows how he did it 'cause there're three or four different versions—he gets out to the street and, running his ass off, makes it clear back to campus, climbs in his bunk, and, exhausted, goes to sleep!" Deafening din and more howls. "You know, though, of course, he was rearrested and the cracker judge threw the book at him. But then Haley Barnes—who else?—went to bat for him, said he was a rough country boy and a Gladstone student and all, and he ends up doing only thirty days. But meantime he'd been kicked out of school. Man, you can imagine how a scared handkerchief-head black college president like our esteemed and beloved Simon Peter Groomes would react to something like this. He was mad *and* frantic!—told Cage to let the doorknob hit him in the back, *now*. You know, of course, what happened then—"

"No, we don't, Roscoe!" somebody mocked. "You go right ahead and tell us!"

"You guys, the girls too, went on a rampage, threatened to raze the campus to the ground, and Groomes let old Cage come on back. He returned as a *hero*, man!—ha, for about five minutes. From then on, though, we started calling him 'the cager!'" Amidst the laughter the jug went around again.

So this is in part the way it was—tragicomedy—according at least to your narrator's admittedly equivocal lights. My memory, though, is sound. But the interpretation of *dreams*, required here, is altogether another matter. Yet in this "history" pray God I prevail.

I finally rose now from that comely Pressman settee in the lounge and went to my room. I needed to go to the laundry and wash some shorts, T-shirts, and socks, but I did not feel up to that tonight. Instead I sat on the bed and ate an apple. I had so wanted, deeply, for Bahr to understand some of what we have just seen and heard. It was important to me. I wished somehow to have conveyed to him, via these purple, hilarious scenes, that, yes, tragi-comedy can have meaning. But he became afraid and ran. I somehow knew then what I had suspected since first encountering him there, that he had a lot that night to be running from. In time my guessing was to end. I would learn—much later, after leaving Pressman—that the burden of his misery stemmed not from the trivial bank fraud conviction that had sent him there. Rather, it was the tragedy of his alienation from his only son, alas brought about by his dalliance (and more) with his son's wife!

Yet, even had I known this at Pressman, would it have to any degree lightened my own load? I have never been sure. There are immense complexities. I only know that there I also suffered from the *physical* symptoms of my neuroses. Here, instead of constipation, my bowels were running off. I constantly chewed bismuth tablets to stop them, but to little effect. This had been going on for some time, though, precipitated, I am sure, by all the unanswered questions involving Carol. There was as well my feeling generally, based on solid enough evidence certainly, that I was completely without intrinsic moral worth. Self-revulsion would then return and finish off the job with stabbing stomach pains and cramps. But I would have died before letting Bahr know, even though, because he too had desolate secrets, we were, unfortunately, and even against our will, comrades—brothers in the bond.

10

WE COME NOW, not fortuitously, to the Archangel Michael. It had been in Sunday school, fittingly enough, that our young hero had first heard of Michael the biblical shining knight, redeemer, chief of heavenly princes, conqueror of Satan—all vouched for in the Good Book itself (see Jude, Daniel, Revelation, and so on): "And at that time shall Michael stand up, the great prince which abideth for the children of thy people (Israel); and there shall be a time of trouble, such as never was since there was a nation; at that time they people shall be delivered, everyone that shall be found written in the book; and many of them that sleep in the dust of the earth shall awake, though some to shame and everlasting contempt, but others to everlasting life."

Thus, as he grew taller, then taller still, Rollo kept his counsel, thought his giant thoughts, dreamed his fantastic, outlandish

49

dreams—of redress, fulfillment, even of defensive "conquest," as well as U.S. Senator Boggs's glorious ethos of "blood, valor, sacrifice, honor"—and, while yet at the high-school stage, sought with a burning zeal to look deeply into himself and, for the task to come, assess the pluses and minuses he saw there. He was of course unaware of how impressionable, sensitive, if naive, he was, yet also of such an iron-willed Spartan cast that although his teeth would fairly ache when, say, in a typical test, on a dare from the other boys, he could chew, then devour, the sourest, most acidic, quince-fruit, then smile.

Nonetheless, he constantly wondered if he were at all equal to these overwhelming undertakings he envisioned and had already assigned himself, as had, eons before, the Archangel. But at once he would fret and fume over the impossible challenge so mighty an exemplar posed, then anguish over his own deficiencies almost to the point of obsession. He now resolved to gain an iron hold on himself, steel his nerves, clear his vision, for what he was certain he must do. They were of course baby dreams. They also consumed him. But he must *learn* more, he thought, find out what great men thoughout history had done, and read, read, read. He was certain, though, there were others, older, stronger, more knowledgeable, who could do the job far better than he. Where were they, though? The people were leaderless—it was an outrage!

He thought of the adults he knew, especially his own father—whom he loved. Amos Lee, the boy confessed, was a good father and husband, and, though often insensitive, was a kind, almost sentimental man. Yet, his sights seldom ever transcended the furrows he plowed, the livestock he fed, the unceasing labor he rendered to landlord Blatchford. His silently rebellious son saw it all as a dismal dead end of which he wanted no part. It made him contrite, however, to realize that his father, too, had dreams, exalted, selfless dreams—for his family.

"Y'see, Rolly," Amos, eyes glowing, would sometimes say, "you're gettin' an education. You'll soon be outa *high school!*—think of that. Time sure does fly, don't it? But I didn't have no chance at an education myself—things was different back then. But look at you—you won't have to sharecrop like I been doin' all my life. You'll *own* your land. Why," he laughed, "you can be a regular Virginia *planter!*—that is, if you want to and set your mind to it! You won't have to split crops with nobody. Then look, boy, what a big help you can be to your mama and your sisters if I'm gone. And what a big purty family of your own you can raise. It's somethin' to think about, I'll tell you, ain't it? . . . *ain't* it, now?" There was such heavy yearning in his tone and look.

Rollo listened respectfully, with love, yes, but said nothing, his mind otherwise occupied with the powerful deeds, utterances, and hypotheses he daily encountered in his schoolbooks. It was during the time he, with the other children of sharecroppers, rode the dilapidated school bus eighteen miles one way to the run-down Negro high school and, en route and returning amidst the violent horseplay of the students, studied his textbooks, grimy dog-eared volumes discarded by the white high school, but inside which he had met Alexander and Charlemagne, Frederick the Great, Napoleon, Karl von Clausewitz, and of course, again, Robert E. Lee—in these books always Lee. But he had met other greats as well, not in his books but in the class discussions his teachers (Negro) led, in which he had come to know the great black men and women of history—Crispus Attucks, Phillis Wheatley, Nat Turner, Sojourner Truth, Frederick Douglass, Marcus Garvey, W. E. B. DuBois, Toussaint L'Ouverture, others.

But, far more crucial, it was from these Negro teachers that he finally came to know the heinous particulars of chattel slavery. Since childhood he had heard not a little about "them bad, bad old slavery times" from Granny and the others, but only by vague, almost folkloristic, if awing, references. Now he learned it systematically and directly, from documented sources—quite different and well beyond those found in the cast-off white textbooks —and taught by well-informed, conscientious, indeed intrepid, teachers not unwilling, moreover, to buttress their discussions by gruesome anecdotes passed down to them from family forebears, many of whom had experienced this horrible history firsthand. To astonished, heartsick, and outraged Rollo the shock was total. For a time, then, he refused to believe what his teachers told him though he soon found he had no alternative.

He would therefore never be the same—having learned of the centuries of horror through which his ancestors had come, abducted in the African homeland and transported to the New World in the horrible slave ships, fed strange worm-riddled food, lashed with cat-o'-nine-tails, many in the process driven to suicide by leaping overboard to the trailing, waiting sharks, the others finally on arrival impressed into the brutal southern work system of cotton-field hands or cane-sugar plantation labor gangs, the victims numbering over the interminable span of generations in the millions on millions, a ghastly four-centuries ordeal which, said zealous teacher Mr. Thatcher, was by all odds the most gigantic crime perpetrated in the annals of human history and constituting a multicontinent slave-labor presence the enormous megaprofits from which largely financed the Western industrial revolution itself. How could this all *possibly* have happened? asked the stupefied young Rollo of any and everyone who would talk to him about it. By seventeen, then, he was already assembling a host of the most involuted, Byzantine theories about this freshly learned history and how it had come about, and also how, at any and all conceivable costs and sacrifice, it could be not only challenged but, if necessary, bloodily rectified. To him this could never be too late. Late? Yes. *Too* late? Never. Often, also, many of his bizarre potential remedies occurred to him in dreams, begging to be sorted out, studied, dissected, mulled over—even, who knew, *tested*!

One Sunday morning, eager to communicate to his father one such far-out dream he had had during the night (it had actually been a nightmare fragment, about which he had already told the womenfolk of the house), he cornered Amos with an avalanche of words and questions. But Amos, in a hurry, a dither, really, not to be late for church—he had promised Rev. Minnifield to bring a vase of roses for the pulpit—barely listened at all, disengaging himself, sidling away, as the boy still talked. His father loved the church, though, he knew, and may have loved roses even more. Roses were a passion he cultivated in a tiny grassy corner of his truck garden back of the house. His wife, Effie, however, despite her tolerance of his whim, never really understood it—a man's passion for roses! Amos's fancy in this took varied guises: Five of their seven children were born in the warm months of the year and invariably, within hours after delivery and the midwife's departure—sometimes even when, exhausted, Effie still lay sleeping off the labor struggles—Amos would enter the bedroom with a few roses, pink and yellow as well as red, in his calloused hand and gently wake her. But Rollo, their second son, had been born in bitter January (the eighteenth—thereby doomed, said the old folks, to a lifetime of nightmares), and on that fateful day Amos came in the house with, instead of roses, a mason jar of thick, nourishing navy bean soup from the kitchen of none other than landlord Blatchford. Yet, when the month of June arrived, he still brought Effie the belated roses, presenting them to her at the back door now, and, besides, a large gunny sack of crab apples for making his favorite jelly.

But of all his offspring Amos Lee understood his January male child least. The boy's idiosyncracies, particularly the strange, barely suppressed force, the zeal and bizarreness of his character, especially his objectives and longings—his idée fixe—entirely escaped him. Nor was Rollo, absorbed as he was in all his visions and strategies, in any way attuned to Amos's own hard past, the father's frustrations, blighted hopes, the years of ceaseless labor, all now taking their certain toll. Although only fifty-seven, but with already unsteady hands, frequent needlelike angina pains, and a hollow wheeze in almost every breath, Amos had long since placed his future, earthly and beyond, in God's (that is, God's local surrogate's, Rev. Minnifield's) care by his presence in the country preacher's little church every time the doors opened. Yet, Rollo had time only for the titans of history he encountered in the grimy cast-off schoolbooks and riveting class discussions, figures who, according to his interpretation, had at great and gory sacrifice, many with their lives, vindicated—as had the Archangel Michael—the rights of their people. He even sometimes communed with these "shining knights"—General Toussaint L'Ouverture among them—in the wild dreams and nightmares that, except for his father, regularly woke up the house. For example:

Trembling with excitement, eager to acquit himself bravely, the young soldier crouched low under the hail of musket fire and scurried to the rear. But it was in search of Colonel Gascar commanding the scant eight cannon available to Toussaint's forces, artillery the general wanted and needed brought forward immediately. "Hurry, lad!" called out the great military commander and patriot-savior. "We must have them!" Running in the crouch through the smoke of battle to carry out the order, he stumbled over the bloody corpse of a Santo Domingan infantryman and went to his knees before recovering his balance and then continuing past a neighing, wounded horse which had just thrown its rider. He was anxious to deliver his message and return up front to the fighting. Yet, he was frightened; nor had he ever known such exhilaration, either; it was almost elation, standing beside his brave commander, his idol, the grand Toussaint L'Ouverture, prepared to die if necessary before accepting defeat at the hands of the cruel French invaders. The year was 1801 and the black Haitian general Toussaint had rallied the people of Santo Domingo to drive out the violators of their country. Moreover, the general had chosen him, yet a teenager, as his aide-de-camp. The boy's pride was now boundless. Soon the eight cannon had been advanced into their new positions and were firing heavy salvos into the ranks of the regrouping French. Toussaint, a man of heroic bearing, perfumed, periwigged, in full parade-ground dress, though the gold epaulets of his crimson tunic had been singed by gunpowder, was directing two of his columns in a daring flanking manuever. The din of battle was deafening but the boy heard the general in his fiery French exhorting his officers not to follow but to lead their men. "Be an example!" he cried. "We fight for our dignity as men, as black men, and for the protection of our women and children on this island! We also fight for our heritage, which is African! Yet, if it be our fate to die, then we embrace death—a bras ouverts!" Toussaint then plunged ahead and led the assault.

He was closely followed, however, by his young aide-de-camp, who now pleaded with him not to so flagrantly expose himself, crying out, "What would happen to us, sir, if you were to be killed?"

"Someone else would take my place!" shouted Toussaint. "Maybe you!"

A gasp. "Oh! Me, sir?"

"Yes, you! Are you not worthy, Rollo, lad?"

The boy was dizzy with euphoria. A great smile came on his face— just, then, as he suddenly lurched sideways. And fell. He did not know why. He looked around for Toussaint, but he had gone on. He tried to get up but could not. At last he saw the blood oozing through his trousers—at the crotch. Terrified, he realized he had taken a musket ball in the groin. He screamed.

He woke up and sat bolt upright in his bed. Dripping sweat, and feeling for his "private parts," he cried out for his father. Finally, at no response, he called then for Granny, for his mother and sisters too. Soon all the women came running, but his father slept through it all.

Next morning, however, before Sunday church, it was still his father he sought out. It was then he found Amos in a great hurry to be off with the pulpit roses in his hand. At last Rollo, frustrated, desperate, went in the kitchen looking for Granny, who, after hearing a tedious repetition of the nightmare, vowed it was a "sign" and threw cayenne pepper over her left shoulder. What had happened in the nightmare, she testily told him, proved the truth of what she had tried these many years to get through his head. Then she closed her toothless mouth tight and would say no more.

Later that morning, alone in the house after the others too had gone to church, he once more stripped naked and studied, contemplated, his body in the mirror. In the end, though, he remained as baffled as before. He finally put his clothes back on and went

54

out for a lonely walk in the fields. The back acres were waist-high in tender corn and to his right the creek meandered between banks overspread with dogwood and oak sprouts. He went on. Soon he told himself he should have gone to church with the others, instead of now idly plodding along beside this rusty wire fence. His heart, though, had not been in it. Yet, standing quietly, pensively, he whispered a brief prayer—for understanding.

Suddenly then the biggest, blackest crow he had ever seen swooped down and, as if waiting to speak to him about something of great urgency, perched precariously on a fence post just ahead. For a moment they eyed each other as he resumed walking, now toward it. Apparently unafraid, indeed defiant, it did not move. At last then, from motives of which he was actually unaware, or could not in any case have possibly explained, he abruptly turned from it and with a jerk of the head completely ignored it, cut it dead. At once the burly bird began a wild squawking and ranting before flying off in a great to-do and commotion—as he turned to watch its furiously flapping wings on the sky.

11

I, YOUR PERENNIALLY AGITATED, confused, yet ever verbose narrator, now ask you to vouchsafe to me (for quite sound reasons, I assure you, but which at first, though only at first, you may not readily grasp) the high privilege, yet necessity, of introducing to you that most atypical of history teachers, stoical, messianic, autistic, and in residence at Gladstone College—viz., one Haley Tulah Barnes.

At once, though, I feel an urge to brace myself. He, his role, has always been a thorny challenge to me. I have lately realized how in this process my mind often falters, becomes easily muddled, distraught, although little of it can be attributed to Haley alone but rather to his fortuitous, indeed fated, involvement in a mission of human salvage—the target, our hero Cager. This in turn raises the hairy question, difficult to parry, of the origins of Haley's vulnerability. My speculation on the issue has at least never escaped the outer reaches of my imagination. Yet now it bores in, in, seeking the very core. It, then, paradoxically, is in this context that my thoughts somehow hark back to those halcyon days when I was, putatively, a "man of God." Ha!

I still easily reconstruct my career back Down East—a section of the country, naturally, I love—with its sedate environment, bright students, its classy, secure denizens. Also I see the collegiate pulpit I occupied, hear my own voice rhapsodizing, oh, so mellifluously, from sermon notes before me couched as they invariably were in all my elaborate dictionary polysyllables. Indeed, as it were, through the mists I descry—as if aboard Ahab's *Pequod*—myself draped and preening in my crimson robes of office as I speak of, say, Christ's Eucharist, His body and blood, or the rites, or rigors, of transubstantiation.

Meanwhile, in the brackish recesses of my mind ever hovers the sterling image of Haley, his life, especially his quietly frenzied youth, that early phrenic quagmire in which, haplessly, he found himself while still in his teens was to shape for him what he would become. This challenge confronting me, yes—of *origins*—even now, a generation later, when he is dead, inorganic, unnerves me.

Born in 1895 forty rural miles out from Moultrie, Georgia, he was destined—vis-à-vis Cager—to bear the freakish brunt of attainder, indeed guilt, on which, like a mad raven, rode the special curse which to this day the existentialists insist does not "exist." We shall in this chronicle, in due time, have occasion to test their premise. Possessor of a B.A. degree, Morehouse College, Atlanta (later Dr. King's school) and (eventually) an M.A., Boston University (the Doctor's graduate school as well), Haley's first marriage, to Carrie Porter, failed—largely, it is said, because he felt threatened. It is established, though—at least according to two other Gladstone faculty members—that he recognized that Carrie saw through him. This was anathema to him and the marriage was doomed. For she had told him that he brooded too much and was basically insecure, that his life was one big cover-up. Which it was. She told him, moreover, that he claimed to like people, when in fact, despite the vaguely sunny front he sometimes put up, he was distrustful of them, also uncomfortable, if not outright bored, with them. Then he married Roxanne.

As I say, he had well known what Carrie had said was true and that his slant on life and human nature was fatally skewed. Actually, the older he got, and the more widely he read, the greater grew his conviction that life was essentially a frame-up, which at times made him both sad and angry. But—another paradox—it somehow also flooded him with a strange, overwhelmingly emotional compassion. His life-view, however, had not always been so funereal. There had been an earlier time, even if briefly in his teens,

56

when he was unaffected, sober optimism itself. The sunny future, like Circe, beckoned and he longed to respond. Then, almost inexorably, came the converse side of things, metamorphosis set in, night descended. What had become passionately involved he, recoiling, would refer to as "the waste . . . of a young life, the horrible waste!" Nor did he mean himself. It had begun in that early Georgia country winter of 1912.

It is when his sister Yolande, a comely, slender, brown child, captious yet tender, is thirteen; and smart; in school the teacher's pet; even this early in their lives Haley is awed by all her bright agile aptitudes, her absolute promise. Tomorrow their father, Sam Barnes, will perform the ritual of "hog-killing time." Three shoats will be butchered after being felled each by one rifle shot between the eyes; no knife slitting, no squealing, no rivulets of hot blood, just a spasmodic, twitching, plumping to the ground; Sam the expert. There will then be sizzling chops, side meat for curing, snouts, ears, and tails to be pickled, and cracklings for corn bread to go with the maws, chitterlings, and buttermilk. Sam will then bring out the walnuts and blackberry wine, a good time for all—he, Johnetta, his wife, Haley, the oldest, and the three other children, including Yolande. But later that afternoon they chase Yolande through Jacoby's bare turnip patch, twice around the Barnes's leaning fodder shed, past the grape arbor, and almost into her own house—the three panting white boys. They are at least seventeen—Haley's age—and turn back only reluctantly after spent gasps of laughing among themselves. Yolande, her heart about to burst from the hurtling speed, collapses in the house in a chair but with a grin on her face. Her mother Johnetta flies into a fit of bitter wrath. "You little hussy, you!" she cries, then turns on Sam and tells him that if he does not do something, does not go see Mr. Crumpler about "them damn no-good nasty boys"— Crumpler's and his neighbors'—she will go herself; that he, Sam, ought to be ashamed of himself for not looking out after, protecting, his family, especially his womenfolk. Then she gives Yolande a running, wild whipping—for the grinning. Haley looks on in shocked horror and sorrow. Afterward he goes to Yolande's room and talks to her, tells her she must be more careful, not go out alone like that anymore, stay closer to the house; that she is his baby sister whom he loves and expects great things of, that what almost happened to her was bad, very bad, certainly nothing for her to be smiling about, but something for her fear, anger, her utter contempt. Sniveling from the whipping, she listens, seems truly contrite, and promises tearfully to heed his advice. Then one day when burgeon-

ing, fructifying April comes around—she does not run as fast as she might have—the boys catch her.

Years swallow one another and it is indigenous Atlanta Negrotown now. Summer heat, clutter, noise, rank inhalations, all abound; yet there is also the sweet aroma of fried chicken, buffalofish, barbecued ribs, mustard greens, cold home brew, all which equally abound. Haley, suitcase in hand, intent, earnest, plodding, looking neither left nor right, is heading down the street to catch a streetcar to the railroad station where he will then take a train back to Boston University. His parents are dead, the family scattered. The girl and the man with her lurch from the alley and, colliding with Haley, almost bowl him over. But they are both blind drunk and do not even see him. He at last avoids them and goes on. Strangely, though, he feels he wants to pause, yet does not; then before he realizes it he has paused, and turns around. Again he sees the disheveled man, chin straight up, laughing, baying, at the scorching firmament, before stumbling and slumping to the curb, where he sits groggy and limp; then he vomits. But soon he is laughing again, howling straight up as would a dog bemoaning, then ridiculing, a full moon, all as the woman, not old, not ugly, but untidy, and almost convulsive in her own coarse laughing, stands over him. He grunts and groans, then retches up his insides. She continues laughing, yet managing in the same breath obscenely to revile him, before sliding down beside him and scratching her ribs. Haley, embarrassed even by two perfect strangers, at last turns around again and goes methodically on his way. Suddenly he freezes, stops dead in his tracks for a moment, then wheels wildly around and, in shock, in horror, recognizes . . . he starts running but is soon stumbling, almost limping, back toward the drunken pair—just at the same instant as the girl recognizes him too and screams. She throws both arms wide now and cries out tearfully, hysterically, "Haley! . . . Haley! Oh, my God! Haley, sweetheart! Of all the streets in this town, why did you have to be going down this one? Oh, Haley, I'm sorry, I'm sorry! I've tried, but I can't help myself! I've tried, Haley, honest to God, I have!" Then she screams again and begins sobbing. It is of course Yolande.

Fifteen months later he is finally located—in Boston—and summoned to Birmingham, Alabama. There he identifies her on the cold morgue slab. He is shown the suppurating knife wound under the delicate left breast. A fortnight later, still dazed, in shock, he is back in Boston where at long last he gets, after all these summers of graduate study, the anticlimactic master's degree.

58

At Gladstone years afterwards he still carries the psychic wounds—"the waste, the utter waste"; it horrifies him; the squandering of a young life so full of promise; prodigally, maniacally, thrown away; it need not have been. He hopes never again to have to be a witness. In this, of course, he will be disappointed. Meantime, his second wife, Roxanne King, herself divorced, has come along. She turns out to be exceptionally good for him—largely in that she successfully feigns lacking his first wife's insight for fathoming his true, his morbid (with cause), makeup. He considers this a heaven-sent change, an escape, bringing him a quieter, less badgered, indeed less tortured, reality, a chance to conceal the symptoms, or at least the vestiges, of the past. But of course he is being duped—and by a good wife, who extravagantly admires him. So Roxanne also sees through him, therefore it will go on and on. It is only he who thinks his camouflage is working—even when from the wings the young hero enters. Cager, tall, ungainly, a mahogany-stippled specimen of the raw freshman, arrives indeed.

Haley has been a Gladstone faculty member for twelve years now, when, on this warm September afternoon, the boy accosts the professor just inside the entrance of Stovall Hall and asks, simply, where one registers for ROTC. Haley looks tired, rumpled, jaded, and brings out a handkerchief to swab his brow. "We don't have an ROTC program at Gladstone," he finally says, though kindly enough, still eyeing the galoot. "Did someone tell you we did?"

"No, sir," says Cager—"nobody told me. I just figured you would. That's why I came here. It's sure what you'all—what we'all—need more'n anything else. More'n any English or chemistry or fraternities. Thank you, sir." He turns and leaves the building, as Haley, at first merely curious, bemused, is somehow now taken aback—as if just fingered by some unholy premonition. He is disquieted.

Eighteen months later he was still so. Only worse. He knew more now, knew the facts, or some of them—though yet not enough, by far. At home of evenings he would talk to Roxanne in the kitchen before dinner. "Groomes is looking for some way to get rid of Rollo Lee," he said. "He's trying to get enough on him to expel him. Only thing is, he's afraid of the students. Most of them, especially the hell-raisers, think Rollo's great." Average in height, nonetheless pudgy, facial skin of biscuit color, half bald, bespectacled, addicted pipe-smoker, Haley sighed, then sat on the high stool in the corner, as Roxanne, peering at a casserole in the oven, gave no sign she had heard. "It's a damn shame," he said.

59

Roxanne turned around, removing her oven mittens. "Lord, here we go again. What's that clown Cager done now, Haley?" Stocky and healthy-looking, quite dark, cheerfully irreverent when not riled, she too was faculty—head of Home Ec. "And get off of Groomes—you're not president, he is. How'd you like to have to be responsible for that crazy Cager Lee? What's he done now?" She finally laughed.

"Who knows?" said Haley. "Maybe nothing. Groomes is on his trail, that's all. I try to tell him the boy's going through a phase. Then next day Rollo will find some brand-new way to mess up. I told you last week he cussed out a white plumber in the dorm, then wanted to fight him, for calling him 'boy.' The company called Groomes and raised hell. He's serious this time."

"Fix me a drink, Haley. You're nuttier than Cager."

"The boy's dumb as hell to play into Groomes's hands like this. But the students love his shenanigans, the girls too; he's popular. It makes no sense. Groomes is smoldering, claims Rollo's polluting the campus, which is preposterous; he's only polluting himself." Haley was grim.

Roxanne slid some rolls in the oven alongside the casserole. "Go empty the garbage, will you, Haley?"

Oblivious, he went on grimacing. "There's something very peculiar about all this—mysterious. Something's gone radically wrong with Rollo. I can't figure it out. He used to practically live in the library. He was serious, almost fanatical—ask others who had him; he's got a mind. He ate my courses up—loved all about the wars and strategies and politics, and so on. Made straight A's—sometimes I felt like giving him A pluses." Haley heaved a sigh. "Now he's not interested in studying at all, just goes around goofing off and playing the fool. And won't talk to anybody about it. Holds everything in. He of all people, though, should know Groomes has had it in for him ever since he led that march downtown and afterward got in the scrape with the police and went to jail. Groomes hasn't forgotten."

Roxanne grinned. "Groomes hasn't forgotten you got him out, either. Haley, why don't you stop worrying yourself about that crazy boy? Stop being such a do-gooder. He's a screwball, I don't care if he was making straight A's. You yourself said last year all he wants is to be some kind of black general and raise a big army of jigaboos to go out and smite the white folks with the jawbone of an ass or something!" She threw her head back laughing.

Haley, still grimacing, was twisting on the tall stool—in torment. He began waving his arms. "I tell Groomes it's a phase the boy's going through! It requires patience, understanding. But he won't listen. Can't you see? . . . It's the awful waste, *the waste!*"

Roxanne shook her head and lit a cigarette. "Go fix my drink, Haley."

12

AT PRESSMAN MY RELATIONSHIP with Bahr can only be called a continuing one if are included its fluctuations and mis-givings—in other words, its headaches. Some days his moods could be forecast, that is, mostly all superior and withdrawn, but on others he could be jaunty to the point of cheerfulness. Yet any time you saw on his face the trace of a smile there was a twinge of innuendo or sarcasm to go with it. One day in the library, with some such mocking smile, he said to me—forcefully, boldly— "Barry, you don't talk about Flo much anymore. How come?"

This at once threw me on the alert—Flo. But first he was talking too loudly. The little library was much used by the "residents" (inmates), many of whom, as I have indicated, were formerly im-portant people—business executives, public officials, including two judges and an ex-governor, even a brilliant, if half-psychotic, psychiatrist. I of course was the only clergyman, and black, and predictably, even aside from the uncertain factor of race, was anything but highly regarded—the theory apparently being a judge may sin but never, never a preacher. But what little library talk there was was kept to whispers, otherwise there came brief frozen stares, as if instead of in Pressman you belonged in the other type institution, with guard towers and ironclad cell blocks. It gave me the excuse to take Bahr back out in the hall and soon up into the lounge where we sat in the bright sunlight. Of course my real, even if subliminal, reason in getting him away was (I well knew) his licentious impropriety in bringing up Flo Ransom, who—in that nostalgic long, long ago—had been Cager's off-campus, or "town," girlfriend and my unforgettable, star-crossed nemesis.

We had barely sat down when Bahr resumed. "If your man Cager had turned out to be such a failure, if he, as you say, was a

61

lowdown scamp (I had certainly said no such thing), the campus clown, to use your words, then what did a good-looking gal like that in town see in him? I gather she was anything but the unsophisticated type—in fact it sounds to me like she was probably pretty slick." He now raked his fingers through his hair (which when he arrived had been dyed a rather demonic saffron brown but was now returning to its true salt-and-pepper cast), fidgeted in his chair, and watched me suspiciously—while I tried to camouflage my deep displeasure at his remarks, all of which, however, I had myself made possible by even, relatively, what little I had told him about my life and those who had figured in it. I also, incidentally, very much disliked his referring to Flo as a "gal." Yet, but for me, he would never have heard of her. He still watched me, though, as if trying to read my mind.

He was of course no fool. Throughout our various conversations about Cager and Flo he always seemed unsatisfied with my account of Cager's sudden strange behavior, his dramatic and radical change from a serious, a superior, student to an eccentric, driven buffoon. Most of all, Bahr was suspicious about what had brought it all on, including the role, if any, Flo had played, which he apparently thought gave him license to use any semblance of pretext to bring her into our discussions. The sick ghoul was rabid for her— that is, for her ghost, her dust. It was also evident, however, that he was mistrustful of me. As well he might have been. For I was dissembling. I had a lot to hide. It was unthinkable, though, despite all my desperate psychic needs to externalize the history of my misdeeds, that I would ever tell him the *whole* truth. I did finally decide, however, to give him, in what was at this point a restrained, even-handed, a judicious second installment, a further glimpse at least of the part I said I saw Flo as having played— which, though, was less than ten percent of the part she had actually played. But even this turned out to be a mistake. For soon, as I have intimated, she was all he wanted to hear or talk about.

But addressing myself to his original question and comment, I began cautiously. "Cager had a way with women," I explained, "up to a point. Besides, Flo herself, there from the big wayward town of New Orleans and at least five years older than he, probably had quite a bit to do with their coming together. She wanted to look after him, I think—sort of like a mother would have maybe." Bahr smiled. "At least," I said falteringly, "there may have been some of that in it. But most people, especially women, were like that about him when they got to know him. Even his womenfolk at home had babied him. So Flo considered herself his town girlfriend, although she knew he also dated a girl—a very nice girl—on campus his own age named Mabel Foster. But Flo didn't mind that. She knew she had the upper hand. Cager, though—"

Bahr's sly, irreverent laugh had stopped me. "Barry," he said, clearly exasperated, "when are you going to get around to taking up Flo in earnest?" He showed his (also cigarette-yellowed) teeth but the laugh had failed. "You make her sound like such a fascinating gal, then you drop the subject altogether."

Deeply resenting him now, I was glad indeed to tell him more—*some* more, that is—for I could almost read his lecherous thoughts and wanted to tantalize, pain, him. "But I've already told you," I said, really exulting inside, "how terrifically good-looking she was."

This brought him quickly fumbling out his little pad and pencil stub and, expectant, excited, he began scribbling. "I hadn't got it all down, though!" he complained, frantically, almost sorrowfully. "Yes, I know you told me she had green eyes! Ha, I remember *that*."

"Green eyes in a golden-beige oval face," I was glad to affirm. "Lovely teeth too, and a smile simply out of this world. Also crinkly coppery hair, with a very light spray of freckles saddling her nose—a rather broad nose it was, too. Then she had this *dream* body. And her Negro blood showed so marvelously not only in her nose but in her full, luscious lips." All this I threw at him as he feverishly scribbled. I was putting it on thick, of course, overdoing it some, though not much, for Flo required little if any exaggeration. But I wanted to punish him. I was quivering inside. How *dare* he pule over our Flo—Cager's and my Flo!

At that moment a stomach cramp hit me—as he watched me with his curious, penetrating gaze. My raw, nervous colon then began churning and knifing until I knew my face showed my agony. The pain made me grip the arm of the chair as he still eyed me archly. Although the Pressman doctors, especially since blood sometimes appeared in my stool, had given me every test imaginable, including a series of those hated barium enemas, they could find nothing, not even a provisional ulcer. So I held onto the chair arm and, suffering, looked into Bahr's pale, desperate face.

"I can see you're concentrating," he said. "There's more to come, all right. I can tell."

"I may not have mentioned it," I said, a death grip on the chair, though careful to avoid saying anything crucial, "but Flo had been married and had a child, a little girl—Annette—although she'd

63

been divorced by the time Cager and I knew her. She'd had a pretty rough time of it. I don't think she'd ever more than finished high school, if that, but it was no handicap in her case, for she wasn't just good-looking, she was plenty intelligent."

"How did she live, though?" he frowned.

I smiled and almost said, "By her wits." In a way it was true. Instead, though, I pretended to have misconstrued the question. "Well enough," I said, which for the most part was also true.

"But *how?*" he almost angrily pressed me. "Where did she get her money?"

Right or wrong, I still attributed his heated suspicion to a weird sexual jealousy, of, moreover, the unhealthiest, ex post facto kind. Flo had been dead for almost fifteen years and he knew it. "She had a *job,*" I said hotly. "*That's* where she got her money." Immediately, though, catching myself, I brought my voice down, saying, "She was, as she liked to put it, 'in state government.' She looked after old folks, Negro senior citizens, and also had some connection, never quite clear, with a home for blind colored children, all people getting some kind of public assistance. It was like, in some ways, being a social worker, I guess, although actually it was a political patronage job. This was unusual for a Negro woman, *or* man, in the deep South at a time when so few Negroes could vote." I did not tell him that there was more to this phase of Flo's life than I had divulged—that is, the matter of her sponsorship for this political preferment. I was also trying hard for aplomb, even breeziness, but, nervously twisting in the chair, he was decidedly irritated with me and began scratching his head—rather it was a kind of manic clawing, for he had dandruff, and every time his hand went up, flakes littered his shoulders. It was unsightly but I knew, even as yet without the facts, that it came from ravaged nerves and I was now surer than ever that he was—as, alas, time would confirm—at least as bad off as I and not as good at disguising it, either. Then another pain hit *me.* But, shivering, I somehow held on.

Suddenly there came from out in the corridor a terrible vocal racket, then a loud clatter of falling, breaking plateware on the floor, followed by a shrill, apoplectic voice of bitter recrimination. At once disgust disfigured Bahr's face. "The Jew is throwing things again," he said. "*Your* friend."

"Have a heart," I said. "The poor guy's in trouble"—I could have added "too"—"and needs help."

"Oh, hell, show me somebody here who doesn't need help. He's a shrink, isn't he? You've got to need one of those just to *be* one. Let him help himself—'Physician, heal thyself.' Shit, and they call this a minimum-security place. That guy ought to be in a padded cell."

At that moment a lithe body came flying down the corridor. The man, razor-thin and pale, with staring, bespectacled eyes beneath a shock of silvery hair, suddenly stopped in his flight long enough to retrieve fragments of the dinner plate he had hurled to the floor. "Pieces, pieces, pieces!" he cried out in what was almost a muffled scream. "Our smashed lives!"

I went over to him. "Bernie, take it easy," I said. "You'll be going home soon. That in itself should get you through the few weeks you've got left. Think of me. I've got almost eight months more."

He stared at me incredulously. "But you and I shouldn't be here *at all*, Meshach! You know that! You know why we're here, too! Different, *harsher*, standards were applied—that's why!"

Bahr, scowling, interrupted him. "Barry here didn't even appeal his conviction," he said. "Neither did I mine. What's that mean?" He clawed at his head. "But, no, you took yours to the *United States Supreme Court*. They wouldn't even hear it. So we're all here together, right? And we're all guilty as hell—*of something*. What difference does it make?"

"Speak for yourself, Bahr!" cried Bernie. "Oh, what a muddled mind you have!" He turned to me again then, both extended hands laden with plate shards, which he now seemed offering me. "Look, Meshach! Look at these broken pieces." He stared at his hands. "Here *we* are! . . . you and I . . . our lives!" Now he let the plateware fall to the floor and rushed off down the corridor.

"What I wonder sometimes," said Bahr, "is who's going to protect us majority from you so-called 'minorities.'"

I said nothing. Soon he made a brief note on his pad before scrutinizing me again. I knew then he was ready to return to Flo but I did not cooperate. I vowed to make him bring her up. I yawned. "I've got to go write my daughter," I said.

"It's pretty clear your pal Cager was an old smoothie," he said, half chuckling now. I didn't know what was coming next, so I remained silent. "But you think Flo was something of a mother figure to him. Pardon me if I laugh. I think they were sleeping together."

This sent me back against the wall. I was furious. I don't know why I was so offended, though. He was right. But he had gone too far now. Then I remembered how critical it was that I not lose my cool. "She did have a certain influence on him," I said guardedly, yet too almost as if his remark had gone unheard. "She kept on him to study harder, tried to get him to buckle down again, stop fooling around so much. Sometimes she'd even make him bring his books in and study at her house."

Bahr let out a guffaw and slapped his knee.

I was seething inside now but I somehow suppressed it. "It was pretty tough going for him all around, though," I said. "He was trying to stay in school and had a variety of odd jobs like most of us at Gladstone. We had to pay our own way, you know."

These obvious irrelevancies only vexed him more. At last, giving up, he put his note pad and pencil stub in his pocket. But not without a parting shot. "I'm sure he was screwing her," he said, as his clawing hand went to his head and the dandruff flew.

From that incident on, though, I realized our talks were fruitless and doomed. Besides, the psychological demands on me were too great, in fact unbearable. True, our sessions continued for a while, but I could no longer bring myself to tell him anything about the crises I was struggling with or make revelations that would in any way lighten my burden. What good was he to me, then? I asked myself. He may somehow have sensed this, for within a few days he had made a complete about-face, become very friendly and cooperative, actually ingratiating. I was certain then that he needed me as much as I had thought I needed him. But it was a little late for us both.

No matter, he now seemed more eager than ever to pull out his little note pad and pencil stub and begin scribbling down anything I felt called on to say. There were no more signs of his boredom, spleen, or mistrust. It was as if he felt our relationship was fast fading and that he must record as much of my forlorn saga as possible while there was yet time. Indeed, I had reason to feel flattered. But I did not. Rather, I felt uneasy, actually a little scared or alarmed, he was now that intense about things. But why, you ask, would he be taking notes in the first place? At the time I was not sure, though I had long speculated on it. In any case, it is well to realize he is not easily analyzed, for he was somehow unbalanced, a little mad. His taking notes had become a kind of ritual, a rite, the unique cachet of his sometimes cloudy vision of life.

But I could not bring myself to believe he had ever had any real interest in what I had to say about Cager—except of course when it also encompassed Flo. It goes without saying Cager was my *sole* interest—if you include the impact, with ramifications, his life had had on mine. What, I think, did most interest Bahr was listening to as much of my tale of pain as I was willing to tell—which, in any concrete or clinical sense, was never much. Yet he was willing, later even avid, to take down as much of it as possible, in order later in his room, as best he could, to study, minutely examine, it with the fanaticism of an undercover anarchist. He wanted, I then believed, to determine whether what he had heard, or what could be deduced from it, at all bore any similarities to his own grave misdeeds. Later, however, these easy surmises of mine were to be considerably altered. I would pity him. But by that time many events would have passed. And even more made plain.

13

IT BEGAN, INNOCUOUSLY ENOUGH, one Saturday morning. "Cage," I said, "wake up." I had come up to the second floor of the dorm and was shaking him in his bunk as he still slept. He finally opened one eye and looked at me. "I need some money," I said. "I've got to go downtown and get my shoes fixed. Could you let me have the twelve bucks you got from me?"

He opened the other eye and slowly sat up, then stretched, scratched his head, and yawned. "Oh, Lord, Rev," he said, shivering, though the room was warm enough, "I sure did let you down, didn't I?"

"No, no, it's not that," I said. "I just need the money." I lifted my left foot and showed him the hole in the sole of the shoe.

It was ten o'clock but there were also others around him, including Roscoe Lomax and Dred Scott Mullins, still sleeping. I disliked waking him like this but I needed my money. Although I had two jobs—washing dishes in the men's dining-hall kitchen, plus pushing a broom in the college power plant—they were barely enough for me to make ends meet despite the occasional small money order Mama Maude was able to send me. I also, inevitably, had the other problem: I found myself frankly puzzled, if not downright disenchanted, with divinity school; my heart was not in it at all. But I knew my little mother would hear of nothing else, so I had reluctantly decided to try continuing and do the best I could. I was

67

therefore having anything but an easy time of it, and now here I was broke again. Moreover, besides the shoe repair, I needed two more textbooks and politely told Cager so.

He was wearing his long underwear for pajamas and sat now on the side of the bunk pondering the general demoralized situation and rubbing his jaw. "Lord have mercy, I ain't got a sou to my name," he said. "I even owe Ma Moody money and I work for her. I *sure* should have paid you before now." He put his chin on his hand and sat gazing forlornly out the window. He sighed— "But let's put our thinking caps on, maybe we can come up with something, get something going. Huh?" He got up and stood staring fixedly out the window now. "Say, y'know," he said, "I just might go in town with you. We ain't got nothing to lose. I got an idea right now." He grinned, stretched, and yawned again, then got his toothbrush and went off to the washroom. He seemed somehow in one of his relatively rare—better—moods, about which, however, I had mixed feelings, for this was no indication necessarily that he was really committed to producing any money. I was soon, though, to gain a clearer understanding of this brief lift in his spirits.

After breakfasting, on Spartan cereal and rolls, we then started out for downtown, walking. The day was bright and crisp, however, and soon he was talking, prattling, really, in a foolish way I was not accustomed to hearing from him. And by the time we were half-way there he had assumed such an outlandishly happy demeanor that it seemed at times bordering on the frantic or driven, as he laughed, capered, and played the fool the rest of the way. I saw then why lately they had been calling him the campus clown. What he whooped and babbled about as we walked was such utter trivia and nonsense—the usual trite hilarious students' gossip and scuttlebutt and other silly goings-on, on and off campus—that I was soon not only bored but exasperated. Before long I was wishing he hadn't come—until, that is, I began to sense something phony about all his clowning and buffoonery, that throughout it he seemed really agitated, desperate, about something. It puzzled me. In any case, I considered our prospects for turning up any money as now nil.

"Where are we headed, Cage?" I asked when we arrived downtown.

"There you go!" he exulted. "Never you mind where we're headed. Say, what're you so curious about, Rev? Does it make any difference as long as I come up with your money. Huh? I can't go to Ma Moody, though—haven't worked in that dive long enough to hit her up again. Ha, she'd fire me—which she's already threatened to do a couple of times. But you stop asking questions." He laughed—emptily—again.

"Okay," I said, "you just come up with my money and I'll be quiet."

But somehow now he grew pensive. "You don't know it," he said, "But today you're in for the treat of your life. You're going to meet an *awfully* nice lady. I called her before we left. Her name's Flo."

"Yes?" I said. I of course had never heard of any such personage and my interest was less than keen.

"And I'll bet you'll like her," he added, and again somehow desperately.

His prediction, however, was to turn out to be the understatement of the century.

When we reached the Negro section, then, he began whistling, and when we finally arrived in front of the little frame house Flo rented, he was merrily—though, I realize now, nervously—humming. We mounted the tiny porch and he knocked. Then, waiting, he gave me a monstrously exaggerated comic wink. I don't recall ever seeing anything so hammy. Strangely then, however, nearly at once, he became subdued, reflective, his expression somber, maybe even sad, before he uttered a great sigh. Flo then opened the door and I almost fainted.

I had never in my whole, if then short, life, of course, seen any woman like this. As the saying goes, she would have caused me to "throw rocks" at Cass Nellis back down home in Sheets, Texas— she was that terrific. Naively, I had thought Cager, now speaking of this "awfully nice lady" named Flo, was referring to some woman among his wide acquaintances possibly in her fifties, somebody's aunt, say, or seamstress, or maybe favorite Sunday-school teacher. I was totally unprepared for the lovely phenomenon, there framed in the door, confronting me. She was everything, or certainly almost so, I was decades later—when poor Flo was no more—to portray so graphically and extravagantly to Bahr.

Her greeting to us was smiling and friendly enough, yet I caught the trace of formality, reserve, in her manner, too—although she was wearing a tightly belted housecoat, mules, and was, unceremoniously, chewing food. "Come in," she said, instinctively raising a hand to press down her thick, slightly crinkly, coppery hair. "We were just finishing lunch."

On entering I saw, in the next room, the kitchen, her little Annette, age seven, at the table. I also noticed that Cager, now in Flo's actual presence, had become so flustered and self-conscious he was almost tongue-tied. "What you saying, baby," he finally got out, much too gleefully, and loudly. "We won't keep you long, hon. This is Meshach, friend of mine."

She smiled at me, but with a half-condescending benignity, as if I were her kid brother. "Hello," she said, though scarcely, really, observing me with those outlandishly concupiscent emerald eyes. "You new out at school?"

"I came this year, yes . . ." I said, jittery to my toes and fingertips. For some bizarre reason Cager then let out a guffaw, which soon, however, even more strangely, degenerated into a titter.

"What're you studying to be?" Flo asked me.

"*Hah!*" Cager broke in. "Tell her, Rev. No, honest, hon—I don't lie—he's in *divinity* school!" She stared at me in such gaping wonder that Cager thought she had not understood. "He's studying to be a *preacher*, baby," he said. "I ain't kidding!"

Flo now gave me that benign smile again. "You'd better change the company you're keeping, then," she said.

Cager's eyes flew wide as he repeated his loud clownish laugh. "Whatta you mean, baby? It's the same company *you* keep, ain't it?"

But she had already changed the subject: "Rollo, you said you were going to come paint my kitchen. You've been saying it for a month now."

"Wait, now, hon!" he laughed crazily again. "I ain't forgot." He then launched into a series of such ludicrous excuses, denials, and promises that Flo only looked at him and, indulgently, smiled. I, though, was following little of it, I was so flabbergasted by *her*. "I'm coming in here tomorrow, Sunday, baby!" he said. "Without fail. I'll paint that dadbloom little kitchen there in an hour."

"I've heard that before." Her smile, though, somehow hovered over him—permissively, humoringly, fondly.

"It's that plantation, that doggone college, out there, hon—yeah, that blankety-blank sweatshop—that keeps me so strung out all the time. Those books, baby! Remember you're the one that's always after me about grades—all the time grades, grades! Well, I'm trying to bring you some grades this time. But I'll be in here in the morning, and when you and Annette get back from church that kitchen will be cool, sweetheart. Now—his voice lowering—"can I speak with you for a minute in private?" Flo seemed not at all surprised. Almost as if by prearrangement, she went ahead of him into the kitchen where they briefly conferred, but out of my line of sight. Immediately, though, my hopes soared for my money.

It was at this moment that little Annette darted from the kitchen into me in the living room. But I really could not handily tell what she looked like—her face. This was because her eyes were somehow encased in this huge pair of leather goggles— which on the child looked bizarre and ghostly, reminiscent, even without the looping corrugated tracheae, of a gas mask and the devastation of war on children, emblematic of the crossbones and skull.

"Hi!" she said, very unabashed and forward. I smiled my return greeting. "I can see you but I bet you can't see me," she said.

"No, not very well—your face," I replied. "Where did you get them?"

"From my mama. She's got some too."

"Why do you wear them?"

"We need them when we go *out*." She seemed exasperated I did not know. Nor would I know for some time to come.

But I was going to pursue it—when Flo and Cager now returned. She was smoking a cigarette and smiling at him. I thought, and certainly hoped, this augured well for my money. "Okay, now," Flo admonished him, "I'll expect your knock tomorrow morning before Annette and I leave."

"Nine o'clock, hon!" he said. "You got my word. That's all you need, ain't it? Now Meshach and I have got to cut. Ha! ha!—got to go see a man about a dog! We'll be seeing you, then, hear?—*right*, baby?" His smile was brilliant, again desperate. She looked long at him now, an odd look—once more indulgent, forgiving, tender.

Finally she turned to me. "Come back, Mee . . ." She could not pronounce my crazy name.

"I will, I will," I said, though. "*Thanks.*" I liked her. I liked her a lot. I felt really happy.

Cager and I left then. He had borrowed twenty dollars from her and gave me my twelve and kept the eight. We went then and got my shoes fixed and afterward had a delicious soul-food meal at Shorty George's little restaurant. I felt terrific now. I was so proud of Cager too now and was sure—alas, too sure—that I would be his most loyal friend forevermore. I was also in love with Flo. Or thought I was.

14

What pipes and timbrels? What wild ecstasy!
—KEATS

It don't mean a thing [however] if you ain't
got that swing!
—DUKE

A SHARP, CHILLY, FRIDAY EVENING, already dark, the campus dead and buried. Certainly that for those of us students now boarding the downtown bus and rarely lucky enough to be leaving campus for a few hours of off-limits fun and games (so we hoped) to spell the tedium of the daily-nightly book grind. Prospects of excitement! Yeah! Of "Ecstasy!" "Swing!"

There were nine of us—five boys, four girls, including Mabel Foster, Cager's campus girlfriend—and, not uncommonly, we had to stand most of the way as our Jim Crow section of the bus was full to overflowing. Cager, though, was already in town, gone on ahead, as he put it, "to arrange things," meaning of course "things" at Ma Moody's jumping Jehoshaphat cabaret. (By Groomes's on-pain-of-death edict a no-no.)

The designation "Ma Moody's," however, despite its almost universal use, was not the real name of the place at all. Rather, the name in lights outside on the front of the building was THE MIDNIGHT CLUB. Ma, originally from Houston, financed the enterprise, but her spouse-equivalent, Keen Smith (nicknamed "Spats" because of his winter footwear), an ex-dice-and-card shark from Dallas, had much to do with running it. An affable man (that is, when uninterferred with) in his late forties, popular with the trade, he most frequently lounged in the bar, pearl Stetson pushed back off his forehead, ragged gold teeth bared in a smile, as he greeted the customers and sipped his Vat 69 scotch and water. But Ma, almost sixty, was less popular. She was inclined to be irascible, except with certain people, of whom Cager, her part-time employee of sorts, was one. She berated and bullied him, but most of the time it was all in her own rough, humorless brand of fun. The fact was, he amused her.

72

Cager, as he waited for us to arrive, sat talking with Spats in the bar/lounge adjacent to the restaurant section, both of which were already crowded even though activities in the larger cabaret annex were yet to begin. Cager drank no alcoholic beverages of any kind, not even our cheap dormitory wine, so he sat with a Coke in his hand as Spats talked about Jimmie Spinks's band which provided the hot jazz music in the cabaret section for dancing and the floor shows. "Jimmie's got a new tenor sax man," Spats said. "Name's Sonny Pemberton. You shoulda heard him when they was rehearsing back there today. Sounded like he was tryin' to blow the roof off the place. Jimmie says he played with Basie for a while."

"What's he doing here, then?" laughed Cager.

Spats arched an eyebrow. "That I couldn't tell you—Jimmie didn't say and I didn't ask him. But don't play Jimmie cheap. His band's reputation's growing all the time. He says he's in beautiful shape now with Pemberton with him. Smooth-lookin' cat, too—Sonny. Great favorite with the ladies."

At this point all nine students from campus trooped in. When Cager saw us through all the crowd and cigarette smoke he feigned a great arm-waving, welcoming jubilation as he went into his sad, fake clowning act. "*Hey, hey!*—look who's here, will you?" he cried, trying to beckon us over. When at last we had all pushed through to him he greeted us effusively, kissing the girls on the cheek, Mabel on the lips, and maddeningly shaking the hands of the boys—all before, a comic smirk on his face, he began deriding us. "What took you'all so long?" he said. "I been here all this time cooling my heels." He glanced at his watch. "Where'd you'all come from—Washington, D.C.?"

"No," said Mabel, "it'll surprise you to learn we all came from Gladstone College. That's not so far from here—ever hear of it? We came on the bus and had to stand up most of the way—with the white section only half full."

Cager's laugh turned unpleasant, mean. "Tsk, tsk," he said, "ain't that a shame. Why didn't you'all go up and sit in those empty seats? Huh? But, oh, I forgot, you didn't have any menfolks along, did you?—in case something happened. Yeah, yeah, that makes a big difference, don't it?" His roguish eyes surveyed us five males standing there.

"Go to hell, Cage," laughed Daryl Wiggins.

"Second the motion," Willie Sparrow said.

"Yes, we had menfolks along," Mabel said, "but they don't have

73

the fondness for jails that some people around here I know have. Neither do I."

Cager, again going into his weird, manic laughing act, threw an arm around Mabel's shoulder, play-wrestled with her briefly, then led us all over in the direction of the big door to the cabaret annex. At the same time warning us: "Ma Moody, you know, don't like Gladstone students coming in her place—especially the girls. She laid me out when I told her I was bringing you'all in here tonight. She's afraid Groomes will make trouble for her—which he sure would if he knew. So she's set a curfew—said we had to be out of here by eleven."

"*What?*" said Newt Gaines.

"That's right," Cager said, "unless she happens to get busy and forgets about us for a while. Maybe we can make out till twelve if we're lucky. We'll just have to play it by ear and not let anything keep us from having us a ball if we can while we *are* here. You'all dig me?" There was reluctant assent.

Entering with the others the spectacular cabaret annex now, I was awe-struck. Moreover, I was soon wild with exhilaration, excitement, and joy. I had never in all my short life been in a nightclub before, of any kind, and I was overwhelmed. The room was large and almost square, flaunting a profusion of colors, with three-fourths of the space taken up with tables bearing immaculate white cloths and artificial floral centerpieces. The four expansive walls were a mass of great blown-up photographs of famous black jazz artists—Duke Ellington, Billie Holiday, Louis Armstrong, the Mills Brothers, Fats Waller, Jimmie Lunceford, Coleman Hawkins, others. In the center of all this was a smaller floor space directly in front of the bandstand for the floor shows and for patron dancing. The room was already fast filling up with customers, and at first there was confusion about where our somewhat large party could be seated, until Cager and a waitress solved the problem by pulling two tables together, though we were still located far in the rear of the house.

But I was so busy staring and gawking that I was completely unaware of any of these mundane goings-on like tables and their location, for I had never seen so many good-looking women before, some of them not only pretty but lusciously worldly-looking and who gave me all kinds of fleshy fantasies, erotic palpitations, and plain old carnal desire, until, that is, I remembered I was studying to be a minister. My heart sank then. But not for long. One reason was that I was so happy and again so proud that I knew

Cager and was, I was sure beyond any doubt, his true and faithful friend. Wasn't I here tonight due solely to his generosity? For I was flat broke again and had told him so when he had invited me to join them. He would hear of none of my excuses. "Don't worry about a thing, Rev. Be my guest. My ship came in yesterday." This meant, I later learned, that Mabel Foster's father, an Atlanta caterer, had sent her a check which she had received the day before. "Willie Sparrow's got a few bucks too this time," he said. "And also Daryl. Maybe next go-round we'll catch *you*, when *your* ship's in. Huh?" He laughed.

Oh, what a terrific guy! I thought—overjoyed. What a friend! I vowed I would find some way to do *him* a favor, show my appreciation. I meant it.

Now, addressing our waitress with his customary endearing "Baby," Cager ordered the drinks, most of them, by his guests' choice, saccharine-sweet, and another Coke for himself—just as a huge tipsy woman two tables over jumped up and, shaking her fist in the air, let out an inebriate yell: "Look out! Here comes the band! . . . Here we go!"

Cager leaped up to see. "She ain't kidding! Hey, now!" Soon we all saw. Jimmie Spinks and his men were drifting in from various parts of the premises and heading up toward the bandstand. "All right, then!" cried Cager. "Let the good times roll!" When, then, the ceiling lights dimmed and the bandstand lights came up, he was not long in spotting, in the front row of the band and now taking his seat, the new tenor sax player Spats Smith had extolled- —Sonny Pemberton. Dapper, trim, "cool," with smooth tawny skin and a hairline mustache, Sonny urbanely viewed the crowd— as Cager studied him.

At last now came a long, loud drum roll, followed by a crashing cymbal—to get order in the house. Jimmie Spinks, in a loud, natty orange jacket, his hair processed and gleaming, stood at the microphone. When the noise had sufficiently subsided, Jimmie, not only band leader but master of ceremonies, his alto sax strung from his neck, finally spoke with an overused rasping voice into the mike: "Ladies and gentlemen! Welcome, one and all, to the Midnight Club—Ma Moody's gift to this backward cracker town!" Everybody laughed. "You'all relax, then, and enjoy yourselves while we bring you some music and our show tonight. We think it's all cool and we hope you'll think the same. Tonight you'll see Foxy Scott, the one-legged tap dancer. Also the Catlett Sisters will do their raunchy little skit, 'Two Old Maids in a Folding Bed,' that'll

75

have you holding your sides in the aisles before they're through. Then you'll meet that clever magician, July Jamieson, the now-you-see-it, now-you-don't man, brought here by Ma and Spats all the way from New Orleans. And, of course, last but not least, our own great lady of the blues, Miss Cuba Armstrong, who you'all love *so much*!" Heavy applause. "And, as always, backing up the show will be the band—your humble servant and his 'Royal Sounds.' By the way too, starting tonight, we have a new addition to our band, a great tenor sax man and artist, Sonny Pemberton, whose way-out horn solos will give you'all thrills you never had before!" Spinks turned around. "Stand up, Sonny, so the folks can see you." Pemberton, self-possessed, almost impassive, stood briefly and acknowledged the applause, as Cager, eager to hear him, more excited and expectant than ever, still watched him.

"Okay, now," cried Spinks, "to get things started, the Royal Sounds will rap out a little number that's got that hard bop beat you'all like so! It's 'Salt Peanuts!' "More clamorous applause. "Stay with us, then, folks, while we *ride* this gig!" His men were ready. "One, two, three," he said, his foot stomping the beat as the music broke sharp, punctuated, frantic. The delighted crowd's hand-clapping with the hard-driving rhythms soon seemed ringing the very ceiling beams. I was in heaven, wildly patting both feet and pounding my hands together in time with the music's beat, as Cager, gleefully pointing to me, again went into his riotous laughing. How I wished now that instead of a preacher I was going to be a great jazz musician! The crowd was soon in ecstasy, and when finally the Royal Sounds ended "Salt Peanuts" with two earsplitting rim licks from the drummer, a great guttural shout went up, followed by more frenzied hand-beating.

Next Spinks, his alto sax swung high, led the band in a "concert" number—"Marie"—chosen primarily, however, to show off Sonny Pemberton's tenor sax prowess. The moment Sonny stood up and began soloing, Cager shook his head in disbelief and sighed, as if in grudging admiration of the way Sonny built his "chords," the intricacies of his harmonies, and his stark, angry tone almost totally devoid of vibrato. "*Jesus!*" cried Cager, "this cat's got his dander up, ain't he? Yeah, swingin' like a Seth Thomas."

But when the music stopped and the floor show began, I noticed his sudden abstraction, his eyes elsewhere, observing a ringside table up front full of Sonny's fans and friends, people who seemed not only enthusiastic well-wishers but a rabid claque who had often stood up to interrupt his solos with boisterous cries and applause. Cager watched them until stopped by Mabel looking in the other direction, toward the door. "Oh, Lord, there's Ma," she said.

Cager turned. Then laughed. "Yeah, makin' trouble for somebody, you can bet on it." We all saw Ma Moody now, edging her way through the tables with apparently no particular destination in mind—a heavy woman though not tall, wearing a hairpiece, a chignon, at the back of her head and a white knit dress far too tight even for her firmly girdled large hips and high derriere. Smoking a cigarette, her dark massive face expressionless, she deigned in her meanderings to speak to but few, if any, of her customers. Cager, his eyes following her, laughed again. "Look at her—casing the joint. She ain't seen us yet. She will, though."

The floor show continued. After magician July Jamieson's penultimate act had come and gone, Jimmie Spinks again stepped to the mike. "And now, folks, we come to the pièce de résistance of the evening! You know who I'm talkin' about, all right! *Home talent!*" This set off such a joyful clamor Spinks could not make Cuba Armstrong's name heard above the din.

Cager had already cried out: "Here she comes! Oh, Cuba, baby! Hey, hey, hey! Sing me the blues, sweetheart!"

"Cool it, Cage," Mabel said.

Spinks's rasping voice was still trying to make itself heard. "Here's your treat, ladies and gentlemen! Here she is!—our *own* queen of the blues! *Miss Cuba Armstrong!*" The place went wild. Whistling, stomping, shouting, and riotous applause inundated the house.

Despite an ancient "battle" scar over her left eye, Cuba was a handsome woman—robust, smooth dark brown, with a gleaming, yet set, smile. Tonight she wore a gown dripping pink sequins, enhanced by glittering pendant earrings, and as she came forward the crowd roared its delirious affection. Yet, except for smiling as she stepped to the mike she—apparently out of high artistic self-esteem—did not further react to the adulation. The din only increased.

Cager—genuinely now—was beside himself with rapture. "That woman can make you *cry!*" he implored us to understand. "Just wait till you hear her! She'll tear your heart out! Lord God Almighty!"

Cuba began with "The Sweet Cider Blues." The band's accompaniment, though silken and mellow, especially in the saxes, soon took on a deep melancholy cast in the brasses, the piano, however, having strangely introduced the melody in a stream of florid arpeggios and rapid chromatic runs just before Cuba glided into her plaint. Her voice was at first high, yet cool and sweet, with a slight tremolo. Then almost at once it darkened, grew passionate and desolate. Her eyes closed now, arms out wide pleadingly, open mouth showing two gold-capped incisors, she moaned, shrieked, and wailed out of her soul the true blues:

"My man done gone, gone, gone.
Left me with nothin' but a jug of sweet cider.
Give his money to a grinnin' high yaller,
Who'll leave him soon as it's gone.
Oh, Lord, Oh Lord, how I miss him!
Miss his teasin',
Miss his snorin',
Miss his fightin',
And oh, how I miss his lovin'!
But now what am I gonna do?
What am I gonna *do*, Lord?
'Sides live with my lonesomeness
And drink his sweet cider!

If anybody axe you
Who sing this song,
Tell 'em it was ole Cuba
Done been here and gone!"

As much tragedienne as singer, her voice often faltering, cracking, under the emotion (some of it self-generated), Cuba seemed in her stagey grief about to break down. The house was hushed now, moved, my own blood throbbing, while Cager was near tears. "Remember Haley Barnes's lecture on the blues?" he cried. "And where they came from, how we got them? . . . what we've been through, and all that? Wasn't old Haley something that day, telling us about it? Lord, but he oughta be here tonight and hear *this* woman! Huh?"

"Calm down, Cage," Mabel said.

Cuba went on regaling the patrons for a half hour, chanting, exhorting, preaching in song, crying out her tumultuous blues, gospel, and work songs. Ma Moody, an acknowledged admirer of her star performer's art, though still patrolling the crowd, occasionally stopped whenever applause overwhelmed the house to say to herself, yet out loud, "Sing it, honey—go on sing them damn blues."

78

When the show was finally over, the patrons surged onto the floor to dance. Spinks was more than ever featuring Sonny Pemberton now. Sonny, his wild sax quacking and quivering, had at last shed all his cool hauteur and was outdoing himself in a weaving, bobbing, trembling fervor, as the heavily imbibing, unruly guests at his ringside table wildly cheered him on. The crowd's frantic dancing seemed to charge him up, spur him on to an even greater frenzy, almost as if he were suddenly possessed by demons. Many of the dancers had now stopped in front of the bandstand, merely to look, listen, and joyfully stamp their feet and clap their hands. And when Cuba Armstrong, rejoining the band to further spur the dancers, began the strains of "He May Be Your Man but He Comes to See Me Sometimes" all hell broke loose. It seemed as if Cager, in the middle of the floor dancing with Mabel, had gone stark raving crazy and berserk. He was doing a wild, hip-slinging, rubber-legged dance called "The Hucklebuck," his version of which, however, no one before or since has ever seen, much less danced, and which defied any description or classification. In his exertions he seemed transported, delirious, and poor harried Mabel, as if appealing to be rescued, spent.

As they all danced, Jackson Dawson, another in our party, and I, neither of us with dates, remained at the table enviously looking on, watching it all. We often tried to talk, or exclaim, about what we were witnessing, but there was such pandemonium from the frenzied music, wild outcries, and dancing that we could only with difficulty hear each other. It was then we saw shouldering her way through the crowd this inky-black old woman, at least in her mid-seventies, her dingy white hair wrapped in a head rag, stopping at each table and haranguing its occupants about something or other we could not hear. Then we saw that she was accompanied, on either side, by two pensive-looking children, a boy and a girl, no older than ten or eleven. But, to our astonishment, the boy carried a big, unhappy, meowing, black cat in his arms. They had all approached to within earshot before I saw the Bible in the old woman's left hand and the lidless cigar box in her right, as she continued loudly lecturing the seated patrons. I knew then she was hawking religion and in that connection making vehement money solicitations. "Oh, cripes," complained a woman customer at the next table, "here comes the *pest!* Old Hattie and those poor kids again. Why does Ma let her come in here? And keeping those children up all hours."

But Hattie was busy canvassing another table, as she inveighed against sin and the Devil and panhandled the merrymakers. Brandishing the Bible and thrusting the cigar box in people's faces, she now stopped at the table to our left, crying out: "Gawd, you know, can tell what's goin' on here! He ain't blind, He ain't deaf, and He ain't dumb! That's why I'm here preachin' His gospel to you sinners the same way my pastor, the Reverend Pilate G. Walker, that sent me here, would be preachin' in this hellhole and den of iniquity tonight if he could be here like me tryin' to save souls! Here is my message to you—*The way of the transgressor is hard!*"

"Amen," said the shy, sleepy-eyed, little bronze girl at her side, as the boy with the cat, who looked nothing like the girl's brother, innocently observed old Hattie's preaching and said nothing.

"The wages of sin is death!" cried Hattie, in her fervor her grimy hair shooting out from under the head rag and her lips peeling back off a jungle of green, decaying teeth. "Sleepers awake, then! Give heed to the word of the Lord!" At this table to our left now she pushed the cigar box into the face of a man trying to light a cigarette, his hand unsteady from drink, and started her spiel. But he interrupted her with a loud, irreverent laugh, then fished some coins out of his pocket and tossed them in her cigar box. "The Lord sure will bless you, sir," she said.

"Amen," now said the boy at her elbow, before stroking the restive black cat in his arms in a vain attempt to keep it quiet. "The Lord sure will, sir."

At that moment Ma Moody appeared out of nowhere behind old Hattie. "Watch your step, now," Ma warned her, frowning. "Don't overdo your damn nuisance or you'll be outa here fast. I let you come in here once in a while to pick up a few dimes and quarters, which—I don't care what you say—that damn woman-chasing pastor of yours, Bearcat Walker, never sees. I just hope you spend some of it on these two poor raggedy foster kids you bring in here to soften up your victims, but who happen to be my customers! I want you outa here in fifteen minutes!" She turned to go then—just at the instant that she spied the black cat. Her mouth flew open but she was speechless. Finally she got out a yell. "*Oh!* How *dare* you bring that thing in here! Take it out that door quick!—but it's already put a sign, a hex, on my place! Oh, get it outa here!" But the boy holding the cat was cowering and looking instead at old Hattie, whom Ma resumed berating— "Why, that's the worst thing you coulda brought in a place like this! Ain't you got any sense at all? Look around you, woman!— everybody here's got a sign on 'em of some kind as it is! Then you let that child bring *that* thing in here!" She advanced on the trembling boy as Hattie leaped to intervene, which brought her a hard shoulder shove from Ma, and soon they were wrestling, as the two frightened children cowered back from them both.

"Ma," cried Hattie, "don't you dare touch that cat! It ain't no sign. It's a pet!"

"Get it out!—get it *outa* here, I say!" yelled Ma, conclusively now, still trying to get at the struggling animal in the boy's arms.

It was then that Cager, Mabel, and the other dancers from our table returned. At once Ma, as if having a seizure, began railing at him and pointing at the cat. "Cager, Cager! . . . get ahold of that thing! Kill it—*kill it*, I tell you! Why, you oughta know it's as bad for you as it is for me or my customers in here! Colored folks already got enough to contend with without another 'sign' on 'em! *Especially you!*"

Cager, though, as were the others with him, seemed frozen in his tracks, only staring in complete bewilderment at the cat, before also finally getting a contagious look of fear and doom in his face as though really wanting to turn and run or hide. He seemed perfectly helpless, mesmerized, turned to stone—as was now Ma, who was unable to speak.

The cat then let out a loud meow, followed by a kind of high, keening wail, just before old Hattie snatched it from the boy and vengefully thrust it first in Cager's, then Ma's, face. "Take *this!*" she said to them. "And *this!*" Yet, it somehow seemed a weird, static pantomime in which neither Cager nor Ma was at all able to react. Only Ma's jaw had dumbly dropped. But suddenly now Hattie dashed out of the Midnight Club she had so thoroughly hexed, the hapless children scurrying after her.

Cager finally dropped in his seat, by some means shaken, as Ma, as if even yet fleeing a departed ghost, quickly vanished in the direction of the kitchen.

But before anyone could remark on all the commotion, Jackson Dawson at my elbow gave me a swift nudge in the ribs, then pointed toward the entrance. I looked. As for me, then, the rest of the evening was a gigantic blur. Flo Ransom had just walked in.

The woman of my dreams, my emissive fantasies! Inside I was euphoric. My loyal friend Cager no longer existed. Casually threading her way through the crowd, she was apparently heading up front—toward the bandstand.

At the same instant now, it seemed, Dawson and I, as if only now remembering, looked across the table at Cager. Had he seen her? I wondered. I rather concluded he had not—yet. He still seemed too shaken by the drama of the black cat. Mabel Foster, however, was another matter. Dawson again leaned toward me, whispering, "Man, oh, man, stick around."—as if I were going any place!

But just as my eyes were devouring Flo, she was swallowed up in the crowd. She had looked so marvelous. She did not have many pretty clothes; she could not afford them. Yet, she never tried to make up for it by overdressing. It only made her more attractive, sexier, heightened her already outrageous appeal. (Years later even, during my narration of some of this—not all—to him, Bahr became very excited, at once fumbling out the habitual writing materials in order to begin his feverish scribblings, the turbulent fantasies so clearly showing in his jiggling Adam's apple, the glowing eyes like coals, and flaking dandruff when inevitably his hand went to his head. Vividly I remember he was both voracious and demoralized. I myself, though, in relating selective parts of this episode to him, became affected, moved—across all those years—by the power of Flo's imperishable image, its magic presence.)

I have tried to reconstruct, after having later seen her that night, how she then really looked—entering the cabaret annex and slowly working her way forward toward the front. She was bareheaded tonight, her expression calm yet intent, her dark gray coat, worn with white gloves, plain but on her extremely attractive. One would never have suspected—from her cool, self-confident manner—her vast, intricate complicatedness, much less her myriad hesitancies and vulnerabilities. So there she went, head high, though not haughty, and looking neither left nor right as she proceeded. Yet, I could only sit there—at Cager's table, too, and as his guest—watching her with mooning eyes. Soon, though, my equilibrium, indeed cunning, began to return. I fell to thinking, even plotting—though well knowing I could do nothing at the moment—about how I could get near her. I was soon, though, seized with a nearly unmanageable urge, a sudden madness—as if my rabid tongue were hanging out—to follow her *now*. I was on fire. Yet, and wisely, I did nothing.

For a brief time, then, I lost sight of her in the crowd. But before long I saw her emerge and, my poor heart shuddering, head straight for Sonny Pemberton's ringside table. I was dumbstruck. An acrid suffocation welled up in my throat that for a moment I thought would choke me. Now I saw her being greeted by the boisterous people at the table, who appeared by no means strangers to her and only too glad—almost as if her arrival had been eagerly awaited—to make room for her snugly beside Sonny himself there socializing while the band was taking a break. I could not escape suspecting something then, and any remaining scales fell from my eyes when I saw Sonny, courtly and smiling, lean and kiss her on the cheek. My bitter heart sank. I felt grievously wounded, and finally resentful, even vengeful, toward her—with never a thought of how Cager, assuming he had seen (though I dared not turn and look across the table), might also feel. I only knew, with Mabel present, he was severely, if not disastrously, handicapped. If, then, or so I reckoned, I had any chance at all, I must bide my time—until, on resumption of the music, Sonny had returned to the bandstand.

When ten minutes later, then, the terrific music had resumed and undecipherable, unreadable Cager, Mabel, and the others were again leaving the table to dance, Newt Gaines, a most considerate fellow, asked me if I wanted to dance with Grier Johnson, the girl he had brought. Spluttering a spate of hurried, nervous nonsense, though thanking him, I of course declined, whereupon Jackson Dawson danced with her, while Newt and I remained at the table—I now in a perfect tizzy of indecision and confusion. I realized, though, I was losing my nerve by the minute, that if I did not soon act, whatever mixed-up resolution I had had would be gone. I then forced myself to act. Telling Newt I would see him in a minute, I got up and, knees shaky, throat dry, headed up front.

But finally on arrival there I saw that Flo's back was to me, as she sat talking to a man and woman who, besides herself, were the only ones at the table not at the moment dancing. I stood there breathlessly waiting then, mortally afraid to interrupt, the soul of discretion, respect, and trembling like a leaf. But at last when she turned and saw me her face was strangely a blank and I thought she had not recognized me. "Flo," I said shakily, "I'm Cager's buddy . . . Meshach—remember?" The gall, the irony too, at the moment altogether escaped me. "He brought me by your house one day."

She finally nodded and gave me that negligent, kid-brother smile I so well recalled from our first meeting. "I remember you, yes," she said. "How're things?"

But I had rushed on. "The music's really great, isn't it?" I said. "Gee, it's terrific! . . ."

She replied with her level, wry gaze cum half-smile: "What's somebody who's going to be a preacher doing in Ma Moody's dancing and drinking highballs and goodtiming all night?"

But I was so flustered I barely heard her, and said, "Oh, never mind that. *Gee*, it's good to see you again! You sure do look great! . . . I saw you when you first came in!" All my resentment and vindictiveness had vanished into thin air. "Flo"—I at last then got it out—"would you mind if I spoke with you, just for a minute?" My heart was in dire fibrillation.

She hesitated. She seemed slightly taken aback, yet hardly unpleasantly so. "You sound like a preacher already," she said at last, patting the seat of the empty chair beside her in invitation. "Okay, speak."

Elated, I then, nervously, sat down and proceeded to commit my first of a series of stupid, disastrous blunders. Like a fink, I leaned close to her and whispered, "Cager's here tonight—did you know? He's out there dancing—now."

She showed no surprise and little interest. "Is he?—I hadn't seen him," she said, as if she might shrug.

It was my dogged genes that impelled me to persist—in my snitching: "His girlfriend Mabel's with him."

She stared me straight in the eye. "So what?" she said. Yet, soon, that strange expression came on her face that I had seen the other time when she had gazed at Cager—indulgence, solicitude, tenderness. She almost laughed. "What's he using for money tonight?" she said.

But by now the music had become so hot and groovy, the sharp rhythms overpowering, the dancing so frantic, that, ignoring the flip question, I blurted out: "Flo, *Flo*, will you let me dance with you—just once?" I was quaking.

She looked at me, really startled now—by my distracted manner—and took a deep breath. "Okay," she finally said, and got up. Blinded by euphoria now, I too rose, led her onto the jumping, crowded floor, and took her in my arms. Oh, heavenly wonders!

But soon, as we began moving about, I suddenly became aware that she was not talking, that in fact she seemed in some kind of distress. Then it hit me. My dancing. I had not danced more than a half-dozen times in my whole life. I had gotten carried away on a streak of temporary derangement—or maybe moon madness—in even asking her to dance. Dancing had been frowned on by my superreligious little mother. Besides, I was by nature as clumsy as an ox. I was appalled now to realize what a disaster I was sure to be in the throes of all those dynamic and complicated rhythms Jimmie Spinks and his colleagues were sending off that bandstand. Yet, something had happened which, temporarily at least, took my mind off my predicament and everything else—including both Cager and Sonny Pemberton. For a time I did not really care anymore. It was that Flo was in my arms and our bodies were in powerfully close contact. I was dizzy, though, not only with rapture but with a wild concupiscence. She felt so firm, yet somehow willowy, pliant too, against me as I stumbled about the floor in a blind dither.

But at last she pulled back from me and gave me a harried, disheveled look. "Who ever told you you could dance?" she said.

"Nobody," I murmured meekly. But soon a strange boldness, even brazenness, came over me and I felt by far the better for it. I suddenly found I wanted to pour out all my problems, frustrations, the chronic headaches of my life, to her, all the afflictions that had baffled me since adolescence, my psychic itching, explosive libido, and more; confess to her freely, extravagantly, even foolishly; humble and humiliate, indeed castigate, myself before her. It was a delirium; it was neuropsychosis; I wanted to confess to her as one would to a holy priest; there were thus so many complicated ways in which I wanted to use her. Of course, though, no matter that I craved to, I did none of these things. I knew it would have been repellent to her. So I tried to return to normalcy, no happy state for me, and talk rationally. "I'm from the country," I said—"A little farm down in east Texas. I didn't know anything about cabarets or dancing. It's all new to me."

"I can believe you," she said, moving her feet nimbly to avoid my stepping on them.

Meantime, I was still stumbling about, rudely bumping into people, and dragging her with me. Occasionally our thighs would bang against each other, or my knee for a split second would enter between her legs, as I wrestled and manhandled her about, all to Jimmie Spinks's loud, driving, reckless music. Although my groin sweetly ached, I was almost swooning from the sheer transport of these infrequent but, for me, utterly blissful rubbings. She could not possibly have missed feeling my case-hardened member against her, for she soon backed off from me and became wary and even more silent.

Finally, though, even I became embarrassed and I think she

sensed it. Yet, despite everything, she somehow did not seem insulted, though by no means amused, either. Could it rather have been—I abhorred the thought—that she was otherwise preoccupied? Say, with the bandstand? Now as I swung her around once more, still badly out of step with the hot boogie-woogie rhythms of the band, my rapturous gaze collided head-on with Cager's stunned, unbelieving stare. Although it had occurred well across the width of the packed dance floor, it for a moment filled me with a strange physical fear. Yet, he had not looked angry so much as shocked. I wondered now if he had really seen Flo come in. At any rate, I came to in a hurry, awkwardly swinging Flo back around in the opposite direction, only to find myself directly under the cool, dispassionate gaze of Sonny Pemberton on the bandstand. Sonny's expression, though, if not blasé was not necessarily hostile, either; he seemed mildly curious, maybe actually amused. As for long-suffering Flo, she was aloof, above it all, as if she had seen none of it, not even Cager, or else did not care. But finally, her patience absolutely depleted, she pulled back and looked me in the eye. "Come on, let's stop these calisthenics," she said with finality. "Haven't we had enough? God, haven't *you?*"

But I had the gall to feel let down, treated unfairly, though I reluctantly led her back to the table and was about to sit down beside her again, when I realized I was not at all welcome. Besides, across the floor again I saw Cager's now outraged look and knew I could not tarry. I uneasily thanked Flo for the dance, though really still feeling hurt, stupid, and more confused, and finally, as she looked much relieved, started back to Cager's table to face what I was sure would be his explosive ire.

When I arrived there I found them all ready to leave to return to campus—it was past midnight—and Cager was already paying the check. His mere glance in my direction told me he was in the foulest of moods. I naturally thought it was against me, until, malevolently grinding his teeth, he said to me, sotto voce: "You take Mabel on back to campus with the others. I can't come right now."

"What's up, Cage?" I said, sensing, actually, a minimum of displeasure toward *me*. I could only think then of Sonny Pemberton as the object of his wrath, and that he had seen plenty, including Flo with Sonny.

He frowned. "Don't you worry about 'what's up,' Rev. Just do as I say."

What I, in short, sensed now was a dangerous situation develop-ing. He gave me another angry, yet somehow fishy, look. In all my years I have never known a poorer liar than Cager Lee. "Why can't you come on back with us?" I said.

Again his fishy look. "I gotta hang around here for a little while. Ma wants me to still do some things for her."

Well knowing him, I knew now what he really meant to do, that is, stay and make trouble, plenty of it—especially for Sonny Pem-berton. I could readily feel his violent, suppressed fury. I also knew he was on the verge of making more trouble for himself than for anybody else—considering his already current situation. I realized, then, I had to get him out of there—fast. So I played my next sleazy trick of the evening on him. Under the guise of going to the john, I quickly left and found Ma in the bar. Knowing by now it was long past her curfew for us, I snitched again. I told her what he had said.

She hit the ceiling. "He's a liar! Oh, no he don't stay, neither!" She looked up at the clock, which showed almost 12:30. "You'all shoulda *been* outa here! You tell him I said so! And the rest of you little snotty-nose college kids go with him!"

When I went back and, whispering, tried to reason with him, then told him what Ma had said, he did something he had never done before and would never do again. He cursed me. Then he wanted to fight me, furiously charging I had betrayed him. Al-though he was not any more specific than that, I was scared. When I continued to try to calm him down he turned and, muttering a string of profanities, ran, bolted, out the front door, as alarmed Mabel, then the rest of us, followed. On the bus going back to campus he sat beside Mabel and silently glowered straight ahead all the way. We did not disturb him, either.

Next day he came to the Gladstone power plant, where three afternoons a week I was one of the janitors, and, trying to conceal a hangdog look, apologized. *He* apologizing to *me*. Ah, Cage. . . .

Indeed Bahr, who did not even have the whole story, especially about Flo, was moved. "How in the hell are you going to figure out a guy like that?" he said, almost irritably, to camouflage his lapse into emotion. "He couldn't figure *himself* out, hell. But what difference would it have made, anyhow?—*in the long run.*" He heaved a heavy sigh, then tried his damnedest to grin.

Powerless before his judgment on Cager—which I had not entirely understood anyway—I said nothing. I only itched.

15

ALONE ON THE STREET CORNER under the bleary light—it was past midnight—he stands waiting. Has he missed it? he wonders—the final bus back to campus. He painfully hopes he has not—his fatigue is too real for the interminable journey on foot. Also the threat of rain hovers in the night air. He yawns. Suddenly, then, it is as if some sepulchral bodiless voice from out of the black void, or escaping from some far-off ominous cave of winds, addresses him in tones both admonitory and sad: "Cager, Cager, for shame. Why—though you call it a job, your meal ticket—why do you continue squandering your days and nights in a bawdy cabaret, run by that chief harridan of the world's proprietresses, when your neglected books, to you once so precious, now pitifully cry out for both your reform and return? Or have you no more capacity for shame?"

He wishes to mumble some feeble defense, cite some extenuating pretext, like: I have, yes, to eat, live, somehow hang on; the crummy job is my sole means. True, it is low, menial, exclusively flunky work, for example, scrubbing pots and pans, mopping floors, unloading heavy supplies, but—no matter that I too often get carried away with the place's raunchy, exciting entertainment fare—what alternative is there? He feels utterly trapped in his present life and at times considers giving it up completely and returning home to the Virginia tidewater—only then to recall the high, if now futile, mission that had first brought him here. Now he leans heavily against the light pole and tries to shut off the grating tumult in his head—until the bus in fact arrives at last.

He boarded, dropped his coins in the fare box, and in long, weary strides made his way down the aisle past the movable WHITE/COLORED sign and on into the mandatory rear—in the process passing the four lone sleeping white men passengers, one of whom was snoring. Almost at once, in deep self-communion again, he sat staring out the window at the night ghosts and shadows of what seemed an unending, a worldwide, nighttime. The bus now stopped again, to take on two more passengers—a white woman and her seven- or eight-year-old son. The strange child had soon utterly monopolized Cager's attention. It was first the bizarre way the boy was dressed, entirely in macho adult-looking clothing: Tyrolean hat with feather, leather jacket, its green plastic belt almost as wide as a sash, plus sharply pressed little trousers and tiny, highly polished jackboots. He seemed at times not a child at all but some freak fascist midget out of a circus or movie, until the rosy, cherubic face was observed.

After paying their fares, his mother, a tall, pale woman with lantern jaws, brought him over halfway back into the white section where they sat down. The child at once climbed up on the seat, faced to the rear, and curiously studied lone Jim Crowed Cager. The two for a moment looked at each other, before suddenly the boy brought up both arms, as if holding an imaginary rifle, took dead aim at Cager, and, feigning pulling the trigger, cried out exultantly: "*Bang! Bang! Bang!*" He then went into gales of childish laughter. The behavior seemed to have so completely stunned Cager that he did not at first react at all. The child soon fired three more phantom rounds, all the while crying, "*Bang! Bang! Bang!*"—then, still laughing, turned to his mother for her commendation. But, appearing tired and bored, she only went on staring straight ahead.

Cager reacted at last. Jumping up, he seized the movable Jim Crow sign in front of him and went and affixed it directly in front of the mother and child. Then, heedless of whether or not the bus driver or other riders had seen this insurrectionary, unthinkable act, he returned to his seat and, grinding his teeth, whispering to himself, plopped down again. Suddenly the mother, realizing what had happened, that she and her son had just been gerrymandered into the COLORED section, blanched, even paler, then opened her mouth, gaping with shock and incredulity, yet somehow could not speak. At last, though, after frantically darting her eyes up front for help, but where apparently no one had yet noticed, she turned furiously on Cager, under her breath spluttering a string of racial epithets just as her son again trained his ghost gun on Cager and, squinting down the barrel, repeatedly squeezed the trigger— "*Bang! Bang! Bang!*"

Astonishingly now, Cager let out a series of strange manic laughs, not strident, not even loud, but which almost at once changed into a menacing growl. The woman, however, had jumped up, grabbed the Jim Crow sign in front of her, and, muttering more imprecations on Cager, returned it to its former place in the rear—her son all the while covering her actions with the withering fire of his imaginary automatic weapon until his mother was safely back in her seat. "Bang! Bang! Bang!" he cried out again and again.

The commotion had finally now awakened the riders up front, who were turning around to stare. Also, the bus driver, at last glowering into his rearview mirror at the ruckus, hollered back to Cager: "Boy, you better stay back there where you belong before I git the cops on here!" Strangely, though, Cager was so fascinated, so engrossed, by the child's actions he seemed wholly oblivious of everything else. Finally, pointing up front toward the white passengers, he said to the boy, "Hey, my man, why don't you shoot up in *that* direction once in a while?" Whatever anger he may have felt before seemed somehow now to have vanished, supplanted, however, by a deeply serious and conscientious curiosity.

But the child had all but lost interest now and was looking around for something new to occupy him. Finally, though, he replied: "*If I shot up there, they'd shoot back.*" Then, bored, he glanced idly at his mother. Cager stared at him in awe, until soon the bus approached the mother's destination, whereupon she pulled the signal cord and herded the boy forward to leave. But not before Cager had leaped to his feet, raised both arms high as if he too now held a powerful firearm, and aimed it straight at the departing pair. "*Bang! Bang! Bang! . . . Bang! Bang! Bang!*" he shouted hoarsely at the top of his voice.

The passengers up front now had spun around scowling, as the bus driver outshouted Cager: "*Set down!*—you damn drunk nigger, befoh I pistol-whip your head myself!" All this as he slowed the bus and finally stopped.

The child then, just before alighting ahead of his mother, turned around to Cager and, calm, composed, doubtless sleepy also, raised both hands high above his head in the classic gesture of capitulation, surrender. Then he and his mother stepped down and disappeared into the night.

The bus went on now. Cager, quiet, subdued, in a deep study, almost a trance, sat staring through the window out into the blackness. He had been so absorbed in what had happened, but most of all by the child's hands-over-head submission in surrender, that the bus driver's slurs had not fazed him, had hardly registered. Soon he was moving his lips, though not quite silently, murmuring in a kind of grand, wondrous affirmation: "Yeah, yeah . . ." he breathed, almost in an awed hush. "Clausewitz, ah . . . yeah, he was so right, wasn't he?—I can see it now plainer than ever. Oh, Lord, I got to try to get myself together again, somehow. *I got to.* Even that little bastard, just a baby, but already wearing jackboots—even *he* knows what it's all about. You heard what he told you, didn't you? Whew!—those folks sure learn early, don't they? Yeah, and that's why they're where *they* are and we're where *we*

are. Huh? Lord, Lord, help me, won't you? . . . help me . . . help
us. . . ." Emotion had closed his throat. He could no longer even
talk to himself.

16

IT WAS FOLLOWING a late Friday afternoon's Gladstone
faculty meeting that Haley Barnes and his wife Roxanne gave
Helen Stubbs, who taught English, a ride home in the throes of a
gorgeous west Tennessee sunset. The subject of their conversation was their institution's president, Simon Peter Groomes. "Do
you ever notice," said Helen in the backseat, "that in reporting to
us just after returning from meeting with the trustee board how
nervous, how really drained, Groomes always looks? It certainly
must take a lot out of him trying to deal with that bunch and
retain some semblance of his own personal dignity."

"Wait a minute," laughed Roxanne, driving, with Haley riding
beside her, "it's impossible; there's no way. Best proof is, *Groomes*
can't do it, and he's a past master. To have to deal with an all-white
board like this, that's also coming up with most of the money that
keeps the place going and our chintzy salary checks coming, has
got to be the no-win situation of all time. You're just a figurehead,
for the board makes all the decisions, big and small."

Haley partially demurred. "It's improved some, though," he
said. "You should have been around when I came here. Old Judge
Dabney was alive then and a board member. He and some of the
others wanted to make the place a glorified manual training
school—teach bricklaying, shoe repair, chicken farming, crop rota-
tion, and all that." Haley laughed. "I'll never forget all the stink
raised when Moses Wardlow started teaching things like Comte's
positivism, Veblen's *Theory of the Leisure Class*, and stuff like that.
Wow!—the feces really hit the fan. Judge Dabney and his board
cohorts threatened to resign en masse, almost half the trustees.
But you know the others weren't going to let that happen, with the
money it represented. Groomes of course had no say in any of
this. But he didn't give up and it wasn't long before his slick
maneuvering in dealing with some of the Dabney members
turned the tide, to some extent anyway, and we eventually got a
curriculum containing a few different things—like more language
courses, and literature, as well as an expanded history program,

and some math, and so forth. It was definitely to the good and Groomes is the one who pretty much masterminded it. These smart-aleck students here can call him a Tom if they want to but they're the ones who've benefited. Groomes has a unique skill, a sixth sense almost, in handling wealthy white folks, and sometimes it pays off. He couldn't budge old Dabney and a few others of that faction on some issues of course, so he would manage somehow to deal around them—sleight of hand, sort of, and Dabney never knew what happened, it was that slick. Still, the old judge remained frustrated and unreconstructed to the end. But, Lord, his wife—who was not a board member, thank God—was worse than he was. In fact, she was the one who ran things, including him. She was—I should say *is*—a real . . . a—"

"Go ahead and say it, Haley!" Roxanne laughed—"a real bitch. Helen, I'm sure you've seen that old woman driving around town here in her chauffeured long shiny black Cadillac. But it was none other than our friend Haley who, after the old judge died, still got some money out of her for Gladstone. I don't know how he did it—he must have a little of Groomes in him. Yes, maybe just a wee bit of Tom!" Both women laughed.

"After the judge died," Haley explained to Helen, "they invited old Mrs. Dabney—begged her, actually, for the family had always given a lot of money—to take his place on the board. She flatly, almost rudely, refused. Said her husband had been badly treated, misused, by the college—especially its board, whose policies she said were all wrong. That was that. But when the next Gladstone fund drive came around, I told Roxanne the old lady might, as sort of a parting shot, still give us something. At least we had everything to gain and nothing to lose. So I asked to come see her. She received me in the kitchen, of course, and throughout, for the grand total of the five minutes allotted me, in the presence of her mammy cook, who I well recall was making corn bread that day, and listened stonily yet somehow patiently to my fund solicitation pitch. She answered by saying that if she did give anything—in memory of her husband—it would certainly be the family's last gift to Gladstone, that his long and dedicated service to the college, indeed to 'nigra' education generally, had gone largely unappreciated. She didn't beat around the bush. She said what was on her mind. There was something about her I've never figured out, or forgotten. Maybe nothing really good, but something uncomplicated, candid, even fearless and combative, and utterly frank. I hate to call it integrity, or courage, or compassion for those less fortunate, for you know what she thought of us—all of us. Yet, as I was leaving her (in the kitchen), she actually complimented me, as a faculty member, for, as she put it, caring enough about the college to engage in fund-raising for it, and wished me well. So I went away with a grudging impression that maybe she wasn't *all* bad. Later she sent in a check for twenty-five hundred, considerably less than formerly, but a last gesture that was at least positive."

Roxanne, now turning the car left into Jasper Street, laughed again. "Come on, now, Haley honey. Are you sure you didn't do just a little shuffling and head scratching—a little Tomming—in that kitchen?" They all laughed.

They were coming into the Negro section now. "What in the world's going on over there?" It was Helen Stubbs pointing. On their right they saw the familiar unfenced vacant lot which they passed each day, but where there were now at least twenty or more adult Negro males assembled. It appeared they were receiving some kind of instruction, earnest and loud, from a very short, squat man no more than five feet two inches tall. There were also a dozen or more Negro children, mostly fascinated, eager boys, watching and cavorting on the sidelines.

"Slow down," Haley said to Roxanne. "What's all this?" She had soon slowed the car to a crawl.

The short man was still shouting his orders, in response to which the men, previously in a ragged formation, began now crowding together, shoulder to shoulder, closing and dressing their ranks in anticipation of the next command, which came at once: "Platoon, atten-*shun!* Forwerrrrd *harch!*" They stepped off smartly (followed by the gleeful, imitating boys) and, swinging their arms, marched in step to the short man's cadenced counting: "*Hut*, two, three, four! *Hut*, two, three, four!"—until they had crossed the length of the lot, where their runt drillmaster then cried, "Platoon, to the rear, *harch!*" They wheeled, faced to the rear, and marched back to the spot whence they had started. "Platoon, *halt!*" cried their sawed-off leader. "At ease!" He smiled to them as they stood resting for a moment. "Not bad, not bad, you guys," he said, now beaming. "But just wait till we get our uniforms! Lord, them beautiful new uniforms! You've already seen the design so you know how they're gonna look—hey, even on *me!* We'll be somethin' to behold then. We'll march downtown, then around the *courthouse square!*"

"*Say*," suddenly said Haley, "I know who it is. That's Shorty

93

George! But what in the hell's he doing? Maybe those fellows have to go in the army soon and he's teaching them close-order drill."

"Who's Shorty George, Haley?" said Roxanne.

But he was oblivious. "This doesn't make sense, though," he said, still staring at the men. "Most of those guys wouldn't be going in the service—some of them are fifty years old. I don't get it."

"Haley, who's Shorty George?" Roxanne repeated, exasperated.

"He's got that dinky little restaurant over there back of Cannery Alley."

Other people in cars were passing now, some slowly as they encountered the strange sight, one a paintless Dodge jalopy containing three white youths. One of them, loudly laughing, leaned the entire top half of his body out of the car window and yelled at Shorty George, "Hey, boy, they'll march better if you'll put a mule in front of 'em! *Ha-ha-ha-ha!*"

Shorty stood glaring after them and finally turned to his men. "That's what I'm talkin' about, you see?" he said. "We're gonna put a stop to that! Wait'll we get our uniforms! These rednecks won't be hollerin' at us then!"

"Right, Shorty—right on!" someone in the ranks called up.

Shorty now beckoned to his fifteen-year-old son in the formation. "Manville, come go to the car and get that flag, our ensign," he said. "Hurry, son." He turned back to the men. "We need it— we need somethin', *anything*—till we get them uniforms and stop these peckerwoods from messin' with us, makin' fun of us, like that. It'll be different, you watch!"

The boy went to Shorty's wreck of a car, got the six-foot cane fishing pole with a tarnished, ragged, red-and-black pennant wired to its top, and returned. He then took the emblem to the head of the platoon where he stationed himself and raised it high for all to see. Now Shorty gave the command: "Atten-*shun!* Forwerrrrd *harch!*" He twice marched them around the lot, their faces serious, intent, full of purpose, almost as if it were the bedraggled red-and-black ensign itself proudly leading them.

"That's got to be the weirdest sight I've ever seen in my life," Roxanne said, shaking her head. Finally she laughed—yet as though it were an afterthought—put the car in gear, and drove off.

Haley sat silent—stumped. "I don't get it," he repeated. "It's more than weird. The marching, the drill practice—what's going on? I can't tell because I don't know, but it's nothing negligible. It's like some kind of grim, static pageant, only it's not static." He finally laughed. "And because of the pageantry I get the funniest darn feeling the only figure—that grand, martial personage—missing from it is Cager Lee! But maybe we should have waited another five minutes!" All laughed.

Haley was more right than he knew.

17

As I, YOUR NARRATOR, have already indicated, what my mother Maude, down on her little farm in Texas when I was sixteen, meant was merely what she had said, namely, "Meshach, I want you to become a minister."

"Oh, Lord, Mom," I said, shocked.

"I mean an upstanding, cultured minister. Not an ordinary preacher, like your father was, the old-time roving country jackleg that liked a lot of women and, in his case, hornswoggled a poor dumb farm girl like me into letting him, a married man almost three times my age, have his way with me. Yet first thing I knew along come old bright-eyed you, sweetest baby ever was, but your daddy by then was long gone, on to his next church and his next women. I got you in the bargain, though, and that wasn't bad. And to keep my brothers from catching up with him and killing him, he did eventually buy this little farm for you and me, though he didn't tell us how to get somebody to come and help us run it, like we finally got a couple of field hands like Lamb and Doc to do. No, no, no jackleg preacher, Meshach baby. I'm talking about you being a minister—an educated man. I think a real man of God out to do good needs an education, because *he's* telling a lot of other people every Sunday what *they* ought to be doing. It's a big job, no kidding—a real responsibility. I know an education by itself ain't going to make a man good, but it helps. Sure don't do no harm."

"Oh, Lord, Mom," I repeated, already unhappy.

"But, you see, I want to start you out headed in the right direction. You're a strange boy, anyhow—I can tell already. You're the jumpy, uneasy type, nervous all the time about nothing, and, on top of that, inclined to be secretlike. That's no good. So you're going to need God's guidance, all right—plenty."

Learning what my life's work was going to be was a great blow to me—compounding the fatal drawbacks I had already been born with—yet I did not even once consider resisting Maude. To me

95

her word was law and always had been. Even today, though, I wonder whether my life would have been any different had, say, she done nothing, just let me drift into anything that would eventually have suited my wayward fancy. How could things have been worse? I ask myself. The fact of the matter is, however, they may just have been vastly better, I don't know. Certainly I would not have encountered the hero. *Nor Carol.* It was the two of them—in tandem—who finally destroyed me.

Years later, of course, in the complicated interim, Lisbeth was quite another matter. When I was courting her I thought my conduct exemplary, which it was, for, surprisingly, I had at that time become somewhat ambitious, even if in an alloyed sort of way, and ambition dictated conformity—marriage. Deep down I really cared little for pomp. I very much wanted to get married, I told myself, only because of high principle, yet maybe, as well, I conceded, as a practical right step. I had recently gotten my second, and considerably better, church—this small but definitely middle-class pastorate in Indianapolis—pending, as I have elsewhere said, my imminent move on to even bigger and better things. Lisbeth, two years older than I, was a social-work supervisor in the Indiana capital and lived with her sister and widowed mother. She was not at all, however, regular in her church attendance, until, that is, she married me (considered by many, under the local circumstances, something of a catch), when at once she became quietly, if somehow still visibly, devout. It was as if she felt it a solemn duty expected of her, and eagerly threw herself into all the varied activities of the church. With the result, not amazingly, that she became invaluable to me and to the rather practicable view I took of my clerical duties. Her now zealous work was interrupted temporarily only by Carol's birth. I have already spoken of how closely I thought the two of them eventually came to resemble each other, though I now think that in fact Lisbeth may have been a trifle plain. Indeed, had it not been for my arrival on the scene, plus what I saw as my quite pragmatic pastoral obligations, she may in time very well have gone into a wistful, hard-eyed spinsterhood.

I remember rather vividly my little family, the three of us, having dinner at home one Sunday—we were by then, over a decade later, in Philadelphia and well ensconced in this new and larger (also better-paying) pastorate—after I had, that morning, preached (particularly well, I thought) on the biblical subject of Christ's miracle in feeding the multitude on the mere five loaves and two fishes. Carol, now twelve and a happy, saucy, if somewhat spoiled (by me) child, during dessert initiated some rather extraordinary (even for her) talk. It was still—my heart is heavy merely conjuring up the thought—almost four years before I would forfeit my soul, and hers, to Charon, netherworld ferryman deep in the sluices of Styx's blackest hell. As she ate her strawberries she chattered as merrily as a magpie, before, out of the blue, she asked, "Father, do you like being a minister?"

I of course had not been ready for it—this solar plexus blow. For in a flash it required that I reassess things, although the truth is that in recent years I had become rather more acclimated to my imposed profession, and not at all unskilled in its practice—actually, it would have been overly modest of me to deny I had been an outstanding success. And I more and more—although I would have done so in any case—revered the memory of my dear departed little mother, who had all but taken me by the hand as she led (or conducted) me into this calling. Yet now I hesitated. I still did not know how to respond to my daughter.

Lisbeth, however, invariably my fanatical booster, came to the rescue. "Why, of course he likes it, honey," she said to Carol. "What kind of question is that?"

"Up there in the pulpit this morning he looked funny," smiled Carol mischievously—too vigorously masticating her strawberries.

"What do you mean by 'funny'?" Lisbeth bridled. "I should think you would have more respect for your father than to make such a remark."

"I do respect him," said Carol with a half-smile. "He just looked sort of out of place, that's all—wearing that long red and black robe, and big ring on his finger, and the cross on a chain around his neck. He looked like he was trying to be somebody he really wasn't. I think it takes something away from him. He's not like that at all—so pious. He's really a good Joe." She smiled at me, then laughed—it was actually a titter. "Aren't you, Father?" She turned again to Lisbeth. "I just wished he laughed more, and played with me some, and took me to the movies maybe, things like that. We could be buddies."—Again her smile to me, mischievous and very stubborn.

My heart had stopped. Oh, bless her, I thought. Then I was plunged into gloom.

Lisbeth was struggling to keep a level voice. "Carol, where on earth do you get these ideas?"

Carol smiled at her mother. "Did you see how almost embarrassed he looked when he was preaching about Jesus feeding all those people with a few loaves of bread and two fishes and had food left over? He really looked unhappy—as if he didn't believe a word of it. I know *I* didn't."

Lisbeth gasped.

Carol turned to me. "Did you, Father?"

Lisbeth exploded. "Carol! I won't have you saying things like that to your father! . . . It's blasphemous!"

Carol said no more. Her mother's vehemence seemed to have frightened her.

Poor, innocent, decent Lisbeth. She would have made such a perfect wife for a sincere, honest clergyman—a real man of God. Carol was right—of course I did not believe in the miracle of the loaves and fishes, and in little else of what I preached. Instead, then, of having married, as she thought, a devout servant of the Lord, Lisbeth had taken a moral cipher. And Carol had some of my genes. Lisbeth not only deserved someone better than I, she deserved a much longer life than, alas, she was in the end to have. Is there no rationale for all the *merde* of this world? Before Carol even reached eighteen Lisbeth went off and left us—via a malignancy called Kahler's disease—and thereby bequeathed to me a sick season of travail, remorse, and guilt I was never to outlive. By her mother's death, under *all* the circumstances, Carol was of course psychically destroyed, especially when remembering Lisbeth's persistent questioning of her in those final days about her (Carol's) mysterious personality change, the silent, withdrawn, doom-ridden (guilt-ridden) daughter she had somehow become. My sick, villainous heart went out to both of them.

After Lisbeth's death I began to lose weight (even with this, my own, figurative millstone of the sociopath around my neck) and could eat or sleep hardly at all. In my blackly depressed state I was all but wiped out. At last I concluded I was going to die. The prospect should really have been a boon. In fact it was not. I literally rushed to the doctor for help, direly warning him, however, against trying to send me to a psychiatrist. His rather casual advice (as if he were not too much disturbed) was that I consider going for a brief stay to this well-known Connecticut spa—euphemistically called a sanatorium—named Coveycote. As a desperate widower acting on my physician's recommendation, I indeed soon after arrival found my time there not altogether unpleasant at all, even if I did resort to some weeping and wailing.

Yet in the end, therapeutically, it was all futile, a washout, made still more so by Carol's failure, or refusal—she was away at the time, a university freshman—to drop everything and come to me there. But I needed help! *Her help!* I wanted to scream it at her! Yet she was not there, and did not come.

18

"Praise His name!" he cried. He was a poor-white, hill-country preacher, Madden Nelson, by name.

"Praise His name!" somebody else sang out, echoing the prior exultation.

"Yes, teach us the faith!" cried another, echoing also.

"Amen, amen!" others added.

The rest stood looking on. They were tense, expectant, a few of them worried, yet some managed to smile.

The sun was lukewarm on the pine grove and also beyond its edge on into the clearing where they were all congregated in front of the little frame church. Preacher Nelson, tall, skinny, hawk-nosed, deeply-bronzed, in overalls and a railroad engineer's cast-off, faded, striped cap, held open his Bible and again exhorted his flock: "Oh, ye of little faith! What ere ye afeared of? God has ordained that it's the faithful that'll inherit this old earth! I'm talkin' about the ones among us that has faith that He will protect His own! Don't matter how dangerous the situation looks like, neither! Dear ones, I'm talkin' about the faith that *moves mountains!*" He closed the Bible now, passed it to someone, then peered down into the big wooden washtub beside him. It was over half full of hissing, writhing rattlesnakes.

The hero, alone, unseen, stealthy, phobic, watched from the cover of nearby trees and tall grass, his heart wildly bumping, trip-hammering, against his ribs, his whole body shaking. "Lord God!" he breathed. "These rednecks ain't afraid of *nothing!*"

"Oh, ye of little faith," cried Preacher Nelson to his country folk—men, women, children—"how will you answer when the day of reckonin' comes around and all along you have had no faith? I ain't no prophet, I ain't no soothsayer, I ain't no rich man, neither, but God *has* give me the faith! Jesus Hisself told us in Mark 16, verses 17 and 18, that, 'In My name shall they cast out devils. They shall speak with new tongues. *They shall take up serpents!* And if they drink any deadly thing, it shall not hurt them. They shall lay hands on the sick and they shall recover.' It's the *faith*, you see, my friends! Hallelujah!" Whereupon, he reached down, gingerly lifted out a huge, writhing, diamondback rattler, and held it up for all to see.

"Praise His name!" screamed a woman with a baby in her arms.

For a moment trembling Cager would not look, could not bear it. "Jesus God!" he breathed, now finally, out of the corner of his eye, making himself watch Nelson. "That cracker is putting that thing around his neck now! *Whew!* Oh, my Lord—I can't watch it no more! . . ." He had walked the seven miles out from Gladstone to witness what he had read in the local newspaper would surely take place whether the sheriff tried to stop it or not. He had long heard of religious snake handlings, knew they occurred, and considered them a powerful test of the will of the participants. But while these people relied on religious faith, which was a strange, unclear phenomenon to him though he did not negate it, his reliance, he hoped, was in *himself*. He was certain, however, he would never have occasion to take part in such a rite. He had come to see this little band of poor whites test themselves. Could they pass this terrible test?—for he saw now that at least their leader could. But what was more important in his own imagination was whether *he* could have succeeded in such a test—ordeal. He had really—though always possessed of great self-confidence—nevertheless come to witness this ritualistic event to experience it vicariously, thus in his own mind to test himself. It was important for the future that he know. On the road coming here he had felt secure, assured, but now, on the scene, he could hardly believe what he saw. There was no way he could have predicted his terror.

The preacher was holding the rattler on his left shoulder now, following its gyrating head and beady eyes with his own burning zealot's gaze. Another woman cried out: "Oh, Mr. Nelson!—that's enough, enough! . . . *Don't test God no further!* Oh, help him, Jesus! . . ."

But the preacher was now being joined by two men from the crowd. They came forward, warily took a snake apiece from the tub, and held them up over their heads, though all the while closely watching the highly excited and wriggling reptiles. Three more men then came up and did the same.

"Faith, faith, you see!" cried the preacher. "Faith is what this old journey on earth is all about! Hear my words 'cause they're

100

God's words! *Behold the faith!*" he shouted to them, shaking his free left fist in the air.

Cager was so mesmerized by the daring feats of these men he was unaware that as he crept forward, the better to see and hear, he was leaving his foliage cover behind. A woman in the crowd quickly spotted him and jabbed her husband's arm. But now the little gathering had begun singing—"Down at the cross where my Savior died"—and slowly, though with a great inner fervor, clapping their hands and lifting their eyes heavenward, all as the six men up front cuddled their hissing snakes to their breasts, one soon cradling his in his arm and plopping down in the grass with it.

His wife, the woman with the baby, became hysterical again. "Oh, God!" she cried. "Don't let nothin' happen to him! He's all I got! He's the father of my kids, Lord! Protect him! *Oh, Jeeesus!*" Again she let out a high, chilling scream, as another woman tried to minister to her—just at the moment that the couple who had seen Cager were now pointing him out to others.

Cager seemed in a trance, or as if as he walked being pulled by some slow but powerful magnet, for now he had wandered out into plain view.

"I'll be dog," said an old man, gaping, to his neighbor. "Where'd *he* come from? Does he work 'round here for somebody?—never seed him before."

"Sure'in hell ain't—me neither," said the other. "They oughta git his ass outa here—putty quick."

Cager's mesmerized gaze, however, was fixed on Preacher Nelson, who, though, somehow, had not yet seen him. "Faith *does* move mountains, I tell yuh!" cried Nelson, for proof pointing down at the snake handler sitting on the grass, and as he himself, his engineer's cap down around his ears from his exertions, hoisted his huge rattler as high as he could reach. "Come forward, you-all of little faith, and touch, *feel*, the strength of the Lord!"

"Whut the hell's he *gawkin'* at?" asked the first old man, still staring at Cager.

"At them damn big snakes, that's whut," said his friend. "Niggers're afeared of snakes as the Devil is of holy water. Look at him."

"Don't know 'bout that, Ben," the first said. "He's comin' over here, ain't he?"

Ben's jaw was slack. "Sure nuff, now. Ain't stopped yet, has he? Where's he think he's goin'?"

101

Cager was walking slowly, indecisively, yet somehow meditatively, through the taller grass toward them all. Soon as many of the little crowd were watching him as were watching the snake handlers. At long last, then, the preacher looked up and saw him and, his mouth dropping open, he stopped talking and stood, incredulously, staring. "*Whut's this?*" he finally said, and threw his rattler back in the tub. "Whut you want, boy?" he called out. Cager, still slowly coming, gazed at him as if under his spell, but said nothing. Soon, though, when he had passed the edge of the crowd, he paused. "I said whut do you *want?*" yelled Nelson, his face crimson. He turned to the others. "You see, don't you? *Satan* sent him! Old black Belzebub hisself has put his own kin up to comin' here to undo God's work! Get him *away* from here!" There were dark rumblings of agreement in the crowd.

Finally Cager got his first few words out. In a high, tremulous voice, but turning to the crowd, he said, "I came here just like the rest of you-all did. I wanted to see if . . ." He faltered, realizing this was not quite accurate, that they had come hoping to strengthen their faith in God, while he, by merely watching them, sought to test his faith in himself.

"You wanted to see *whut?* yelled the preacher.

". . . I wanted to see if you'all really did do these things," Cager said.

"You're a messenger from the Devil!" cried Nelson. "Yes, you are, even if you do wear a sport shirt! If you ain't one of Satan's minions, if you come here just like the rest of us did—which you didn't—then come up here and take one of Satan's serpents outa this tub!"

Cager's knees went slack. His mouth was dry. He could not move.

"Look at him, folks!" cried Nelson. "You see, don't you?"

At last, though, Cager slowly, from some obscure source, seemed to summon some small strength. He began, though anything but boldly, walking toward the preacher, his shoulders slumped, eyes downcast, his head on his chest, like a condemned man approaching the executioner. A hush fell over the crowd. Soon he was standing directly before his taunter.

"*Here, boy!*" cried the preacher. "Take a look in this tub here!"

Cager finally came forward, looked, and, shivering, saw on top of the undulant pile of snakes the huge diamondback Nelson had just thrown back. His face long, jaw slack, eyes burning and terrorized, he looked at the preacher, then swallowed. At last he

102

glanced in the tub again, then turned his eyes away. Suddenly then like lightning he descended and reached in. The great coiled reptile, loudly hissing, its rattles clattering, struck. But too late. Cager had jumped back just in the nick of time. The crowd gasped. Though one man laughed. Suddenly now, grinding his teeth, Cager lunged at the tub, as his hand went in again, grasped the diamondback, and brought it out, the great snake writhing and threshing. His face now grotesquely contorted, Cager held the snake aloft for all to see.

"Praise His name!" someone cried out.

Cager, the agony ravaging his face, continued holding the struggling rattler high above his head.

"*Praise His name!*" This time it was the preacher.

Cager finally turned and dropped the snake back in the tub. Then he fainted dead away.

19

"HEY, THERE, GIRLFRIEND," he said, his face in a wide grin. "What's cookin' around here today?"

The nine-year-old child, though unable to see him, nonetheless also smiled. It was the mere tone of his voice—warm, familiar, comical—that so pleased her. "Hi, Cager," she said.

A knapsack slung across his shoulder, he had just entered. "Say," he said, "y'know, you once told me your name. Then what did I do? Why, I went right off and forgot it. What kinda guy's that? What'd you say it was, sugar?

Still smiling, but chin now sharply elevated, dead eyes wandering along the ceiling, she stood twisting two fingers. "Ophelia," she finally said.

"Ha!—Hamlet. There you go! Ophelia what?" She hesitated— still twisting the fingers. But at last, unable to come up with an answer, she instead put out both hands, gropingly, toward him, yet could not touch him because of the row of empty chairs separating them. "What's the matter, hon, the cat got your tongue or something?" he said. "Ophelia what?"

"Just Ophelia," she said. "Nobody told me *what*." She laughed.

"Yeah? I'll bet Mrs. Baker knows." Annie Baker was matron here at Billups School for Blind (Negro) Children, a neglected state institution with which Flo Ransom had some never-quite-clear connection. The school, however, had acquired an almost obsessive hold on Cager ever since Flo had taken him there with her on one of her "official" visits. He came alone now, regularly; indeed he could not stay away.

Soon Annie Baker, a tiny, prune-colored—and very conscientious—woman, entered leading ten or twelve more of the children. "Okay, boys and girls," she smiled. "This way. Follow me."

At once Cager began laughing and clowning, even making faces as if the children could see him. "Hey, what's goin' on here?" he cried. "Where're all you-all coming from?"

A boy about Ophelia's age raised his shrill voice in challenge. "What did you bring us, Cager? Any candy? Any peanuts? Where you at, Cager?" He too now began a groping motion in the direction of Cager's voice.

"Just listen at that," said Cager. " 'What did you bring us?' Virgil, don't you know candy's bad for your teeth?"

Ophelia gave a squeal of laughing delight. "No, it ain't, either! You bring it all the time. What else did you bring?"

"Brought myself, that's 'what else,' " he laughed. "That's enough, ain't it? But I can see you'all don't want me coming out here empty-handed. You'all are smart. You know what makes the world go round, all right." He glanced at Annie Baker. "Whatever it is Mrs. Baker here is teaching you'all it sure makes sense." He circumvented the row of chairs now and began mingling with the children, gleefully poking the girls' ribs and kneading the boys' heads.

"What you got in your sack today, Cager?" two or three more asked.

"There you go again," he said. "Is that all you got to say on that broken record?" There were shrieks of laughter as they crowded around him, some pawing at the knapsack. "Okay, okay," he said, feigning a sigh. "I give up." He opened the knapsack and began passing out an assortment of cellophane-wrapped goodies.

Annie Baker, observing the groping, shoving, pawing, and shrieking, laughed in alarm to the children, "My goodness, you'd think we starve you to death here."

When Cager had depleted the knapsack, he uttered a loud "Whew!" and went over to the bench against the wall where he sat watching the children milling around, talking, and eating their sweet knickknacks.

But soon he heard Virgil calling him. "Cager! Cager, where you at?"

He started to wave the boy over but immediately brought his hand down. "Over here, my man," he said. "By the wall." Virgil soon came bumping and jostling his way through, followed by Ophelia whom he had by the hand. But now they stood idly, reticently, before him. "What's up, you'all?" he said. "You lost your voices? Tell me what's going on around here. You'all studying thos Braille books hard like Mrs. Baker tells you to? That's all you got to do to make it, you know. Study hard and you'll be cool, huh?—ain't that right?" Ruefully, though, he thought of himself. But neither Virgil nor Ophelia answered, although both seemed reflecting on what he had said. "You'all see what I'm saying?" he asked.

"We can't *see*," Ophelia said, and smiled.

"Oh, there I go again. Excuse me, will you? I didn't mean it like that. I meant do you understand what I'm saying."

"I guess so," Virgil said.

"What do *you* see, Cager?" It was Ophelia.

"I see *you*, for one thing, honey. Why?"

"What else do you see?"

"Yes," said Virgil. "What else?"

"I see this room," Cager said. "And all you children. Hah, hah, hah!—and I see candy wrappers, and peanuts, and Cracker Jack, all over the floor! I also see Mrs. Baker frowning!"

"Do you see the sun?" asked Ophelia. "I ain't never seen the sun."

"Neither have I," Virgil said.

"There is no sun today," said Cager nervously.

"There's no sun *any* day," Virgil said.

"Okay, okay," Cager hastened from the subject.

Ophelia, though, said, "I don't see the sun but I see Jesus up there where the sun *is*." She pointed vaguely overhead.

"Yeah?" said Virgil dubiously. "What's He look like?"

"Oh, He's beautiful." Her opaque eyes roved the ceiling.

"What's He *look like*?" Virgil said.

"He's got nice, long, brown hair," said Ophelia. "It's way down to His shoulders. He's got a soft, brown beard, too. And blue eyes that love you. He always wears a robe. And sandals on His feet. He's got soft white hands, too. And a gentle, loving, white face."

Cager had stiffened. He sat erect now, his face dour, stony. Soon he spoke gravely. "Who told you this, sweetheart?"

"Mrs. Baker," Ophelia said.

"So when you see Jesus, that's what you see, huh?"

"Yes, I see Him very plain," said Ophelia. She lifted her filmy eyes straight up. "I see Him *now*. He's our friend. Jesus is love."

"That's right," Virgil said eagerly now. "Jesus can make the *blind* see if He wants to." He turned to Ophelia. "We can see *Him* all right, can't we?"

"Sure can," smiled Ophelia.

Cager rose. He stood there for a moment, his expression cold, forbidding, angry. Then he headed for the door.

At once the children sensed his absence. "Cager," cried Ophelia, "Where are you? Have you left already? Come back, Cager. . . ."

"He's gone," Virgil said glumly. "Why'd he go so quick? . . ."

"I don't know," said Ophelia, now almost sorrowfully. "I hope he comes back."

20

WHAT I HAVE TO SAY at this juncture was written, again by way of therapy, during my second, and longer, sojourn at Coveycote, the first, yes, having come just after my wife Lisbeth's death. The second, though, had been necessitated, if it can be believed, by something somewhat more severe, namely, a suffocating neuropsychotic version of the underwater bends, following my release from the "penal servitude" of Pressman—some four months, incidentally, prior to Bahr's, and at the close of what had turned out to be (as I had both intimated and forecast) his and my utterly failed collaboration. But Bahr, three weeks following his own release—alas, I must tell you—killed himself with an ice pick. However, I did not learn of his death for almost ten months, as I was having my own chronic self-harassments and personal unrest far, far away. Yet, even as I write this, I somehow still feel as if it were not Bahr's hand, with its little pad and pencil stub, but my own that had been stilled, my own slant on things obliterated, *my* woeful imagination, my vision, dispatched.

As I was about to go off and leave him at Pressman, he came and brought me, his eyes averted, a large manila envelope containing his sheaf of notes of our conversations—which, despite this account's limited mention of our talks, had been numerous, and (even if, though just, below the surface) impassioned, despairing, mutual cries for help—by which, I now realize, he (not I) had somehow sought for the last time to right his course, pull back from the brink, before it was too late. All the while, though, he probably knew it *was* too late. "You take them, Barry," he said of the notes. I of course did not understand that he had by then very nearly given up, washed his hands of affairs, reached his high resolve. I protested receiving his papers. "No, you take them," he said. So I did, and later stowed them away with the journal I myself had been keeping at Pressman. But—as I, due to my own continuing botched existence, was soon for the second time to enter Coveycote—I did not get around to reading his materials until well after his death.

I was stunned. He had reduced not Cager's but *my* life story to a series of utter grotesqueries. Then he had tried to psychoanalyze me. Yet, his accuracy was uncanny. At the time, though, I was furious—I am of course no longer so—for I felt I had been outwitted and betrayed, conveniently forgetting that it was I who had been most eager for our sad and futile confabulations. His papers, however, made it clear that all along his opinion of me had not been high. But I confess I had all along sensed this. Therefore, one of my principal aims of the silly experiment of our talks (that of somehow making him—or anyone!—understand, even, if possible, extenuate, my sad preordered life) had early failed.

But, as I say, I had additional problems, ailments which eventually sent me to rest, hopefully to heal, at the well-known sanatorium in Connecticut named for the thousand-acre wooded estate of the John M. Severnses, the quite mad husband-and-wife team whose money had founded the treatment center. Thus Coveycote is significant in my life and this chronicle because it was there that I formed the resolve to rediscover (not, realistically, to rehabilitate, nothing so ambitious as that) myself through Cager's life, his great works, and, above all, his sacrificial example.

Perhaps, though, deep in my unconscious, I really sought only expiation and regarded the place as a center for penance. I had read, though only cursorily, from *Pensees* and a few other things of Pascal's, as well as random portions of Schopenhauer's writings, both while I was at Yale, yet now, at Coveycote, I had adopted these two great thinkers as part of my ongoing regimen. "The finite," Pascal wrote in the seventeenth century, "is annihilated in the presence of the infinite. It becomes a pure nothing. The larger light blinds it—and us! But it is only then that we truly gain our bearings. Yet, finite or infinite, we have our own choices between them which we must, and do, make. We should not then reprove for error those who do the same." I thought this so apt, so rarely profound, that, in my direly unsettled mental state, indeed my neurasthenia, it never failed to move, to stir, me. Actually, I shuddered with rapture and for a time my lifelong itching ceased.

There were also, however, what, at first impression (though only first), seemed lighter moments, as when Joe Rattle talked his crazy talk. Joe was the rich and famous black pro basketball star, but who was now—due to his riotous white women—a Coveycote patient. One day he was looking out the window watching one of the institution's gardeners at work. "Say, man," he said to me, pointing, "what's that cat out there call himself doing?"

I came and looked. "I think he's putting fertilizer on the strawberries," I said.

Joe, still pointing, doubled up in a loud, raucous, sidesplitting laugh. "Haw! Haw! Haw! I thought that! Here's this clown out there putting cow shit on his strawberries and you and I put sugar and cream on ours and they call *us* crazy! Haw! Haw! Haw!"

But his corny joke, preceded and followed by his desperate laugh, unnerved me, then briefly somehow made me sad, for I was almost certain, depending on definition, that we both *were* crazy.

But to you, Bahr, my perverse ex-colleague-in-pain, yet somehow friend, I say *requiescat in pace!* It took me months to track down your son, then another grueling effort to get him to talk. It turned out, though, contrary, ironically, to what you had thought, that he had *not* repudiated you. He knew you had—as indeed had I, though far more strongly—been early marked for a life of petty, then not so petty, ignominy. In the end then he was forbearing, even forgiving, and spoke once or twice of—his word—your "preordination." Yet, this seemingly innocuous word made me shudder and called to mind the bleakness of Schopenhauer.

Here is the dyspeptic, reclusive, old metaphysician of Frankfurt am Main: "Everyone [*The Wisdom of Life*, I, 147] believes himself *à priori* to be perfectly free, even in his individual actions, and thinks that at any moment he can commence another manner of life, which just means that he can become another person. But *à posteriori*, through experience, he finds to his astonishment that he is *not* free, but subject to necessity; that in spite of all his resolutions and reflections he does not change his conduct—cannot!—and that, from the beginning of his life to the end of it, he must carry out the very character which he himself condemns, and, as it were, play the part *imposed on him* to the very end." (My italics.)

I therefore insist that you, my quondam friend Bahr, should not have taken your precipitant action. You despaired too quickly. I, an aborted "man of God," yes, a failed preacher, somehow held on. You should have tried to do likewise, with—except for one rather grave, indeed startling, transgression—your relatively innocuous, indeed piddling, record: pummeling your long-suffering wife, embezzling funds of your bank employer, patronizing racetracks and an occasional too-expensive call girl. That, though, of course, as I say, was not quite all. But we shall not belabor it. Many have done worse—I, I repeat, for instance. You need not then, I insist, have acted so hastily, and rashly. And so gruesomely! *Aughhh!* Desperation is the lot of man, remember. I have a daughter, who is my Schopenhauerian destiny (and, alas, I hers), by my first wife, the latter who died, and a mongoloid son, now in a Michigan institution, by my second wife, a Eurasian, who left me after seventeen months. Yet, I have refused to jump ship. I have held on to this existence, stubbornly discountenanced denying or repudiating any part of its corrosive life force. It would have done no good. Besides, why should I have? The present tenuous life is all we have, or shall ever have—never mind my pulpit blatherings—and after it comes the eternal black void. *Eternal!* . . .

I sometimes reread parts of your notes, your myopic little pencil-stub scribblings on that tiny ruled notebook paper, and almost want to laugh, or cry, about what we were each vainly trying to do by these peevish, distrustful confidences of mine. You were trying, by comparing your misshapen life with what you strongly suspected, correctly, was my own sordid one, to make yourself in your own mind look better than the base individual you had considered yourself to be. While I, so hard pressed in comparing my own offenses, my dirty perfidies, with the sterling life and character of the hero, was trying to "burn and purge away" what I can now, if logical, only call (can it be possible?) a gray ghost.

The ghost of the double (or single) standard. Or if I, the wretch, am an automaton, why then is not he, the hero, one also? But no, I do not want this. I abhor the very possibility. It robs him of his worth and me my crutch. The hero must live on—in his perfect virtue and saintly martyrdom. I need this. It has become a driven necessity. Yes, even if in insisting on it I repudiate both logic and history. Let both be damned. I want to believe in miracles. Yes, even that of Jesus and the loaves and fishes. I know that history does not support my longings. But what is history? Pascal said that if Cleopatra's nose had been an inch longer or shorter, history

109

would have been vastly different. Yet, here even my great French seer stumbles into error. Whatever the shape of Cleopatra's nose, history would have been the same. It is never different. History is man. There may even *be* no history. Only biography.—(Emerson)

21

IN THE DORMITORY HE LAY, fully dressed, in his bunk—waiting. A few lights were still on for those studying late—though he was not one of them—and once again he peered at his wristwatch. He would not leave until about eleven-thirty, fifteen minutes from now, for he did not want to get there before midnight. Just *at* midnight, if possible, would be the ideal, the symbolic, hour. He could no longer hear the rain now and surmised it had stopped, or slowed to an all-night drizzle. He got up and looked out the window but, aside from the dripping trees, saw nothing but the few misty campus lights. Yet he could not rid himself of the uneasiness. He would have denied that it was fear. At eleven-thirty, then, he put on his long, below-knee-length overcoat—he owned no raincoat—a poncho over it, a knit cap on his head, and stuck a borrowed flashlight in his pocket. Then he left.

Calvary, the cemetery for whites, was not too far—about a twenty-minute walk even in the pitch blackness and rain—so he trudged purposefully. Absorbed in his thoughts, his mission, he had little cognizance of the passage of time and was over halfway there before he realized it—*and* before he became aware of the headlights of a car approaching from the rear. Glancing once over his shoulder he thought nothing of it until he sensed now that the car was moving very slowly, indeed almost leisurely—cruising. Then as if suddenly the occupants had made sure of their decision, it sped up—pounced—and the next he knew it had come directly alongside him and with its powerful spotlight had pinned him in a freeze.

"Hey, boy, come over here," said the heavy male voice from the front seat.

Blinded by the spotlight, Cager did not at first react.

"Did you hear him—are you deaf?" called a second male voice now, this one from the steering wheel seat.

"Who're you'all?" Cager said. squinting hard into the flood of light.

110

"You know who we are," said the second voice. "Git over here."

"I can't see with that light in my face. Are you-all the police?" The spotlight's beam was then moved up into the trees behind him, still barely leaving enough light for him to see POLICE on the side of the car and the two uniformed white men inside.

"Yeah, you guessed it," said the heavy-voiced one sitting beside the driver.

At last Cager went over to the curb to them.

"Where you goin' in this neighborhood this time of night?" It was the heavy-voiced one again.

Cager hesitated. "For a walk," he finally said, thinly.

"Say, listen, don't play with us, boy." It was the driver getting out of the car. He came around. "Where're you goin'? What're you up to?"

"I'm not up to anything, Officer," Cager said.

"Frisk him, Luke," said the heavy-voiced policeman still in the car, apparently the senior of the two.

Luke patted Cager down, found the flashlight, and brought it out. "Hey, what's *this*?" he said, as if he had found a pistol.

"Nothing wrong with carrying a flashlight on a night like this, is there?" said Cager.

"Naw, if you ain't getting ready to steal something with it. Where you live?"

Cager pointed vaguely. "Over at Gladstone College."

"Hear that, J.C.?" Luke said to his partner in the car.

J.C. grinned. "What's he do besides live there?"

Luke, also grinning, turned to Cager and waited.

"I'm a student," Cager said.

"How'ya like that, J.C.?"

J.C. smiled up at Cager. "Tell me, has you did yoh Greek yet tonight, boy?"

Cager at first said nothing. Finally then, "I don't take Greek."

"Oh. Scuse me."

But Luke, leaning against the car, was looking at his watch. "Hell, it's almost midnight, J.C." He turned to Cager beside him. "At this hour what you doin' over *here*?"

"I'm on my way to Calvary," Cager said, his voice somehow dark, sepulchral, prophetic.

"*What*?" Luke burst out laughing and turned to J.C. "You hear that? He says he's on his way to the *graveyard*!"

But J.C. was not laughing.

"Here it is midnight," said Luke, "and it's rainin', lonesome, quiet as a mouse pissin' on cotton, and he's payin' a visit to all them ghosts and hants and tombstones out there in Calvary!" Nor was Luke laughing now. "What the hell's goin' on here? You believe that, J.C.?"

"He's lyin'," J.C. said. He turned to Cager. "Boy, prove to me you go to that college over there. I don't believe it."

Cager slowly got out his wallet, at last found his Gladstone ID card, and handed it over to J.C. The two policemen, using Cager's weak flashlight, now studied the card minutely. Finally J.C., in a surly mood, returned the card and the flashlight to Cager, then sat in silence. But suddenly, as if a thought hit him, he reached behind him and opened the car door to the backseat. "Climb in, boy," he said. "We'll see about you and the graveyard. Come on, Luke. We're gonna take him and put him out right in the middle of the damn graveyard. That'll learn him not to lie to police officers. Come on, boy, get in."

But Cager stood there as if in a trance.

Luke, now climbing under the steering wheel, said to him, "That was a command from an officer of the law, college boy. He said 'get in.' Do you understand that?"

"I understand it," said Cager. "I want to go to Calvary by myself, though, on my own—not be shanghaied there." But then, inexplicably, and now silently—as if at last resigned—he climbed in the backseat and they drove off.

Later, though, on arriving inside the cemetery, J.C. and Luke had great difficulty in agreeing on just the right—the most scary— spot in which to leave their captive. They assessed one location after another, before moving on to the next, earnestly conferring and making constant use of their powerful spotlight, yet still without finding the ideal place, until, finally giving up, they settled for a nondescript gravesite overgrown with persimmon, thistle, and briers, on whose headstone, along with the name of the deceased, was engraved a lone human hand, its forefinger pointing straight up, heavenward. Beneath it the legend read: I'LL NEVER MAKE IT. Here, laughing, they ordered him out of the car and, their boisterous hilarity echoing up into the dark treetops, drove off.

Although relieved and glad to be free of the law's dangerously mercurial and arbitrary clutches, Cager was stoical. "They thought I was lying, they really did, didn't they?" he mused half aloud, but soon almost gloating. "Didn't believe I was already headed right here when they stopped me. Huh? Yeah, thought I was too damn scared to ever be coming to a graveyard at midnight.

112

Me. Us. Ha! Huh?" He repeatedly stretched his arms, legs, and torso in an effort now to relieve or dissipate the tensions of the experience just past, then he got out the flashlight. But it needed new batteries and its puny yellow light was of small help in getting him oriented among the wet, dripping trees, the murk and mist— the saturated blackness. He knew, though, his first task was to get outside the cemetery again, then come back in. He must enter it his own way, he thought, on his own, as he had told those redneck cops; it must be entirely voluntary; he must even *want* to do it, be a true believer, smash the shibboleth that "niggers (including himself) are afraid of night graveyards worse than death and anything the devil himself can conjure up." This was the very canard he had come here to negate, explode, blast, and defeat! He was spluttering, grinding his teeth, and anxious to get on with it.

Now holding out the helpless weak beam of the flashlight, he started forward, willy-nilly. He knew, whatever the direction, he must, if he continued straight, eventually come to the cemetery wall. There he would exit, then return in his own fashion, according to his own instincts and will. Soon now, at a caretaker's gate, and congratulating himself, he made his way outside. "I know what I'm doing, all right," he whispered feverishly, boastfully, though his heart was racing. He doused his light and stood for a moment to catch his breath. Although momentarily the rain had stopped, a wind had risen and as he waited outside the low stone wall he could hear it blowing through the wet grass, the soaked, threshing trees inside, indeed over and through the cemetery's entire vampirish reliquary, all with a most unearthly and eerie effect. He found now he was uneasy, his skin creepy and clammy, and wondered if rather it was really fear. He prayed it was not. Outside he followed the wall now for nearly eighty feet, then scaled it easily. He groped ahead, trying to locate the meandering roadway used by the hearses and procession cars, but could not find it.

Soon he threw the feeble yellow light on a large perpendicular stone slab with the name HENDERSON cut into it. Next to it rose the ornate mausoleum of the Phelps family, notably: LAMAR EDWARD PHELPS, 1862–1935." Fifteen feet beyond he came upon the ancient small stone marker bearing the name BABY ELLEN SUE MORSE, 1880–1883. Soon he began to mutter and make other strange vocal noises to himself as he went from grave to grave, examining each headstone with the sorry light, commenting on each one in a nervous yet almost exultant tone. "Ah, but look at you'all now," he

113

said, intoned, to the decaying headstones—especially the one of BREVET MAJOR HENRY SILER TULLS, 1837–1864. "Yeah, yeah," he breathed, "you'all had your day, your time of glory, of history, all right. Now let others come on and have *theirs.* Huh?"

Suddenly then he thought he heard a strange sound behind him. He wheeled and, trembling, futilely threw the puny light around him, but saw nothing and heard nothing more. Yet, before thinking, he called out shakily, "*Who's there?*" No reply, no further sound, nothing. At once then he felt guilty. "Just listen to that—*me*," he said. "'Who's there?' Lord, Lord. It's just like those damn cracker cops thought—scared of my shadow. Yeah, but I'll bet you a span of mules it won't happen again—*no, sirree.*"

He went over and leaned against a slippery tree and, again dousing the light, stood resting, though somehow still breathing hard, excited, if not scared. He could not remember such a pitch-black night, with the dripping of the water and the mournful whirring of the wind in the trees. Despite all his vows his heart now was pounding. But soon he resumed his roving among the dead, his jaw set in a new and grim determination. "Who's afraid of a bunch of dead rebel peckerwoods anyhow?" he said. "Nobody that's got any sense." Throwing the sickly light around right and left, he began a slight swagger as he walked, still talking to himself, until he felt calmer, less afraid.

It had begun to rain again now, slowly, steadily, but he continued his roaming among the dark, bleak "ghosts and hants and tombstones" until he was aware of bladder discomfort. He stepped over and urinated on what he thought to be the next grave, then threw the light on its headstone. It read: ROBERT E. LEE BONNARD, 1900–19–" "Good God!" he breathed. "Well, I'll be damned! . . . Whew! And he ain't even dead yet." He hurried away.

Yet, during the next three hours, back and forth, up, down, and obliquely, he traversed the entire ghostly reaches of Calvary cemetery. Finally, wet and exhausted, he returned to the grandest, most imposing, and largest, almost the size of a house, granite mausoleum he had encountered in all his nervous, rainy wanderings, its huge family name—DABNEY—cut into the rich, red-mottled marble over the entrance, and for a moment stood there somehow contemplating that fateful name in the flashlight's frail glimmer. At long last then he spread down his poncho against the wall of the edifice, leaned back, his face to the drizzle, and stubbornly sat out the night.

22

IT WAS NOT WEDNESDAY AFTERNOON'S rain that had caused the postponement. Far from it. There were no plans that day anyway to use the big vacant lot for drill practice. Rather, the arrangement had been to move indoors for an evening session. But now, just after dark, throwing off his dripping poncho as he entered Shorty George's little restaurant, Cager, in frustration and disgust, had to explain to Shorty the actual, and highly unsatisfactory, situation. "The lodge hall's not available. And I only just now found out about it. They've canceled us out. They could at least have told us sooner!" His anger flared. "But you know them simple lodge niggers! They're an ignorant bunch of clowns. Bad as it's got for us in this town lately, the only thing these backward-ass fools can find to do is meet in their hall and go through a lot of childish gibberish and lodge ritual like some kind of ignorant voodoo— flashing crazy signs and signals, winking, giving each other the grip, and all that shit. It's pitiful, man! Jesus Christ!" He was walking the floor.

Shorty, worried about the four customers in the place, pulled him over to a sequestered table in the corner. "Keep your shirt on, Cage," he said.

"Instead, then, of letting us hold our meeting like they'd booked us to do, and for a fee, they revoke us till some other night so they can get together and go through all that crazy irrelevant rigmarole like a bunch of coons in a minstrel show! It's a damn disgrace! What they oughta be doing is coming to our drill sessions, learning what's *really* going on, what our people have to put up with in this cracker burg!" He took a deep breath. "Well anyhow, we can't meet tonight. So the unit's dismissed till Friday over in the lot again. Will you get the word out, Shorty?"

Shorty was glum, disconsolate. "Yeah," he finally said. "But it's just as well, for I got worse news for you. Togo Jackson's lost the new uniforms."

"*What?*" Cager took a step back almost as if reeling.

"Somebody stole 'em out of the trunk of that pile of junk he calls his car."

The waitress, Shorty's long-suffering wife, came over to see if Cager was going to eat. "Hold it," Shorty said to her. "Later."

Cager was still staring incredulously at Shorty, then began wringing his hands in utter anguish. "What the hell're you *talking*

115

about!" he at last shouted at Shorty, as the latter's wife looked on in alarm and the few customers stared.

"You oughta know," snapped Shorty. "Togo was your idea. We all told you he was dumb as hell, a moron, but you wanted him in the organization anyhow, said we needed everybody we could get. Why would anybody but a moron leave twelve brand-new jackets to our uniforms out in his car all night less'n he's dumb as a fence post? They wasn't even paid for yet, just the down payment. We still gotta pay Nate Goldberg for 'em."

Cager heaved another heavy sigh, sank into a chair at the table, and stared out at the rainy darkness.

The "organization" did not even have a name yet. Presently it was still what Cager, its founder and leader, with Shorty as early financial backer, called the "drill unit." But, with Shorty's concurrence, he had already designed a uniform and matching cap for the members—gray-green jacket and trousers with red and gold accouterments, including a gold forked-lightning bolt on the left sleeve and crossed Ashanti spears on either lapel. The trousers, with red and gold stripes down each leg, would come later when the money was available.

The "unit" nevertheless met at least one evening a week to drill and confer—in either the customary vacant lot or the Negro lodge hall. In the latter, in addition to an hour or so of close-order drill, much time afterward was devoted to what Cager referred to as "briefing sessions." These, invariably led by him, included discussions of subjects like the town's physical layout, which they sedulously studied, including the location, even floor plan, of the courthouse, its situation and distance from the police and fire stations, the armory (and its contents), the radio station, gasworks, electric generating station, and sundry other sites, all referred to by leader Cager in his briefings as "strategic installations." His eyes fairly shone as he told the seventeen or eighteen men usually present: "It's all in case any trouble starts. We won't be starting it. It's in case *they* do. We got maps of everything. We know just about all that's going on, too. That's the job of our intelligence section. Shorty here and I have also designed a uniform for us even though they're not over twenty-five of us as yet."

This brought some affirmative nodding among his hearers and smiles of gratification.

"Speaking of Shorty," Cager said, "we sure wouldn't be much without *him* and what he's done for the unit. He's showed how important *he* thinks it is. He's put his *money* in it, ain't he? That's

116

the best proof there is. He came up with most of the down payment for the uniform tunics, didn't he? I know you-all know that and are going to come up with your part when you can. But he'll get every nickel he's put on the line for the unit—we'll see to that. My hat's, then, sure off to Shorty. Now there'll be more guys than ever coming into our army, you mark my words. We're building from the ground up—solid. When we get a couple hundred or more of our troops signed up, and all of us have our complete uniforms, we'll march down Main Street to the courthouse on a Saturday at *high noon*, man!"

"Tell it like it is, Cage," somebody said.

"It'll be a warning to 'em, I'll tell you," said Cager. "It's the uniforms. Don't forget, we're no damn lodge, or club. We're not just some marching unit, either. *We're an army!*"

That had been four or five months before. Now Shorty George pulled out a chair across the table from Cager and sat down. He spoke in a low, earnest voice. "But, Cage, forget about the uniforms for a minute, will you? Nate Goldberg ain't pressing us. He's sympathetic—for a white man—and the only one around here making uniforms that wouldn't run blabbing to the white folks on us. He's almost one of us, says so himself, and I believe him. So skip the uniforms for the time being, Cage. I been meaning, though, to talk to you about some other things . . . just in general like." Shorty swallowed. He was clearly having difficulty tackling the subject. "I been thinking a lot about what we been trying to do all these months. Sure, I've put a little money into it but I ain't making no big deal outa that. The organization was your idea from the beginning and you're due the credit. Nobody's gonna take anything away from you on that score. Back then we all thought it was a helluvan idea and long overdue. But lately—and this ain't got nothin' to do with the bad luck with the uniforms—I been thinking a lot about what's down the road for us, for our organization. Is there any honest-to-God future for what we been callin' our 'army'? Is it practical? Does it make any sense at all? See what I'm sayin'?—or askin'."

Cager, already struggling to control his incredulity and deep offense at this startling heresy, indeed apostasy, sat studying Shorty for a moment, hard. "Yeaaah," he finally said, his fierce irony dripping, "it's practical, it makes sense—if, that is, being *strong* makes sense." Soon, however, he was glaring furiously at Shorty. "You believe in *strength*, don't you, man?"

"Sure, Cage. Only thing is, how strong does it look like we're

117

gonna get? Strong enough to do some real good? Or are we just gonna go out in the street in a bunch of monkey suits and get our heads whipped and throwed in jail again like when you whipped them two cops and locked them up only to have the judge put you *underneath* the jail—we just gonna do that? See what I'm tryin' to get at? Sure, strength is practical, *if* you're strong enough to win. But seems to me you gotta think about what your chances are, too. Am I right? The thing is, though, I ain't seen no big surge of people tryin' to come join up with us, and we been recruitin' for these many months now. Tell me, what's on your mind, Cage? How do you see this thing shapin' up? I need somebody to tell me somethin'."

Now, in the struggle to control himself, Cager was writhing in the chair. He liked and respected, almost loved, Shorty and abhorred the thought of losing his friendship by treating him unjustly or speaking rashly any more than he already had. "We ain't going to get strong just overnight, you know," he said. "It takes time. It takes a lot of work, too. But look, Shorty, if you're getting fed up, if you want out, there won't be any hard feelings. Honest." But his emotions were overwhelming him, making his voice falter, then quaver. "You've been our friend and backer. *My* friend, too. You've put your money into this thing that I know oughta been going into your business or to your family. On top of that I know how lucky we been to have an old ex-army sergeant like you around to teach the men how to really drill and learn discipline. How're we ever going to forget these things, any of 'em? We can't. You're sure entitled, then, to a voice of your own. But getting strong—I'm talking about *militarily!*—ain't easy. Nobody said it would be! Good God, Shorty!" He was writhing again.

"By 'militarily' do you mean with an army, Cage?"

"How's anybody gonna get strong without *eventually* having some kind of army? Look at history, Shorty!"

Shorty seemed to have lost patience now. He looked at Cager, shook his head, and tried to smile. "Cage, you really believe that, don't you? Lord have mercy. And you had me believin' it, too. We was both nuts. But you're the one that's nuts now—not me no longer. But you've always had your head so high in the clouds on this thing it wouldn't never let your feet touch the hard ground. Lord, *an army!* Why, it don't make no kinda sense. I think we oughta just throw it all outa our minds and chalk it up to bad experience. No, no, I ain't all of a sudden lettin' you down—I hope

118

you understand that. I'm just askin' you to think about it, study it a little, and see if I ain't right."

Cager would not even look at him now.

"Some of the other guys are thinkin' the same way as me, too, Cage. Even talkin' among themselves."

Cager bristled. "*Who?*"

"Never mind who. But they're gettin' bored, losin' interest like. Most of 'em, anyway. Cage, we gotta face up to it, all of us. It's a crazy idea. Christ Almighty—*an army*! Always was. Like kids shakin' a bare crab apple tree at Christmas—with nothin' comin' down. Where we been all this time? Good God, I don't know. You had this vision, I guess, and we went followin' along."

Cager took another deep, deep breath, then observed his erstwhile colleague. Finally, swallowing all words, he reached for his poncho.

"Don't you want something to eat?" said Shorty. "We got ribs and collards tonight."

Cager, now grinding his teeth, made no reply. His eyes were glazed over, slightly wet, as he finally shook his head in the negative. Then he rose from the chair. At last, though, he tried to speak, to argue, his eyes flashing fire. But he was unable, and soon, swinging the poncho around his shoulders, averting his gaze, walked out.

23

DIRECTLY FROM SHORTY GEORGE'S, still fighting tears, he stormed out of the rain into Ma Moody's place—talking to himself, also reviling himself as well as the whole world and all mankind in it. Oh, Shorty, Shorty! he thought. "How'n the hell could you do it? You were my right-hand man!" He was heading to find Ma now and wondering about her mood, though well knowing that Wednesdays were slow business nights even in good weather, and that the pouring rain now only made customer prospects even bleaker, invariably sending Ma into one of her mean, dyspeptic tempers from which she might not recover until next day and then only when she had finally seen some sun.

His poncho still dripping, he found her in her "office," a tiny partitioned-off cubbyhole wedged in between the dining room and

119

lounge, and in tones both suppliant and demanding, the words gushing, told her of what he characterized as his "bound obligation"—to Shorty George. This of course was a grave tactical error, for the moment Shorty's name was mentioned, Ma mashed out her cigarette, picked up a pencil, and, all the while keeping her eyes away from him, began a dry, impatient—vindictive—drumming of her desk. Shorty was a business competitor, even if a pitiful, almost negligible, one. Ma, though, in such matters was relentless. "In other words," she said, "you want money from *me* to give *him*, is that it?"

He was impetuous, reckless. "Shorty made a helluva sacrifice, Ma! He didn't have much money, hardly any, but he came up with what he had! He's poor as Job's turkey—you know that. His place barely takes in enough to stay open. I don't see how he takes care of his family. As it is, he's the cook and his wife's the waitress! But I couldn't have started the organization without him. He even scraped up the down payment for our uniforms. Now *they've* been stolen! Oh, Lord! He'd siphoned that money off his business, Ma! The organization was my idea but right away he jumped in and helped me. But, sad to say, he wants out now. He didn't ask for his money back, though. He's written it off. But he's entitled to get it back—he can't afford to forget it. You can see that, Ma! It was *my* idea!"

Ma's eyes flashed angrily. "You don't have to tell me that! *I* know it was your idea! Who else could come up with anything that simple-ass and dumb?—a bunch of grown niggers out marching in a vacant lot!"

"But he wouldn't be out this money—about a hundred and seventy-five bucks—if it wasn't for me!"

"Of course he wouldn't! Which shows he dumber'n you—which ain't easy to be!"

"I gotta see that he gets it back, though, Ma! If you could let me have it, I could pay you back in no time—I could put in more hours here, some days now as well as nights. So you'd be *guaranteed* your money back!"

"Oh, now, would I? Boy, when the Lord was handin' out brains, you musta been behind the door, or out to lunch, or some place." Ma had already resumed studying a stack of invoices on her desk, merely adding, casually, "Y'better let me think about it some more and get back to you." She did not look at him again. He stood waiting. Finally, though, regarding it as hopeless, and knowing protests would do no good, he left helplessly muttering to himself.

Soon he found himself in the adjacent dining room ordering a sandwich before returning to Gladstone.

As he now sat waiting for his food, his frustrations and fatigue seemed to have settled painfully in his neck and shoulders, even down his spine, though he yet dreaded the thought of having to return to campus and all its ecology of blasted hopes where his string of comedies had now all but been played out and himself consigned to utter nadir. Soon his sandwich and milk were brought but they at last seemed to him as having little taste. Yet, he slowly chewed the food and tried to confine, narrow, even hedge in, his thoughts in order to make them somehow more manageable. This too in the end remained equivocal.

It was then, as he still ate, that the girl entered the dining room. "Cage, baby!" she cried, swooping over to his table. He sighed. It was Hortense Bangs. Embarrassed, he wanted to look around to see if any of the mere dozen other diners had noticed. Hortense was somewhat notorious. Even Ma cared little for her patronage.

"How you doing, Hortense?" he finally said.

She was standing over him now. "I'd join you, sweetie," she said, "but Silky Thomas is meeting me here to eat." At this he tried to grin. "How're things, baby?" she went on. "If you ask me, you look like you just got back from your mama's funeral or somethin'—and I *don't* play the dozens! Ha-ha-ha!" She passed on to another, yet nearby, table.

Although loud and brash, she was not bad-looking—slender, neat enough, young, her facial skin slightly pitted yet a pleasant saddle-brown. It was her eyes, however, that were most arresting—alert, intelligent, with a definitely worldly, brassy and brazen, almost defiant, glitter. She was, alas, also known for vending her considerable charms for cold cash.

Before long Silky Thomas, a "colleague," duly arrived—a laughing, boisterous, lighter-skinned (squash-colored) girl—and within minutes, abetted by some bonded bourbon whiskey, the pair were off on a flight of loud, hilarious talk and gossip, comparing notes on a variety of escapades, including every recent male encounter either had had or could remember, all of it, though, heard not only by nearby Cager but by the other diners in the place also. As time went on and Hortense had disposed of her third Manhattan he noticed her occasional neglect of her conversation with Silky in eyeing him. Again embarrassed, he looked away. But when she—obviously the lavish hostess—ordered T-bone steaks for herself and friend he was impressed.

121

Now Spats Smith, Ma's live-in boyfriend and Midnight Club straw boss, ambled in. "Spats, baby!" cried tipsy Hortense. "Come over here, honey—*look!*" She opened her purse, took out a double sheaf of ten- and twenty-dollar bills, and waved them at Spats. Cager's mouth fell open. "Come on, Spats, baby," said Hortense, "I'll buy you some of your favorite Vat 69!" Spats, habitually smiling and courteous to all customers, at first hesitated, but at last then, obligingly, came over. "I'm flush tonight, Spats!" Hortense said. "Set *down*, I say!"

Spats still smiled his gold-toothed smile but remained standing over her, saying, "Lemme take a rain check on it tonight, will you, baby—I'm workin', y'know. And why don't you stop wavin' all that cabbage around? That ain't good. Ain't you got a boyfriend that takes care of business matters like this for you?"

The two steaks arrived now. But not before Hortense, by way of reply to Spats, let out something resembling a high, shrill, almost braying, horselaugh of derision. "Spats, you got better sense than that! Ha! Ha! Ha! Christ! Do I look that simple?—to have some damn nigger pimp spendin' my hard-earned money for me? Don't believe it for a minute, baby! Like last night, I caught me a real live pigeon. Didn't no damn pimp help me do it, either. This drunk cracker came to see me just after he'd left a big poker game he'd cleaned out! Ha!—and promptly got *himself* cleaned out! I bet when he sobered up this mornin' he wished he'd gone straight home instead of first comin' to my place! I changed his luck, all right! Now, how come I need some damn pimp to help me spend this money? You tell me that, Spats baby! Ha, ha, ha! What?"

"Okay, okay," grinned Spats, anxious to quiet the uproar, "but just stop wavin' that wad around and put it back in your purse. There're a lotta people around, y'know, that'd like to get their hands on some of that loot."

Cager almost winced. He watched Hortense with feverishly burning eyes. At once, catching him in the act, she gave him her strident, lascivious laugh and again stuck out her quivering tongue. It as quickly aroused him and immediately he hated himself for it. Spats Smith had moved on now. It reminded Cager that he too should long since have left. He seemed powerless to move, though. He lingered indecisively, as if somehow waiting to do something he dreaded. But Hortense, in the euphoria of her bourbon, misread his mind and stepped up her flirting. It made him sick, more desolate than ever. But smiling, she still watched

122

him, her manner ridiculing him; then, laughing, she made more faces at him. Now he would not look at her.

Yet, when she and Silky had finished their steaks and were eating dessert, Hortense tipsily called over to him. "Cage, I been watching you ogling me all night—I ain't blind, you know. But when I start ogling back, you act like you wanta get up and run somewhere. What's the matter with you? What you scared of?— Ha! Ha! Ha!" Silky laughed too. He could only grin though it seemed a grimace. Shortly Hortense called the waitress over for the check and once more, his eyes popping, he saw the tremendous wad of bills she ostentatiously pulled out of her purse. "Come on, Silky, honey, let's go," she said, rising after she had paid and had heavily tipped the waitress. "And that means *you too*, Cage baby! Come along, now—you're goin' with me. Ha!—Silky's got a car out there and she'll drop us off at my place. Then you and me are gonna have us a ball—*all night long!* Hey, hey, now!" She raised both hands and, snapping her fingers, did a raunchy little dance.

"I can't! . . ." he tried to say. "I've got to get back out to campus!"

"Don't hand me that! You've had an hour to start back out there. Instead, you been setting there undressing *me*. So don't act so upset now." She gave a high, excited, unsteady laugh. "I've had my eye on you ever since you started workin' here! Ha! Ha!—yeah, I've had you slated for a killing a long time, old string-bean Cage! You come on home with me and I'll learn you some things them damn professors out at Gladstone ain't never heard of. 'Cause what I'm talkin' about ain't in any damn *book!* Hey, now!—I'm talkin' about the *sweet* life!" In attempting to give her little dance again she reeled and almost stumbled. Cager was trembling with shame. He was also thinking of that huge wad of money in her purse. Soon, therefore, drooping, limp, his gaze downcast, he got his poncho and left with them out into the driving rain.

The moment he and Hortense were alone in her flat, she threw off her coat and, smiling, stood triumphantly before him. "What's the matter, baby?" she tried to coo. "You didn't say a word all the way here. Now you look scared as hell. I sure don't know why. What could a little woman like me do to a big handsome galoot like you? Ha!—except maybe take him in that bedroom there and ring his bells for him right good! *Ding-a-ling! Ding-a-ling!*" She reeled back on her heels laughing and again almost

123

stumbled. "You oughta be lookin' forward to me," she said. "Yeah, shakin' with excitement like I sure know how to make a man feel. But instead you stand there lookin' like a ghost or like you just took poison. Lord, baby, tell me what's the matter." He only observed her and said nothing. "Let me fix you a drink, then, Cage. You sure need *somethin'* for whatever it is that ails you."

"That's true," he said, "but it's not whiskey." He finally sat down on the sofa.

"Well, *I'll* have a drink," she said, and left the room.

He sat gazing around him and hating the oppressive, cloyingly-sweet smell of the living room deodorant. The apartment, though tidy enough, was small and boxy and reeked of this weird incense in the midst of which were a half-dozen subdued multicolored lights strategically placed to create "atmosphere." When she finally returned with her drink he saw that she had also changed out of her street clothes, reappearing now in a negligee so sheer he could make out, even in the incense-laden murk, her stark-naked figure underneath. His blood jumped, then began furiously pounding. He wanted to run over and grapple with her, kiss and caress her—the smooth tainted young body, the protuberant breasts, the wiry pouting muff between the thighs, her sweet musk. But at last, drink in hand, she sat down beside him on the sofa, though not yet close to him. "To save my life I can't understand you," she smiled impishly, seeming now, despite the new drink, to have somewhat sobered. "You knew when you came here what the deal was. 'Cause I told you. You knew I was goin' to be a bad influence on you—*college boy*! Ha! Ha! So why're you now acting so damn innocent—or plain scared? I didn't bring you here to turn a trick with you, you know. This is *my* night to howl—and yours. If I was workin' I sure wouldn't be drinkin'. That's dangerous. In this business you got to keep your wits about you—*all the time*—or you'll end up some night dead." She sipped the drink, lit a cigarette, and sat back observing him. Both were silent for a time.

Finally she said: "I told you I been watching you like a hawk, didn't I? Well, I have and you know it. What do I care about you and old Flo Ransom? Hey, you didn't know I knew all about you two, did you? But that woman's another story. Ha!—another whole *book*! But I won't get into that—what she does is her business. Only thing I can say, though, is that you're as naive and country as they come, Cage baby. You need somebody to wise you

124

up, look after you, somebody that's hip to the tip—like *me*. You need protection. What can Flo Ransom do for you? Nothing. That's why I brought you here—at least one of the reasons—to talk. About *us*. I need a boyfriend, Cage. And I don't mean no damn pimp. And you need somebody to look after you that knows the ropes. I *will* say, though—ha!—that Flo Ransom knows 'em better than a lot of people give her credit for! But *you* sure don't know 'em, Cage honey. Lord, have mercy, no. But as for me, I need a man I can like for what he is, somebody I can look up to, like you, an educated young guy—and I bet I ain't two years older'n you. What I *don't* need—and don't want, and won't have— is some roughneck bastard that's only thinkin' about takin' what little money I get ahold of now and then, like last night. They forget I'm flat broke sometimes, too. But that's when a pimp wants to start mistreatin' you, beatin' up on you, when you ain't pro- ducin' for him. None of that for me. I want somebody that needs me as much as I need him. Y'know what I mean?"

Cager at last solemnly nodded, then took his eyes away.

Hortense bridled. "Why don't you *say* something, for Christ's sake! You sure get on my nerves! You ain't all that damn dumb. I hear at one time you was smart as hell out at Gladstone. Well, you at least must've been able to *talk!*"

He frowned, shook his head, then spread his hands futilely. "I don't know what to say, that's all. . . . "

Yet, before long, she had moved closer to him on the sofa, her voice somewhat softening now. "I didn't mean to scold you, Cage honey. That's my trouble, I run my mouth too much for my own good. I've been talking to you like I was putting some kinda big business deal to you. I don't feel that way about it at all. It's more like a nice warm feeling that I've got—I'm tellin' you the honest-to-God truth, Cage. It's like the way you feel when you really like somebody. And need 'em, too." She raised her face toward his and looked at him. "I'm a girl—no, a woman, I guess"—she laughed— "and have got feelings like anybody else." Suddenly then, nerv- ously, she leaned over and tittered in his ear: "Would you like to have sex with me tonight?"

He started. Frightened, he looked bewilderedly at her. But at last, his eyes staring now, piteous, afire, he could not speak. Yet, he longed to say, to cry out, to her, "*Yes, yes!*"

Soon she moved still closer to him, until now their shoulders and hips touched. "Honest," she said, "I ain't trying to make a

125

customer outa you, or anything like that, you know." She gave another uneasy laugh. "I *told* you it ain't business. That it won't cost you nothin'. I just want to have sex with you, that's all. What's wrong with that? I want to see if you like me like that. I *am* a girl, or woman, and I'm healthy. And I also like you a lot, so it's natural, ain't it, that I'd want to sleep with you. Have I got to tell you again you're my type? It's because you're intelligent. And a good guy. You're not rough-acting, either, like a lot of these clowns I know. *Ha!*—yeah, you can be *my* pimp any time! But ain't you got the least bit of feeling for me? Ain't you just a little bit excited, setting close to me like this—Ha, ha, ha!—and us rubbing asses?" Then without any warning at all, before he could possibly have known what was happening, she slid her hand along the inside of his thigh to his genitals. They were throbbing hard.

He jumped straight up. Then stood before her quivering and mortified.

"What'n the hell's wrong with you?" she cried. "Do you get all upset about a little foreplay like that? You act like you've never been to bed with a woman! I know, though—I can tell—I excite you, all right. I could feel—for a second or two there at least—that you was hard . . . or was somethin' . . . Lord, I don't know what, to tell you the truth. What kinda guy *are* you, Cage?" Then, as he still stood before her, numb, speechless, quaking with both confusion and desire, she shot out her hand to touch him again. He jumped back as if she had had a white-hot poker in her hand. "Cage baby, I swear before God I've never run into anybody like you before in my life. You sure got me up a tree. I've seen all types—at least I thought I had—but nobody like you. You like women, don't you? You ain't a faggot, are you?—tryin' to put me on. You don't think I ain't met a lot of them, do you? Two of my closest buddies—Art and Sammy—are flits, what're you talkin' about? Tell me, are you one of *them?*"

He scowled, then glared, at her.

"Okay, I take it back. On the other hand, though, don't be so quick to lose your cool. It don't look good—like you're overreactin' or somethin'. There're a lot worse things you can be than a sissy, I'll tell you that. But what *is* your problem, then? Good God, let me in on it—if you know. Which I doubt."

"I *am* a pimp!" he finally blurted. "I came here only to get some of that money you were flashing around at Ma's!"

She gaped at him. "Cage honey, I know you're dumb about

126

some things," she said. "Not all, but some. But, Lord have mercy, I didn't know you could be *that* dumb. This thing's gotten outa hand. It's crazy. Money? What kinda numbers are you talkin' about?"

"A hundred and seventy-five dollars."

"That ain't a fortune but it's still money—somebody else's, mine." She had scooted back from him now, to her original place at the other end of the sofa, and sat staring at him, as if baffled. "I guess I ain't as surprised that you'd want money from me as I am that you'd think—just for half a second!—that you could *get* it, talk me out of it. You sure don't know *me*, honey. I never gave a damn man a quarter in my life. Even if I do say it myself, you're dealin' with one of the hippest, hardest-hearted, most street-wise, women you'll ever come across. I'm young, sure, but I started early. I've dealt with every kinda no-good type there is, every one of 'em— and, yeah, right here in this hick town. Niggers and crackers alike. Crackers that after they screw you, want to kill you, or tell you they gotta mind to. Or while they're screwin' you call you all kinda dirty coon-breeding, filthy nigger bitches, saying all niggers oughta be burned alive, all this while they're gruntin' and carryin' on, fuckin' you, gettin' their nuts off. I tell you, they're crazy, they're sick. People to be really afraid of. Oh, sure, they're mostly drunk when they're sayin' all these things but, oh yeah, they're speakin' their sober thoughts right on."

Although Cager now seemed strangely to have little interest in what she was saying, the words, he still somehow watched her face with awe, and finally revulsion.

"Then, of course," she said, "there's the niggers—oh, my God. They're just as bad, in other ways. Some big filthy black ape, drunk, or right off a garbage truck, will want to screw half the night for five dollars. When you tell him no dice and cuss him out and order him to *git*, then he wants to beat you up, cripple you. I've coped with all kinds, I tell you—black and white—and all of 'em are the same, a bunch of low, no-good, horny dogs. They're all dogs, yeah—animals. Still they think they can look down on you, talk to you, or treat you, any damn way they want to—just because you happen to be a whore. It *is* happenstance, you know. Well, there you are, that's what the scene's like, and I been dealin' with it, too. So here comes old country boy Cager that's gonna take advantage of *me*, talk *me* outa some money. Right?" She was not smiling.

127

"Why do you live this kind of life?" he said abruptly, frowning. Then the horror and disgust returned to his face. "Good God, *I've* got sisters. I'd shoot one of 'em first. How can you live this way?"

"Because it's how I was cut out to live. I told you it was happenstance. You ain't got any choice. You gotta play the hand you was dealt and not bellyache about it—just hope things will be better next time around, in the next life. I'm a religious gal, you know—even if I don't go to church, where they wouldn't want me anyhow—and pray all the time. Ha! Ha!—I mean *all* the time. Maybe it's because I'm plain scared—scared that some night one of these misfits will cave my skull in, or cut my liver out. See what I mean? Sure I'm religious—I *better* be! If I had *my* way, though, I'd be a *queen*, settin' on a damn throne somewhere—cool! Ha! Ha! Ha!"

He gazed morosely at her, then said something not quite audible.

"So what's your story, Cage baby? How'd you think you was gonna con *me* outa some money?"

"I was up against it," he finally said, almost apologetically. "I needed the money bad."

Hortense smiled. "Why didn't you go to your old girlfriend Flo? She's a big shot around here, ain't she?—my, my, works for the *state*. Now, don't make me have to tell you how she *got* with the state, sweetheart—ha, ha! But where was she?—old green-eyed, freckle-faced Flo."

Except for grinding his teeth he sat mute and would not look at her.

"Oh, but maybe she wouldn't have had the kinda money you're talkin' about, eh? Right, Cage baby? Wow, a hundred and seventy-five smackers. You ain't knocked up one of those little gals out at Gladstone, have you?"

"I wanted the money for Shorty George," he said. "He put it up when we were starting our organization and ain't been paid back yet."

"Christ, I thought that dumb outfit had gone bust by now. I sure don't hear about it anymore."

He stiffened, almost bristling. "We've had a temporary setback, yeah," he said. "Shorty's probably dropping out—that's why he oughta get his money back—but we *ain't gone bust!*" He glared at her.

"Oh, Cage, come off it. That outfit was a joke. Instead of protecting us it was the laughingstock of the town—and most of all by

128

these rednecks, the ones you was tryin' to scare. How'n the hell did you'all dream that thing up? It was a scream, Cage—honest. You' all out there trampin' up and down that empty lot like a bunch of clowns, people passing by laughing their asses off—even the niggers."

He jumped up. "That's a lie! Don't you say that about Negroes! It's not true! It was a good idea—a *great* idea!—I don't give a damn what you'all say! Ain't you got any pride? To hell with all of you! . . . You don't deserve any better!" He had grabbed up his poncho and was running to the door.

Suddenly she pursued him now, trying to intercept him, head him off.

"Get to hell out of my way!" he said, his arm throwing her aside.

"Now, you just wait a minute, there, Mr. Cager!" she cried. "I'm sorry I said that, even if it was true! I'm sorry, I say!"

But his hand was already on the doorknob.

She tried to jerk it away and then they struggled. "You can have the money! . . ." she said, panting. "Hell, that's no sweat! I'm sorry for what I said. Don't you leave—I'll go get my purse right now! Do you hear? You wait, now, Cage!" She was pleading as she turned him loose.

"Come back!" he said. "I don't want it! I won't take it!"

She returned. "You listen to me, Cager!" Her pleading had strangely turned to panic. "What money I handle is all bad—bad money! It comes from the bad and as soon as I get it, it goes right back to the bad! Can't you see that? I want you to take that hundred and seventy-five bucks and give it to Shorty like you said. For once money of mine will be goin' for something that at least had good intentions! I told you I was wrong, didn't I?" She had now become hysterical. "Give me this one chance, won't you? *Oh, Cage! . . .*"

But he opened the door and fled down the stairs.

Next morning she went to the post office and sent Shorty George a money order for a hundred and seventy-five dollars. The sender's name was stated merely as "Cager," for she knew neither the real first name nor any version of his last. Only "Cager." But that was enough. Cager, though, did not know that she had done it.

Two days later, with clearing skies, Ma Moody called him in and, in one of her rare better, indeed generous, moods, returned of her own volition to the subject of his recent request for a loan. He glumly thanked her but, lying, said he no longer had need of it.

129

24

OH, FLO! . . . OF MY DREAMS! Of, yes, my, your narrator's, emissive fantasies! In this steamy self-gratification I have persisted in reveling until now it has become habitual. Despite your unfavorable opinion of me (I would tell her by way of telling myself back then), you are nevertheless my constant partner, my idyll, my masochistic joy! In this interim of dragging time since that wild night of cabareting and dancing in the Midnight Club, I have been no more able to forget you than formerly I could that dangerous (even to *think* of it!) Cass Nellis back home in Sheets, Texas. So now here at Gladstone it is all you, Flo, only you, who limns my carnal obsessions even if my satyr's lust for you is somehow coupled with an admittedly schoolboyish idolatry hardly justified by your caustic treatment of me on that never-to-be-forgotten night in Ma's place of the music riots—this even conceding that your displeasure had ample cause. Yet, it has only stoked the fires of my determination. Ever since then I have vowed never to abandon my pursuit of you, even if in saner moments I realize how utterly implausible, indeed ridiculous, the idea, that it is more than likely that I shall not even see you again. Ah, but that has been so many, many years ago. I *did* see her again.

There ever remained, then, that strain of vindictiveness, perversely commingled with love, I felt for her, my craving to even the score, actually punish her, that I would not be able to control. Strangely, Cager's presence in the equation seldom crossed my mind. Nor did thought of the likelihood, if not certainty, that he would find out (what he doubtless knew or suspected already). It was, though, possible, maybe probable, that on that memorable night at Ma's he had even been not so much angry over my brazen wooing of Flo as he had my betrayal of him to Ma in order to keep the peace and Sonny Pemberton's hind parts intact. In which case my anxieties over his feelings about Flo and me could only be presumptuous, and I, in his mind, in this context, a harmless cipher—to which of course Flo would have heartily agreed. There was even the possibility she might herself have told him of my silly antics.

Yet, all this only heightened the secret rancor (cum love) I harbored toward her, which, however, diminished not one scintilla my rabid panting after her. One day I even summoned the gall to phone her, twice, though when each time there was no answer I experienced an almost fainting, breathless relief. It was fear, not so

130

much of Cager, but of her almost certain unpleasantness. How foolish all this fatuous plotting, I told myself, and how absolutely devoid of hope. It was of course at this juncture in the weird scale of events, and life, indeed fate, that I suddenly, and in the bizarrest of circumstances, encountered her again.

Imagine, if you will, Flo's owning a bicycle. Imagine further, if you can, seeing her—in her grave dignity—*riding* one, and in the business district downtown and elsewhere. The phenomenon can only be appreciated when, in turn, the phenomenon of her various and complicated mind is, at least to some degree, understood— plus, more mundanely, the fact that she could not afford a car, not even a jalopy. No matter, one would have thought, in light of her natural self-possession and reserve, plus an inordinate pride, that she would have considered a bike, to put it modestly, unbecoming—especially a big gaudy red contraption with a professional's plenitude of accessories, including a second seat close up behind her for little Annette, and which, at least apparently Flo thought, required that they when riding, each wear a pair of huge leather goggles.

On the other hand, her basic, her bedrock, reasons for choice— no, necessity—of this mode of transportation had largely to do with her quibbling but unyielding views of not only civilized comfort and sense of well-being but the bleakness of her speculations about her and her daughter's chances of making it in that dice game of intricate, entangled, that is, *the race-segregated,* life. Although the city buses were but one example, she hated them and all they told her about her career of chance-taking with color as stakes. Yet, a paradox, or irony, she harbored a vague feeling, if only thinly disguised, of superiority over the rank-and-file Negroes—domestics, laborers, general underclass, and so on— daily herded and crushed together in those foul, repellent Jim Crow sections and all that the custom, enforced by harsh laws rigorously implemented, connoted, a negation of her total pride and selfhood. She therefore took for herself and child the necessary, if quixotic, step toward circumvention—avoiding completely the use of public transportation. Her means, then, was her purchase of this brand-new vehicle, together with the two pairs of formidable-looking, but largely unneeded, goggles, by all of which she sought to keep intact her dignity, her very persona.

On the day of our astounding new encounter I had gone into town to cash a small postal money order my little mother Maude had sent me in her dogged furtherance of my religious education.

131

Poor deceived dear! Forgive me, Mom! But, alas, as Hazlitt tells us: "The repentance of a hypocrite is itself hypocrisy." Leaving the post office, though, that day I saw, a half block down the street, this small gathering of spectators surrounding some happening, incident, or other, which I, however, because of the obstructed view, could not quite see. Out of curiosity, though, I started walking toward it. It was then that I saw the light-sorrel-hued young Negro woman, wearing big goggles, frantically remonstrating for some reason with the white onlookers around her. Next I saw the Negro child, the little girl, lying prostrate in the street yammering and apparently crying great tears, her monstrous goggles now violently askew across her face. It was then I felt the shock of recognition and almost tripped—I had identified Flo only after first recognizing Annette and was furious with myself as I now started running toward them.

As I neared the scene, Flo's harsh, strident, excited voice was unmistakable. "Won't you call an ambulance, or get somebody's car!" she cried out in appeal to the spectators. "You can see my little girl's hurt and I can't leave to get help! My goodness!" Now she pointed to a sour-looking, bewildered farmer standing beside his rusty little truck, its motor still running. "He ran into us!" she said, finally snatching off her goggles. "All of you saw it! It was his fault—he hit *us!*" Halfway under the truck then I saw the big beautiful bicycle, its shiny red paint badly scuffed, the rear wheel twisted and mangled. Annette, still crying, was lying near the curb and holding her left shoulder as if in great pain, as the bystanders, not hostile, not necessarily unsympathetic even, appeared nonetheless immobilized and almost embarrassed, glancing at each other as if more from discomfort than heartlessness. Yet, they did nothing.

At this instant I rushed up. "Flo!" I cried. "What on earth's happened?"

She whirled around with a stupefied look on her face. Then: "You can see! . . . oh, you can *see!*" Wailing desperately, she pointed the huge goggles in her hand at little Annette lying in the street. "She's hurt! . . . Can't you tell? Oh, help me get her to the hospital! I need an ambulance!"

"Now, now, take it easy," I said, rather magisterially, all the while laying my hand on the soft fleshy part of her upper arm. "Don't you worry, now! I'll find some way to get her there." I had not, however, the slightest notion of what to do as I too now looked around at the staring witnesses. "You stay right here," I finally

132

said, but in a hopeless dither. "I'll be right back!" Yet, I did not move. I had no idea what to do or where to go for help.

At last a bewhiskered old man in overalls, his beet-red face now wrinkled and sun-parched, moved his cud of chewing tobacco from his right to his left cheek and pointed up the street a ways. "That fire station up there's the quickest way to git a ambulance over here," he said. He pointed down at Annette then and said to Flo, "Shouldn't nobody touch her till it gits here. Might be some bones broke."

"Oh, my God!—that's what I *know*!" cried Flo, almost in tears.

But now I felt more confident with the benefit of the old man's tip. "I'll be right back," I repeated to her, and took off on a run—to the fire station.

"Oh, thank heavens, Meshach!" she called out after me. "Hurry, hurry, won't you?"

I was euphoric! She had called me by my *name*! I found myself now running faster than ever. The fire station was about two and a half blocks up the street. As I ran I thought about how helpless poor Flo looked now and how overwhelmingly appealing it made her, and maybe too, for all I knew, more vulnerable—my obliquitous mind conjuring up all sorts of fancied opportunities for at long last working my will on her.

The fire station was a small redbrick building. I was not only out of breath but also now nervous, even scared—about having to go in this unfamiliar, probably unfriendly, place and ask for help. But the moment I entered I was promptly greeted—welcomed—by the station mascot, a beautiful Dalmatian dog, a bitch, which ran forward to me waving her handsome ropy tail and uttering excited little whines and blatherings of delight. I hurried past her, however, and went over to the two firemen playing gin rummy at a table against the wall. "Excuse me, please, sirs," I said, very hesitantly, very politely, "there's been an accident just now, down the street from the post office, involving a small truck and a woman and her little girl on a bicycle. The child is hurt and needs an ambulance to get her to the hospital. A man there told us the quickest way was to ask you if you would please call for one." At once then I realized I had made a mistake in using the word "us," for both men had looked curiously hard at me.

"She hurt bad?" the tall, saturnine one, a cigarette hanging from his lips, finally asked.

"I don't know, sir," I said. "She was lying in the street and seemed to be in pain.

133

The other fireman, with bushy red hair and a pencil behind his ear, looked hard at me again. "Do *you* know her?" he said.

I knew what he meant, all right, and saw the opportunity to rectify my blunder, lying like a champion. "Oh, no, sir," I said. "I just happened to be coming out of the post office and saw the bystanders down the street. I told the lady, the child's mother, that I'd run up here and tell you."

At last he tossed the pencil on the table, pushed his chair back, and, lackadaisically, went over to the telephone.

Meanwhile it seemed the beautiful Dalmatian bitch had not once taken her eyes off me. She came quickly now and squatted on her haunches directly in front of me, observing me whimsically but clearly with approval, before rising to nuzzle my knees. Her hair was fine and sleek and her myriad black spots, the size of half dollars, were randomly distributed over her immaculate coat of white. Finally she leaped up on me, leaning heavily against me, her paws almost reaching to my chest, as all the while she gazed mirthfully into my eyes. The tall, saturnine fireman, who had remained at the gin rummy table, sat watching her with a strange, indescribable look, though not yet quite a frown—until, that is, he suddenly, apoplectically, yelled at her. "*Blanche!* You gawddamn tramp!—you whore, you! Git your ass over here before I come and give it a good whackin'!" He was not smiling. Blanche, almost knocking me down, bolted and ran to him, sadly leaving me in the lurch, and, reaching him, dropped down contritely at his feet—yet even at this distance observing me as wistfully, and mischievously, as before. I like dogs but she had made me more nervous even than I had already been, although, I must say, somewhat less so than had her saturnine rebuker—who really frightened me. But now the other fireman returned from the telephone and, as he sat down to resume the gin game, told me curtly that the ambulance was on its way and picked up the deck of cards again. Whereupon I thanked him, again very politely, almost effusively, and at once got out of that menacingly uncomfortable place aptly indeed called a firehouse.

When I arrived back at the scene of the accident, a motorcycle policeman was there interviewing the sour-looking, bewildered farmer, the accused, and others, as I ran up breathlessly to Flo and announced my great success. "The ambulance is on its way! The fire station up there called for it!" I was triumphant, so proud of myself.

"Oh, good for you!" she said. "The cop there just called for one too. But bless you—I don't know what I'd have done if you hadn't come along!" Yet, she spoke hurriedly, her eyes and attention many places elsewhere, especially on little Annette, before she abruptly left me to go give the policeman another scrap of information or two she had just recalled. I was deeply disappointed, even offended, wounded, for I had returned fully expecting to find her still in utter distress, maybe a crying, bewailing wreck, and thus more than ever dependent on me. I had thought then of how I would console her, perhaps putting my arm about her lovely figure and discreetly hugging her to me with unlimited, softly spoken expressions of reassurance, comfort, and my personal protection, as I told her I was sure Annette would be found to be all right, not hurt badly, maybe even able to go home with her. But instead she had, after a few kind but now hurried words, practically ignored or dismissed me. I was crushed, and also vindictively angry, though careful, very careful, to conceal both.

After Flo had talked briefly with the policeman, who seemed unusually jaunty and bantering with her, his sportive Clark Gable eyes all but consuming her, she returned to Annette, who had by now stopped crying, though still lying at the curb, her head resting on a car seat-cushion which one of the onlookers had silently supplied. I started over to the farmer's little truck now to drag Flo's damaged bike from under it but, suddenly remembering the policeman's investigation still in progress, quickly desisted. Instead I went up to Flo and Annette and, like an oily, unctuous undertaker, tried to speak to them as solicitously and comfortingly as, considering my true dudgeon, I could bring myself to do. Flo perfunctorily thanked me again but, as before, was too occupied with Annette and other pressing things to notice me further. Then and there once more I vowed to have satisfaction—in more ways than one.

The ambulance finally arrived. There was no commotion or confusion as the two stony-faced attendants brought out a stretcher and placed whimpering Annette on it. When they had loaded her in the vehicle, Flo, excited and scurrying about all over again, scrambled in behind her, as I, officious and ingratiating to the very end, got in behind Flo—when suddenly she spun around to me. "Oh, my bike!" she said. "Meshach, will you go back and ask the cop if you can take it to my house for me? I may be able to get it fixed—I'm not sure. Will you please do that?" I could only glumly accede and was already swinging down as the ambulance pulled off. "And leave it chained to the back stoop, Meshach!" she called out just as they turned the corner. Ah, but I was all too well aware that I could not carry out her urgent request. In her haste and confusion she had forgotten to give me the bike's safety chain padlock key. Now I was free to take the bike to her house and, in guarding it, wait there until she came home. I felt a touch of vindication already, though only a touch, for it took over three hours of this endless waiting—and of my resenting, and scheming, yet ghoulishly hoping. But always vowing.

But when she did—at long, long last—arrive home, I immediately saw that she had been crying and was otherwise in an extremely nervous state. It turned out that she had not only had to ride a hated Jim Crow bus back but had been told by the doctor it was uncertain how long Annette would have to remain in the hospital, that her left shoulder had been dislocated. Flo herself had sustained only three lacerated knuckles. Despite my efforts to console her she remained inconsolable and for a time stood at her kitchen window—whose frame bore Cager's pale green paint—snuffling, gloomy, and uncommunicative. Oh, how I loved her like this! She seemed so right—and *ripe*—for me! I could hardly control myself.

Eventually, though, she began talking about lawyers, wondering how she would be able to get one, what treatment she would receive if the case had to go to court, even, God forbid, to a jury, if a settlement could not be reached with the careless farmer, and, above all, how much it would all cost if she failed. She looked so downcast and distraught. How I marveled at her! Finally she invited me to stay while she tried to find food with which to fix a quick dinner. But I was not at all so brainless as to misread this gesture and was quick to contain my elation, realizing she so badly missed Annette that she dreaded eating alone. I appeared to assent reluctantly—of course for a definite and pregnant reason. My desire for her was so overpowering, so outlandish, really, that I feared, at this critical point, making some disastrous blunder (to which anyway I was genetically prone). I wanted no repetition of the night at Ma Moody's where in my stupid ardor I had spoiled everything. I was then, as I say, determined to be cautious, extremely careful, and, above all, patient—even if cunning. So now despite her bandaged hand, she prepared two ham omelets, with toast, and with this we drank the one bottle of orange pop she had in her little icebox. But as soon as the meal was over I cere-

moniously rose, thanked her, and told her (the truth) that I had a
lot of homework back on campus to get done before morning.

"Oh, sure," she said, "I understand." She seemed relieved that I
was going. "I'm glad you're studious." She grew pensive. "I wish I
could get Rollo to be that way—like he used to be. But . . ." She
sighed. "Oh, well." She led me to the door, thanked me again, and
I left.

I went down the street in a daze of elation, as if walking on
diaphanous atmosphere and white clouds. But soon my feelings
began to settle, deflate, grow sober. I was beginning to feel sorry
for her. She seemed so helpless and troubled. I then myself became briefly confused and distressed. Ah, futility!

I of course recounted absolutely nothing of this episode to Bahr.
He would have wanted—in his sad, sick, secret heart—to maim
then kill me. He too was that addicted to that phenomenon—that
miracle!—we call Flo.

25

"YOU'VE GOT TO LET GOD come into your life, your
heart," Mabel Foster told him. "He's the only One who can help
you. You won't talk but everybody knows just the same that something's happened to you, upset you, and changed your whole life,
turned it around in the very opposite direction—the Devil's direction. You need God, I tell you, Cage. That means the Church. I'll
bet you can't remember when you've last been." These are some
of the things his campus girlfriend told him—to which his answers, if any, were both hesitant and ineffectual.

His mother, however, in her halting letters, had perhaps been
less sure of herself than Mabel—or maybe only more oblique. Yet,
Effie Lee's concerns had preceded the present phase by many
years. She had long been unclear about what she knew to be the
uniqueness—and complexity—of her son's religiosity. In a recent
letter to him, nonetheless, she had been, in her own quaint way,
somewhat more direct—by quoting lines from the old gospel song:

Not my brother, not my sister
But it's *me*, Oh, Lord,
Standing in the need of prayer.

137

To Effie also, though, as with Mabel, prayer, and God, meant—required—the Church. It likewise meant and required that God's message come through one of the chosen He had called to preach. All the above Cager ponders, until—

Sunday morning the preacher is preaching, preaching and the church is rocking, rocking to the preacher's banshee cries and wildly gesticulating arms and hands, even fingers, sending out from the pulpit a message all their own, before he rears back and in his bullhorn voice delivers a thunderous repetition of his text: *"When the great day of His wrath shall come, who will be able to stand?"*

"Not many, preacher!" somebody cried back up at him. "Praise Jesus, then!"

Traversing the wide width of the rostrum, then back again, the bullet-headed gospeler, an ear cocked for a still louder congregation response, paused in his gamboling strut, arched his back, and cried out, "I cain't *hear* you'all! Remember, I'm talkin' about Gawd's *wrath*!"

"Yes, he is," said one deaconess—seated in front of Cager—to another.

"I know it," the other replied. "Preach, Bearcat!"

"Yeah, *teach*, Pilate!" hollered a third.

"Look!—look at him strutin'!" somebody else loudly volunteered. "Tipping like a Maltese kitten on a snow-capped mountain! Go on with your bad self, Bearcat!"

Cager sat with a curious, startled, yet not unreceptive, expression. Although he had often heard of it and its colorful (to say the least), ubiquitous leader, this was his first time ever inside Shiloh Missionary Baptist Church, the biggest Negro church in town, the Reverend Doctor Pilate Goodings ("Bearcat") Walker, pastor—and also where Ma Moody and Spats Smith, good friends of Bearcat, "worshiped."

The preacher, now prancing, highballing, and grimacing, showed a mass of perfect-white horse teeth as again, in his heavy, loud-quavering voice, he exploded: "In the thunderin' and the lightnin', in the brimstone and the fy-yah, when the frogs done come outa the hail clouds and the bats done cut out from the barn—Oh, Lord, chilren!—when Hell itself rips open and Satan shows his cowerin' face, who, church, *who*, will be able to stand?"

"Only sweet Jesus!" cried Sister Alberta Broadnax. "Don't overdo it, though, now, Pilate!"

"No, no, leave him alone!—turn him loose!" cried Poolroom

138

Mary, who then yelled up at the pulpit, "Keep on with your fast self, Bearcat! Keep on keepin' on!"

But a more sedate lady, Mrs. Charlayne McGillicuddy, a sprig of artificial leaves and cherries on her white hat, called up decorously to the rostrum, "Hum up, Doctor Walker!"

The big old swayback structure of a church had been packed and jammed since eleven o'clock. Besides the pastor, there were six or seven other, lesser, divines seated up behind him on the rostrum, all handpicked by Bearcat for their long fealty to him and their eagerness at the slightest provocation to jump up as he preached and loudly egg him on, men clad in the shiny blue serge suits and white bow ties of (except Sundays) a gnarled-handed, hod-carrying clergy. But not Bearcat—he of the velvety hands, manicured nails, and Memphis-monogrammed shirts.

He was still preaching when next someone, hands clapping, started up a jaunty hymn:

I want to be ready,
I want to be ready,
To walk in Jerusalem
Just like John!

Promptly the gospel singing and clapping were taken up by the others, soon swelling into a shouting chant throughout the church.

Bearcat, his eyes half closed now as if he were in a trance, continued his traipsing back and forth across the rostrum, urged on by his corps of platform prelates. But soon he stopped and faced the congregation. "But we *all* wanta be ready, church—not just some! I'm talkin' about when *Judgment Day* comes down on this old earth! When, yes, Lord, Your wrath done struck! You have commanded me, your unworthy servant, to preach hellfire and damnation, baptism by immersion, and Christ crucified, to Your peoples, Lord, so that they'll be ready when their record is brought before You who'll be judgin' both the quick and the dead! Hear me, flock! When that day comes, then, *Oh, Lord, who will be able to stand?*"

Someone—rapturous, impetuous, carried away—began the familiar long-meter hymnal response:

There is a fountain filled with blood
Drawn from Emmanuel's veins
And sinners plunged beneath that flood
Lose all their guilty stains.

Singing broke out afresh now, powerful, plangent, keening, soon engulfing the entire congregation.

Cager, deeply moved by the mighty singing, yet sat watching the preacher with a puzzled, and soon somewhat displeased, look on his face—still, however, expectant, hopeful.

Following Bearcat's lurid, strident Book of Revelation's blast and warning, then his loud misquotation from First Thessalonians, another hymn refrain was taken up by all: "The Storm Is Passing Over, Hallelujah!"

At once resourceful Bearcat, walking, talking, declaiming, seized on this theme as if it were a brand-new text. "Gawd's sunny light *does* shine through after the storm, church!" he cried, lifting the blatant whites of his eyes to the rafters. "You can see it up there! You can spy His mighty hand rolling back them old black clouds to let the sun come on through! Praise His name! Take heart, then, disciples! Serve Gawd and He'll never forsake you!"

Some woman in the rear let out a piercing wail not quite a scream.

"All right, now!" affirmed a man nearer. "Warm 'em up, Pilate!"

Cager turned around to get a glimpse of the woman. Heavy, grizzled, jet black, old, she was standing, her eyes tightly closed, shaking her fist at the ceiling. "*Show* us the Redeemer, Reverend!" she cried. "It's *Him* I wanta see! I wanta put my old eyes on Him just once, Reverend Walker! You been tellin' us about Him but now I wanta *see* Him, face-to-face, Mista Pilate! 'Cause time's runnin' out on me and I'll be meetin' Him 'fore long! *Reveal* Him to me, Reverend!" She opened her eyes wide, though staring blankly, then somehow even wider. "Show me the face of my *Savior!*" she pleaded. With a start Cager recognized her now. It was old Hattie, late-night frequenter, with the two pitiful foster children, of Ma Moody's cabaret where she hustled nickels and dimes for Bearcat. "Show me your *face*, Jesus!" she screamed now, soon then shuffling and shouting in the aisle, which before long required two white-gloved women ushers to subdue her and lead her back to her seat.

"Gawd will never forsake you, chilren!" bawled Bearcat, ignoring old Hattie's pleas. "If you'll only serve Him! Just when life is darkest, and meanest, and when we feel, like old Job, beat down to the ground, when our so-called friends tell us to curse Gawd and die, then's when—if we know *Jesus*—we begin to see that old storm movin' on away from here!"

"Oh, no, now!" cried a deaconess in the second row.

"Bless Jesus!" said another.

One of the platform prelates, a man of almost three hundred pounds, stood and loudly encouraged the preacher: "Keep this old wagon goin' on up the mountingside, Pilate, whilst we chock for you!"

Now vain Bearcat momentarily paused to pick a speck of lint off his lapel. His dapper black suit, the pearl stickpin in his tie, the high sheen on his Florsheim shoes, the Lay-'em-Straight on his hair, his conspicuous masonic (diamond) ring, to say nothing of the gleaming Oldsmobile parked out behind the church, all attested to his stellar pastoral (fiscal) accomplishments with the church—likewise with a goodly number of its female parishioners. But the church, giver of gifts, felt proud—while at last Cager was filling up with a sickening disgust; and this was where he had come for help.

Now Bearcat, perspiring, took out a large linen handkerchief and mopped his brow. "Oh, yes!" he cried. "The storm passes on over when we accept Christ as our savior, when we turn our backs on this old world that stands for nothin', the world the white folks own lock, stock, and barrel! But let 'em go on and have all their gold and silver, church, their flashy sinful trinkets, the society playthings they love so much! They're welcome to their yachts, their country clubs, their big banks! *Just give me Jesus!*"

A great guttural shout came up out of the congregation.

Cager, grinding his teeth, now curled his lip in scorn. Soon, violently twisting and turning in his seat, he began a furious whispering as, hardly able to contain himself, he glared up at Bearcat.

"Preach it, Pilate!" someone yelled. "Have mercy, Father!"

"Down at the cross where my Savior died!" sang a tiny but pregnant woman in a high, shrill tremolo, only soon to be drowned out by an avalanche of cries of "Amen!" for Bearcat, incited by the now standing platform prelates.

"Look out, now, Bearcat!" cried up Sister Alberta Broadnax again. "I tell you, don't overdo it! Hep him, Lord!"

Bearcat was still walking, talking, and, with his fine handkerchief, mopping his sloped-back brow. "What did old Job say, brothers and sisters?" he cried. "Job said, 'Naked came I out of my mother's womb, and naked shall I return thither! The Lord giveth, and the Lord taketh. Blessed be the name of the Lord!'"

"Tell it like it was writ, Bearcat!" cried Poolroom Mary. "Come on up a little higher, now!"

"Oh, yeah," somebody else yelled up, "tell it like it are!"

"We're still chockin' for you, Pilate!" now exclaimed the huge one of the rostrum divines.

"Hear me out, church!" Bearcat cried. "Jesus said, 'Lay not up for yourselves treasures upon this earth, where moths and rust doth corrupt, and where thieves break in and steal! But lay up for yourselves treasures in *heaven*'—Praise Gawd!—'for where your treasure is, *there will your heart be also*'" From the congregation came a great hoarse roar of affirmation, now setting off general stamping and shouting in the aisles. "Gawd is tellin' us, flock, to stop tryin' to copy the white folks! If they smite you on the left cheek, go on and turn 'em the right! Why get mad at 'em, why bring in the NAACP, why try to fight 'em?—all for *nothin'*! It ain't worth it, church! Our time's comin' way on down the line—when Gawd's good and ready!"

"There you are!" called out someone.

"Don't quit now, Pilate!" said another.

Cager in his blind rage sat glaring and trembling.

Bearcat, waving his arms, flashing the whites of his eyes, bleating like a bass billy goat, continued: "So stop covetin' the white man's riches, church! Stop pining after his old Dow Jones stocks and bonds! Stop yearnin' to take over his mints and big corporations, his armies—his *worldly* might, Lord! What's worldly might and power gonna get *you*, church? A lot of headaches, that's what! You don't need it! *Gawd will protect you!*"

"Keep on helpin' him out, Lord!" yelled a woman.

Cried Bearcat: "We got Gawd's grace 'cause we been lookin' over into the *next* world! We been *closer* to Gawd! The white man can't understand that! He's too busy thinkin' about *this* world! He wanted it, didn't he?—wanted it *all*! Well, he's got it all! But what's he got? He's got a *bear* by the tail, that what he's got! He can't handle it, neither! It's givin' him Hail Columbia! Ain't it, now, church? You'all hear me, all right!"

"I wanta tell you!" someone affirmed. "*Been* hearin' you!"

"That's why," said Bearcat, "he's always fightin' wars! One right after another! Remember, though, church, what he's fightin' *for*! Money! Power! That's what his problem is! That's why he just *loves* to fight! And he'll conquer or die, too—one or the other! He don't want nobody steppin' on *his* neck! But remember, church, it's the *meek*, saith Jesus, that shall inherit the earth! Yes, oh, yes, the *transformed* earth, flock!—Jesus' earth! So you can have this old world—I keep tellin' you—*just give me Jesus*:" Bearcat then

142

began prancing and dancing again as a tidal wave of new singing broke out, sweeping the church.

Cager jumped up. Scowling, lips quivering, whispering the fiercest obscenities and blasphemies, he plowed his way through, bolted up the aisle, and out of the church. It was not until he had gotten almost two blocks away that, in his blind fury, he could speak at all—even to himself. *"He's* why we're in the fix we're in! *His* kind! Where're our *leaders? If I had a gun I'd kill that motherfucker!"*

26

THE TRAVELER SWUNG DOWN, his feet hardly touching the ground before he glimpsed out of the corner of his eye the train's brakeman already swinging his lantern, signaling ahead to the engineer that all was clear again to proceed. He realized then that they had never really stopped to let him off, had merely slowed enough to allow him, gripping his suitcase, to quit the Jim Crow coach and hit the gravel running, running almost past this flag stop of a station on a damp, raw night in December. The hour was already past eleven and he still had four miles to walk to reach home. Gladstone seemed altogether another, an inapposite, world.

The road he soon traveled went past the now desolate fields of Judge Timothy Carr, a power in this part of Virginia and a man hated by the upstart Nathan Blatchford whose father had been a dirt farmer with a shackful of pellagra-ridden children. The bad blood between the two men, one the aristocrat, the other the poor white populist, had often been the subject of table talk at Amos Lee's house. "When they gets to fightin' amongst they selves," laughed Amos, "they forgets all about *us.* That's good, ain't it?— even if it's jes for a few minutes, 'cause then they lose track of us. We gets a breathin' spell then, don't we? Ha, ha, ha!"

But, as he walked, Cager doubted that his father had really been all that amused and was sure he knew that, no matter what, "they" never forgot "us." "Our" labor, thought Cager, was the foundation of their primal ascendancy over "us." So how could they ever forget "us"? Alas, though, now none of this mattered to his father, for whom any and all subjects were at last moot. Yet, the son was still overwhelmed by the fact of death. Although he had known from his mother that Amos Lee's health had drastically worsened,

143

he still had been as unprepared for the inevitable as for the telegram from home that announced it and enclosed his meager train fare to the rural obsequies. He knew little or nothing of death. As with so many other things, his tired, harried father had not instructed him on it, had not the time, not even when Granny had died. The fact was real now, though.

Making his way along the lonely country road with midnight approaching, he gazed up at the sky as if for some kind of guidance or light. But there was no light, although a sliver of new moon appeared occasionally in a nest of nomadic clouds. It had been during the long train ride from southwestern Tennessee that it had occurred to him again that he loved his father. Yet, it was not now so much grief he felt as confusion. He had never really admired or looked up to his father, had never felt dependent on him, either, even when as a child he sat at the table eating his hard-won bread. But now he felt perplexed, and strangely let down. He also felt guilt.

Soon a noisy old car approached from the opposite direction, its headlights sweeping everything—trees, pastures, telephone lines, fence rails—before them. When it passed him he turned and watched the taillights glowing even as they receded into the distance. The night seemed blacker now; then the slender moon briefly reappeared as he continued down this gravelly road of seeming oblivion. He could not recall such unearthly silence, such solitude; it was eerie and he felt strange, though not afraid. He only knew he did not wish to think. He had been doing too much of that lately. Soon he caught himself yawning and realized he was so exhausted he could easily have sat down, wrapped his long coat closer about him, and slept. He knew, though, he must go on.

His anxious mother Effie was greatly relieved to hear his knock, then see him standing in the door, at well past midnight. The two of his sisters at home were equally consoled. The main reason was that Amos Lee had already been dead four days. While the scattered grown children were being sought, time, despite the sharp December chill, was fast running out. But Effie tried to dwell on other things.

"At the last there Daddy would sleep all the time," she said as he ate her rabbit stew by the kerosene lamp's light. "He had this loud wheezing in his chest, though. And didn't have no appetite hardly at all. Just wanted some horehound candy once in a while or a little piece of pound cake. We had to almost make him eat a little soup. He talked a lot about Granny, too. Said he knew his mama was in heaven, all right. Then when he started having fainting spells, and got so weak that even at night he couldn't hardly get out of bed to make it to the slop jar, Claudine there and I milked the cows and cut the stove wood and fed the stock. Your brother Ordie, you know, now works over at Mr. Collins's place as a hired hand. But Daddy would set there looking out the window at me and Claudine chopping wood and just cry. Finally Mr. Blatchford got the doctor to come out from Cook's Grove to see him. Doc Spiess said it was a catarrh of the heart and lungs but that it didn't just *have* to be fatal. He left some big old green pills—the things was as big as the vets give to horses—and told us on top of that to use chest poultices and plenty of strong hot sassafras tea. And make sure he got plenty rest. But going out the door, not looking any of us in the eye, neither, he said for us to pray, too. That was about a week before your daddy died."

Restive, irritable, already in distress, Cager looked about the room, frowning. "Where *is* Daddy?" he said.

Effie shook her head. "We figured it would take some time for all you children to get here, so Mr. Zeglis, the undertaker from Cook's Grove, said it would be safer if we carried the casket out in the barn where it's cold." Cager started up, incensed. Effie then pointed to the potbellied stove. "That thing there throws out so much heat it made us uneasy," she said.

"Oh, Mama, did you have to do that? You desecrated Daddy!"

"It's cold in the barn, Rolly. We couldn't take any chances waiting on you'all to get here. We ain't located your brother T.M. in Detroit *yet*. We can't wait much longer, though, Mr. Zeglis says."

Cager stood over her now. "Let's go out," he said.

Effie went and lit the lantern and they went out. But, entering the barn, he took it from her and held it out high in front of them. There in the center of the hay-strewn floor, on a pair of trestles, rested the cheap gray casket. Yet, when they had nearly reached it he hesitated, then stopped, seeming afraid, or about to recoil. "Oh, Daddy!" But it was a whisper, the cold air making white wraiths of his breath. He advanced then.

"You can open it," his mother said, tenderly, reassuringly, and took the lantern back from him.

He finally lifted the upper half-lid of the casket and locked the hinge in place. Effie raised the lantern higher. But daughter Claudine, when shaving her father, had taken the razor too high at both temples, creating the look of an Abyssinian tonsured monk,

145

though Amos lay in his dark Sunday serge, the only suit he owned. Cager leaned forward now the better to see in the lantern's sallow glow. Suddenly he jerked back and turned to Effie. "Mama, he *smells!*"

"That's what I've been tryin' to tell you we've been up against," Effie said. "We can't wait no longer. Come on, let's go back— you've seen him now." She brought the lantern down.

Oblivious, he continued standing there, gazing into the casket in the murky half-light. But soon, gently, he let the lid down, though still remaining for another moment as if in a daze or reverie. Finally, following her out of the barn, he said grimly, "I got to go somewhere and find Daddy his roses."

"Oh, you can't, Rolly," said Effie, "it's wintertime. There ain't no roses."

They were well outside now. High over the barnyard not even the sliver of moon was in view. Chilled through, he walked docilely behind his mother, his long arms hanging helplessly at his side. "No chance," he murmured to himself, but just audibly. "He never had a chance—worked to death." He stopped and, turning his grimacing face up to the sky, said, "Daddy, I ain't forgot what you went through all these years. I'll never forget, either. Please forgive me, Daddy, for the way I acted sometimes. No, I'll never forget!. . ." His voice faltering, he sniveled once. But then his face changed, again grew stony, forbidding, as the whimpering ceased.

Effie turned around to him. "Come on, now, Rolly. You need sleep, a heap of sleep."

For a moment he did not move. "I ain't forgot," he repeated—to his father—his jaw grimly set. "*I never will!*" It was a furiously muttered vow.

Innocently blind to his meaning, Effie turned to him again. "I know you won't, Rolly, I know. None of us ever will forget him. Come on, now." She kept the lantern and led him away.

27

"SO WHAT IT ALL BOILS DOWN TO," said deeply serious Haley Barnes, "is that somebody ought to go on and put him out of his misery."

Roxanne came up with another of her irreverent laughs. "You mean you want to shoot him, eh?"

"I mean of course something drastic that will *help* him," Haley said. "Everything that's been tried so far has failed. If something's not done, he'll soon break under the strain—with all his unknown, his secret, problems, plus now his father's death, which I understand he's taking hard."

Roxanne was waiting for a break in the conversation to start the vacuum cleaner again, but Haley, a malingering partner in their weekly Saturday morning housecleanings, and standing holding a dust cloth she had thrust in his hand, instead wanted urgently to talk and now plopped down on the sofa. "No, no, you don't, Haley," she said. "Let's finish this work."

Haley finally rose, saying, "He should merely be talked into leaving Gladstone, that's all—before he's thrown out."

"Poor, poor Cager," Roxanne said in mock commiseration, then flicked on the ancient Hoover cleaner, flooding the living room with raucous noise.

"Shut that cement mixer off, will you?" Haley yelled over the din. "Listen to me for a minute, Rox!" The sweeper stopped. "It would be the humane thing," he said. "He's in terrible shape psychologically. It's because of the kind of peculiar earthling species he represents."

"Cager's not that bad, Haley," Roxanne laughed.

"Be serious, will you? He's sensitive, high-strung, ultraserious. He's a made-to-order victim for whatever it is he's going through." Haley paused and stared vacantly out the front window onto the porch, at last adding, almost parenthetically, "I've had this big, but vague, idea—sort of a wild brainstorm—that's come to me out of the blue, or the bowels of the subconscious, I don't know which. As if it made any difference. Yet I've had it, given birth to it. But it seems to have come to me in two parts—or phases, the second of which, alas, however, was stillborn, a perfect blank. The first, and the easiest, at least on paper, would, as I say, call for his voluntarily leaving Gladstone before he flunks out. If he keeps on hanging around and has to go because of bad grades or more goofing off, his chances of getting back in, especially with Groomes on his tail, are about nil. If, though, he could be persuaded to go along with Part One of my blurry plan he might be able to return—of course after makeup exams and all, which I think, with study, he could do okay on."

"I can already see about three dozen drawbacks," Roxanne said. "For one, what would he *do* if he dropped out? Where would he *go*? Back home?"

"Good God, no! That would be the end of him. He'd think, out of family loyalty and his father's memory, that he should stay home and try to carry on there. It would be a calamity for him. It's the *waste*, Rox! That's the terrible thing about it. It's what we want to try to prevent if we can. Am I right?"

"Haley honey, one minute I admire you so—for all your fine qualities and everything—and the next I think you're nuts." She lifted her eyes to the ceiling. "Dear God, in Your infinite wisdom, please deliver me from all do-gooders."

"You won't listen," he said. "The second part of my plan, is, as I say, a no-show. But I do know that after he voluntarily dropped out he'd still stay around town here, where we could keep an eye on him, encourage him along, and, above all, get him some kind of work. I'm not talking about in some honky-tonk dive like Ma Moody's, either. But with the right kind of job he might come out of this . . . whatever it is that's got everybody—including himself, probably—stumped." Haley paused to think more.

"Go on, I'm listening," Roxanne said, finally backing up and sitting in a chair.

Haley, in his agitation, remained standing—as if the better to harangue her. "Unfortunately, though, that's where my brainstorm ends," he said. "The question is, how do you occupy him and keep him out of trouble during the waiting period when he's preparing to try for a comeback?"

"My God, Haley, what an *impossible* thing to speculate about! It's goofy!"

Haley hurried on. "And of course we've got to assume he'd cooperate with the plan. That's not an easy thing to assume, though, I realize." He smiled broadly. "Unless, that is, part two, when and if it takes shape, has something to do with raising a huge black army to go out and whip a lot of white people and put a black man in charge of the world!" Haley thought this funny and now laughed uproariously.

"You miss *my* point, though," Roxanne said with a straight face, "which is that you're every bit as nutty as Cager—any day."

"You tell *me*, then. What should I do? Nothing? Just walk away from it? Let him go to the dogs—even more than he has already? Okay, if that's how you really feel about it, then I will. You say stop and I'll stop. No kidding—go ahead. *Say it*."

Roxanne gave him a deeply anxious look now.

"I challenge you!" he said.

"Oh, Haley," she sighed.

He knew he had her then, and smiled, as if he had beaten her at checkers.

At once she bristled. "You go to hell, Haley! You sure get on my nerves—you damn do-gooders!" She jumped up and turned on the thunderous vacuum cleaner again.

In the end, then, as sometimes happens, that archfiend Irony was to have his way. It would of course be Roxanne—who else?— who would come up with the entirely inspired "missing idea" of part two, to make Haley's plan whole and thus turn an innocent brainstorm into fateful reality.

It was of almost equal irony that only the evening before, with a full moon watching, Cager had paid the Haley Barneses a rare visit, his trials and confusions now so acute he was driven to talk to somebody—yet not anybody. Actually only Haley would do. But Haley and Roxanne were out at the time—at a faculty dinner gathering—and Cager, finally realizing after repeated knockings that no one was at home, became desperate and irrational, feeling somehow betrayed, before then flying into a rage on the front porch. Swept by new passions of loneliness and defeat, he began such a furious pounding on the door that it rattled the windowpanes. At last, though, aware of the futility of his actions he stopped and sat down on Haley's porch steps, where, moaning as he dove his face in his hands, he remained until his pulse rate began to slow some and he regained a measure of control. After almost a half hour he finally got up and headed for Ma Moody's.

He walked as if in a stuporous daze and, despite both the moonlight and the streetlights, he seemed groping. But then, making his way down Jackson toward Glasgow Street, he suddenly came to, became alert. It was the sound. The strange sound, or sounds, like the muffled voices of a crowd somewhere ahead, although still some distance. It was not clamorous, there were no shouts, no cheering, only one steady buzzing hubbub—until, that is, he heard the train's whistle. He strongly suspected then the human noise was coming from the vicinity of the railroad station, though the second whistle sounded not so much like a whistle as a throttled exhalation, yet strenuous and dogged, accompanying the shuttling of boxcars or passenger cars—perhaps some engine backing or switching coaches into a station siding. Then again came the low vocal din of the crowd. Strangely now, fully alert, he began walking faster, toward the weird commotion, his now curious and purposeful mind somehow reaching out toward it, this unseeable, and therefore unknowable—undefined—materiality. Soon he was trotting, loping, and at last, as if goaded by some omen, running. How did it happen he was doing this? he wondered—where was this magnet pulling him, and why?

He was near now. He was running back of the low brick warehouse fronting on the railroad station with only the tracks in between them. Now he turned the corner and came into the crammed prospect of the station ablaze with lights. The first objects he saw, though, were soldiers. But they were not Americans, he realized, startled. They wore boots or heavy shoes, jaunty caps with jutting bills, and long gray-green overcoats. Strange, strange, he thought, these cool, taciturn, self-possessed men, especially when, even more puzzled now, he saw they were under heavy guard—by helmeted American soldiers, white, in their drab brown uniforms and carrying their carbines at the ready. The guarded soldiers, many of them blond, most of them clean though needing haircuts, had, he realized, just detrained and were standing crowded together on the station platform, waiting . . . waiting for something, he did not know what. Some were sullen, contemptuous of their guard contingent, and especially of the milling, buzzing throng of local townspeople forming a huge crescent in front of the platform as they gawked and talked.

Cager had stopped short, mouth agape. "What the hell's goin' on here?" he whispered to himself incredulously. Then before it could even dawn on him it hit him. These dour, impassive soldiers in their gray-green uniforms were not only prisoners of war—they were *Germans!* At once Clausewitz flew into his mind. How come they were prisoners? But he realized now they were en route to some American internment camp. How come, though, they surrendered? He could not understand it. Turning now, he saw still more of them, but these were inside the station building, in a long, waiting queue—ah, yes, he told himself, the *cafeteria line*. "Well, I'll be damned! . . ." he breathed, his mouth still open.

The fascinated crowd was still busy looking on and making its hushed yet enthusiastic comments, none of which, however, that he heard, were in any way hostile or even unfriendly toward the prisoners. A tall, rural, red-faced Tennessean said in his flat drawl to a neighbor, "Yeah, it was all in the paper this mawnin' that they was comin' through. They're from the Africa Corps, y'know. *Rommel* men." He said it almost proudly.

"Well, I'll be dog," said the other in awe. "Sho-nuff?"

Cager, watching the Germans and thinking of Clausewitz, was

sure he recognized the Prussian indoctrination and ferule stamp. In a grudging way, he was awesomely impressed. "Lord, Lord," he whispered, "they sure don't *look* like prisoners, do they? Don't act like it, either. Look at 'em lookin' down their noses at these crackers, like instead *they* were the prisoners—ha. Whew!" He looked around at the crowd again now. It too was all curiosity and awe. "Well, well . . ." he breathed, and inhaled deeply.

Finally he turned and faced the cafeteria wing of the station where inside he saw now still more queued Germans, trays in hand, inching along toward their turn at the food steam table. Grinding his teeth and chattering maniacally to himself, he began on tiptoes to rubberneck, raising his elongated body and neck, like a giraffe, as high as he could extend them, straight up, craning, peering, over the heads of the crowd in his futile attempt, if only symbolically, once more to see, on the cafeteria's door, that legend, that painted shibboleth of a sign, a warning, he knew so well from past experience certainly still to be there though presently he could not see it because the townspeople and the haughty, hungry Germans obstructed his view. He well remembered what it said, though—WHITES ONLY!

28

As WE LAY IN HER BED, I caught her, out of the corner of my eye, watching me. It was high noon and, having just had our strenuous little tête-à-tête (our party for two), we were resting—she having a postcoital cigarette. "You know," she said, her voice hollow and resentful, "I wonder sometimes what's up the road for a young guy like you." Her look was severe and disapproving. She added, "You never think about anything or anybody but yourself, your own pleasures—your kicks. Tell me, Meshach, do you ever have a really unselfish thought? I doubt it. Am I right?"

I was no longer surprised by anything Flo said, or did, for by now I had learned so very much more about her than I ever thought I would, or could. Among her vagaries, her curlicues, of personality, even character, was this sudden, mercurial, perverse streak, her lightning turnabouts as well—of which theretofore I had been entirely ignorant. They still surprised me, though—even now. Indeed when I really got to know her she turned out to be, as I have said, anything but the cool, confident, self-assured person I had

151

become so smitten with. The more, as today, she participated in our wild gymnastic sex bouts (which, I have always been convinced, were so savagely, so piteously, against everything she held in her heart and will), the more caustic and accusatory, toward me, became her talk, her diatribes, afterward—today being no exception—so that I have long since, across all the intervening years, ceased trying to solve the riddle of her harassed, shrewish, sex-guilt-driven mentality.

In the bed, her bed, yes, still staring at me, she now raised her beautiful, naked, slightly freckled body on her elbow and said, "Meshach, are you aware you're as phony as a three-dollar bill—and always will be?"

"No, I wasn't aware of that," I said, smiling patiently, secure now, supremely so, in the knowledge that it was *I* now who was in the driver's seat, who had had full satisfaction for all his slights and humiliations. But my smiling smugness would make her flame with anger, whereupon she would berate me with even greater, more savage, bitterness. Actually, secretly, however, her bitter tirades made me furious inside, if only briefly, even if I did my best to seem calm, amused, or even indifferent toward them. But during this period I did really feel outlandishly smug and appeased, at times secretly arrogant, even vainglorious, over my long (interminably long, it seemed to me, though it had been only weeks, yet, I assure you, *another whole book!*—that is, the range and variety, and doggedness, of my pitiless pursuit of her), as I say, smug over my long but successful effort, too much so now certainly to let myself appear uneasy, thin-skinned, or insecure. I was the victor! Though young, you see, I was, inherently, the Devil! My work was cut out for me! And I took to it like a duck to water. Poor, poor, Flo! Across the years you are ever in my memories. But I was busy, busy, as Hortense Bangs would have put it, playing the hand I was dealt! Also, at the time, I was fatuous enough to think I understood her. What presumption! In fact, she was in such a state of confusion and guilt, indeed panic, that she tried to free herself of my evil spell by more and more pressing Cager to assume again a larger place in her life. But he was so mired in his own Sturm und Drang that he needed her more than he cared to admit even to himself, so, ironically—his desperate pride—he did his best to stay away from her. The effect of this was to send her into long periods of pique and spite, then deep gloom. All of this of course only played into my hands. In short, and to somewhat oversimplify

152

both a complex situation and a human being, Flo, she succumbed to my panting, horny pursuit out of sheer desperation and anguish—which, again ironically, for the most part involved Cager. Ah, irony!

But the bedrock nub is this. Flo was an intricately formed woman, psychologically, but she (her flaw, her Achilles' heel) was also a wonderfully healthy woman and almost as powerfully sexed as I—making her of course something of a monotype, a grotesque—and over the years bringing me, as if some dual curse on us were involved, to pity her as I have only pitied myself. But from the very beginning her life had been anything but easy—like myself illegitimate, reared by an aunt in New Orleans, and married at eighteen, she had been brought, pregnant, to Tennessee by her worthless four-flusher husband, Harlan Ransom, much older, and whom she left not long after little Annette was born. Since then she had fended for herself and her child in circumstances almost always hard and discouraging—even after she had met, in some mysterious way never clearly known to anyone I ever heard of, a certain well-off, influential white man. In the Negro community, however, the relationship, though known, soon became shrouded in veils of innuendo, gossip, and rumor. Cager, victim of callous remarks, even taunts, about her—from the likes of Hortense Bangs and Ma Moody—was therefore not himself entirely ignorant of the talk. Even I had encountered at least one somewhat solid bit of evidence when one day, approaching Flo's little house (on nefarious business of my own), I saw a car that had just pulled up and a rather handsome white man, fortyish, get out with a bushel basket of fruit, peaches and plums, I think, which he went and deposited on her porch before, with no further ado whatever, driving off in a quiet, almost businesslike manner. It was only later that I learned he was State Senator Christopher ("Christy") Bends. All this, though, I think, somehow left a strangely morbid, even satanic, mark on her, of which she was never, so far as I know, to rid herself. This, then, was the Flo I knew, in all her uniqueness, misadventures, her flightiness, sullied virtue—ah, her sweetness and loveliness.

It was also of course an inexplicable paradox that although she finally surrendered to me, she deeply resented me. Typical complicated Flo! In bed, for instance, in the violent throes of sex, naked except, in her case, for stockings rolled to just above the knees (at my urging), or wearing only earrings, or a necklace (also my idea), she could be all whining milk and honey one minute, then, the next, a grasping, grappling tornado, between short gasping intakes of breath crying out to me and, through hot-breathed teeth, uttering the most savage and maniacal recriminations. "You phony, lucky, little preacher, black bastard, you!" she would say all in one breath. It is true, as I have said, that, having been born, as was she, out of wedlock, I am a bastard. Yet, I don't know why she would say I'm "little," in any sense. I am five feet ten, and at that time weighed 185 pounds. Nor is my skin black, but a caramel brown. To the rest of her impassioned description, however, including all implications, I merely plead nolo contendere. "I really don't like you, you know! . . ." she, between the embattled sheets, would cry out, almost wailing, vixenlike and wild, all the while gasping and making a wretchedly beautiful face. "You can see that, can't you? *What?* Oh, look what you're doing to me . . . Oh, you're so bogus, Meshach! I never would have thought it that first day Rollo brought you by here, but you are, you are! Oh, my God, what a fraud you are, Meshach! *Oh! Oh!*—this last as if I had suddenly dashed her stark nakedness with a pail of ice water. This was of course when I had her in our frenzied wrestling out from under the sheets, pinned flat on her back, down near the foot of the mattress, where our struggles had now brought us, and, in my powerful, smothering embrace, when I was really bearing down on her with all I had—which, if I may say so, and as I have implied, was considerable—penetrating her to the hilt. Finally then at climax, both of us fighting, keening, yowling, and at last in the gestalt of the moment, giving up the ghost, a great paroxysmal seizure would take her and she would shudder and shake, then try to throw me off her (to no avail, of course; I wasn't going for that), all the while crying out in the bitterest tears of self-castigation: "Oh, *why* did I finally give in to you! *Why* have you done this to me, taken advantage of me in my weakness and miseries, hounded me to the earth like an animal of prey! And *why*, in God's name, have I *let* you! Oh, I'm so weak! *I'm dirt!* Why are we like we are in this world?—and can do nothing about it! . . ." On and on it went like this. It was unnerving—actually scary. Yet, it gluttonously gorged my huge appetite and short-lived ego—yes, my Pyrrhic victory!

One such day, though—a fateful day it was, too—when, finished, perspiring, exhausted, we lay limp across her bed, and as usual little Annette was still at school, I tried to mollify her, assuage her tears. I asked her why she was so unhappy. She would not answer. Whereupon, pretending to pout, I said rather sharply, "Okay, then, keep it to yourself."

Fire leaped in her tearful eyes. "Look who's questioning *me*," she said. "But I'll answer by asking *you* a question! When we're together like this do you ever think of Rollo—your supposed close friend, your buddy? Do you?"

I was surprised—and hesitated. "Is it fair to bring him into this?" I said.

"Yes, it's fair! He *should* be brought into it. Oh, Rollo makes me cry!—like now, real tears. Do you know why? Of course you don't—you wouldn't. Well, I'm going to tell you, because you're so lucky, and have got so much brass, and you're, yes, so damn phony, you deserve to be told. I cried just now because I wished that instead of you being here that it was Rollo!"

This bowled me over. I was cut to the quick. Then at once I tried not to show it. My brief ego, though, was shattered.

She continued her philippic. "It's just that Rollo is what he is. Absolutely unphony. He's got character. Do you know about character? He's a *man*—a sweet man. His character shows in everything he does. In my whole life, which has mostly been a big hassle, I've never met anybody like him—never." She paused then—as if for effect. To punish me.

But I waited. I could somehow, though, feel the tension. It was strangely, I remember, in my throat, my vocal cords. It was as if something . . . an epiphany?—I cannot possibly describe it—was coming. Yet I waited.

"But he's in deep trouble now," she said, "and I'm to blame for it."

Another pause. She seemed as if she felt she had blundered now. She stared at me. It was portentous. I dreaded even so much as breathing, though, for fear she might not go on.

"It's the saddest thing that could ever have happened to him," she finally said. "To *him*—of all people. To anyone, though, for that matter—any man. But I'm the culprit! It couldn't have happened if I hadn't done it to him—the dumbest, craziest thing I'll ever do in my life if I live to be a hundred. Now he doesn't care about anything. He's an altogether different person now." (As if everybody in town did not know *that*.) "And his schoolwork's gone down the drain like everything else in his life. *I did it!*" She was crying again now and wiped her nose and eyes with a corner of the bed sheet—as I lay there afraid to part my lips but wanting to kill her for not getting to the point. "Do you really like Rollo, Meshach?" she finally said, snuffling. "I mean, do you really understand him, appreciate him for the kind of person he is; yes, his character?"

"I know damn well I do!" I said, bridling. "What're you *talking* about!"

She sighed then. "I believe you," she said, almost contritely. "Otherwise, I guess I wouldn't be telling you all this. Maybe I shouldn't have said those mean things about you—but lately I've been so miserable."

"Why take it out on me, though?" I said, feigning hurt and resentment.

"I feel so guilty about our relationship, Meshach—you and me," she said. "And so sorry for Rollo. Now I don't know what I'm doing half the time. It's just that I envy you so—*for Rollo.*"

"For *Rollo!*" I said. "Look, will you stop talking in riddles? . . . Will you go on and say what you're trying to say?" Then I wanted to choke myself—she might, I thought, clam up on me, tell me nothing. I was somehow surer than ever now she was on the verge of revealing something momentous. But now she did in fact stop talking. Instead she rose from the bed, put on a robe, and lit a cigarette, then went and sat in a chair near the window, as far away from me as the tiny bedroom would allow, yet staring stubbornly at me before going into a grim-lipped dudgeon. I had given up hope.

"It's his penis." But she had almost blurted it—as if otherwise she would not have been able to give up her secret.

Of course my jaw had fallen.

She thought I had not heard her. "His *penis*," she repeated. "It's too short. Do you understand me? It's so short and small it's hardly one at all. He's deformed. It's no bigger around than a pencil, and only two, certainly not more than three, inches long at most—even when it's hard."

When she saw me speechless, with my mouth open, a great woebegone expression came on her face, then another tear glistened in her eyelashes. I took a gigantic breath and held it until I was giddy. Nothing helped. She had so overwhelmed me that my disbelief, for the moment, was total. Suddenly then, against all logic and likelihood, I contracted the weirdest of all possible urges. I wanted to laugh. But just as suddenly I was horrified. I swallowed. "Go on," I said weakly.

She blinked back the tears enough to say, "I don't think anybody had ever really told him about it—explained it to him. He didn't know he was different. That's hard to believe, I know, but *I* almost believe it. You've got to know Cager—and I do. He mentioned his home folks. I gather they hinted at it to him, at the same time, though, indulging him, trying in every way they knew how to protect and shield him. Although he didn't come right out and say it, I think he felt everybody had known it—that is, before I, like a fool, told him—except himself. I'm sure I'm his first woman, the one that took his virginity."

This to me, your narrator, raises many questions. But on that of whether or not he knew about his condition, I have never believed that he did not. Maybe on one level he did not—he had the strangest, most complex, of minds—but on other levels he had to know. An uncanny parallel could have been his dogged insistence on the possibility, if not feasability, of raising a great all-Negro army. A preposterous idea, of course. Maybe on one level, though, he believed all things possible—or, that is, refused to accept, even deign notice, the bald, hard countenance of reality. Nothing could curb or exhaust his great dreams, his mighty longings, for a better day. It was instinctual with him, or as if his rational mind were at constant warfare with a vision so powerful, so grand, as on some levels to have entirely overwhelmed pure logic.

No matter, on still other levels—despite all of Flo's evidence and what she thought and felt—he could not, beforehand, have failed to know and understand. (What about, to cite just one minor instance, the baths, the showers, in Gladstone's dorms? There were no stalls; they were all communal. He had eyes to see others.) But Flo now, maybe for the first time, in her oddly callous way, had really brought it home to him—in a manner so graphic, sudden, so telling, that it jolted him like a long-delayed electric shock, made him actually see, in a new, far more grave and startling way, his predicament, indeed the symbolic dilemma present for the whole black struggle itself. In truth, then, its effect could have been, for all intents and purposes, hardly less jarring, devastating, than had he actually just been made aware of his bizarre imperfection for the first time. Yet, one more complication even, if not inconsistency, lies in the fact that although Flo's jolting revelation to him, if that indeed it was, ruined his career as a Gladstone student, there still was no detectable change, before or after, in his obstinate passion to field his black army. His zeal in this, in fact, may have been only heightened. Therein, though, lay the Aeschylean tragedy, in the thwarting confusion now assailing him, the frustration, mental torture, together, inevitably, with all that these ruinous factors symbolized, namely, the ironical self-image of the great

157

fearless young black war leader, reincarnation of Clausewitz, plus that of the new (black) Archangel Michael, savior of his fellow blacks, all rolled into one composite and mighty hero—and he then possessed of a two-inch penis!

This, knowing him, is my deep conviction about his reaction to the evidence. I regard it as having been, for a time, utterly crippling to him—though not forever. Yet we shall never really know—although I have pondered the riddle for thirty-five years. We only know that, given impossible alternatives, he still somehow persevered. This was his natural code. To that there was indeed no alternative.

Now Flo was saying, "When I first hinted at his condition to him, that he was really small, he didn't right away seem to catch on to what I was talking about. It may have been because of the stupid way I put it, for I was feeling really sorry for him now and may have been vague. But then he used to kid around with me, poke fun at me a lot, some of it pretty rough, until one day when I wasn't feeling good I got peeved and started kidding him back, pretty hard, like he had me, finally ending up telling him he needn't think he was so hot with a pecker like a seven-year-old boy's. He looked at me until, laughing, I told him again. He couldn't speak, he was so shocked, and the stricken look stayed on his face for the rest of the time. When I saw how it had floored him I got scared. But soon I was sick, realizing what I had done to him. I was so disgusted that I hated myself. Then suddenly, like an even bigger fool, I tried to take it all back. It of course only made things worse—he tried to laugh it off. But this was the most pitiful sight of all, for you could tell he was wiped out. Oh, Rollo talks big but actually he's as innocent as all outdoors. I just *know* I'm his first woman—I know it! You'd think, then, after I told him about himself that he'd hate me, but in a way, although he fights it like hell, it's only made him more than ever dependent on me. He'd die before admitting it, though, but that's why he doesn't come around much anymore. Of course, he won't touch me now, physically. He's ashamed. He hasn't had anything to do with me like that since that day, he's so mortified. Sure it's wiped him out—made him lose all interest in his studies and everything else. And *I* did it! So it's no wonder he's changed! He's ruined!" She shot me a baleful look. "Why couldn't it have been somebody else?" she said. "Like *you*."

I said nothing. What was there to say?—I was so stunned by her revelations and, at the time, too puzzled by what Cager's predicament, though it explained many things, really meant. But at last, by way of mild rebuke, I said to Flo, "Why would you wish something like this on me? You didn't have to say that." She looked at me, then looked away, saying nothing. "You may, though," I said, "be overestimating the harm done him. He's not physically impotent, or anything like that, is he?"

"Oh, for heaven's sake, *no*," she said. "That's not the problem at all. The problem is what he *thinks* of himself now. I've told him again and again that his condition doesn't make any difference to me—that length isn't everything to a woman. But, looking at me, he just smiles, as if to say, 'Liar.' Can't you see why I hate myself so?"

It was then that I came up with the most inane remark of all. "Are you in love with him?" I asked.

She started. Then gave me an unbelieving stare. "You're not serious, are you? Of course I'm in love with him! What do you think I've been talking about all this time? My God!"

Again I had taken it on the chin and my old vindictiveness returned with a vengeance. "Then why have you just now been in bed with me?" I said. And I had the gall, indeed cruelty, to smile.

She was now so filled up with her rage and sorrow that she began a loud wailing, actually caterwauling, that must have been heard out in the street. Alarmed, and now contrite, I tried everything I knew to mollify and console her but nothing would staunch her virtual inundation of tears. But, oh, how appealing she was to me now!—sitting there by the window, clad only in a half-open pale green robe the color of her eyes, with those big pearly tears falling on her lovely freckled breasts. I craved to take her again. I knew, though, she would have murdered me first.

Yet, if for only a moment, I somehow felt a heady triumph— only quickly to have it collapse, thinking of my base role in this sad, unseemly affair. Ah, Flo. I shall never forget that dear, unique, passionate, wonderful creature. How mixed up, how vulnerable, unhappy, she was. Even Bahr, across thousands of miles and decades of time, was to feel the kinetic power of her presence before his own chilling quietus. She knew much less about life, was not half so sophisticated or worldly-wise, as she let on, or indeed thought she was. It is true, in recent years, with a consciousness heightened by my terrible guilt trials and crises since those days, that much of my admiration—my love—for her stems from her passionate devotion to the hero and all he symbolized.

Of course she never let me come near her after the day of this

159

stupendous revelation that cleared up so many mysteries. It was our grand finale, the absolute end of a most unlikely affair. Yet, across the years, I still think of her with the tenderest memories and emotions. She was Cager's Flo, all right, no doubt about that, but no matter how she treated me, I shall always believe, even if there is such scant, or no, evidence, that a little, if only a tiny, place in her heart belonged to me. This is important to me today, when so few people—though, bless her, I shall always have (ah, my moral millstone) Carol—think well of me. I yearn to believe—I almost insist—that were Flo alive today she would somehow feel compassion for me in all that has since happened. I believe—I *must!*—that in her more tranquil, less harried and outraged moments, she would, or might, somehow comprehend. It is a grasping hope I yet cling to, this ceaseless try at self-affirmation, which—unlike the case of Bahr—is my means of survival.

29

I CALL IT, though not without some sense of parody, the "zenith of my career." I was in Academe in a big way—Dean of Chapel—as late as 1976. Except for my two terminated marriages—the first, of course, by Lisbeth's untimely death, the other by (the Eurasian) Pin Lee Stolz Barry's early outright repudiation of me by divorce after, as I have said, seventeen months and a mongoloid son who ever since has been institutionalized—except, I say, for these two heavy misadventures I considered myself, with or without justification at the time, as soaring like an eagle. Soaring because of my then recent religious educational honors, the scholarly, indeed literary sermons I preached in the fine old heavily vined campus chapel, its organ famous for its thundering, exalted Bach preludes and fugues, and the new exhilarating academic responsibilities attendant on all this. I was so pleased and flattered that I experienced one of the few happy, heady periods in my rocky life. Alas, however, it was not to last. A few short months would bring the knell of this state of things and the onset of my crack-up, my fall from the eagle's heights, as a result of my involvement in the piddling difficulties, heretofore touched on, which, though, eventually sent me for a year and a day to Pressman—and to Bahr.

Nevertheless, one fine day, just before the debacle, I had had this migraine headache for hours (possibly a harbinger) which, however, around three in the afternoon was finally showing signs of abating, when as I sat in my office (that of the chaplain of this chic, venerable, old Down East college), I was paid a visit by one of my charges until then unknown to me. But what struck me about her, before I even saw her, was the dulcet tones of her voice when, speaking to the young man, a student assistant, outside my office, she said, "I don't have an appointment, but, if it's possible, I'd like to see Dean Barry. Is he in?"

My door was open but neither of us, for the moment at right angles, was in the other's line of sight. The student assistant, though, came and got my nod to send her in. She was a comely, sedate girl of obvious class and breeding but now somehow pale, yet giving one the impression that in healthier times her color had been a rich tawny pink. Her hair, parted dead center and falling to her shoulders, was ash-blonde and straight; too straight, in fact, almost lank, though doubtless temporarily so and matching the recent sickly pallor of her face. No matter, she was extremely attractive, and carried two textbooks and a large loose-leaf notebook.

"Good afternoon," I said pleasantly and motioned her to either of the two close-up chairs directly across my desk from me.

She hesitated. "May I close the door?" she said, though diffidently, depositing the books in one of the chairs.

I hesitated then. I did not usually close the door when counseling students, for my office was spacious enough to keep any normal conversation safely from the ears of my secretary outside or of any of the student assistants. Another, and more compelling, if secret, reason, however, was that I did not feel at all comfortable, and therefore *never* closed the door, if the student was female. Do not ask me to be more specific. It is much too involved, as well as, I'm afraid, somewhat tedious—yet, by now knowing me, you may already have your surmises. Yet, finally relenting, I said nervously, "Very well, you may close it." I had tried to add a cordial note to my voice but am not sure I succeeded.

She went then and, unobtrusively, though, I thought, with extreme care, eased the door shut. I was really uncomfortable now, and made no less so when, as she returned and sat down, I thought I detected her trace of a sigh. But soon she smiled—wanly—and introduced herself. "Dean Barry, my name is Deborah Hastings."

161

"I'm pleased to meet you, Miss Hastings," I said, and finally smiled.

Then followed a long awkward pause during which her eyes searched my face, as if she were asking herself whether, though knowing me to be the chief spiritual adviser of students, I still were really the right person to be coming to with her particular problem—whatever it was. I sensed her hesitance, reluctance, her critical weighing of the matter, but, according to my rule of practice in such situations, I sat and waited. "I assume," she finally said, though frowning with a gravity rarely encountered in students, "that you, as our chaplain, believe in prayer."

Say, what's going on here? I thought. I studied her. Then quickly I remembered to smile again. But I had not expected a question so fundamental. Then I thought, though, I might well seize this opportunity to put her more at ease—by laughing: "That presumption, Miss Hastings, is what we might call an *irrebuttable* one. Ha! I do indeed believe in prayer." (This of course was not the first or last time in my life I would tell this lie.)

She smiled wanly again. "I do, too," she said. "I was taught to, anyway. I wonder, though, if prayer is really any good in everyday, or practical, situations." She paused again. I thought she might go on and explain but she did not. She only sat there with flickers of doubt still astir in her eyes, yet as if she still thought I had the happy faculties to read her mind and eventually help her in spite of herself. It seemed to me obvious, however, that her purpose in being there were anything but frivolous. But I was determined to wait her out.

As I say, I had this rule in counseling students—especially females!—against asking questions of them. I was extremely chary about giving any impression of prying into their private affairs, quick to remind myself that I was not their confessor. I much preferred dealing with them more or less on the basis of information they freely volunteered. Besides, I well knew the efficacy, if not necessity, of tact. Ah, yes—tact. The watchword. True, the recent civil rights revolution had opened up heretofore nonexistent opportunities for, if I may say so, well-prepared, discreet persons of color, like myself, yet tact was still very much the order of the day, especially, as in my case, an Afro-American occupying the chair (even if it was, actually, an innocuous position, one of negligible power) of Dean of Chapel at this famous old white prestigious institution. My response, then, to yet another of my visitor's pauses was no response myself, except possibly an earnest, interested expression on my face.

"You're probably wondering," she said at last, though speaking very slowly, as if feeling her way, "what I mean, in asking if prayer is any good, in 'everyday, or practical, situations.' I mean one, say, when the house mortgage payment is long overdue and you don't have it and don't know where you're going to get it—that sort of situation. I'm not talking about praying for things like greater wisdom, or faith, or for one's soul. But immediate—*very pressing*— things!" The poor child, I saw now, was almost pleading with me. (Oh, she was so attractive now.) "So," she said, "would it do any good to pray for help in a practical, a real–life situation?" At once then she attempted to camouflage the intensity of her feelings by trying another wan smile, but it was clear her heart was not even in that.

I was quick, though, to respond now. "Oh, absolutely," I said, smiling. "I might at the same time, however, do some other things. Like, in the case of the mortgage, calling up my brother, if I had one, which I don't, in Des Moines or wherever, and asking him for a loan to tide me over. Or I might decide I could no longer afford my car and sell it to raise the money. I might try any number of things, in fact, until I got the payment so they wouldn't foreclose on me. But afterward I'd probably think about making other, longer–range economies, or even getting a better-paying job. Things like that."

"But doesn't that show," she said, very earnestly and with genuine innocence (the poor dear!), "that you don't really have much faith in your prayers? I mean, you'd do all the same things you mentioned, wouldn't you, if you were an atheist?"

"I might, yes," I said, much amused, for, unwittingly, she was hitting home. "But prayer is the powerful additive available to us that the atheists don't have. It of course, though, presupposes our belief in a personal God, a God capable, if so moved, of intervening on our individual behalves. But we must remember God doesn't act willy-nilly. We ourselves must at least show some signs of worthiness. And how better to show this than by taking, volitionally, a few steps calculated to help your own cause? No, there's no inconsistency here at all, Miss Hastings. It works." How very clever I had become with these sophistries, I thought, consummately pleased with myself and of course believing none of them.

She said nothing now, only sat staring at me, as if straining to

163

control herself, keep from saying more. But soon she seemed about to burst, her paleness slowly metamorphosing into a deep emotion-dredged crimson. "It doesn't work for me!" she finally said. It was plain she was in great torment. At this I began to feel really uncomfortable again. I wanted to get up and go open that damned door but I dared not. I only sat there and, helpless, nervous as a cat, ever libidinous of course, watched the child struggle with herself and her God. "I've prayed, and prayed, and prayed," she said, "but it doesn't do any good! God may hear me but He doesn't care, or if He does He doesn't do anything to help me. He may even be punishing me. What should I *do*, Dean Barry? That's why I came to see you, to get your advice—you're our adviser."

Things were getting out of hand now. I was so disturbed I suddenly realized my migraine had returned with such ferocity as possibly to be some kind of penalty or damnation. Hastily, I got up, went to the table across the room and poured her a paper cupful of cold water from my thermos jug. She took it and, sipping, gazed mournfully out the window, as I realized how utterly ineffective I was being. I began now to feel a really chaste pity for her.

At last I lamely volunteered: "Sometimes, you know, it takes great patience on our part. And, I might add, great faith. I must say your faith seems to have become somewhat eroded, Miss Hastings." My heart was pounding, hammering, now.

"But I've prayed, night and day, for three whole weeks," she said. "Ever since I found out." At once she looked stricken, destroyed, her hand going to her mouth too late. But I was adamant. I smelled danger and was more determined than ever to stick to my inviolable rule of no questions, no probing. The ensuing silence, though, was so oppressive and my own discomfort so real that I may well have felt almost as much pain as she.

Finally, palms down, she put both her hands flat on my desk in front of her—as if bracing, buttressing, herself—before saying it: "I'm pregnant."

I panicked. My throat closed on me. "Oh, heavens!. . ." I said. "I'm sorry but you've come to the wrong place. You must go over right away to the Dean of Women's office—I'll call and tell them you're coming. You'll find Dean Moore a wonderful, helpful, a most understanding lady. I'm merely the students' *spiritual* adviser. This isn't that kind of situation at all." I was already standing, trying to contain my panic.

164

She shook her head sadly. "No, I've come to the right place," she said. "This is something, if it can be solved at all, will only be solved by prayer and spiritual guidance. You must take my word for it—it *is* a spiritual matter, only that, and I've come to you to advise me."

I felt like the coward I knew I was, but I would not, could not, relent. I would ask her nothing. There was too much at stake—my own mortal infirmities—and I could take no chances. "I *am* advising you, Miss Hastings," I said. "I'm advising you, imploring you, actually, to go see Dean Mary Moore right away. Tell her the whole story—who the boy is and everything."

She gazed sadly out the window again. Finally her voice was hollow, almost ghostly, as she spoke. "It isn't a boy, Dean Barry. It's my father."

30

I AM MORE THAN CONVINCED that the visit my daughter Carol finally, in her own good time, paid me during my second stay at the Coveycote sanatarium in Connecticut was in retaliation for something, months earlier, I had done to her—namely, insisted, against her weeks of resistance, that she accompany me on a visit out to my son Bertie, now fourteen (her idiot half brother!), who, as I have said, was, of direst necessity, confined in an institution in far-off Michigan, in a small bleak town on the northern peninsula called Wallpere. The visit, as she had feared, turned out to be a bad, very bad, experience for her (his harrowing mongoloid condition), for he recognized no one, not even the attendants, could not talk, only mumble as he drooled, had to be fed by others (sometimes force-fed), and was totally incontinent. Carol hated me for making her go and thought I had done it deliberately, out of spite, to punish her for some fancied slight or other. The truth was I wanted her to witness for herself the depth and enormity of my own punishment and suffering, in order somehow to bestir her sympathy, her compassion, for me, neither of which recently had been much in evidence. It did not work, of course, and she still held it against me even as at long last she came to see me during this, my repeat sojourn, at Coveycote.

By now my bubble had indeed burst. The "zenith of my (mad)

career" had finally overreached itself and now lay in rubble. The devastating incident with the student Deborah Hastings, just related, and its telltale shock—and import—for me, sending me to bed for three days, would almost of itself have been enough to produce the present debacle and send me off packing again to the therapists. But then quickly followed the second of the one-two punches, that is, the unraveling of my failed conquest of this gorgeous Antiguan woman and fellow faculty member, who, of course, in the end, directly or indirectly, involved me with Uncle Sam, Judge Jeffreys, and his jury, and finally Pressman and Bahr. But now, my sentence duly served and release accomplished, that was all over. My new confrontation with Carol, however, was only now to begin. Could I, at this late date, be saved? I was to ask that first of myself, then of the Coveycote doctors, and at last Carol. My own answer to myself was to amount to hedging; it was also self-indulgent, and finally inconclusive. As for the kind, smiling, yet somehow aloof doctors, they would be merely agreeable and noncommittal. And Carol? It is far more complicated.

Although I had sent her my usual flurry of SOS's she had not responded until the very last. And now that she had arrived, for all the comfort she gave me or even had the capacity to give, she may as well have stayed on her job in New York State—White Plains. Why had she come, even so late? I asked myself. Certainly not because of my maundering appeals. Was it then her aim to hound and obsess me, never let me forget, hover over and around me like a hollow-eyed ghost or ghoul? Or was it her genuine filial love? In light of our history, could the latter at all be possible? But, grasping at any straw, I refused to rule it out—for did I not also genuinely love my daughter? My answers to all these questions were of course undependable, because our talks turned out to be too self-conscious—understandably—and also a little dishonest. How else, though, could they have been?

One evening we sat at this small sequestered table in Coveycote's petite dining room. Occasionally she would observe me—quietly, dispassionately—as she picked at her chop suey. It had been, since her arrival, a mercurial forty-eight hours for me and my protean temperament and I never knew a few seconds beforehand how I would react to any given bit of stimuli. This evening I felt especially nervous, strung-out, and sullen, though only two days before at her first appearance, I had been actually overjoyed, almost in tears. Now I was only stolid, at times truculent.

166

"I assume you won't be here much longer," she said. "There's no need for it. These places can become addictive." She sipped her iced tea. "What will you do when you leave, Father?" I looked at her blankly. "I mean, with your life?" she said.

At once I bristled in defiance. "*What* life?"

"Well, isn't teaching now out of the question?—even maybe preaching too, for a while."

"That's right," I said curtly.

"Will you still, though, later on, possibly, be able to get some kind of church?"

"I don't know," I shrugged. "Maybe so, maybe not—depending on how closely they check. Being here at this place, though, could be just as bad as if they found out about Pressman. This may be a highfalutin retreat, all right, a resort with doctors—mediocre ones, by the way, with their phony sunny dispositions and who talk to us all the time about Freud, and Jung, and Adler. But it's still a crazy-house. Carol, can I really be saved?"

She looked dejected, or perhaps displeased, and futilely shook her head. "It's unfair to ask me that," she said. "How would I know?—I don't even know how 'saved,' as you use it, can, or should, be defined." It was somehow all I could do to suppress my unaccountable anger. I could not possibly reply civilly to my daughter and remained silent. "What will you do now, Father?" she repeated.

"When I leave this place," I said, "I'm going to go somewhere and try to save *myself*!" I said it in a great huff, than sat fuming, before adding, "Certainly no one else gives a damn! I've already picked out a likely place, though. I found it on a road map with a magnifying glass—in rural Kansas, a place named Berlin, population fifty-eight hundred. That will fix you. I'll go out there and take any kind of work, even menial, that they'll give me as long as it's enough to pay rent and eat on. Though I'm not flat broke yet, I'm not flush, either—after all I've been through. But I'll go out there and hole up for the rest of my miserable life. And I've got a little secret for you. Out there I'll be able to do something I've wanted to do all my life—write poetry. Yes, it's true. I could then tell the rest of the world to go to hell!"

Carol shook her head disconsolately. "I'm not surprised about the poetry at all," she said. "It's no secret. Your sermons were always full of poetry quotes, especially Milton—some, I'm sure, were your own, too. But if you think this would be satisfying to you as a way of life, and for the rest of your life, you don't know yourself as others, as *I*, know you." Her face grew long, cheerless. "How old are you, Father—fifty-five now?"

"Yes."

"I think these plans you've thought up are a little romantic. They're certainly not in keeping with your makeup, your character, at this stage of your life. You're not an old man. If you were seventy-five, or even maybe sixty-five, I might see it, but not now. It's far more likely you'll go on being yourself for quite some time yet. How can you change at fifty-five? Why, no more than Niagara River can flow back up its falls. These quixotic plans you have—of burying yourself out in some place called Berlin, Kansas, so that you can write poetry and thumb your nose at the rest of the world—are just not *you*. Besides, this won't bring you what you really want—peace of mind."

I did not comment out of fear of exploding. She had insulted me deeply, implying I would have to wait until my mid-sixties, or even seventies—when, presumably, my libidinous fires had cooled, was really what she was getting at—before I could lead a life of selflessness and purity. I thought it outrageous and bitterly resented it. Peace of mind! Had she ever resisted me? Hadn't she, a child of twelve, flirted with me right at the dinner table in the presence of her unsuspecting, unaware mother? Peace of mind! Bah! What gall! I have no faith in such slogans, anyway. I do not seek such peace. (Which, of course, was untrue. Why, oh, why, would I tell such lies to *myself*?) The slogan is a sophomoric concept at best, I nevertheless went on insisting. The *hero* was certainly not interested in peace of mind. He believed in the strenuous existence—raising armies! Besides, I know peace of mind is something I shall never have. I don't even deserve it.

Carol was undaunted by my heated silence. "Do you agree?" she said.

"I've told you, Carol, what my unpretentious plans, my ambitions, are. I don't care to be patronized. I merely wish to be left alone." (Which was also untrue. She knew it, of course.) "You insist on steering my life," I said. "I'm a man of some independence, some accomplishment—and pride—you know."

"But isn't it true that we should be viewing things from the same angle?" she said. "I want nothing from you, Father," she added, somewhat inexplicably in the context, I thought. I pondered in vain what she meant. Yet, somehow fearful, I chose not to interrogate her—possibly on her innermost thoughts—and remained silent, though alert. "Nothing except your love," she said

168

then with tears in her eyes. I was of course dumbfounded, speech-less—and moved.

The little dining room had almost emptied. She too now looked around her and began to stir. Our Chinese repast over, she, quite ceremoniously, I thought, dabbed at her eyes with her paper napkin, then folded it and nervously nudged it under the edge of her plate, all the while eschewing my desperate, pitiful glances. She seemed exhausted and sat solemnly drooped forward—reminiscent of her mother—before again looking away.

She left Coveycote next morning, at the taxi rising off her heels to kiss me on the cheek, and I was not to see her, or even hear from her, again for almost two years. But even by the time, five weeks after she left, that I myself departed Coveycote, I had definitely decided on Berlin, Kansas, to which to relocate and fight my demons. I trembled with that rare hope which still refused to succumb to that other clear, crystalline strychnine in my heart.

31

IMAGINE! In the dorm this particular Tuesday afternoon Cager had come looking for *me*. It was a surprise, a most singular event, for I was *his* acolyte, not the other way around. For another reason also I could not believe my eyes. He carried *books*! A great armload of them. I was sitting on my bunk bed studying for an exam and when he saw the amazement on my face he laughed. It was, however, an uncomfortable, self-conscious laugh. "What's up, Rev?" he finally said, dumping his impedimenta down beside me.

"I should be asking *you* that," I said. "Somehow you and books no longer go together. What *is* up?"

His reply was oblique. "I'm hungry," he said. "Want to go over to Campus Grill and get a hamburger?" But instead he sat down and lounged back against my bunk post, looking listless and aimless one moment, preoccupied and meditative the next, yet as if waiting for something, anything, to happen. But I was still looking at all those books of his on my bunk. They baffled me but intrigued me too. "Ain't you hungry?" he said. It was 2:15.

"I guess so," I said, putting my work aside.

Whereupon, idly, he picked up off the little table the book I had been studying—*Commentaries on the Pentateuch*—and began thumbing through it. "You preachers," he said, "have to study stuff like this, eh?" He spoke carelessly, then yawned, before staring off vacantly into space. I began to feel that something important—at least to him—occupied his mind.

"The book's a series of critiques," I explained, "on the first five books of the Old Testament."

"Great stuff, eh?—ha, for you faith-healers and sky pilots!" he said, and tossed the book back on the table.

It was obvious now he was killing time. This too puzzled me. With his constant preoccupation and nervous energy devoted to all his various projects he was definitely not the type to be lounging or loitering about anywhere. Then I remembered he had been hanging around the dorm most of the past week, in fact, and this heightened my curiosity and suspicions. I was soon convinced something was weighing heavily on his mind. It was inescapable.

We finally left for Campus Grill, located back of Stovall Hall and the gym, with him, though, still doggedly lugging the armload of books. It was a chill, bright day and as we crossed campus I could see how clumsily burdensome his load was for him. "Why didn't you leave those things in the dorm?" I said. "Why carry them around like that?"

He gazed down at the books in his arms, ruefully smiling, then at last laughing. "Me and these old tomes are kinda buddies," he said. "At least we sure used to be—when I first came here. Man, did I study these dadbloom things—night and day! Old Haley, and, for that matter, everybody else on this faculty, gave me a flock of A's. These books were dear to my heart, I'll tell you. Still are. Old Hannibal crossing the Alps, getting ready to jump on the Romans, with those big African elephants (ha, *Loxodonta africana*)—those pachyderms, man!—pulling his supply trains. Napoleon at Austerlitz, too—whipped the Austrians' ass *and* the Russians, both! And Lee—oh, Lord!—with old Stonewall Jackson at his side, at Second Manassas! And then, on top of *that*, at Fredericksburg making Burnside look like a schoolboy! Lord Jesus, what men! These old books tell all about those heavy hitters, huh?" As he turned to me his eyes were shining like sapphires. Finally then he added, "But I probably won't be seeing them again soon." He tried to laugh again but it ended in a desperate swallow.

"Yeah," I said casually, shilly-shallying until I could learn more. "Some books do get to be a part of you like that."

"I'm taking them," he said, "to Haley for safekeeping for a while." I waited for him to explain, but he did not, so we went on. Then he said, out of the blue, "Rev, I want you to go in town with me tomorrow. Haley's sending me in to check on a job he might have lined up for me there."

I did not know what to make of this. It was totally unexpected. But I also wanted to ask him why he wanted me to accompany him. I was not the job applicant. But I did not. "Sure, I'll go," I said. I suddenly wanted to oblige him; in fact, I was eager to do it, for welling up inside me were all my feelings of contrition and guilt. I laughed: "And while we're in there maybe *two* jobs might turn up."

"I may really need the job, though," he said seriously. "'Cause I'll probably be leaving Gladstone, for a spell, anyway, you know."

I stopped dead in my tracks in the middle of the campus now. "I don't get you, Cage," I finally said, my heart momentarily stopping—an augury.

"I'm flunking out, anyhow, y'know," he said. "Haley says it's hopeless, that I ought to just go on and drop out on my own. That it might be a whole lot better that way in the long run. Then later—though there's no guarantee, of course—I might be able to come on back. Maybe even next fall. But if I wait around till I do flunk out, he says, there's practically no chance they'll ever let me back in—absolutely none if Groomes gets wind of it. Haley's probably right—he's up on everything, you know."

I started slowly walking again. I was bowled over, of course. I also suddenly found myself sad. Soon I was really desolate at the prospect of his leaving campus—especially when this combined itself with my other feelings, the guilt. I began to feel lonely already, although there were days, even sometimes a week, when we might not see each other at all. But now I felt alone, indeed deserted, and did not know what to say. Apparently neither did he, for there was now a long silence as we walked.

At last, though, he seemed to arouse himself. "It's some old rich white woman in town that Haley's talked to," he finally said—"an aristocratic old widow. Her husband was a big judge around here. He was even a Gladstone trustee, for years and years. How about that? Wow! But Haley said it's only a houseboy's job they talked about. That's better than nothing, though, ain't it—ha! *Damnsight* better—Haley says, wouldn't he?—than this so-called job I've got now at Ma Moody's! Ha, ha!"

It did not seem at all funny to me—nor, in fact, for that matter, did it to him, despite his guffaws. "What's a houseboy do?" I asked.

"Beats me. Just another flunky, I guess. But nothing's definite

171

yet. She wants to look me over, naturally. Ha, that sure makes sense, don't it?—with my reputation."

"You've got a *good* reputation, Cage," I found myself saying, impulsively. "All your friends know that. Even some of them—some of *us*—that laugh at the crazy things you do sometimes."

This spontaneous praise visibly embarrassed him. He ignored it and rushed on. "Her name's Dabney," he said—"the old lady. Haley says she's already got more servants, all darkies, of course, than she needs now—three or four—but he wants me to go in anyhow. So I'm going. When I thanked him for trying to help me, he said he couldn't take credit for it all, that it was really his wife that came up with the idea of old lady Dabney. How about that? So I gotta go in—you can see that. If he and his wife both are in this thing, I oughta at least show some interest in helping myself. Huh?"

". . . That's right, I guess," I finally said, though still so flabbergasted by the whole astounding development that words did not come readily.

"Haley says, though, that if I do get the job I'll have to be on my P's and Q's from morning till night, really handle the old woman with kid gloves, for they say she's a holy terror, or can be when she gets riled up. She's what you call one hundred percent unreconstructed. But, ha, I told him if I can get along with Ma Moody I oughta be able to get along with *anybody*. Huh?"

". . . Well, whataya know?" I said absently, sighing, my mind elsewhere—on my betrayal of him.

He misunderstood my vagueness. "*I've* thought a lot about it myself, too, Rev," he said. "But I've about made up my mind to go ahead and do it. It ain't been easy, though. Yeah, it seems strange, all right—me doing this. But, hell, nothing may come of it, anyhow, and I'll be off the hook then. I don't want to let Haley and his wife down, either, though, by not doing what they say. So, yeah, I'm goin' on in."

"I'll sure hate to see you leave," I heard myself saying to him. But it was the unmitigated truth. I was really unhappy. I felt closer to him now than I ever had. And there was always the remorse.

"Hey," he laughed, "I ain't got the job yet. Maybe I hope I will, though, you know. I want to show Haley I can make it back to Gladstone—then maybe go on and make good like I started out to. Besides, he says the job, if I get it, won't really be all that bad. It will pay pretty good for a flunky job, including living and eating right there on the premises, and the work wouldn't be hard or

172

heavy or anything like that. So . . . that's the deal. Wish me well. I gotta try and make it this time. I've fucked up long enough, ha! *Huh?*"

"Cage," I repeated, "I'll sure miss you not being around here anymore." Again it was the truth if I ever spoke it. "Sure, as I say, though, I'll go in with you—any time." But I felt terrible. I felt abandoned.

By one o'clock the following afternoon—a chilly but sunny March day—we were already on our way into town. Alas, however, my mercurial friend, unlike the day before, was in one of his foulest moods. I was almost certain now that he did not want to go, that something may even be telling him not to. As we walked, then, he was mostly silent, his gaze both dour and downcast, as he answered my cheerful attempts at conversation in gruff monosyllables.

The Dabney address was No. 924 Beauregard Street, in the oldest and most aristocratic part of town—a section neither of us had ever seen. When we reached Beauregard I was wonderfully impressed by the historic old houses, many of them antebellum, and though now venerable, a few even fragile-looking, they were all the more arresting and elegant for it. "Cage," I laughed, "you can tell this street represents *old* money."

"You mean old *slave* money," he growled. "Off our backs. There's nothing here for *us* to be kicking up our heels about."

"I know it," I conceded.

A little farther on he pointed grimly to a lawn ornament in front of one of the stately old houses, a playful cast-iron blackamoor jockey, almost life-size, its racing colors a lurid red and black. "Looka there," he said, "see what I mean?" What was queer was that somehow the frolicsome jockey's right arm was raised absurdly in a gesture reminiscent, of all things, of a Nazi salute. It's boots were black but the scarlet cap and jacket matched the red of its grinning, fawning, sycophant lips. "It ain't no Isaac Murphy, I can tell you that," said Cager. "You wouldn't catch *him* showing all his ivories like that—he had too much dignity."

"Who're you talking about?" I said.

He was glad to educate me. "Isaac Murphy was the great Negro jockey—way back when—who won the Kentucky Derby *three* times. The only thing he could do today, though, if he was alive, is clean the horse shit out of the stables. Huh? We're *retrogressing,* man!" I said nothing, for I could see he was getting more and more upset. But I knew the real reason was less that of the grinning iron blackamoor and Isaac Murphy than of his rebellion against our present undertaking. What a mood to be in, though, I thought, when you are on your way to apply for a houseboy's job. I noticed something else. The nearer we got to No. 924, the slower became his gait. He was almost sauntering now, nervously strolling, as if he had all day and half the night to get where we were going.

Thus, however, we finally arrived at the Dabney mansion. At once I noticed his sudden new and heightened interest, his wide, gawking eyes, the sharpened curiosity, despite the dour countenance. But I was as captivated as he and for a moment we both stood staring at the daunting old house and grounds. Although an antebellum structure, it definitely was not one of the senile, fragile ones, but squarish and solid, the brick exterior a dull greenish-white hue, its windows tall and framed by masses of hoary vines now leafless. There were also four great Corinthian columns across the front adding to the imposing shopworn majesty of the edifice surrounded by its extensive grounds on which I would learn it had stood since the presidency of Andrew Jackson. Yet, these grounds now showed patches of lumpy sod, unkempt bare spots, and other unsightly signs of the departed winter. Then all too suddenly—our hearts beating wildly—we found ourselves at the Dabney ornate wrought iron gate.

But before I knew what was happening, Cager had stepped, almost leapt, in front of me, swung the gate wide, and was heading straight up the walk toward the front door. "Where're you *going*?" I cried. "Don't go up there!" I started frantically running after him. "We've got to go around to the back, Cage!" No wonder he had brought me, I thought. Indeed he needed me. I was angry and really wanted to tell him he was being both stupid and mule-headed but I didn't have time. I was sure, though, he would ruin any chances he had of making a good impression, especially knowing the old lady's bad reputation. I realized now I was trying to protect him from himself, which I thought entirely futile. "You know better than that!" I called out after him.

Instead, with his long strides, he kept right on going, as if utterly disdainful of anything I might have to say, now or later. "We're college students," he said over his shoulder. "We ain't field hands, y'know."

"I don't care. You've come here to see about a servant's job, right? You don't think white help would try to use the front door, do you? What the hell's got into you, Cage!"

But we were already mounting the steps of the graceful old

portico now, and before I could do anything about it he was pushing the doorbell. I was not only angry now but worried—actually scared. Panting from my own exertions and nervousness, though, I was also sure, no matter how brash he appeared, he was scared too. Thus we stood breathing hard and waiting.

Finally he was about to ring again, when we heard a slight movement just inside the door. Then slowly, very slowly, the door was opened by a wizened, old, quite black man who looked all of ninety. His small head was almost totally bald and he wore an ancient cutaway coat, high collar, and formal black string bow tie. He studied us and we studied him. But before he ever uttered a word I could tell he was decidedly unfriendly. He had begun shaking his head already, slowly but in a hostile way, then with a feeble sweep of the arm made a motion around toward the rear of the premises.

I knew what he meant of course, and so did Cager, who frowned and said to him hotly, loudly, almost as if the old servitor were stone-deaf: "We came to see Mrs. Dabney! We're students! We're from Gladstone!"

"Ah doan care ef you're from Tuskegee," said the brittle aged butler in a thin reedy voice, "you doan come in *dis* doh." He then emitted a contemptuous little cough as he shook his head again and gave us the same slow circular sweep of the arm indicating the back door.

For a brief perverse moment I was glad. I had been proven right and Cager both wrong and wrong-headed. I had readily then turned to obey the butler and descend the portico steps, when Cager's outraged stare now fell on me. "Where you going?" he demanded. "We don't even know if she's home or not. I ain't about to go around to no damn back door when I don't even know if she's here." Now he turned hostilely on the old butler. "What I wanta know is, is Mrs. Dabney *in?*"

Once more the old man shook his head. "We cain't talk no moh at *dis* doh," he said. "I ain't got nothin' more to say to you *heah.*" Again he waved us around to the rear and closed the door.

"I told you so, Cage," I said. "Come on, let's go around—like we should have in the first place." I turned again to go and, although he was muttering all manner of blue expletives to himself, he finally—slowly—followed me. It seemed, though, that, deliberately or not, he was doing everything in his power to make the mission fail.

But when, after traversing the paved walk of the unsightly yard,

175

we arrived around at the back door, we found our nemesis, the old butler, already there, waiting for us. He opened the door and, sniffing testily, faced us with an arch, imperial air. "Yas, now," he said, "de lady of de house is in. Ef you'll give me yoh names and whut it is you want, I'll go tell huh."

I hurried to speak first. "One of our professors out at the college has spoken with Mrs. Dabney and says she might be considering hiring a student on a temporary basis." I pointed to glowering Cager. "That's why he's here—to see about the job." I gave him Cager's name, which I am sure he promptly forgot, as Cager stood beside me, his breast rising and falling in his highly offended (yet somehow spurious) agitation—and dread. The old man's rheumy, beady eyes still studied us. At last, then, curtly, he said, "Hold on"—and closed the door again.

Cager was furiously grinding his teeth now. "Yeah," he said, "right off old Massa's plantation. A real-life, old-timey, house nigger. A *relic*, man! That old bastard's older'n God." I did not deign to answer.

But soon the old man was back. He opened the door, slowly again, grudgingly, stepped aside, and motioned us in. "Foller me," he said, his voice raspy and fractious, as he led us forward. Before we knew it, then, we were in the long, ornate hallway-gallery of the house. It was a spacious, overawing, oak-floored corridor, with both walls lined with great portraits, almost all of them magnificently uniformed military men. Cager had stopped stunned in his tracks. Staring, gaping, now, he seemed suddenly transfixed, a standing effigy in stone. Bearded, austere, yet serene (especially Lee), and clad in the burnished full-dress of Confederate general officers, they gazed down on posterity from prodigious scroll-worked gilt frames. Then we saw mounted on the left wall, extending under the tremendous span of at least four portraits, and flanked by two dramatic clusters of scarlet battle flags, an enormously long Confederate Enfield musket, its gleaming bayonet, which seemed at least half as long as the musket itself, fiercely affixed. Cager, his jaw hanging now, as in awe he stared up at Lee, Jackson, Jeb Stuart, and others on the wall, had not moved one inch. His legs seemed paralyzed.

At last I elbowed him rudely. "Come *on!*" I said.

This was just as the old butler's reedy voice also cut in, sharply, impatiently—"Dis way!"

We followed him down the hallway-gallery and finally—directly across from the majestic parlor—into the Dabney library. I still remember, vividly, how, as we entered this stately room, the sunlight streamed in through the tall windows and onto the high walls shelved, from floor to ceiling, with solid masses of books, historical and Civil War memorabilia, musty histories, maps, and strategy memoirs of the 1861-65 military campaigns, as well as a profuse miscellany of other tracts, treatises, and heavier volumes.

Then, at long, long last, from an elegant Louis Quinze writing table, a gold fountain pen still poised in her hand, she sat observing us as we entered. Here unmistakably—white-haired, somehow pristine yet magisterial, but also forbidding, already past her mid-seventies, strong-featured though pink-jowled, her pince-nez glinting in the brash sunlight—here indeed sat the grand doyenne of western Tennessee: Mary Eliza Fitzhugh Dabney.

Cager, scarcely able to breathe, had frozen in his tracks, become totally immobilized. He could only stand there—astonished—staring at her. He had at once recognized, remembered, her, he later vowed—recalling that sultry September afternoon, her long black Cadillac coming down Culpeper Street toward us at the courthouse, her black chauffeur impassive, she, the handsome old aristocrat, alone in the backseat gazing straight ahead, her rich, ruddy countenance shielded by fierce pince-nez, before there had come the sudden, mutual, surprised, then fixed stares between the two of them decreed by fate. Standing here now in her magnificent library, he was suddenly weak. But why? Somehow he also wanted to turn and run. I, though, at that moment, remembered none of it. Nor, of course, did she.

The frail old butler, stepping slightly aside now, let an arm fall petulantly, in a gesture of silent if grudging introduction, yet as if he wished he might say to her, "You the one that had 'em come heah, not me."

"Very well, Caleb," she said to him and, frowning, turned to Cager and me. "I wasn't told there would be two of you," she said. "Which one of you is Rollo?"

Cager swallowed. ". . . I am," he finally got out.

She scrutinized him from head to foot. Finally she turned to me. "You may leave with Caleb and wait," she said.

At this Cager looked terrified, as if about to panic. Yesterday his premonition had told him to bring me along, but now it was all for naught, for he had not reckoned with the possibility he still might have to face her alone. I could feel his envious, miserable—frightened—eyes on me as Caleb escorted me out of the room. He was, alas, on his own now.

177

32

When old Caleb went up front to answer the doorbell he found Augusta Coombs outside vigorously stamping her wet shoes on the doormat. "Mawnin'," he said, letting her in.

"Good morning, Caleb." Entering the foyer, she gave him her collapsed, dripping umbrella. "Where is my mother?"

"She in the pahler. Ain't long come down."

"Tell Phoebe not to put my name in the pot. I've got to leave before lunchtime."

"Yessum."

She went down the hallway-gallery of portraits but looked neither left nor right. These cool martial countenances had gazed down on her since her birth forty-four years ago upstairs in this house. She soon entered the parlor where M. E. F. Dabney sat in the satinwood Hepplewhite chair before a cheerful fire reading the *Memphis Commercial Appeal.* "Hello, Mother."

"Hello, Gussie."

Augusta, thick-set, tweedy, handsome, went and, momentarily, stood before the blaze. "It's foul out there," she said. "The fire's wonderful. April's been worse than March, even February." She still wore her coat for the moment.

Dabney put the newspaper aside and removed her pince-nez. "Did you bring Johnny's letter?"

Augusta laughed, but then sighed. "Why do you think I came?" She sat down, took a letter from her soldier son from her purse, and handed it over.

"Why on earth did he take his commission in the infantry?" complained Dabney. "He could have gone to Fort Sill—to the field artillery officers' school. Instead he chose Fort Benning."

"He *wanted* the infantry, Mother. Don't ask me why."

Dabney had put her pince-nez back on in order to read the letter. "It's because that's where the action, the fighting, is, bless his heart," she said. "That's Johnny."

Augusta's face became distressful. "Oh, I dread to think he'll be going overseas as soon as he graduates, but he will. Some nights I can't sleep."

"Just hope it will be Europe and not that awful Pacific," Dabney said.

"I wish he didn't have to go anywhere—at all."

"Of course you do—you and a million other mothers around the

178

globe—but, sad to say, it's not like that." Dabney began reading the letter.

Augusta, waiting, crossed her legs, smoothed her tweed skirt, and again sighed. Married to a local surgeon, mother of four—Johnny and three girls—she herself was the youngest of the three Dabney children, *all* girls. "This war's awful," she fumed as her mother silently read. "It's so terribly disruptive. It's spoiled so many lives. Just think, Johnny would be finishing Vanderbilt this year, not Benning."

Dabney, still reading, said in an oblivious aside, "He says he likes the Georgia people. That's good. Families like ours there have opened their homes to him and some of the other southern boys like him. That's as it should be. The army has all kinds in it—some are bad eggs. But I worry far less about Johnny than you do, although he's just as dear to me. It's his strength of character. That will bring him through. It's in his blood, of course. So stop worrying so much. Besides, it does no good." Having finished the letter, she returned it to Augusta.

"That's easy for you to say, Mother. You had only us girls."

Dabney acted as if she had not heard. "You call the war 'disruptive,'" she said. "But wars are much worse than that, Gussie. I was a child growing up in Virginia soon after the South was defeated. It was a terrible time and worse still in the deeper South. Horrible things happened. We were a completely helpless people and our Yankee conquerers didn't let us forget it, either. Southerners today are too prone to forget this. We were a different people in those times, though. Endurance, pride, honor, all meant something. But now, as a region, as a people, we've atrophied. Courage and self-sacrifice, even defiance—the old virtues—have all but disappeared. We had nearly won the war despite the fact that we were greatly outnumbered and outequipped. But it was the kind of people we were that had made the difference. We were superior. Southerners sprang from a superior stock, from the Normans, who were a noble, fearless, conquering people, while Northerners, Yankees, came from a far lower stock, the Angles and the Jutes, who were largely serfs. In the War Between the States one Southerner was the equal of any three Northerners. But we have now as a people lost most of the old virtues that made us great. Still, some of us have been doing what little we can to preserve the old traditions, yet with only limited success. It's discouraging. But we've somehow kept at it. We've had to—when you consider the alternatives."

She was referring to three organizations in which all or most of her life she had been an active, if not zealous, member or leader—the Presbyterian Church, South, the United Daughters of the Confederacy, and, more locally, the Shiloh Battlefield Memorial Association. The Shiloh Association, until recently, she had headed—indeed fiercely dominated—for twenty-three years. Even now, as president emeritus (by her own choice), her retirement was anything but total. Despite a capable and energetic successor, hand-picked and trained by her, she nevertheless continued from habit and, in her view, necessity to chart most of the association's course. She spent much of each day in the book-crammed Dabney library in spirited, hortatory correspondence—invariably using her wonderful Sheaffer gold instrument—as she hurriedly penned letters of inquiry, encouragement, or sharp admonition, the last to that group of members she commonly referred to as "malingerers" or "lightweights."

"But, Mother," said Augusta, "don't you think a time finally comes when you have to turn over these headaches to others and say, 'Look, I've done more than my part, now you take over and carry on from here?'"

"Oh, I know I'm not indispensable, Gussie. I'm gradually easing off."

Augusta, who idolized her mother, smiled. "Yes?—not that anyone can see."

"There's still so much to be done, though, so much yet at stake, in trying to preserve even the vestiges of our old way of life. Your father used to get after me the same way—about what he called my 'zealotry.' Yet he believed in these things every bit as much as I do." She grew solemn, pensive, as if, silently, to herself, communing with a ghost—"Now, yes, you did, Nathan. Don't deny it, dear." Nostalgically, then, she gazed down at her tawny, wrinkled left hand, at the plain gold band on her wedding ring finger. Her father, fifty-eight years before, had refused to let his only daughter, Mary Eliza Fitzhugh, accept the large spangled wedding diamond that her affianced, the brash young Tennessee lawyer, Nathan Poole Dabney, at the apogee of his ardor, had sought to give her. They had all then agreed, Nathan reluctantly, on this far less ostentatious gold band—which, however, at once he had had engraved on its inside surface: "Darling M.E.F.D." This was the ring she gazed at today. Yet, on their silver anniversary he had given her the selfsame diamond, which all the while he had kept stashed away in the bank vault, now mounted on a small platinum brooch. For by then both Timothy and Lucinda Fitzhugh, her parents, were dead. Again now she looked down at the simple ring, thinking, still silently communicating, "Although I've always loved it, it's still not you, Nathan. You thought bigger. You wanted the best for me, the most spectacular, as well, and I admired you so for it. You may have felt rebuffed by Father but certainly not by me. Dear . . . dear Nathan!"

"Mother, what are you daydreaming about?"

"I was thinking of your father. And also of my own. They were exact opposites. I doubt if my father ever realized that he was really a poet at heart, or a classical musician, or even a painter. I don't think there was anything in the world, including even his family maybe, that he loved more than he did Shakespeare, whom he read daily just as he did the Bible. He also at last renounced war, you know. On general principles. It wasn't because he'd lost an arm at Shiloh, which he had, and was afraid. Not that. As you intimate you do, he simply abhorred it—even if he did know there were times when it couldn't be avoided. That is, if a nation or people was to preserve its honor. Ah, but not *your* father's family. They, and he, dealt in no such niceties. His being a Dabney, a Tennessee Dabney, explains so much. Although he was too young to fight in the war against the North—in fact, he was only a baby—he nonetheless lost seventeen, I believe he said it was, cousins, uncles, brothers, and the like, to say nothing of those maimed. The Dabneys had so many amputees among the survivors waving stubs for arms at their friends or hobbling around the state like Coxey's Army that people called the family the 'peg-legged Dabneys.' I want to say for *my* father, though, that he was twice decorated for bravery—at Shiloh and before that at Ball's Bluff—yet he hated war and finally ended up a pacifist. Poor Papa."

"I repeat, Mother," said Augusta, "that you had only us girls. You haven't had the experience of a son going off to war."

"No, but, as I said, don't think my heart's not in my throat every time you mention Johnny. I know it hurts, Gussie. But he's got Dabney marrow in his bones. He'll survive as most of them did. Remember they originally came from the roughest Tennessee pioneer stock but were shrewd and aggressive and in time, beginning with about the Martin Van Buren administration, came to own plantations, slaves, and much bank stock. Yet all the while of course they were raising big families, although the men also found time to carouse, and wench, and fight duels, the duels, however, signifying they were now regarded as gentry."

Augusta's florid face puckered grotesquely in an attempt to stifle a yawn. What her mother was saying she had heard all her life. Indeed she now felt constrained to mention her own husband's family—the Coombses—for an accolade or two. "Ned's family was *always* gentry, you know, Mother. But their being South Carolinians explains that."

Dabney went on obliviously. "*My* father and mother, though (she was a Randolph, as you well know), came from much older, more genteel Virginia stock. The Fitzhughs were great readers and thinkers, patrons of the arts and letters. My great-grandfather taught Thomas Jefferson to play Mozart on the violin. Actually, the Fitzhughs were inclined to be visionaries and idealists and never became great politicians or what you might call really wealthy. Still, the Dabneys were mightily impressed with us. And I, though not Father, with them. I liked their go-getiveness, and also their riotous sense of humor, but was at first frightened by their hot, dangerous tempers. Nevertheless, I soon became a real Dabney myself. Poor Father in the end, I think, was a little dismayed. I shall always, no matter, revere his memory in the tenderest way— although by the time of his death he had not only renounced war but had voiced approval of the Emancipation Proclamation! *And* the Thirteenth, Fourteenth, and Fifteenth amendments!" Dabney heaved a heavy sigh and shook her head. "But," she said, "I guess just about all of us do now, except possibly a few unlettered backwoods diehards still around. Times change so. Father saw this, saw it coming. Ah, my father . . . a most virtuous man. Yes, a dreamer, who so wanted a better world."

Augusta observed her mother seriously. "Goodness, Mother, you're certainly reliving the past today."

Just then Caleb—who himself could have boasted, had he wished, of service in the Dabney family for sixty-six years now— entered the parlor and, sniffing irritably, looking away, said to his employer: "You got any letters to go? Ahm sendin' that boy downtown to the hardware stoh. He kin drop 'em in the post orrfice."

"Yes, Caleb, there are some on my writing table, a half-dozen or so," said Dabney. "Give them to him."

The tails of his cutaway coat hanging lank off his frail buttocks, Caleb went out again.

"How has the new boy turned out, Mother?" Augusta asked.

182

Dabney paused and thought. "It's too early to tell," she finally said. "He's a riddle. He has very little to say. So I can't tell whether he's just nervous and uneasy about his new job or if he's being impudent, uppity. When he first came to see about the job, he brought another boy with him. I thought that was strange and dismissed the other boy. This really upset Rollo. He would hardly say anything at all after his friend left the room. It certainly irritated me. I had to pry information out of him. I thought a long time before I told him he could start—I'm in no pinch for help."

"Goodness, I wouldn't think so," Augusta said.

"Yet, I finally ended up hiring him—on faith, I guess. Even he himself, though, seemed uncertain about whether he ought to take the job. It was really a strange meeting. But I'm still inclined to think it was just fear or nervousness—he was tongue-tied. He's turned out to be a good worker, though. But he came well enough recommended, as I told you, by Haley Barnes, one of his teachers out at Gladstone. I have a measure of confidence in Barnes. Caleb, though, can't abide Rollo."

Augusta laughed. "Whom can Caleb abide?"

"But I guess the main thing is that the boy does the work well —is conscientious and thorough. He's just quiet—maybe has things on his mind. A strange one, really strange, yet has his good points."

"You say you may have hired him on faith, Mother. What does that mean? It's almost as if you felt you *had* to take him—that you were being dictated to. The truth is, you don't need any more help. With Caleb, Sampson, and Phoebe here, what's there for Rollo to do?"

"To his credit," said Dabney, "he's found plenty. I was surprised myself. Of course you know how trifling Sampson is. The only thing he's interested in is sneaking his half-pints of gin back there in the garage and then driving me around town in a long, shiny, black car, and, on the sly, nodding and grinning to his darky friends on the street. After that he thinks it's beneath him to do anything else—like cleaning."

"Mother, I've told you that you should *fire* him. Someday, full of his gin, he's going to have a car accident and hurt you."

Dabney sighed. "Well, your father hired him. How can I fire him? It's not all that easy, unless he goes *too* far. And Caleb's a perfect cipher now. He can hardly get up and down the stairs. Phoebe looks down on anything except cooking—especially cleaning. She thinks she's here just to stay back there in the kitchen and munch on leftovers—she must weigh two hundred and fifty pounds."

"Mother, you've let these darkies take over. *They're* running *you.*"

"Haven't they always run us? We just think we're in charge. They're our destiny. It's an irony that Rollo's turned out to be the only plus in the whole picture. He puts in a full day's work and the results show. This is very helpful to me because I've still got responsibilities here, Gussie. I must keep this house up, maintain it in the fashion it's always known, as it was in the old days, as long as I'm alive. Your father, now with God, would be sadly displeased otherwise, and rightly so. This is a historic house, I don't have to tell you. It was in this very parlor where we sit that one fateful evening in the spring of 1861—May, to be exact—that a caucus of the state's leading political figures gathered to acknowledge the stupendous crisis already upon them, the black storm clouds of war overhead, and to discuss the process which was soon to lead, in early June, to Tennessee's secession from the Union. Your father's granduncle, hotheaded old Dowland Dabney (he had killed two men in duels), house speaker in the legislature, was one of these leaders. The state of Virginia was going through the same trauma and seceded two weeks ahead of Tennessee."

Augusta laughed. "I remember Father's saying how you liked to brag about that."

"But you can see why I say this house is history, Gussie, and that I must behave toward it accordingly. What happens after I'm gone is quite another matter. Today's such a different world from the one I've known. You and your sisters may have other ideas about this place, may not care to take on these problems—like, for instance, trying to get more responsible help in here. The darkies, the reliable ones, like everybody else these days, have gotten very choosy. I hired Rollo, yes, probably, on faith, but also because Barnes is one of the few people out at that Gladstone with any sense. But the boy's only to be here anyway until he gets over what Barnes says is some difficulty or other he's had with his studies. Heavenly Father, I can understand that. Oh, that place out there —I can imagine something of the poor boy's predicament. They teach *French* out there. *And*—though over your father's angry remonstrance—the Elizabethan drama. Heavens!"

Augusta was laughing. Her mother was not.

"But Rollo," said Dabney, "will probably have to be going in the army soon, anyhow. I haven't talked to him about it but it's a wonder he's managed to stay out this long. What I should have done, I realize now, was talk to Barnes more carefully, in greater depth, about all these various angles and complications before I hired Rollo. But I didn't. I may regret it."

"You know, Mother, sometimes you worry me." Yet Augusta was all smiles.

33

SPRING, AUTHENTIC SPRING, though late, had arrived at last—with a warmer sun, fledgling grass, honeysuckle, hydrangeas, azaleas, the sweet perfumed air, and garter snakes. Impishly, chauffeur Sampson stood in the door of the garage behind the Dabney house smoking a cigarette and chewing cloves. He would not, however, let himself get near officious cook Phoebe (of the 250 pounds and balloon derriere) coming from the smokehouse with a side of bacon. He was determined today not to give her the opportunity to detect his breath. He knew she suspected the usual—gin—even if he had had only a taste, certainly not enough, to himself he argued, adversely to affect the performance of his duties.

Why don't you get yoh big ass on back in that kitchen, he thought, but of course did not say to her, instead of hangin' around out here in the backyard tryin' to smell my little gin so you kin run in there and tell her I'm at it again and not to let me git her kilt in some accident, which I ain't about to do 'cause I ain't had but a thimbleful, and it don't hinder me none—do it, now? You kin see I just got back with her, didn't I, from takin' her to make a talk at one of her Confedacy meetings. Ain't that right, now? How kin I be high, then? But, Lawd, wouldn't she skin me alive if I was and she caught me. Wow! Whew!"

Phoebe watched him, then came closer. "Hummph, just like I thought," she said. "I can tell by your eyes wobblin. That's your gin, I don't care how many cloves you done chewed. You better watch yourself, Mr. Big. You better watch *her*, too." She spoke as if she were reading his mind off a ticker tape. "Yeah, but not only her," she said. "There's somebody *else* around here you better be watchin'. That old boy Rollo's catchin' on fast, you hear me? *She* sees it, too—I can see it by the way she watches him, just like a hawk. And never gits after him about his work, like she does you, which is some kinda world record for her. He does his work, don't fool around none, and keeps his mouth shut. Besides, he's a college boy. Long as she's been puttin' up with your carryin'-on she just might be gettin' him ready for somethin' else, who knows?—like drivin' her big car for her. You guessed it—*he* don't drink nothin' but milk."

"Haw!" uttered Sampson. "You must think I'm the world's biggest chump. Well, I ain't. First thing I done when he come here was check out his drivin'. He kin drive, all right—a span of mules. So what's he goin' to be doin' behind the wheel of a great big long new shiny black Cadillac that ain't even got any numbers on the license plates, just letters—L-E-E! Tell me that."

"I ain't tellin' you nothin'," said Phoebe. "Can't nobody do that."

Meanwhile, inside the house, Cager, on his knees, was vigorously buffing the oak floor of the portrait gallery—when suddenly M. E. F. Dabney came up behind him before he saw her. "Rollo." He almost jumped. "Are you registered for the draft? I've been meaning to ask you why it is you haven't been called into the military service."

He straightened up, though still on his knees; then, seeming to himself to be kneeling before her as if she were some monarch, he awkwardly got to his feet and, shiftily, looked at her. "No'm," he said, "I'm not registered."

She frowned. "Don't you know you could go to jail for that? If you want to continue working here you'll have to obey the law and go downtown and register. The country's at war—I don't have to tell you that. My grandson, who is your age, just arrived overseas, in Europe, to fight. But you wouldn't even be required to fight, for you'd doubtlessly be sent to one of the service supply units—far behind the lines. So the least you can do is go register."

He reflected on this. And finally said nothing.

"What about all those other boys out at Gladstone?" she said. "Have any of them gone?"

". . . Some have." He spoke tentatively, though.

"But not many, I'll bet. Well, tomorrow you go down to the draft board in the courthouse and do your duty—get on the rolls." She turned to go on.

He stopped her, though, by pointing up at one of the portraits over them and asking, "Who's that, ma'am?"

She looked. "That's General Jackson." But she was impatiently

186

sidling away as she spoke, though adding, "General Thomas Jonathan Jackson—Stonewall Jackson."

". . . Oh," he said, his eyes widening in awe, *"that's* who that is, is it? I know about him but never saw his picture. He's from Virginia. He was killed at Chancellorsville—yeah, yeah." Next he pointed to the adjacent portrait which hung directly above the long, gleaming bayonet fiercely affixed to the interminably long Enfield musket. "He's from Virginia too," he said eagerly—"General Lee. I know quite a bit about him."

She at last returned and, reverently, gazed up at Robert E. Lee's white-bearded, unruffled countenance. Suddenly then she turned and said, "You studied about him out at the *college?"*—her voice harsh, unbelieving, though also as if a yes answer might in her estimate somewhat redeem Gladstone.

"No'm," he said, "in high school—back in Virginia."

She stared at him. *"I'm* from Virginia," she finally said. Then with a quiet dignity yet a slight arch of the chin—"My forebears have been there since, you might say, almost the time of Captain John Smith and Pocahontas." She did not smile. "One should always be proud of being a Virginian. It's had such a long and fruitful history, and produced so many great men—including more presidents than any other state in the nation. Then of course there was General Lee. . . . Ah, no more can be said after him. What part are you from?"

"The tidewater."

"Well . . . indeed. So was my father." She spoke gravely. "He was born near Elberon. And my mother in Smithfield."

"My father sharecropped on a place between Rescue and Moonlight," he said. "That's not too far out from Smithfield. We were closer to Cook's Grove, though."

She sighed. "Most of those names are no longer familiar to me. It's been such a long, long time."

Leaving him standing there with the piece of buffing wool in his hand, she continued toward the library. He followed her. But unaware, she entered, sat down at her writing table, and reached for a sheet of stationery and her gold fountain pen. Meanwhile, as he could never refrain from doing whenever in this room, he stood staring around him in wonder, amazement, at the four great high walls of books—most of them in some respect or another about war. They hypnotized him. She looked up now and, startled, saw him standing almost directly over her. Instant displeasure showed on her face—at both the intrusion and the presumption.

187

"Ma'am," he said—it was almost an accusation—"you got more books here than we got in our whole library out at Gladstone."

She bridled and reddened. "Your trouble out there is not the paucity of books. It's the kinds of books they are. Impractical, foolish books—*French*, my goodness! And Shakespeare. Greek mythology, social etiquette, the so-called African 'civilizations.' That's what's wrong out there—and not only the library but the whole college. Now, please leave me—I've got work to do. And don't you forget about going to the draft board—tomorrow!"

Somehow he did not move. Rather, he still stood looking at her, not challengingly, not defiantly, only knitting his brow as he wrestled with the problem, also as if debating whether or not to articulate it. Finally—"Yessum, I'll go register, but to tell you the truth I'm not too interested in *this* war." He stopped and swallowed, as if to garner strength, indeed the daring, to say more. "This war," he said, "is not the one I carry around in my head all the time. Sure, ma'am, I think about war, all right, the past ones and the future ones, too, but not much about the present one. This war's for other people—you folks." He spoke quietly, sincerely, even confidently, as if what he was saying was so patent, so logical, it was unarguable, something she would see at once if only he took the time to spell it out. "We're not like you-all," he said— "we don't have much stake in this war. That's why we got to start raising an army of our own. I hope I, or somebody that's got more on the ball than I got, will be able to do it. We'll fight *our* war, then. Do you know the writings of General Karl von Clausewitz? Do you get what I'm saying? I'm dealing with how my people can get the wherewithal, and the know-how—the *power* is what I'm talking about—to wage *our* war, wage it to victory. You can see that, ma'am!" He was almost pleading now.

The utterly shocked and dumbfounded expression on her face had first caused it to blanch. But as the anger, then outrage, hit, it flushed an engorged ruby red, almost purple. Now, her jowls quivering, she snatched off her pince-nez. "What in heaven's name are you talking about! Where on earth did you learn such absolutely stupid drivel! Out at that Gladstone? No, I don't know that German's writings—I never heard of him! And, no, I don't get what you're saying! Or maybe I *do* and see how dumb or insane you are—really both! You talk of raising a nigra army, fighting your own war, winning some kind of silly minstrel-show victory, I guess. Is that it? Good God! 'Wherewithal!' 'Know-how!' 'Power!' 'Victory!' Have you lost your childish mind? Well, let me tell *you* a thing or two! You've already got your 'power'! You've already won your 'victory'!" She was pointing wildly toward where they had just come from. "You got them when those generals out there in that hall-gallery could no longer hold off the Northern hordes that so outnumbered their barefoot, starving men and overran our prostrate Southland!" She was shouting, almost shrieking, now. "They destroyed our way of life, completely and forever, and impoverished us till this day! *That* was your victory! And it was won *for* you, not *by* you! Your fancy notions, wherever you got them, are asinine! Absurd! Actually, they're laughable if it weren't for the gall they show. So now you—and 'your people,' as you call them—are living on the fat of the land and in the greatest civilization that ever existed at any time or in any place! And you—and 'your people'—are here only because you were brought here and placed down in the very midst of all of it! Certainly, a little of it was *bound* to rub off on you—not much, but a little! Yet that's when you began getting all your fancy, highfalutin ideas!—that you could demand the rest, or go about raising an army of your benighted shirttail nigras and take it—instead of thanking your lucky stars you'd been exposed to any of it! Otherwise today you'd be running around somewhere over there in the African bush in a loincloth with a bone in your nose!" She stood trembling. "Now, you listen to me! My grandson is over there somewhere in the very thick of the fighting, while you, and those others out there at that Gladstone like you, are whiling away your time reading Homer and Voltaire and playing squash! Well, I won't have any of your preposterous nonsense in *this* house!" She was shouting again. "You get down there to that draft board tomorrow and register or else take your clothes and leave here now! At once! I mean every word I say! *Now, that's all!*" Apoplectic, she waved him out—as frightened Phoebe and Sampson, even old Caleb, peered around the corner from the base of the stairs.

Sampson finally turned and grinned triumphantly to Phoebe. "Don't look like to me she got him in mind fuh anythang—'cept maybe lynchin'."

Cager left the library. But he had been strangely numb, could not feel anything. Her sudden savagery had surprised him, left him limp and ineffectual. At last as he had left her presence he was stooped, his head bowed, and he shuffled as if partially paralyzed. He seemed less resentful than bewildered, then finally numb again, though soon once more utterly confused, as if, due to his own fault, he had somehow failed to get his point—a point to him so clear, logical, so rational—across to her, convince her he was right. The anger, the bitter hurt, and then the fury, like the delayed fuse of a time bomb, would come only later.

34

AT HIS NOON BREAK he was anything but hungry and refused Phoebe's food. Instead he climbed up to the tiny cubicle in the servants' third-floor quarters he called his room and sat on the bed for a while—still dazed from her insane outburst that morning. It had taken him completely unawares, though now he realized he had, even if unthinkingly, provoked it. He was still numbed by her fury. But soon after she had driven him from the library he, hastily, rashly, had concluded he should come throw his few clothes in the suitcase, forget it all, and go home to his mother before she left the farm to live with his married sister. It was no use, he thought; all of Haley's fancy, ingenious plans had misfired, and now there was only the sting of defeat. But then his consciousness seemed suddenly plunged into conflict, struggling, warring, within itself, as he found himself at last overwhelmed by this recurring impulse to stay just long enough to complete what in the past few weeks he had, stealthily to himself, come to call his "education" in this house—that is, his feverish use of her library. How, *possibly*, he thought, could he go off and leave certain of these great war books unread?—books and other materials so crucial to his (on-again, off-again) mission. That afternoon, wrestling with these trials, he worked in a fog.

Finally, that night, lying across the bed in his pajamas, he tried, stubbornly, to read, think, concentrate, thus shield his mind from what, ironically, it at last seemed prepared, indeed almost eager now, to accept—namely, that he had no alternative but to stay awhile longer. He *must* accomplish the immediate task he had set himself, he thought, as, symbolically, he gazed at the Civil War book, titled *Morgan's Raiders*, in his hand. It, like the other books and documents he now regularly (temporarily) "borrowed," had come from her library downstairs. "What I must *not* do, though, damn it, is panic," he told himself. "I can't let her get the best of me again like she did today. I got to keep my shirt on, 'cause she's got what I need, what I got to have, in some of those books and papers down there. Lord, Lord, that library's a *gold mine* for me! Whew!—all those history books, and biographies of the generals, memoirs, and other things like that, battle strategy and tactics, maps to illustrate them, and all that! It's a godsend, man! So I just got to go on and put up with her ranting and raving for a while. I also got to learn to stay out of her way, not aggravate her like I did today, not even get in any more conversations with her. Instead just bear down on these *books* of hers. I hate to say it—when I think of Haley and all he's done for me—but now it's good-bye to Gladstone. That campus is history now. I'm finally studying at Dabney War College. From there, Lord willing, I'll get my train back on the track, tackle my mission again, no matter about my condition, all I've been through, and what Flo did to me. I got to overcome all that. Sure, I'll go downtown in the morning and register for the draft if that's what she wants. Hell, that's no sweat. But they'll never get me. They'll never take me and put me in *their* damn army, when pretty soon I'll be putting one of my own in the field—*if*, that is, things work out after I stay here a couple or three more months and cram the books I already got picked out down there in her library to study. Huh? But I got to work at it, can't fool around, got to burn the midnight oil, stop goofin' off, no more feelin' sorry for myself. Yeah, I got to finish a *crash* course, man! There's no way, though, I can stay here any longer than that— three months at the most. Otherwise it would kill me. I'm suffocating as it is! Then I'll shake the dust of this damn cracker town off my feet, like recently I've been planning to do, and take off up to Chicago and my recruiting drive. I mean to pull off a *miracle*, man! Huh? *Ah, Chicago!*"

To go back. This dramatic change in direction had begun only two weeks before. Chauffeur Sampson, of all people, had unwittingly been the initial catalyst. Entering the garage one day with a bag of trash for disposal, Cager had come upon the seated Sampson so engrossed in reading a strange newspaper—including its huge bloodred headline—that he did not hear Cager approach. Soon Cager, silent, curious, was peering over Sampson's shoulder. The lurid headline read: BLACK SOLDIER IN UNIFORM BARELY SAVED FROM MISSISSIPPI MOB. "Whew!" Cager said before he thought.

Sampson almost jumped out of his skin. "You git outa here!" he whispered fiercely, snatching the paper protectively to his breast. "You damn sneak, you!"

"*Samps*, listen, man," said Cager, "where'd you get that? . . .

What kinda paper's *that*? Let me see it." Wide-eyed, he was already reaching, and soon they were wrestling, Cager's trash on the floor.

"Git outa my face!" Sampson stage-whispered. "You wanta get us both fired? And maybe beat up in this town besides! Let go, boy. . . . This sheet's dangerous! Let *go*, I say!" Cager finally desisted. "Ain't you got any damn sense at all?" Sampson said. "Why would I be slipping and reading this thing out here in the *garage*? This rag's dynamite, that's why! It's *The Hawk!*—a nigger weekly outa Chicago. You ain't never heard of *The Chicago Hawk*? Boy, you're *really* country. But if you don't know about it, you better hurry up and learn—to stay away from it, that is. My simple-ass brother up in Chicago keeps sendin' this thing down here just to be braggin' about all the great, the terrific, things he claims we're doin' *up there*, but so *down here* I can get my head bashed in if any of these rednecks was ever to catch me with this sheet—to say nothin' about what *she'd* do!" He nodded toward the house.

This, then, was Cager's sudden, rude introduction to *The Chicago Hawk*. By both cajolery and threats, he eventually induced Sampson to let him take the paper upstairs to his room to read, and there, merely scanning the sensational front-page editorial, he was thenceforth transformed. "Our Negro people here in Chicago," said the editorial, "unlike in many other places in the nation, are *alive* to what's going on around us. We are not asleep! We see and we understand! We are no longer passive and gullible! We *make* our opportunities, then *seize* them, and we urge other black communities, North and South, to do likewise! In the last six years Chicago has *organized*—throughout the Negro section—and the bigots are on the run! Here every black enclave has its own constituent organization, each with its leader, assistant leader, and governing council. These councils have recruited what they call their 'day-and-night watches' to protect their people against possible outside marauders and backlashers. Yes, it *is* a paramilitary operation! We make no bones about it, or apologies for it! We've found it's the only way to salvation and our rights! There will now be change, or hell to pay, one or the other! It's up to *them*! The time for weakness is past! We now look only to *strength*! We exhort Negro communities throughout the nation—and especially in the *South*—to emulate our example! Our watchword now is, yes, STRENGTH!"

Cager was beside himself—on fire. He began walking the tiny floor of his room, chattering and babbling to himself like a highly excited, addled magpie. "*Oh, man!* That's what I been saying all along! *Somebody's* waking up—finally! Good God Almighty!" He grabbed up the newspaper again and began reading, devouring, other parts of it—only then to have the query hit him of how he would now be able to get future issues. At once he was plunged in despair. No answers came.

One result, however, was his redoubled effort, his zeal, in his studies. In his room each night some new book, treatise, or other document, all smuggled up from the library downstairs, was eagerly examined. On one such night, among other things, he opened a dusty, brittle, old scrapbook, whose dry mucilaged spine required his gentlest handling, to find an item of telling interest. He first found inside the usual early Dabney family photographs and snapshots, now musty and faded, numerous party and wedding announcements, a few pressed flowers, brown and dried, pinned to the pages, and a variety of yellowed newspaper clippings. Then he saw the surname Dabney in the caption of a 1923 clipping from *The Atlanta Constitution:* MRS. DABNEY DELIVERS RINGING CONGRESSIONAL APPEAL. The story began: "The second day of the United Daughters of the Confederacy's Atlanta convention was made memorable by the stirring address of Mary Eliza Fitzhugh Dabney, wife of Tennessee Appeals Court jurist Nathan P. Dabney. Mrs. Dabney's impassioned attack on the anti-lynching bills now pending before Congress brought the convention to its feet—women as well as men—with shouts, cheers, and applause." He slammed the fragile scrapbook shut and pitched it on the bed. "Sounds just like her, all right," he muttered. "She ain't changed a bit, either. I gotta read her war books and get *outa* this place!"

He leafed through two bound books now, put them aside for later attention, and picked up a third, whose title, *The Families of Man,* had intrigued though puzzled him as he had plucked the book off its shelf downstairs. What, however, had impelled him to bring this nonmilitary title up to his room was his recognition, from frequently handling her outgoing mail, of its copious annotations and margin comments in the unmistakable handwriting of his employer. He opened the book now and was scanning the table of contents, when he realized he had noted neither the author's name nor credentials. Going back one page then, he read: "By Professor Merriweather R. Stimson (1803–1862), College of William and Mary." "Ah, the Old Dominion," he said to himself.

"It is altogether feasible and useful," wrote Professor Stimson at random page 83, "to take, say, the following simple and unassailable proposition—indeed mainly because it is truth: There *are* families of mankind. But who can contend that amongst them there is unity? It is all to the contrary. Plurality is the key factor here. Each family (of mankind) is different. It can be said, however, to be a phenomenon which indeed may be of lesser complexity than most investigators, heretofore interested in this vital question, might at first have thought. This is because that before we even come to the respective abstract capacities of the human brain amongst these various, above-referred-to families, we are compelled to recognize the vast divergencies in the outward physical attributes of the subjects. Who can dispute this?

"If, then, there are such inordinate differences in the outward, the physical, characteristics—the skin hue, hair texture, nose, the lips, the legs and feet, and, beyond all that, the cranial conformation—how then, according to this, do we find the aforesaid families grouped? There are but three categories possible. They are called, in the scientific language, 'proto-types.' The cranium of the true Caucasian, for instance, bears the shape of the smooth egg seated on its smaller cone. That of the Mongolian the likeness to a pyramid. But the negro shows us something vastly apart from either of these. Indeed, he is called in the science texts 'prognathous man,' an expression deriving from *pro*, meaning 'before,' then *gnathos*, meaning 'jaws,' or 'mouth,' all having reference to the head, which slopes sharply back from a facial jutting jaw. Or, to cast it in an alternative mode: the mouth coming before the brain. (Are we not all—to be not entirely humorous, either—familiar with this symbolistic penchant of the negro's?) His 'prognathous' head shape then gives him the physical profile of some of the lower species—the gibbon (genus *Hylobates*), the ape, the brute, for example.

"Yet, beyond doubt, he is an authentic human being, though woefully, organically, strapped—his mouth extending out well beyond the frontal portion of the skull, which latter, as is well known, houses the cognitive lobule of the brain, or, to state it alternatively, the conceptual capacities of the type or genus. This, it need not be said, is his grievous lacking. Who amongst us has ever encountered a negro capable of abstract thought—of conceptualization? It is true there are some mulattos, a few octoroons, say, having something akin to this capability. But the pure, unadulterated negro—prognathous man—no, never. The genus can no more contradict itself in this than the leopard may change its

194

spots. It need not be added that the deeper implications are both pervasive and momentous."

Cager suddenly began blinking his eyes. Soon he seemed either on the verge of crying or going blind, all the while—his lips drooling spittle—feverishly whispering, "Oh, God! . . . *Oh, God!* . . . Oh!" For a moment then he put the book down, feeling the necessity to rest, to spell himself, from the force of its ghastly hypotheses. He only sat there now, weaving from side to side, salivating and mumbling, as the weak ceiling light bulb seemed casting the room in an eclipse, a sinister gloaming, before he opened the book again—to another random chapter, captioned: "A Dissection of the Theory of the Prognathous Genus, Or a Vital Answer to the Vast Northern Hypocrisy."

In his incredulity and outrage he was about to slam the book shut, when on the flyleaf he saw what until now he had overlooked, the book's gift inscription, in the ancient ink now mottled, brown, and faded: "To my beloved son, Nathan, from a loving and, it is to be hoped, instructive father." (Signed) "Josiah West Dabney, February 10, 1879." Then below it, in a much later, and bolder, scrawl, the ink only now yellowing: "In turn, to my beloved wife, Mary Eliza, I pass along from my father, of fervent and affectionate memory, this most excellent and influential book of science." (Signed) "Nathan Poole Dabney, May 28, 1921."

He then went forward in the book again, finding a plethora of pages where the said "Mary Eliza" had heavily underscored certain words, phrases, sentences, even, twice, whole paragraphs, together with frequent lengthy annotations and emendations, indeed one in her audacious hand across the top of the page and down the vertical margin, this time in red ink: "This passage," she writes, "clearly shows that in the importation of the African to our shores our colonial, and later, forebears, out of sheer material greed, committed a most fundamental and horrible sin against us, their heirs and posterity—*indeed betrayed us!*—having no thought for the country's future and immense promise but only for their own grasping avarice. They took no pains to foresee the terrible fire storm of a war among soverign American states, hideous and tragic in its proportions, which would result from their greedy rapacity. Nor in their wildest mercenary dreams did they anticipate that these hordes of blacks—God-abandoned, helpless wretches all, who breed like flies and who will soon overwhelm and inundate us all—that they would one day be freed and made full-fledged American citizens, *forever,* thus sowing the seeds of the nation's eventual, *but certain,* oblivion and foreclosing for eternal time to come all its former glowing promise of achieving that pure and unique state which can only be truly described for what it is, *Anglo-Saxon civilization!"*

Later that night—near 3:00 A.M.—he had his first nightmare in the Dabney household.

35 NEXT MORNING, reeling from sleeplessness and fatigue, still dazed by the experience of the night before—which had then been eclipsed only by the horrendous nightmare—he finally reached, just after ten o'clock, the second floor of the courthouse downtown. To his surprise and puzzlement he found a crowd of people. They were milling around in the hall outside the entrance to the draft board's office—from which a great cloud of plaster dust now billowed. Was it some sudden catastrophe? he wondered—or just workmen tearing the place up under the guise of repairs? But why the crowd? He moved forward to the edge of the onlookers and, taller than most, peered directly into the office.

Heavy, ancient ceiling plaster had fallen, most of it apparently only minutes before, plummeting to the floor in a hail of detritus and rubble. Now there was much scurrying about by the office's personnel as, decorously as possible, they tried to shoo off the curious while attempting to clear chairs, desks, and file cabinets, of the debris, as well as minister to one of the typists, a scrawny red-haired girl who, though apparently not really hurt, had been showered by much of the lighter fallout. Shock, consternation, and confusion reigned, however, though there was also some laughing when it was finally determined that no one was injured.

Suddenly then from inside the office, from the very midst of the swirling dust, clutter, and disorder, burst, like a racehorse from the starting gate, a seedy, greasy scarecrow of a black man covered with plaster dust. "The sky's fell in in there, folks!" he cried as he tried somehow—as if the abrupt disaster had interrupted him in the Jim Crow men's room—to adjust his suspenders underneath his grimy jacket as he ran. "Judgment Day's come!" he bellowed. "The Lawd's tryin' to tell us somethin' about this old courthouse, heah?" Coughing, laughing, flapping his arms, he railed, "Git

196

back, folks, git back! This dust'll kill you ef the fallin' ceiling don't! It's the devil to pay in there! Sure won't be no draftin' done heah today! The Lawd's stepped in, y'see, and stopped it. He's shuttin' this whole operation down for a while—all the killin' and maimin'—and puttin' a hex on this sinful old courthouse itself where all these hundred years and more so much dirt to *certain* peoples has been did. You'all heah me?" he laughed again, though it was really a grimace. An indulgent titter went through the crowd nevertheless.

Cager, still staring at him, suddenly stiffened, then began scowling—the scowl of positive recognition. At once he wanted to turn and flee downstairs, back out into the street—as if some far worse calamity than a falling ceiling impended—for he had just recognized old Joshua, the street vendor of toy Trojan horses, who now, for weal or woe, had reentered his life. At the moment, though, he seemed only able to stand there and watch the exhibitionistic old scarecrow.

A laughing white man in the crowd now called out, "Joshua, where was *you* when the lights went out?" The crowd laughed again.

"Mist' Dawkins," cried Joshua, "I was thinkin' about how to git down to that cellar, suh!" He then wilted in a sycophant laugh.

"Are you talkin' about the cellar of this 'sinful old courthouse,' as you call it?" asked Dawkins, unsmiling.

"Sho am, suh," said Joshua. "Any ole port in a storm." At that moment he looked over and saw glowering Cager on the edge of the crowd. "*High Pockets!*" he cried, rushing over—as Cager recoiled. "Lawd, ef it ain't ole Slim again! So you finally come to register to go help Uncle Sam, eh? Well, I got news for you. You're too late! You ain't needed—you ain't even wanted no more. We already got more'n enough colored boys for stevedores and truck drivers! Too late now for you, Slim. But you oughta be glad, too. The Lawd has closed us down heah for a while—even for the young white fightin' men. The sky has fell in on us. I tell you the Lawd works in mysterious ways. He do, now, for a fact!"

Chuckling, Dawkins called out to Cager, "You follow *his* advice, boy, and you'll end up in jail a draft dodger. Old Uncle Joshua here's crazy as a loon—been that way for years! Calls himself a draft board official and carries around phony papers to try and prove it. But he cain't. He's just a broom pusher around here, and part-time at that, when he ain't outen the street sellin' a bunch of knickknack junk and toy animals to colored folks, tellin' them his junk's *alive*, that his birds—*his larks!*—sing and his plastic pigs squeal, and his horses get stole and messed with, and all that kinda crazy stuff. Even thinks he can foretell the future. Haw!—says someday a colored boy's goin' to be president of these *Dis*-United States! Now you *know* he's ready for the kookhouse. So, watch him, High Pockets—don't let him get you in front of old Judge Ramsey and a wool-hat jury. Haw-haw-haw!"

"I kin foretell him this, though, Mist' Dawkins, suh," Joshua said. "That he'll never be drafted. We kin get him signed up all we want to but he'll never serve a day in the service. Not only that, but from this day fouwerd—this goes for *all* you-all!—most of the writs and summons issuin' from this place, this ole courthouse, this ancient pile of stone, brick, and mortar, will be null and void! It's Gawd's will and I'm foretellin' it! Don't you smell that brimstone in all this plaster dust, Mist' Dawkins, suh? This ole courthouse that's been standin' right heah since way back in slavery times, it's gonna go one of these days just like that ceiling in there went. This was a tiny sample, a 'sign,' of what's gonna come, and it's already way past due, *now*! You're gonna see more dust and rubble and bricks and stone and tore-up oak beams than you ever seed in your natural life, Mist' Dawkins, suh. This ole courthouse, that used to have slave pens and slave auctions right outside the front door, will be no more. Yassuh, I foretell it. It'll be the day of reckonin', *of judgment*, suh. We got a little taste of it today, but only a taste!" He turned to Cager. "What you so frownin' and worried about, Slim? When it happens, ef you got any sense, you'll be long gone from heah—and to a happier place, I hope. *You* kin smell that brimstone, I bet! Ah, I kin tell you smell somethin', all right. It's *their* ole courthouse, not ours. We won't be losin' nothin when it goes, heah?" He stepped and placed his grimy hand on Cager's shoulder. "Don't take no chances, Slim. Git outa this town!"

Dawkins loudly guffawed.

Cager still stood frowning and bewildered, looking first at Dawkins then at Joshua. Abruptly, then, he turned on his heel and went off down the corridor—past the closed courtroom, the judge's chambers, jury room, sheriff's office, and finally down the stone stairs and out into the street again. A grim expression had come on his face. He first looked at his watch, then headed up Forrest Street—his destination the railroad station.

Fifteen minutes later, seated on a hard bench in the station's small Jim Crow section, he faced a wait of almost two hours before the Chicago-to-Memphis train was due. But it gave him needed time to think. He was trying to get a handle on all these complicated things happening to him recently. He knew, though, he must—without fail—return tomorrow, when the draft board would be functioning again, and register. He could not afford the risk—in the face of his truculent employer—of failing to do so. For he knew he needed these few precious weeks ahead in which to play out to the finish his crucial role of student in her house—indeed, the books! The station wait now seemed interminable and soon, his heavy fatigue getting the better of him, he dozed off and slept. Much later, then, he was aroused by the stationmaster's loud, harsh call—of the Memphis train from Chicago. Bestirring himself, he rose and went out with the others.

Although the train was not yet in sight, he heard its shrill whistle blow for the Terrence Street crossing and knew that, momentarily, it would be rounding Culpeper Street bend and heading into the station. Somehow he no longer felt his fatigue. In fact, he was alert, his heart beating fast, expectantly, maybe too much so for the smooth execution of the coming effort he had set himself. His mere being here on this concrete station platform, doggedly pursuing such a nebulous idea, was enough to unnerve him, especially when he thought of what it involved, its wider implications, and that right now it, not a little, frightened him. How would his proposition be received? he wondered. Or was it so unrealistic as to be silly? Yet, he thought, he had racked his brain for any other way to no avail, and now felt forced to try what he here hoped might work. It was important.

As he walked down the platform, the giant steam engine, pulling in, finally ground to a halt and, all down the line, the Pullman porters alighted with their portable steps in hand to assist the departing passengers. Already confused, he approached one porter while the man was still busy helping riders and collecting his tips and was promptly ignored. Up front then he saw a U.S. mail truck pull up to one of the baggage cars to load outgoing mail and to receive the incoming and now felt less rushed although no less jittery. He stood aside and waited. At last he sighted an idle porter two cars down and at once left to talk to him. By the time he got there the man had been joined by a second porter. He went up to them. "Can I talk to you'all for a minute?" he said nervously.

199

They stopped their conversation and observed him. "Yeah, go ahead," finally said the first one.

"Is this your regular run—Chicago to Memphis?" asked Cager.

Again they looked at him.

"The reason I ask," he said, "is that I wanted to make an arrangement with you to bring me a newspaper out of Chicago each week. It's *The Chicago Hawk*. Man, that's a helluva paper. Do you know about it? I'd pay you."

"Lord, yes, I know about it, *been* knowin'," said the same porter. "Who ain't? I've *read* it. No, I wouldn't want to get involved in anything like that. First thing, it's too much trouble. But most of all it's dangerous. Don't you know these white folks down here ain't gonna let no damn wild nigger paper from up in Chicago get in the hands of these black peoples down here, puttin' all kinds of crazy ideas in they heads and wakin' them up? You better believe they ain't—no indeed."

"That's *right*," said his friend, nodding vigorously. "It's too much of a hassle just to get throwed in jail for or your head bloodied." He shook his head. "No dice."

Cager looked glumly at them. "Okay," he said. "Thanks anyhow."

He left them and went on to the porter at the next car. With the same curt result. After still two more futile tries with other porters he gave up. Besides, now, the train was ready to pull out. He finally left for home.

When he got there he at once sought out Sampson in the garage. "Say, Samps," he said, "do you think your brother up in Chicago would send us that paper on a regular basis if we paid him?"

"Boy, have you lost your weak mind?" said Sampson, gin on his breath. "Ain't nothin' you'll stop at, is there, to get yourself—*and me*—in trouble. After you took that paper away from me, I wrote him and threatened him with death if he ever sent one of them things down here again. Forget it!"

Forlorn Cager said nothing.

"Say," said Sampson, "there was a guy, colored—a little sawed-off sonofabitch—here lookin' for you today while you was gone. He had a package. But didn't say anything about who he was, and I sure didn't ask him—I don't pry into folks' business 'cause I don't like 'em pryin' into mine, if *you* get what I mean. When this little runt found out you wasn't here, though, he wrote a note and put it in the package, then scooted. I took the thing upstairs to your room."

Cager gave him a puzzled stare, and finally shrugged, then left and went up to his room. There he saw the large cardboard box on the bed. Cautiously, he removed the twine and lifted the lid. Whereupon, the dazzling contents almost leapt out at him—the colors! He experienced utter disbelief. Then came the sadness.

It was a uniform—the beautiful gray-green tunic of the resplendent outfit he and Shorty George had designed for the, alas, now-defunct "drill unit"—and he knew now, even before reading the note, who the "runt" was who had brought it. Shorty's hardly decipherable note read: "Dear Cage, who in hell would have thought it? The damn uniforms turned up after all. Wouldn't they?—now that we ain't in business no more? It sure ain't what some people call the luck of the Irish. That dumb Togo Jackson finally found out his brother-in-law—he must be even dumber than Togo—had went in the car trunk for something and saw the uniforms and took them into the house, get this, *for safekeeping!* He had hung them back in some old dark closet and forgot them. They been there all this time. Anyhow, I went through the stuff and picked out this jacket, which, long as it is, must have been the one Nate Goldberg measured you for, and took it to my restaurant, expectin', sometime or other, you'd drop by and I could give it to you—especially after Nate, as a donation to what we was tryin' to do, wrote off the balance of what we owed him, and also after you sent the 175 dollars, which was damn nice of you and sure did come in handy at a time I was really up against it; restaurant rent was so far behind they was getting ready to throw me out, but this money order kinda eased things. When you never came by, though, I looked up your sidekick Meshach and he told me where you was now. Well, take it easy, and come to see us—you act like you're mad at me, when, what we been through together, we oughta be friends for life. Am I right? Say, my wife's got a new kid on the way—it'll be here in a couple of months. Lord, another mouth to feed, but we're damn glad just the same. So long, then, old man. Best of luck in the world to you. Shorty."

Cager groped for the chair and sat down. He thought of Hortense Bangs and where her money came from. He was undismayed, only thankful. He also thought of Shorty. And Nate Goldberg. But all that was too late, he thought. He was moving on to higher things now—ah, Chicago.

201

36

IN THE PARLOR, seated in the Hepplewhite chair, she was listening to her daughter. "It's true, Mother"—Augusta tried her best to laugh—"I did it. I was just that desperate, that lonely, for him. Oh, I miss him so much. And I'm always thinking of when he was growing up. What do you make of that?"

"It's only natural," said Dabney. "Johnny is such a wonderful boy."

"Yesterday I got out all of his old high-school stuff. Even the football clippings, the year when he was all-state end and caught all those passes. He was certainly the talk of *this* town. Then—oh, my goodness—there were the 'bug books.'"

"Don't I know?" Dabney said. "The crawling things."

"Johnny's zoology notebooks. Oh, I went through them all. It was Ned who used to laugh and call them the 'bug books.' The drawings are amazing. They're so precocious. All the insects, the centipedes, spiders, ticks, and of course the grasshoppers—they're all there. I'd really forgotten how meticulous he was, so painstaking. I was fascinated. Then it only made me feel worse."

"You forgot the snakes," Dabney shuddered. "And the lizards. I'm glad he outgrew entomology and now, like his grandfather Dabney, will pursue the law."

The parlor was ablaze with the afternoon sun, its searching rays finding the remotest corners of the fine old room and suffusing even the heavy damask draperies with its pale golden light.

"Ned used to tease him at dinner until I stopped him," Augusta said. "He'd say with a perfectly straight face, 'John, what would happen if one of your grasshoppers and, say, a black widow spider—which afterwards eats its mate, you know—were to get together?' 'A male or female grasshopper, Dad?' Johnny would ask, ever so seriously—he was only thirteen then. Ned would laugh uproariously, 'Why, male, of course. A female wouldn't be mating with a black widow, would she?' Johnny would smile indulgently, as if to say, 'Come on, Dad, stop putting me on.' Then, to explain, he'd rattle off a string of scientific terms none of us knew anything about—except for a few, I couldn't pronounce them even if I remembered them. 'It's a little more complicated than you make it, Dad,' he'd say,—'The black widow is combative but at the same time very self-protective. She's afraid no matter what the sex of the other creature is. She has all her delicate defensive apparatus to worry about, whether they'll do their job and protect her—the pedipalpi and spinnerets, the cephalothorax, and also the pedicel, of course. On the other hand, a grasshopper, even a male—unless it happened to be an albino, which is very rare, but which, naturally, in this dangerous situation, would be scared half to death—would probably by then also be checking its getaway gear, to make sure everything's in order, maybe almost as fast as the albino, with its antennae, and the two tibiae, its claws and mandible too, as well as the hind wings. This is pretty much what would be going on, Dad.' Ned would laugh his head off (he was so happy and proud), but finally, feigning astonishment and wonder, he'd say, 'Oh, I see. I hadn't thought of *that*. Very impressive!' Oh, how the girls, especially little Sarah, would squeal with delight at the table—cheering their brother on. But Johnny would only smile, knowingly, smugly, and observe, 'The truth is, though, that a black widow and a grasshopper, especially if it was an albino, wouldn't meet at all, or it's very unlikely. It's practically like they were segregated off from one another. They're so different, you know—their worlds. As different as whites and nigras, for example. Or, better, maybe as day and night. It's more than just custom, you know. It's nature's system of regulating things, keeping things straight and functioning—it's sort of ironclad, or Darwinian. Nature's very strong, Dad.' Oh, Johnny's such a brain, Mother!"

"He is that," said Dabney. "I'm sending him a book this week. *The Meditations of Marcus Aurelius*. He's ready for that now. I myself am no Stoic but men in war should know something about what the Stoics thought. I only hope now that somewhere over there it will catch up with him. *And* that he will want to read it."

Augusta's face showed her distress. "Oh, I pray day and night that he'll be okay. Even Ned prays now."

Suddenly a loud whir was heard somewhere outside the parlor. Augusta looked at her mother. "It's Rollo," said Dabney. "Well, he's fixed it. The vacuum cleaner's been out of commission. I was going to have it picked up and repaired. But he said he thought he could fix it and maybe he has."

"Has he had any more nightmares?" Augusta asked.

"Oh, my heavens!" An expression of frightened despair came on Dabney's face. "Don't mention that. He woke us all again the other night. It was terrifying. He's had two more now since that first one. I'm completely at a loss to know what brings them on. I've considered having Maxwell come out and talk with him, to see if he can pick up any clues, but Rollo might not cooperate if I took it on myself to have a doctor for him. He's quiet but he can be stubborn, too. In fact, I think sometimes it's gall—although you never really know what motivates him. But, oh, those nightmares—I have no idea what to do about them. He probably won't be around much longer anyway, though. He went down and registered for the draft, you know."

"I, for one, would feel a lot better if he left. It's pretty clear you're not going to dismiss him."

"Why should I dismiss him?—he's done nothing to be dismissed for. He can't help it about the nightmares. It's only when he's emboldened enough to start talking about what he calls 'his people,' the nigras, and the war effort, and all, that I want to wring his neck. He can say some of the most idiotic, asinine, maddening things!—*Oh!* He wants to raise and lead an army of nigras, but not for this war—to do what, though, God only knows! To fight *us,* I guess. When he gets on this subject he sounds like he's really demented—saying 'his people' have no stake in *this* war, that they've got one to wage of their own, or words to that effect. That's when I could kill him!"

But Augusta went into gales of laughter. "*Ha! Ha! Ha! Ha!* Oh, my! Mother, you and your chocolate soldier!"

"What you see so funny about it escapes me altogether," said Dabney. "He tries my patience with this tommyrot. He's picked it up out at that Gladstone, probably. Well, I'll bet he won't bring up the subject again to me. I read the riot act to him the other day. He'll never forget it, either. I completely lost control of myself. I was thinking of all we've done for the nigras in this country, even if they were in fact brought over here as slaves, and, despite everything, how lucky they are just to be here, that I may have said things to him I shouldn't have. But I was furious. Well, they certainly aren't slaves *today,* when you look at that radical NAACP and all it's doing to wreck the country—with nobody doing anything at all to curb it. It's a terrible development! Be assured I gave your chocolate soldier a tongue-lashing he'll never forget!"

"As you hinted at, though, Mother, he may be a little off in the head—disturbed in some way."

Dabney shook her head decisively. "If I hinted it, I was wrong. I don't believe he's mentally disturbed at all. He's just muddled. It's his fanciful but untutored mind. Plus that awful Gladstone. But I've got to continue to try to help him—as long as he's a servant in this house. It's an obligation I have, a tradition of our family—of our class, really—which we can't shirk or ignore."

Augusta's face grew long. "If you ask me," she said, "this whole thing has been strange from the beginning. The way you hired him. You really didn't need him, even if his work is satisfactory, for you could have put a stop to Sampson's and Phoebe's continual loafing. You went on and hired him, though, just like you had no choice in the matter, almost as if it were something . . . oh, I don't know . . . something you were helpless about."

Dabney bridled. "I was *not* helpless. Barnes said the boy needed a change of scene. I could have said no. But that would have been wrong without knowing more of the facts, and now that he's connected with this household I can't ignore him and his problems. Especially those horrible nightmares! Something's weighing on his mind—he may have burdens we don't know anything about. Long ago I learned from my father in Virginia about our responsibilities to our people—our nigras. I've never forgotten it. We have a duty, he always said, a solemn obligation, in fact, to help them. To be firm but always kind, for they—even the Bible says so—are less fortunate than we."

Augusta gazed at her mother adoringly. "Yes," she said, "and you taught that to all of us, too, just as Grandfather Fitzhugh taught it to you. It's so compassionate and high-minded, Mother. It's really noble."

Dabney, though, still looking perplexed and grim, said nothing.

37

THERE FOLLOWED NIGHT AFTER NIGHT the implacable, voracious routine he had set himself as he sat bent forward in the straight chair beside his bed, reading, reading, poring, over the fierce martial texts plus a constant, almost nightly, rereading of his lone, now fragile, issue of *The Chicago Hawk* which he studied in order to sustain, recharge, his faith, maintain his sense of direction—Chicago. But the puny ceiling light brought a squinting, then an aching, to his eyes, often causing him to have to stop and rest them. Yet he persevered. Nor did the books, documents, and mementoes from the library downstairs treat only of generals, forced marches, river fordings, frontal assaults, or other tactics and strategies. Many were histories, ancient and modern, also memoirs, going even as far back as the campaigns, military and political, of "Andy" Jackson. He found them all gripping and read with the close myopic zeal of the Scholastics, of Saint Anselm, say, or the "Seraphic Doctor" Saint Bonaventure. It mattered not that the yellow light bulb in the ceiling was so weak it still caused his eyes to throb and burn. He merely went out the next day and bought a glaring 150-watt bulb, secreting it alongside the "borrowed" library contraband he kept hidden in the bottom drawer of the ancient chiffonier in his room.

It was during this time that he made yet another discovery. Dusting one day in the library downstairs, he came upon this nondescript-looking little book, privately printed in 1924, its author one Cynthia E. Ambrose, which attracted his attention mainly for its odd and ungainly title—*The Day of Bloody Treachery in McNairy County.* At first he thought it dealt with the Indian wars. But opening it, he saw at once, to his astonishment, the name of the august personage who had written its preface—none other than one Mary Eliza Fitzhugh Dabney. Stealthily, he whisked the book upstairs to his room and that night read its mere ninety-two pages nonstop. It was to be the night of his final obsession.

Yet, even after four successive readings he still could not penetrate what he sensed to be some vivifying, subterranean meaning in all that Cynthia Ambrose was trying to say—or, as it were, trying to rid herself of. Indeed, he wondered if she herself had fully appreciated, grasped, the core—actually, the burden—of the mystery. He only knew now he could not part with this evil little book and, after each reading session, would stash it underneath his mattress, there to keep company with his one cherished issue of *the Hawk.* Nothing, though, had ever filled him with such scalding anger yet exaltation—but then always utter bafflement. Nor did Dabney's passionate introduction throw light on the central enigma.

"I know first-hand," prefaced Dabney, "of the painstaking researches and labor on the part of our own Miss Cynthia Elizabeth Ambrose, my respected and scholarly colleague in our Shiloh Battlefield Memorial Association, that went into the writing of this book, and it is only fitting that its publication occur under the imprimatur of our Association. For it is a phase of our history, in that it records a terrible event, another ordeal, suffered by our people in that great War Between the States. It, moreover, took place on the very eve of the Battle of Shiloh itself, indeed not

206

thirty miles from its memorable and bloody site. Yet, it is not easy for us here now, in 1924, sixty-two years after the event, fully to comprehend the shocking difficulties, the anguish and desperation, of those times. It is true that slave uprisings, if not common, were certainly not unheard of—the famous case of Nat Turner in my own state of Virginia at once comes to mind—yet, no matter, they were rare. But the dreadful crimes of the Tennessee slave Ofield Smalls, chronicled in this short history, may well, in time, and as a result of Miss Ambrose's persevering investigations, become as notorious as those of the infamous Turner.

"Ofield Smalls was a most peculiar negro. He hungered after a way of life that God never intended to be. In his heart he did not consider himself a slave. Indeed this baleful aberration was the wellspring of all his infamies. The seed idea of his depredations did not come to him from dreams or visions. Nor was he a religious fanatic, or unhinged. His cold purposes grew out of a strange, brutish (African) quasi-mentality which quickly reverted to its natural bent. This was of course violence, bloodshed, barbaric savagery. Into his gory scheme, as well, he recruited a dozen or more other, neighboring, slaves of his own ilk. In his infested brain's intriguing he saw his masters, the hapless Smalls family, as minions of the very devil himself. What an irony—what a *tragic* irony! For the Smallses were known far and wide for their leniency and humanity, their succor, their ministrations to their slaves, field as well as house slaves, and for their courageous, sometimes— many thought—officious, unwelcome, counseling of the same in others.

"Another sorry aspect of the despicable Ofield's plotting was that it would be carried out at a time when almost all the able-bodied menfolk, including even overseers, were away at the War and the whole plantation establishment managed by the women-folk and juveniles, with the inept help of the few slaves still loyal. Such was the situation and environment in which Ofield Smalls initiated his grisly work, which not only at last ended in his own, as well as the other miscreants', terrible—and just—deaths at, finally, the hands of our soldiers, though not before the senseless butchery by the black wretches of the Smallses, women and children, master and faithful slaves, alike.

"This slim volume, then, is a frightful but faithful account of the havoc which one primitive mind, leading others of like inclinations, could wreak on its imagined enemies, only because it was a

207

mind which foolishly groped after a conception of things impossibly beyond its natural and God-decreed limitations and ken. All in the name of a mirage—*freedom*! By her labors on this invaluable book of local, yet universal, history Miss Ambrose has rendered us greater service than she, a self-effacing and overmodest person, knows. For what she shows us here is not entirely without its applicability and timeliness today. Indeed, this is its great value and, as well, its worthiness to be studied by every true believer in the old virtues, the settled values, that were once our Southern mode of life and is still our imperishable heritage."

Cager was powerless to speak, or utter a sound, even to himself. Instead he was numb.

In his room two nights later, the powerful 150-watt bulb notwithstanding, his eyes were aching again, but now from the cruel focus, the intensity, of his rereading of Cynthia Ambrose's text in his dogged search for answers. Illogically, nonetheless, he got up and put on his hat as a shield not against the glare but his demoniacal emotions. Soon, in his agitation, he found himself frantically jumping back and forth among the various chapters of the book though by now he knew them all almost by heart. When he finally leafed forward to chapter 5 he felt, all over again, the same seismic shock as before. The chapter was titled "God's Own Charity to All."

In it author Ambrose wrote, "The Smallses' slaves were seldom if ever whipped—after a succession of overseers had been discharged for this infraction—and many of the house slaves were even taught to read and write, in clear and perilous violation of law. The Smallses were also a religious, a most pious, family. Indeed, certain of their slaves were sometimes chosen to be taken with them to church on Sunday and sent up into the loft at the rear of the church to hear the sermon and, actually, join in the hymn singing. Then on returning to the plantation after the service they were read to from the Bible by their master, the aged Obediah Smalls himself, who in the kindest tones possible reminded them of their good fortune to be living and working on his plantation where God had so blessed their joint endeavors. Then their rations for the day were doubled and they feasted on suckling pig, greens, corn pone, and apple cider. What more could they have wished for, even dreamed of? Yet, it was *this* very setting, and *these* very people, the good Smallses—it can only be said to be the most baffling of mysteries—that the evil Ofield selected as the object of his crafty and bloody villainy. Why else would this of all families have been chosen for the gory slaughter? The readiest—if still unsatisfying—answer is that it may have been thought that the Smallses, because of their humaneness and piety, were weak and defenseless masters, easy marks, lending therefore the highest promise to Ofield's murderous schemes. This may in fact have played some small part, yet, surely, it cannot have been all of the wretch's deadly motivation. It was something far beyond that, something perhaps more delicate, ominous, more fine-spun, but consequently also less accessible, in its vow to say something. It was as though the Smallses had been chosen *because* of their good works. Indeed, *singled out!* It was as if the fiendish Ofield was in this way mightily striving to make what can only be called, as hereinafter a chapter in this book is titled, 'A Higher Point.'"

He could not read on. He could not bear it. He closed the little book and, with trembling hands, let it drop on the bed. What *was* this hateful woman talking about? he again, for the n*th* time, asked himself. She was clearly confused, he thought. She was wandering, befuddled, groping for an answer, or answers, just as he himself was. But he had not written the book, *she* had. So she should have had answers. How, though, could *she* have known what Ofield, by what he did, was trying to say? He, Cager, only knew now that somehow, somewhere, across all these years, that Ofield was speaking to *him*. He also knew that he loved this brave, noble titan of a black man whom these two terrible women had so falsely, damnably, slandered by calling him "slave." Yet he loved him with somehow a strange and powerful envy. He reached for the book again and held it in his shuddering hand. Consider, he told himself, how preposterous that these two wicked women, one of whom, at least, still survived, at that very moment, in fact, slept only a floor below him, could think they could possibly have understood a man like Ofield, much less the profound message of his acts. Whatever that message was! Would he ever . . . *ever*. . . know it? The question stirred him. It also made him think. What *if* he were to come to know it? What then? . . . His thoughts would not go on.

He raised the mattress, once more deposited the book beneath it, but alongside *The Chicago Hawk*, and went to bed. The nightmare came late. But it came. Thundering. He heard jarring the very earth the loud summoning drums of Toussaint's legions and cried out in his nightmarish ecstasy—"*Chicago!* . . . I must hurry!"

209

38

IT WAS NO WONDER, then, that the next morning he overslept.

Just after nine, old Caleb came cantankerously pounding on his door. "Missus wants to see you in the liberry. You dead or sumpin?"

He jumped, sat straight up in the bed, then rolled out running—to the servants' bathroom to wash and become presentable. When, without breakfast, he presented himself to her in the library, she was at her writing table and at once put down the gold fountain pen. "Rollo," she said, "You are ill." It was a pronouncement, a judgment. "There can be no question about it. You should have heard yourself about four o'clock this morning. It was appalling, absolutely unnerving! Another sign is that you're late this morning. That's certainly not like you."

He looked away. ". . . I overslept." It was all he could finally think of to say, and that hardly audibly.

"That's apparent. But you're ill. Tell me, is something badly worrying you—that makes you have those horrible, chilling nightmares?"

"No'm. . . . I don't think I'm worried too much."

"I must ask this, then. Has your life been extraordinarily hard? Could this be a carryover from that? Did you have an unhappy childhood? Or has anyone, white or nigra, at some time or other, mistreated you?"

He pondered this and grew crafty. "No'm, I don't think so." He was stalling for time to throw her off the scent. "I may worry about my mother sometime. We don't have much of a family anymore since my father passed. My mother lives with one of my sisters in Norfolk now. I probably shouldn't have come back here but stayed home and taken care of her."

"It seems to me," said Dabney, "that anything would have been better than your coming back to Gladstone. I've wondered why you ever chose to come here in the first place. All the evidence indicates that in your case it wasn't a very wise choice. You've somehow become a very mixed-up person. Those awful nightmares prove that. We've got to try to do something about them and you must cooperate. I think, though, just your being *here*, even if you will soon have to be going into the service, will help you immeasurably—here in a quiet, well-ordered house, where you're not under strain of any kind, and so on. Also, I may want you to

210

answer some questions for Dr. Maxwell when he's here some-time—about your condition. Will you do that?"

He was saved in the nick of time by Caleb's entrance. Caleb crossed the room and, sniffing irritably, glanced in Cager's direction as he whispered something in her ear.

With a look of grave displeasure she turned to Cager, saying, "Someone wishes to speak to you on the telephone. You may go take it but return at once as soon as you've finished."

Puzzled, he glumly followed Caleb out. Soon, though, he was tingling with curiosity, then anxiety, and finally fear. Who, he wondered, would be calling him here? Venomously now, Caleb supplied a partial answer. "Some *woman!*" he hissed. "Use de pantry phone."

Soon, alone in the pantry, Cager heard the familiar voice. "Rollo, I know I shouldn't be calling you there," said Flo, "but it was the only way I knew of reaching you. Where on earth have you been? Why don't you call me once in a while? I get uneasy about you—especially when I don't hear from you for so long. Maybe there's no reason for me to worry, but I do. Even little Annette asks about you. I tell her you've got a new job that keeps you busy, which sounds silly, for she knows you don't work day *and* night. You may not know it, but you need me, Rollo—you always have and always will. I know I've caused you a lot of headaches—and heartaches too—but you yourself said it would never affect our relationship. Now, didn't you say that?"

"Flo, Flo!" he cried out, though whispering. "Give me a break, won't you? I *am* busy here—yeah, almost day and night. You don't know how busy I really am. I'm into some awful big things here—you better believe it—which, though, I can't tell anybody about right now. But, oh, Lord, I'm on the verge of something that would blow your mind. I'm thinking about going to Chicago soon—to live. Honest to God! Do you and Annette want to go with me—huh?" He laughed. "Look, but I ain't kiddin'."

"Rollo, you have lost you mind. I'm sure of it now."

"No, no, all along my mind's been lost. But no more."

"Oh, Rollo! . . ."

"Flo, you gotta believe in me, trust me. I'm leavin' this sad town, I tell you. Yeah, yeah, I might just take you and Annette with me."

"What in the hell are you talking about, Rollo! It sounds to me like you're in some kind of bad trouble. No wonder something's been telling me to try to get in touch with you. I can read you like a book, you know. Just like some people are accident-prone, you're

211

trouble-prone—you and your wild dreams and visions of power to rectify things. But you listen to me, now. You need me. That's why we've got to keep in touch with one another better than we have. Do you see what I'm saying? Now, tell me what's this talk about Chicago?"

"Flo, Flo, I can't talk any longer. This old woman I work for had just called me in when you phoned. I gotta get back in there. Have confidence in me. A little patience. You're still on *my* side, ain't you, baby?" He tried to laugh again.

"Rollo, you're hopeless." On this note the conversation finally ended.

When, hurrying, he returned to the library, Dabney had resumed writing letters. Silently, he stood before her, waiting—his heart pounding. Besides, he was faint from hunger. She spoke without looking up. "So, in a nutshell, Rollo, you've got to start rethinking, reshaping, your life, ridding yourself of all these bad influences you've acquired, many at that school out there, absolutely fantastic notions about some nigra army to fight for 'your people,' as you call them. In all my life I've never heard such nonsense. The influences in your life, whatever they've been, have obviously betrayed you." She finally put down her gold fountain pen now, removed her pince-nez, and sat peering at him. "You say, Rollo, you want to help your people, which is certainly a laudable enough aim, but in order to be a real leader, as you clearly wish to be, you've first got to be able to set an example for them. I'm sure you're aware of that. But what *kind* of example? That's the question. For that you've got to know them, really understand them, their strengths, yes, but especially their weaknesses—how to bring out the best of their peculiar gifts, and try in whatever way possible to make up for their deficiencies, which of course they had no hand in creating. This was all foreordained—set—for us all. It happened ages ago in the long, tortuous sequel of man back at that crucial time when the various races were allotted their respective roles in this world."

He stared down on her with a most painful look on his face. He seemed to want to interject some pleading remark of objection, even moving his lips, but then desisted.

"Remember," she said, "it is from the Book of Genesis, no less, that we learn that Ham was Noah's *second* son. This is full of meaning. But helpful, too, as we each seek to shape our lives, and the lives of others, in your case, those of your people. At this early stage of their development they also, as I say, badly need the right

212

examples, examples of thrift, sobriety, hard work, and especially common sense, which, as to the latter, I'm glad to say many of your people were born with. I believe you to be one of them, Rollo. But you must be careful not to allow yourself to become surrounded with the wrong influences—like having women calling you here on your job, for instance. That's certainly not a good sign. Tell me, do you give women your money, some of your salary? You have no expenses here, you know."

He faltered. "No'm," he finally said. "I don't give my money away." The moment he said it, though, he thought of the blind children out at Billups whom he now gave almost every cent of his salary.

"Well, I'm glad to hear you're careful in that," she said. "You're young and must start thinking about what you're going to do with your life when you return from the service. You'll be faced, you know, with having to get some kind of gainful employment. And there's marriage to think of, a family too of course, and all that that involves—church, community activities, and the like, and, yes, as you yourself wish, maybe even some leadership role as well. But, oh, my heavens, not *military!* Get that out of your system entirely. It's nothing short of lunacy. It's clear, though, you have ideas of one day becoming some kind of leader. And I really think you have some qualities for it. But right now you need direction. Goals must be identified to you that are very different from those you've so far been exposed to—especially the brainwashing you've gotten out at that Gladstone. Oh, that place—their attempts to teach *French!* . . . and Shakespeare, and calculus, and all that; even wanting to build a tennis court. Why, that present board out there must be a bunch of lunatics. It's certainly not like it was in the old days by any means—when my husband was active (and, I might add, *financially* so)—when they had a curriculum that made some sense for that particular student body." She waved a hand around now at the four high walls of books literally surrounding them, then fixed him with her penetrating gaze. "It's no scientific secret, Rollo—there are books up there to prove it" (as if he didn't know) "—that there are vast, yes, fundamental, differences among the various population groups on this big earth. It's not at all a subject to be squeamish about, or one to be ashamed of, or, most of all, angry about. It's merely, as I say, an age-old fact of life and nature. If there are clear, indeed conspicuous, differences in *physical* characteristics among some of the various groups or races—and who can deny there are?—what's so astounding or startling, then,

213

about equally discernible differences in their *mental* characteristics and capacities? I ask you that. The existence of the latter is clearly no more illogical than that of the former. Yes, it's God's ordinance, Rollo. He has His own designs, His plans, in this world, you know—which, I must confess, it's not always given to us to understand—and they are so immutable we've even come to call them *nature* at work. But it's merely *God* at work. And who are we to question *Him*? We must all, then, find our true stations, our natural roles, in life according to our gifts. You certainly never heard anything like this out at that Gladstone, I'll bet. And you won't. They're too busy teaching Ovid, Chaucer, and the Spenserian stanza! I want you to think about these things. It may help solve some of the problems—whatever they are—that are so clearly plaguing you, causing those deafening, those perfectly *mad*, nightmares. Think—*think*, Rollo—about some of these things we've talked about here this morning. They will help orient you, start you out on a new path, save you time and effort, maybe heartbreak, too. Will you do that?"

Like a hapless, condemned prisoner in the dock, somehow containing, suppressing, his blind fury, remembering, too, his vows of forbearance, he stood silently before her—finally even nodding mute assent. He was turning to go then, when, suddenly brightening, she called him back. "Rollo, are you at all musical?" He stared at her in bewilderment. "Do you play an instrument of any kind?"

"No'm," he at last replied.

"Maybe you sing, then. . . ." She sank into a starry-eyed reverie. "Among my fondest memories, as a child and young lady back in Virginia, are those of listening, especially at Christmastime, to our servants sing. They would all assemble before us in the parlor and, after unwrapping their presents, sing spirituals for us in gratitude. Oh, how beautifully they sang! How moving it was! Your people are very musical, Rollo, even if you personally aren't. It's a gift from God, a gift *my* people certainly don't have in such abundance, but which I don't feel the least bit sensitive, or inferior, about. I repeat, it's God's irrevocable decree, which we may question all we like but to no avail. In fact, you might be a lot better off, have a mind freer of torment, if you *were* musical, Rollo. Think about this also."

His mind by now was limp, depleted. "Yessum," he mumbled, and once more turned to go.

Only to have her stop him yet again. "From a remark you made earlier, Rollo, I glean the impression—and I hope I'm right—that you do observe the rules of thrift. That is, that you save most of your salary. If you do, you're to be commended. It shows seriousness and foresight, attitudes that should by all means be encouraged. There's no more useful precept to be taught anyone—and certainly not just your people—than frugality. Accordingly, I've decided to increase your salary. Substantially, if I may say so. As long, that is, as you continue saving it as you've apparently been doing. I want to make it clear, though, that this is *not* an act of charity. I rather prefer to think of it as a kind of moral investment —in you and your potential—as well as a token of the confidence I've come to have in your essential character."

His mouth partly opened. Yet no words came. Obviously straining to control himself standing before her, he shifted his weight from left to right, then back again, but could not bring himself to look at her. Finally, grinding his teeth, he said nothing.

"Is this agreeable with you, Rollo?" she asked. "If it isn't, you have only to say so and I'll understand. I very much admire self-reliance and personal pride."

Before he thought then he blurted it. "I haven't been saving the money you pay me, ma'am. I've been spending it, spending it all— no, *giving* it away."

She blanched, then frowned deeply. "I don't understand you. What *is* this? Giving it to whom?"

"To that little school for blind colored children," he said. "Out there on Ridge Street."

". . . Oh! Yes, of course—Billups. Billups Orphanage." Her stare was still stern, though, forbidding, and also confused. She finally waited for him to go on.

"It's supposed to be run by the state," he said. "But they don't give it hardly any money at all. The kids need everything. Mrs. Baker, the teacher and matron, can't get them most of the things they ought to have. I mean necessities. But there're only seventeen or eighteen of them. Yet the state don't do much even for that few. When I was at Gladstone I used to take them candy and knickknacks and a few things like that whenever I had the money. But since I've been working here I've been able to do quite a bit more—like getting the two or three barefoot ones shoes, or some of the others underwear, or toothbrushes, and a few school supplies sometimes, things like that." He seemed embarrassed and averted his gaze now—as if having just confessed to a series of wanton crimes.

She sat staring at him incredulously. "Well . . . I see," she said at

215

last, heavily exhaling. "Yes, those Billups children out there." Her expression became solemn now, almost grim, but soon, too, a trifle imperious, somehow as though she were bearing a jealous chip on her shoulder. Withal, though, she had become vaguely enigmatic —perhaps even to herself. There was a long pause as she studied him. She seemed as if faced with an absolutely unprecedented situation. "Well, I think that's admirable, Rollo," she finally said, though hollowly. "Quite admirable." But her hesitance, her inde- cision, appeared as though stemming from some deep, lurking displeasure, even envy; also as if here in a most crucial, because symbolic, enterprise she, the savior and conscience, the moral doyenne, of the whole civilization, had been suddenly taken by surprise, outwitted, upstaged, by a mere interloper, or usurper— this "nigra" houseboy. But almost at once, then, the more pragma- tic sector of her mind seemed trying to take over, capture the real, if nearly impenetrable, meaning of these his self-confessed acts— high noble acts all.

It was a turning point. Indeed a watershed. A central moment in her fading, dissolving life-force. He had set in motion deep, re- sidual influences the effects of which on her he would never know, could not even have conceived, much less understood. It was the interposition of something which in the end would cause her, fervently, to pray, then search out herself, as well as God's un- manifested will in the bargain. She had had, as it were, a seizure under the blinding light of fact, that of his *natural* virtue (hadn't she extolled nature's law?) coupled with the *purest* volition—this on the part of the tall, bean-pole-ungainly, crazily visionary black boy who scrubbed her antebellum floors. She had merely—for the brief remainder of her existence, and his—been eternally trans- formed. But, in essence, by what? By perhaps whatever had trans- formed (transfigured) Saul, who would become thereby the Apos- tle Paul, when struck down en route to Damascus.

39

SHE HAD NEVER LIKED HIM. Now she liked him even less —since he had metamorphosed into a prominent local lawyer with considerable political influence as well. To her he was still white trash. He was, after all, Barney (for Barnabas W.) Renfroe, son of old liquor-head Blacksmith Joe, who in turn was son of Dan'l Renfroe, a patroller and slave driver on one of the old Dabney plantations, near Somerville on the way to Memphis, and who, in 1863, was killed when shot off an ordnance mule at Chickamauga.

Even Barney's amused but perennial defender, her late husband Judge Dabney, had conceded all this. Yet Barney had been her lawyer even (or especially) when the judge was alive, and on his advice, if not insistence. This, however, was at a time when Barney was so invariably available and accommodating as to be almost servile. But the judge persisted in seeing much merit in him and had paid him, in the judge's view at least, the ultimate compliment: "He can get things done," he told his wife, if somewhat mysteriously. "He's a wizard at it. If anything were to happen to me he's the one around here I'd want to look after your affairs. He's a good lawyer but he also knows the right strings to pull. Oh, don't worry—he's honest enough. He's learned from experience that over the long haul it's only smart to play it straight, even if he might—no, I wouldn't put it past him—now and then wish to cut a corner. He didn't come from much but he's no fool and never has been."

But today Mrs. M. E. F. Dabney was inwardly furious. When she had telephoned Renfroe's office that morning, announcing herself to the secretary, she had been kept on hold for fully three minutes. This would never have happened in the old days, she thought, before Renfroe had begun to take on such airs. When, moreover, he finally came on the line, there had been no mention by him of her wait, much less any apology for it. Rather, he seemed still hurried and preoccupied, when formerly it had been his habit to laugh, insipidly, she thought, and briefly engage in small talk or an item or two of local gossip before getting down to her business. But not today. He was courteous, even friendly, yet, she was convinced, deliberately professional, in a way, she thought, only a parvenu can be. She was therefore unduly curt as she told him she desired his opinion on a legal matter and would much appreciate his stopping by her house at his early convenience—she had never in her life set foot in his office. Now, perceiving her frosty attitude, he quickly changed, reverted to his old self, and, with an unconcealed alacrity, told her he would stop by that very evening on his way home. She coolly thanked him and hung up.

He arrived shortly after five-thirty. Tall, in his late fifties, with an unhealthy stoop but a sharp, florid face, his loose-hanging, funereal clothes reeking of strong cigars, he greeted her warmly when ushered into the parlor by Caleb, who then looked shocked when what he considered this upstart visitor, having hardly taken his seat, asked him for whiskey—a bourbon and water. True, there was still guest whiskey (since Judge Dabney's death) in this now teetotaling house, but such a presumptuous request made before the present head of the house had even invited the imbibing of spirits in her presence, no matter that it was her own lawyer present at her bidding, was in Caleb's vast experience altogether (outlandishly) without precedent. Nevertheless, though sniffing his rank displeasure, he nodded to Renfroe that he had heard. Whereupon the lawyer, in an apparent afterthought, turned to Dabney. "I hope you don't mind, ma'am. This has sho'lly been a rugged day in the office an' I'm just beat as I can be. Trouble is, I need more help. Business has got so heavy this year." He laughed. "But I guess I oughtn't be complainin' about *that*, ought I?" He took off his glasses and polished them vigorously with his handkerchief while with his now naked eyes he squinted hard at his hostess. "Know one thing?" he smiled broadly, ingratiatingly, then. "You're sho lookin' mighty well. *Somethin'* must be agreein' with you, Miss Mary Eliza."

Dabney flushed crimson. He had never before dared address her by anything except "Ma'am" or "Mrs. Dabney." His gall riled her. "To get to the business at hand, Mr. Renfroe," she said, "I want to discuss with you an idea I have almost formulated. It's a plan, really. Although as yet it's perhaps tentative, I've decided I should explore with you the *legal* aspects of it. It has to do with—"

At that moment Caleb returned with a decanter of whiskey, a crystal glass, ice, and water on a silver tray which he deposited at Renfroe's elbow. The lawyer's hand went up in an expression of extreme pleasure. "Thanks a million, Caleb," he said, seeming now to have forgotten Dabney completely as he poured himself a heavy spate of bourbon over the ice, splashed it with water, and took a generous sip. Soon, though, he again turned to her. "Now, Miss Mary Eliza, will you please go ahead with what you were sayin' befo we were so pleasantly interrupted? Ha, ha!"

Dabney, her face inflamed, spoke quickly, harshly. "It has to do with Billups Orphanage. That's the school out there on Ridge Street for blind nigra children. I want to do something for it."

Slowly, very deliberately, Renfroe put his drink down.

"The state runs it, of course," she said, "but in name only. In fact, it does so little to support it, it amounts to gross neglect."

Renfroe had become markedly subdued, actually grave, ignoring his drink altogether, as he sat observing his client. "I thought they'd closed that place down," he finally said, "and put the few pickaninnies around in cullud private homes. But it's still goin', is it?"

"Barely," frowned Dabney. "It's in a very bad way. It needs even the barest necessities, which the state should be providing—items of clothing, school supplies, better heating of the building in winter, sometimes even nourishing food. I want to arrange to provide it with some financial assistance. But because it's a state institution I'm not sure whether that would be legally permissible. This is what I wanted to talk to you about."

Renfroe still sat studying her. Seeming at last, though, to remember his drink, he reached for it again, but, before sipping, held it for another thoughtful moment. "Ma'am," he said, "I see you're not askin' my advice on what we call in the law the '*merits*' of the matter. I mean the basic feasibility of doin' what you've got in mind. What you're askin', if I understand you right, is more or less what we term a procedural, or adjective, question. Sho'lly you're not inquirin' whether it's somethin' you oughta be doin' in the first place. All you want to know, I take it, is whether by law the thing can be done. If it can, then you probably intend to go ahead and do it. Am I right on that?" He smiled, but when, glaring at him, she did not even deign to reply, the smile, though fading, became somewhat acidic. "Well, ma'am," he said, "just let me say this, then: You can't give Billups money directly. You *could*, though, give the state of Tennessee a million dollars if you was of a mind to, but it would go straight into the General Revenue Fund. There it could be used for any lawful state purposes the guv'ner and legislature saw fit to put it to. But there's no guarantee—there's little possibility—that a dime of it would ever go to Billups. That's about the size of it, Miss Mary Eliza."

Dabney was now full of fight. "That may be the law," she said, "but it doesn't make a thimbleful of sense."

Renfroe was oblivious. "Ma'am, if I may say so with all due respect, your idea is not a very good one. In fact, I think it's a little unfortunate. I'm sho Judge Dabney—oh, land sakes, how I admired that man—would want me to speak frankly to you about something like this. And to think, next month I have the honor—I sho'lly so consider it—of heading up the annual drive for our local YM and YWCA. Our own kids need things, too, y'know. The two Ys, I don't have to tell you, a community leader, are mighty key

219

institutions in this town. They need help. The YW doesn't even have its own swimming pool. The YM has to set aside two days a week for the YW girls to come over and use the boys' pool. You can see, ma'am, that's not a good, a decent, arrangement at all. It's not worthy of our community." He finally smiled. "So, if I could be so bold, I'd like to ask you to consider helping out *these* institutions a little—especially when there's no state angle of any kind to complicate things legally and hamstring what you're tryin' to do. The community would once again sho'lly be grateful, ma'am, to one of its longtime—historical, I might say—leading families, one that has always been in the forefront for the betterment of our little city, if you could see your way clear to give us some help in our Y drive—"

Just then Caleb passed in the hall outside the parlor and Dabney, rising, called to him. "You may serve dinner now, Caleb. But first bring Mr. Renfroe's hat." She turned to the lawyer. "Then, I assume, Mr. Renfroe, your answer about Billups is in the negative, that it can't—legally—be done. Is that correct?"

Renfroe, his face more florid still from having now finished his drink, took his time about rising. "Yes, ma'am," he said, "that's about what it boils down to. I'm afraid, though, my opinion would be the same even if there wasn't any technicality with the state involved in this thing at all. I just honestly don't consider what you want to do as in any way feasible. I don't. So that's about the long and short of it, ma'am."

Dabney sighed. When Caleb returned with Renfroe's hat, she said, "Thank you for coming, Mr. Renfroe. And please don't take so long in sending me a bill. You may also call me when your Y drive gets under way. Good evening."

40

SOMEHOW AUGUSTA, her secret senses and anxieties—though for no solid reasons—strangely mounting, thirsted for information which, if it at all existed, certainly as yet had no point or focus. It was merely, at this juncture, something akin to an extrasensory intuition of some kind that was killing her. None of it, moreover, was to any degree allayed when that week she had twice phoned her mother, inviting herself over for lunch, only to be put off, told she was behind in her work and too busy. Whereupon, on

Friday, taking the bit in her teeth, Augusta made an uninvited pop call. Entering the parlor, she found her mother busy, all right—busy seated in the Hepplewhite chair, hands folded idly in lap, in a deep brown study staring vacantly out the window. Augusta, somehow not at all surprised, began the tête-à-tête with an adroit diversionary maneuver. "Mother, why do you always sit in that uncomfortable chair? No wonder you look unhappy. It's an elegant old heirloom, I know, but it's severe and straight-backed and designed to have no arms. Why don't you ever use any of these more comfortable upholstered pieces in the room?"

"It's not uncomfortable to me," said Dabney. "It was, as you certainly know, my mother's. Even before her, it had been in her family, the Randolphs, since before the Revolution. But when I married she insisted on having it shipped here for me. It dates from around 1765 in England and was of course made by George Hepplewhite himself. It's needless to say that I treasure it—of course I do."

Augusta had sat down, though all the while, furtively but intently, eyeing her. "Do you feel all right today, Mother?" she said. "I told you you don't look very happy—sitting there like that idly staring out the window."

"Of course I feel all right," said Dabney irritably. "I'm not in the business of looking happy, anyway. Take note of the world around you, of Europe in flames, and tell me if you're happy. You have a son over there, too, you know."

"Oh, why do you have to bring that up?" wailed Augusta. "As if I didn't know."

"And Caleb took sick again last night," Dabney said. "He loses ground daily, it's plain to see, but he won't give up, won't even admit anything's wrong with him, even old age. I'm sure he doesn't know his exact age but he's aware it's plenty—over ninety. He's staying in bed today, yet he won't let anyone do anything for him—even insists on coming downstairs to the kitchen for his meals, knowing that afterward he can barely make it back upstairs. I've called Maxwell, who's coming out to see him later today, but you know what Caleb thinks of doctors, that they're all frauds. But what if Maxwell wants to put him in the hospital—where even I know he belongs—and he refuses to go? He's stubborn as a mule. No one can do anything with him. Also, in the last couple of years, he's gotten meaner than at any time I've known him. But he always was haughty as all get-out. It's a good thing that all these years he's been under the protection of this family. Otherwise the

221

rednecks would have made it very bad for him. He's been utterly faithful to us, though—in his own cussed way passionately faithful—but well he might have, considering how we've put up with his ways. In the early days, when I arrived here a new bride, he would even have treated me like an upstart if I'd let him, which of course I didn't for one minute. My family, even if they weren't any longer as well off as they'd once been—which was never exceptional—could have thought the same of the nouveau riche, and less genteel, Dabneys."

"Why has he been like that, Mother?"

"It was the Dabney family. Your father it was, most of all, who indulged him, spoiled him, really, then made excuses for him. He used to say Caleb considered himself nothing less than a Dabney and acted accordingly—with nigras and whites alike. He was married twice, you know (though that's supposed to be—I don't know why—a deep, dark secret), and both times to high yellows. Your father, taking up for him, of course, said neither woman was any good—which may, or may not, have been true. What woman in her right mind could have stood Caleb for a lifetime? But I don't think he ever regretted not having had a successful marriage or a family. He's taken life as it came and, whatever he thought, has kept it to himself and never complained—although I think his opinion of the world in general, and mankind in particular, is not very high. He has no fear of death, either—of this I'm certain—although he knows it's fast on its way and will soon overtake him. The same applies to me, of course, and I'm well aware of it. There are times lately when I tire of still trying to hold things together, like this house and my organizations, as if they were all solely my responsibility, and find I'm ready to pass the torch on—the burdens, for that's what they are—to others now. But that's merely a sign that the Reaper is drawing closer—that, as the darkies say, 'Time ain't long.' Your father used to talk this way during the last year of his life, and Caleb, who admired him so—in fact I think he's the only person, man or woman, black or white, Caleb ever really looked up to—may well now be thinking similar thoughts. As at times I myself do."

But Augusta, frowning, seemed again on the verge of querulousness. "Heavens, Mother, whatever got you in this frame of mind? You seem so moody, and, yes, downright unhappy."

"I'm neither. I'm a realist. But, don't worry, I'm not resigning from life yet. I've still got a thing or two up my sleeve—unfinished business, you might call it—before I present myself to the Maker on the great reckoning day. If I say it myself, though, I've tried hard enough to be worthy, but whether or not I am is up to the Master Himself to judge. However, I'm still trying to improve the record—it's my daily preoccupation. In this connection, I had Renfroe over here day before yesterday. But, oh, that man! In the process he made me so angry I almost regretted I'd called him. No, no, it wasn't about my will—I've tampered with that all I intend to. It's something else—not a big matter, actually, although that goat Renfroe apparently thought it was—but something I want to do while there's yet time. Renfroe's gotten very important now, too, you know, takes on a lot of airs—until I've had to bring him up sharply a time or two to remind him of who *he* is and who *I* am. No matter, it's extremely unpleasant to have to be in his presence for long. I had to have him over, though, to discuss with him this idea I have. Frankly, it came out of a surprising talk I had some days ago with Rollo. It was quite by accident—I literally had to drag it out of him—that he told me he gives the salary I pay him, practically all of it, to Billups School for the Blind. That's that ramshackle little school for blind nigra children out there on Ridge Street. What he says he's been doing sounds incredible but I believe it. He's that way. It's extremely compasssionate and high-minded of him. But it bears out what I've thought of him for some time now. He's really unusual—in a way sort of messianic. He's not aware of it, of course. Just think of his doing such a thing—it's really extraordinary, when you consider he's had almost no advantages, no one to teach him these things or act as examples, and so on, things we were taught from childhood in the bosom of our family and take for granted. It shows that, with him, it's a gift, I think—don't you?"

But Augusta had long now had a look of deep concern on her face. "Yes, Mother," she finally said, "Rollo *is* unusual. This would certainly seem to justify your confidence in him. You must also realize, though, that he's definitely influenced you. Are you aware of that?"

Dabney looked appalled. "Oh, *fiddlesticks*, Gussie! Stop talking such nonsense. Well, anyhow, I wanted to get Renfroe's best thinking on whether my idea for Billups would hold up legally."

The worried expression on Augusta's face intensified.

"The state," said Dabney, "has sadly neglected the school. Rollo says, and I believe him, that the children need so many things, basic things. But it didn't take Renfroe long—after he'd had the gall to ask Caleb to bring him some whiskey—to tell me I couldn't

223

give money directly to the school by law. He didn't stop there, either. He proceeded, as he sipped his whiskey, to advise me on a number of other things I hadn't asked, or wanted, his advice on. And which, in addition, were none of his business. He went on to let me know, by a few unsubtle remarks—despite that he knew we'd given money for years to Gladstone, though a private institution (or maybe *because* he knew)—that he thought what I had in mind, meaning, giving money to yet another nigra institution, no matter how needy its circumstances, was, as he put it, 'unfortunate.'"

Augusta sat up. "Well, Mother, he's an experienced lawyer. Maybe he—"

"—What's something being 'unfortunate' got to do with the *legal* question I sought his advice on, if he's such an experienced lawyer? What, in his low-class presumption, he's really 'advising' me on is how I should live, order, my life, on my moral standards, on how I see my obligations! He began telling me how badly our YM and YWCA need money—for a swimming pool—to which I should have replied, but didn't, that those blind pickaninnies out at Billups often don't have enough to *eat*!"

Augusta too, though, was getting excited. "I know, I know, Mother, but apparently he *also* thinks there are real legal obstacles to what you want to do—despite your good intentions."

"Oh, hogwash! It would have been the same to him if everything had been perfectly legal. He's dead set against my helping the school, period. *He's* the kind those two-faced, self-righteous Yankees up North are always lambasting us about, lumping us all together with people like him. There are other ways, though, you know, that I can do what I want to do and I've hit on one. It's not a bit complicated, either. If I wished to, and I'm seriously considering it, I could, from time to time, give money to Rollo—but considerably more than he's been able himself to give Billups—and he could then see to it that it gets spent at the school for the right purposes." Augusta's gasp stopped her mother not at all. "It's an entirely workable plan, Gussie, and makes absolute sense, Renfroe notwithstanding. Rollo's by now proven to me he's got a lot of good, hard, common sense, and also that he's honest, can be trusted, all certainly to my satisfaction or else I wouldn't be thinking of using him in a venture like this."

"'Venture' is right, Mother—that's what it is!"

"Haley Barnes vouched for his character. In fact, that's why he's tried to help Rollo all this time, even if he doesn't vouch for some

224

of his strange ways and ideas, and I have confidence in Barnes. You say I'm right to call it a venture, but I'm not at all unmindful of at least the possibility that this thing could misfire. There's no doubt that Rollo is the key to the whole plan. But I have faith in him. Besides, the end here justifies the means. And I've prayed over it, Gussie."

Augusta sighed helplessly and gazed at Dabney. "Somehow none of this seems real," she finally said. "Have you talked with Rollo about it?"

"No, not yet. But there's plenty of time for that. Besides, something kept telling me to hold off for a while and I'm glad I did, for I keep forgetting that he's registered for the draft now and could be called up any time."

"Well, my heavens, where does that leave you?"

"Ah, that's where Renfroe comes in again," said Dabney. "Your father used to say Renfroe was such a 'wizard' at getting things done. Well, we shall see. I'm going to put it squarely to him to use some of that influence that everybody, including himself, thinks he has—that 'wizardry'—on the draft board and get Rollo a series of deferments, maybe indefinitely. Knowing Renfroe, and how he loves to impress people, especially us—I've also promised him help in his Y drive—I'm sure he'll find a way to do this. I have no qualms whatever about using the draft board, for the purpose of all this is to accomplish a far greater good. I tell you I've talked to God. I believe He understands it all, knows what I'm trying to do, and will somehow approve. Renfroe of course knows nothing of my plan to use Rollo in this, so will see no connection. No, I have no scruples at all about it. Rollo will be performing a far higher mission, and one he's certainly demonstrated his sympathy with, than if he were somewhere in the Army Quartermaster Corps lifting sides of beef off of a truck or washing dishes in some officers' club."

Mystified Augusta was shaking her head. "Mother, somehow you've changed," she said, now staring in virtual awe at Dabney. "You've never been like this. And no matter what you say—I know you're sincere, too—Rollo, not knowing it, completely in the dark, has influenced you. I said it before and I say it again. You've changed and *he's* changed you."

"Gussie, Gussie, please spare me your cosmic speculations. You've never been good at that sort of thing. I haven't changed at all. I'm acting perfectly in character. Why would I *want* to change?"

225

"Mother, you can't possibly see yourself like others, like I, can see you. You *have* changed, I tell you, and it's happened since Rollo came into your life."

Dabney looked shocked. "Gussie, it makes me wonder if you're quite bright. How could *Rollo* come into *my* life? I should think it a little disrespectful of you to say such a thing to your own mother. The truth is, I've come into *his* life. And he's the better off for it, too—I've been the turning point in that hapless black boy's life, I have."

Augusta merely shook her head again and stared incredulously at her mother. Finally—"Another thing, do you realize that in your zeal to do good, Mother, you may have lost some of your sense of direction?"

"Oh, how you love to complicate things, Gussie—instead of trying to see I'm merely performing a duty. There oughtn't to be anything so complicated, or extraordinary, about one doing one's duty. It's not only a matter of ethics and morality but of respectability—of class. Renfroe and his ilk could never understand this in a lifetime. Gussie, really, don't you also feel this way about some things—that you're different, maybe better, than most people. When you get right down to it, most human beings, white as well as black, don't stand for very much. When you take a hard look, they're rather unprepossessing, with so few qualities to admire; they're small and grasping, even morally ugly—nasty. They're slobs, actually. They of course don't realize this. But they could do nothing about it if they did. The only thing they can do is rail against those of us who're more gifted, mentally and morally, than they, not realizing that if it weren't for us, people who see their duty and go quietly about doing it—often at great sacrifice and the butt of envy, even hatred—that the whole fabric of civilized society would disintegrate and go under and they, the least gifted, would be by far the worst off, indeed first to perish. They should rather be thankful to us. God has made us all different, Gussie—races, classes, individuals—and He has His own purposes. I have faith in that. It has sustained me throughout a long life. I believe in it."

Futilely, Augusta sighed and looked away. "Yes, Mother," she said, almost meekly now.

"Gussie, I want, *I need*, your moral support and understanding. This is somehow a critical time for me, the most critical in my life maybe, though I don't know why. But I feel it. That's why I pray, why I commune with God, try to keep in close touch with Him. *But I haven't changed!* Who could change me but Him?"

Phoebe came in now and announced lunch.

"Only one thing more, then, Mother," said tenacious Augusta. "Even before talking to Rollo, shouldn't you first go out to Billups and take a look at the place for yourself—observe the pickaninnies, talk to any of the darkies in charge, and sort of assess conditions out there—before going any further with your plans. That way you could get some idea about what needs to be done, also about how much it would eventually cost to do all the things you seem to want to do—just how the whole thing could be gone about, and all. Shouldn't you do that?"

Dabney, who had risen to lead the way to the dining room, now paused to ponder this. "You may be right," she said, "—it may be wise to do that."

At once wily Augusta jumped at the opening. "If you liked," she said, none too subtly, "I could even go along with you."

"No, Gussie," said Dabney, "I can manage it. I don't want to make a big thing out of this and scare a lot of people. I'll just have Sampson drive me out there one day. Though that won't be soon—I'm too busy."

Augusta thought this somewhat ironical. Yes, she thought but did not say, busy sitting staring out the parlor window. Oh, Mother, I worry about you.

Indeed the moment that Augusta had left, Dabney summoned Sampson and ordered him to drive her out to Billups. Cager, of course, still knew nothing.

41

THE DEAD OF NIGHT. In his room, however, the cruel, now-hated, 150-watt light bulb—which he keeps hidden during the day but which now fairly blazes overhead—pulsates and palpitates as he reads the book not only by the jarring light's electric current induction but from the book's own transferred kinetic waves linked to his wildest visions and fantasies of Ofield Smalls (the hero's hero), mystery man of grisly deeds, wrathful retribution, but now dweller in the pantheon of true heroes and golden death. Of this much of the mystery Cager is certain.

227

The night is warm and, naked except for his shorts, he lies on his back on the bed as a solitary mosquito, having somehow gained entry, hums about his ear until he draws the bed sheet up over his long torso. But most of all he desperately clutches the little ninety-two-page book in his fist and squints painfully up into the throbbing illumination. Finally he rises, gets his hat again and, vainly swiping at the mosquito, claps the hat onto his head for some protection against the glare, as his body's sweat drips from his armpits. He does all this, though, as if by instinct, so engrossed and chronically agitated has he become in these night-after-night sessions poring over the fateful little book he has, if ambivalently, come to hate more than the light bulb, as he mutters his epithets at what he regards as Cynthia Ambrose's fatuous attempts at analyzing her protagonist's mind and actions and, in the end, Ofield's unfathomable yet titanic statement—whatever that was or seemed to be. The statement is the mystery.

As if he can no longer remember, remember that which is in fact forever branded on his brain, he turns back to reread, reponder, the book's now-despised title: *The Day of Bloody Treachery in McNairy County*. Bloody indeed! he concedes, but why call it treachery? Were they, the Smallses, so deaf, mute, blind, so utterly lacking in any semblance of mentality, that they could not see, or know—indeed, could not *fore*see? Again now he riffles through the book's sparse pages, at last stopping where he begins anew the short, baffling chapter which invariably engages him, grapples with him, sending up his temperature, and finally clutching at him, as if by the lapels, to shout its elusive message yet like some abstract but terrifying principle hovering just an eyelash beyond the reach of his comprehension. There it was—the chapter's still-enigmatic caption: "A Higher Point."

"The Smalls family," a later portion of it reads, "had married extensively into the rich though harsh Oglethorpes (not to be confused with the distant, more famous Georgia Oglethorpes), but had then lived to regret it. These Tennessee Oglethorpes were known for the severity of their treatment of their slaves, among whom they made few if any distinctions. The carpenters, wheelwrights, hostlers, and house slaves, as well as the far more numerous field hands, were treated generally alike—that is, not well, often cruelly, indeed at times brutally. This treatment, however, though inhumane in result, was deliberate, an established policy, on the Oglethorpes' part, though (a seeming paradox) brutality, as such, was not at all their chief aim. It had rather grown out of their wisdom and experience with slaves, especially with the negro's—if you will—life-view, formed in turn by his unique character, temperament, and experience, all three. The Oglethorpes knew that this, as it were, tripartite garment worn by the negro, quaint as it was (is) indestructible, and of purely African origin, made him less inclined to be resentful of this treatment than had he been coddled and pampered. This may seem yet another paradox but it is palpable truth, moreover having besides some strange, refined, and delicate, almost fastidious, aspects which till this day are not clear, but which somehow inheres in the negro's otherwise—so it is widely held though without necessarily my concurrence—obtuse psyche. Examine this case that I, Cynthia Elizabeth Ambrose, have in this book put before you. I hold there is little evidence of obtuseness, though much, indeed an excess, of savage, fiendish niceties.

"Yet in exploring this difficult anthropological phenomenon, if not paradox, we dare not confuse the African's very special, unique, psychological perspective on life and existence with that of our own, the Caucasian's. Theirs is something wholly apart, so different (though, as I view the evidence here, no less complex) as to be, to us, almost bizarre. Yet, as I say, in its essential characteristics it is most delicate and subtle. This is because it is centuries-inbred and not easily perceived without years of observation of, and experience with, the negro himself. I do not wish here, however, to strain credulity. It is not my claim that the slave did not feel real physical pain when punished, or when starved, or, for some infraction, left for a time outside at the mercies of the wintry elements. Physically, he *did* feel this punishment. Yet, when it was all over and the pain or discomfort had subsided, or gone, little, if any, true resentment remained. Why was this? you ask incredulously. To most it is a mystery, yet close study will reveal that the answer lies in how the African, or negro, viewed (or views) *himself*.

"Follow closely, please. He believed that his benighted existence on this earth, including the corporal punishment attendant upon it, was merely a manifestation of his true lot in life. He therefore regarded life as a given, something he was *put here* to bear, a manner of being, of existing, that it made no sense whatever to resist or resent. Even from the Bible he was taught by his masters, people like the Oglethorpes, that, as was mentioned therein, he, as an African, a true descendant, yes, of Noah's second son, was ordained to be one of the 'hewers of wood and drawers of water' of this world, that he could look forward at the end of this life only to

229

the recompense of some slum negrillo heaven—no grand ethereal paradise of winged angels, golden streets, and lilting harps for him.

"Indeed, it can even be quite rationally asserted that he himself felt that not only was this harsh treatment his due, but something which, under God's own ukase, he *deserved*."

"*Oh!*" cried Cager, like a jack-in-the-box springing up from the bed. "*Oh! Oh!*"—as if a dentist's drill had suddenly plunged into the pulp nerve of a molar. With all the violence dormant in his strength, now he hurled the book up against the wall and began moving, stumbling, around in the tiny floor space at the foot of his bed, spluttering wildly to himself, his eyes finally glazed with tears. Soon, however, as if irresistibly drawn by a lodestone or magnet, he went and retrieved the book and sat down on the bed with it in his trembling hands. He realized he was reacting as if reading the chapter for the first, instead of fourteenth, time. Yet, heart racing, he resumed.

"The Oglethorpes, yes, knew all these things," wrote Ambrose. "But, alas, the Smallses did not. They failed to understand how bitterly, even without knowing why, the slaves—who, in their hapless misfortune, considered themselves, in receiving any gesture of kindness or humanity, as being mocked, ridiculed, by both God and the Smallses—how bitterly they resented them. This was of course a poignant consequence. Yet, the family was tragically unaware—in their piety and compassion—of the powder keg on which they sat, the risk, the mortal peril, that daily encompassed them about."

Saliva now forming at the corners of his mouth, he sat literally growling, a grotesque, before heaping a spate of the vilest obscenities and abuses on the author despite his speculation that by now she must be long in her moldering grave—at least so he hoped. Finally he slammed the book shut and cried out to himself in utter despair: "Oh, I can't figure out *none* of this shit! Oh, Lord, it's getting me down! The only thing I know is that the woman that wrote this goddamn book was not only evil but ignorant! She wrote it but she didn't know anything about what the hell it meant! No more than I do. Probably not as much. Even *I* know that Ofield, in doing what he did, what he *had* to do, and well knowing that by doing it he was sacrificing his and his comrades' lives—as sure as the next day would dawn—was *telling us something*, yes, making a statement. Lord, if I could only get a handle on what it was.

"Ofield was most likely looking way, way, into the future somewhere. But, oh, these two terrible women! Neither one of them could see that. That Ofield *had* to do what he did. It was a moral necessity!—and all that that means. But what was the *statement* he was making? What was he trying to get across to us? Oh, Lord, help me to see it, grasp it, then to *use* it. I feel, I sense, something—something that that Ambrose woman sure didn't, *couldn't*, feel. No, no, that can't be right, either. Although she didn't grasp it either, she *did* feel something, because of the very title she gave the chapter: 'A Higher Point.' I only know, though, that Ofield was a mighty man, a great man—*my* man!—and I'll never give up till, some way, I find out where he was coming from, what he was saying, by what he did, what he *had* to do, before he went down in glory. Help me, Lord. Oh, how long, how much *longer,* do I have to go through the torture of this house? When will I learn enough from her evil but powerful books to leave here and try my best to begin my own mission—like Ofield, my *own* life's work? Will I, though, really be able to take charge, *do* the job . . . after what I went through with Flo? I need your help, Lord. Don't let me down. But when can I *begin*. Soon, soon, I hope and pray. Oh, how I *yearn* to leave here and come up there to you, Chicago."

It was next morning, then, that Dabney summoned him to the library and told him of her dazzling plans for Billups School for the Blind.

42

THE TWO WOMEN attired in black, sat well off to themselves in the rear of the dingy mortuary chapel, staring straight ahead as the short service proceeded apace and the portly black preacher, bald, toothless, a gold cross in his lapel, stood above the cheap coffin, its upper half open, and read the Scripture lesson from the Epistle to the Romans: "For he that is dead is freed from sin. If he be dead in Christ, he shall live with Him. Knowing that Christ is raised from the dead, he dieth no more; death hath no more dominion over him." The dull sun coming in at the two grimy west windows made dusty schematic patterns on the center aisle and on many of the folding chairs, predominantly empty, as Sampson, in his chauffeur's uniform and puttees, the gin on his breath again camouflaged by cloves, sat up front beside large Phoebe and tried his best to look alert.

Soon, however, the service over and the handful of "mourners," vacant-faced and unmoved, leaving, the two isolated women in the back stood as Sampson and Phoebe hurried to escort them to the shiny long black Cadillac outside. As they all finally got in and sat waiting for the hearse car to be loaded, Sampson, tittering, whispered to Phoebe seated beside him something about the makeshift service and the unknown preacher who had presided. Phoebe, however, mindful of the backseat occupants, dared make no response whatever.

But M. E. F. Dabney, leaning forward past Augusta, spoke sternly. "Sampson, on such an occasion as this how you find something to laugh about entirely escapes me. We shall all miss Caleb—I dare say even *you*."

"Oh, yas, yas, missus," said Sampson instantaneously. "Beg your pardon, ma'am. Sure will. Sure will miss him, thas for a fact."

"Mother," Augusta said, lowering her voice, "I counted them. There were only eleven there besides the four of us. It's shameful."

Dabney, for greater privacy, reached and slid closed the limousine's glass partition between the front and back seats. "Caleb wasn't well-liked by the other nigras, you know," she said. "He was arrogant with them, therefore had few friends. I myself am putting him away. I'm very disappointed, though, with what I've seen—everything so shabby and impromptu—considering what it's costing. I even had to pay Ferguson, the undertaker, fifteen dollars for that jackleg preacher, Tate, I think his name is, whom nobody ever heard of but who's probably a buddy, or coconspirator, of his, to come say something over Caleb and go out to the cemetery with us. You can see what short shrift he made of the service—twenty minutes, including poor Phoebe's solo, which I thought would never end. Did you ever see such a flimsy coffin? I thought I'd paid for something better than that—it looks like it's papier-mâché. I'm sure I've been grossly cheated. I also had Sampson bring Caleb's very best suit here to Ferguson for burying him in—at least I see he's doing that. But, oh, these darkies such as Ferguson! They're like children. But they can be mighty crafty, too. You've got to watch them every minute or you'll come out a loser."

"It's been a very disagreeable afternoon, there's no question, Mother," Augusta sighed. "Caleb would agree. Although only the upper half of his body was on view, it still was enough to tell by the expression on his face that he was very displeased—or at least in my imagination it seemed that way. He was lying there literally

232

frowning." As they still sat waiting, undertaker Ferguson, along with the preacher and two hangers-on—one of them a seven-foot giant—brought the coffin out of the chapel and placed it in the battered hearse. "But couldn't they have done something about his face," Augusta persisted, "—given it a more pleasant expression?"

"I suppose so," said Dabney, "but that stupid Ferguson was so busy powdering Caleb's face that he had little time or inclination to do much else to it. He had him looking almost white—like he'd dipped him in a barrel of flour or something. Powdering would have made Caleb absolutely furious, as if he wanted to be white, which is something he never had any wish to be, you know. Nor, for that matter, nigra, either—he didn't particularly admire them; except, possibly, Booker Washington down at Tuskegee, whom he thought was great. I agreed with him, of course, up to a point. Oh, Caleb was an unusual person, to be a servant. He was the last link with the past, Gussie—with the life and great tragic times of your father and his family, and of mine. Yes, I shall miss Caleb—very much."

The day was mild, the sun tentative, as the two-car cortege moved out and proceeded down Foster Street toward the town's outskirts and Mount Pisgah (the Negro) cemetery beyond. "Let's not talk about the past, now, Mother," said Augusta. "It makes you too gloomy."

"But it's a past that's dead, anyway," Dabney said. "How somber your father would be today, following Caleb's body as we are here." She sat starkly erect, dry-eyed, grim, pale. "Caleb, as he weakened there at the last, nevertheless knew everything that was happening. He and I had a very frank talk about it. I told him what Maxwell had said, that he was too old, too spent, to get well, all of which he knew. He only nodded his understanding, said nothing. I asked him if he wanted a minister—I was thinking of that nice old darky preacher, Simmons, from the little Methodist church down on Mason (not that criminal from Greater Shiloh Baptist, Bearcat Walker!)—to come out and pray with him. He shook his head no. He didn't seem troubled, or sad, just resigned. I hope I do as well. He was probably glad to be going, wanted to get it over with. I wonder what it's like to be a nigra, Gussie. They don't have an easy time of it, you know, not at all. It seems God's had it in for them for some reason—this *can't* be so, though; it wouldn't be just—yet they're the most religious people in the world. I wonder if God sometimes feels contrite about that. But Caleb wasn't very

233

religious—at least I don't think so; yes, he was just resigned. Proof of it is the way he even nodded his quiet assent when I told him I'd already selected his successor as butler—Rollo."

Augusta gasped. She stared at Dabney in incredulity. "Mother, you can't be serious—*Rollo!*"

"Well, isn't it the most logical thing in the world? Think about it for a minute. Of course it is. Besides, the job may be therapy for him. Maybe he won't be so harassed now all the time. It will be the quietest life he's ever had and may even get rid of those awful nightmares. You hadn't thought of that, had you? Well, I had."

"And you still insist you haven't changed, Mother? Why, some of your actions lately are absolutely beyond belief. You don't believe it's Rollo's influence on you? Sure, it's uncalculated—he's not aware of it—but it's *there*. As plain as a big red barn by the side of the road. You're only doing this for Rollo. You're not thinking at all about yourself, about whether, with all his crazy behavior and silly ideas, he's suitable for the position. Mother, I *do* worry about you—honest. Have you told him yet?"

That Dabney had not relished Augusta's lecture was plain from her stern, drawn face and her refusal to answer. They rode on in a chilly silence. "I told him yesterday," she finally said, sighing. "I must say, though, that at the moment he's still in shock. He seemed terribly upset and distressed for some reason; he looked actually stricken. I was surprised, frankly. It may be that he fears the added responsibilities, lacks confidence in himself, although I tried to reassure him about it, reminded him of the superb job he's been doing out at Billups—which he surely has—and how that proves he has real managerial ability, and so forth. I did my best to impress on him that it's only natural, then, that he should step into Caleb's shoes and take charge of the house. But he looked so pained I didn't press it anymore at the time. He's a strange individual. I brought it up again to him this morning and am inclined to feel he'll gradually maybe come around, though he hasn't given me an answer yet. Oh, Gussie, how tired I'm getting of all these obligations—especially of that great old house of our family's. But what choice do I have? None. My ties are there. You and your sisters were all born upstairs in that house. So was your *father* even. Think of it. It's a hallowed place. No, no, I have to keep on."

They were now finally entering the rough, hilly cemetery— Mount Pisgah. The decrepit hearse ahead bumped and jostled its way along the winding gravelly roadway between the rocks, brush, burdock, pokeweed, and briar on either side, as three of the men, utility pallbearers, rode crowded shoulder-to-shoulder in the front seat and the black giant—whom for convenience we shall, not inaptly, call "Colossus"—lay stretched on his stomach alongside the coffin in the back, his massive chin propped on his hoisted hand as he stared morosely, although also somehow philosophically, out the rear at the long, gleaming Cadillac following close behind.

Augusta looked worried and unhappy, saying, "I really had no idea what a disagreeable experience this would be. Everything's so primitive and unappealing out here"—just as, below them in a sharp depression, they saw the open grave. She shuddered. "Goodness gracious!" Beside the grave stood the wizened Negro caretaker, a blue bandanna handkerchief tied around his neck, as he drank from a dipper of water before heartily waving and smiling to undertaker Ferguson as if to a longtime friend. "I need a drink, too," sighed Augusta—"but not water." Dabney cut her an eye of acute displeasure. "Pardon me, Mother, but this has turned out to be a real ordeal." She waved around at the scene before them. "Do they call this a cemetery? Well, it's not exactly like ours, is it?— Calvary. Where's the green grass. Are there any headstones?—I don't see any, although I wouldn't expect mausoleums. Where, though, is the peaceful quiet—the repose?"

At last Dabney turned on her—severely. "My heavens! Gussie, at forty-four, you're still my youngest child, my baby, yet at times, when you make asinine remarks like now, I'm almost convinced you never really grew up. What an unkind, an unfair, thing to say. You are demeaning the efforts of people less fortunate than yourself, people who are making the best of a bad lot, doing the best they know how under great—natural—handicaps, and shouldn't be ridiculed, much less spoken spitefully of. It's not only unkind, but slightly low-class also. Please spare me any more of this childish claptrap. It's an insult to Caleb—and to your father's memory as well. Besides, my own heart is heavy enough without your making it more so. The servant we are burying today was the faithful retainer to your father and his family for over sixty-five years, think of that. And you prattle about green grass, mausoleums, and repose. If that's all you have to say on this sad occasion, then please be quiet!"

Augusta's face, however, was longer than ever. "I'm sorry, Mother," she said at last, her voice hardly audible. "Oh, poor Father. . . . Poor Caleb."

The beautiful sleek black Cadillac was bucking and bumping along the almost impassably narrow, weedy roadway as now Dabney hurriedly reached and opened the glass partition behind Sampson and Phoebe. "Sampson!" she said, "be careful of those awful rocks, those boulders. Straddle the center ridge in the road, if you can, and don't get so close to the ditch. Beware or you'll dump us all right into Caleb's grave—heavens!" Then, having forgotten just chiding her, she said to Augusta, "Oh, what a place for a graveyard! It's not fit for a mountain goat!" She cried out again to Sampson, "Can't you put it in low gear!—like we did the old car that time on Pikes Peak? My goodness!"

"Yassum, missus—no problem," said Sampson, fighting the steering wheel and sweating his gin, whereupon, blatantly ignoring her instructions, he maneuvered around the now halted hearse and went to the other, lower, side of the grave, where here, though, he then for some inexplicable reason, gin or not, suddenly slammed on the brakes, sending all in the car lurching violently forward in their seats, Dabney grabbing her flying pince-nez and Augusta her prim little black hat, as the consumptive-looking caretaker jumped for his life out of Sampson's wild advance.

"Oh, my heavens!" cried Dabney. "He'll kill us all!"—as the car finally came to a stop down at the very edge of the grave opposite the hearse on the other, steeply higher, side. Sampson, chewing his cloves, now clambered out and ran around to open the car door for Dabney and, incidentally, Augusta.

"Mother," said disheveled Augusta. "do we have to get out? Can't we sit here in the car and watch?"

"Get out, Gussie, and stop whining," Dabney said.

Meanwhile, up above, undertaker Ferguson, preacher Tate, and the other two makeshift pallbearers, including Colossus, were standing out, four abreast, alongside the hearse, facing the grave from the high, rocky ground and waiting for the Cadillac's occupants, now on foot, to reach the grave's edge. When this was accomplished and Dabney and Augusta stood graveside flanked by Phoebe and Sampson, the pallbearers solemnly repaired to the rear of their vehicle, leaving the Cadillac's party below to stare up at them—Dabney as pale, harried, but austere as ever. Ferguson now opened the rear door of the hearse and first took out Dabney's large floral wreath, as the other three stepped forward to join in receiving the coffin, Colossus at Ferguson's elbow. Ferguson then with extreme, almost breathless, caution coaxed the coffin far enough out of the hearse for the other pallbearers to come forward, take a handle each, and, with Ferguson, begin the short but precipitous march down to the yawning grave, Ferguson and Colossus leading the way.

Alas, then, Colossus stumbled. He had stepped on an oversize stone, which now under his foot rolled over once, though no more. But once was enough. Feeling himself about to go down, he panicked. With a mighty grunt, summoning all his herculean strength in an attempt to right himself in time, he yanked, wrenched, his end of the coffin straight up. Whereupon the cheap handle came off in his hand as he heavily fell.

"OH!" came Dabney's stunned, incredulous—primordial—cry, even before she saw that the other pallbearers were now also losing control as a result of the plunging, bull-like weight of Colossus's headlong collapse. Final disaster then hit when the flimsy coffin, now also lost and falling, struck a hillside boulder and broke open like an overripe watermelon.

"OH!" again came Dabney's hoarse, primeval cry. "*You childish, stupid wretches, you! . . .*" she yelled at Ferguson and his colleagues. "Look—*just look*—at what you blithering roustabouts have done! . . . OH! . . . MY GOD!"

In the ensuing catastrophe then the first object seen was Caleb's left leg, bare-naked all the way up, protruding from the now wide-open wreckage of the coffin. Ferguson wheeled around to the two of his cohorts yet standing (Colossus was still on the ground)— "Don't leave me, now, boys," he said, trembling.

Caleb somehow lay twisted and athwart his own right arm as his sunken, white-powdered face, eyes tightly shut as if in a bad dream, aimed, symbolically, toward the grave. It was only then that, as he sprawled, they saw his bared, ancient genitals, withered except for the enormous penis, which, like a blacksnake, even in rigor mortis, reached halfway down his emaciated thigh. Dabney, her face crimson, swollen, engorged, was now at the point of fainting. It was clear that her finicky, irascible butler was being interred—in a coffin showing the upper torso only—minus his (undertaker-purloined) trousers. Then, completely to annihilate matters, Ferguson, quaking, in extremis, snatched the blue bandanna handkerchief from around the caretaker's neck, stepped forward and, touching his hat out of respect to the deceased and/ or his endowment, covered the snake.

Mary Eliza Fitzhugh Dabney, FFV (First Families of Virginia), was beyond fainting—now apoplectic and speechless. She could only turn her eyes away from the truth in crinoline-abashed mod-

237

esty—and purple fury—until her lips could and did form words: "*You filthy, thieving crook, you, Ferguson!*" she screamed. "*You scum of the earth!*" Augusta was trying to pull her away toward the car but Dabney fought her off. "*You low-life crapshooter, you!*" she railed. "*You cur!* . . ."

"Mother! . . . Mother!" cried Augusta. "You'll be ill, you'll have a stroke! *Please* let's go! Can't you see we've been disgraced and humiliated enough already?"

But Dabney was still screaming at hapless Ferguson. "*You swindling dog, you!* . . . I'll have you behind bars before the sun goes down, *you filthy field-hand reprobate!* . . . Stealing clothing off a corpse! *You scavenger!*"

Stone-sober Sampson's eyes were large as silver dollars. He seemed wanting to flee her wrath as much as Ferguson.

Augusta was wrestling with her mother. "*Please,* come get in the car!"

"*You low ornery hound!*" Dabney still yelled at Ferguson. "You gather up that corpse and take it right back to your place! You'll never bury him like that! You're going to do all this over again before you go to jail, you low hound! In proper attire and in a coffin representing something of what I paid you! I'll be there tomorrow to inspect everything you've done! Oh, you ought to be horsewhipped! . . . *Or worse!* Yes worse! You're not fit to *live!* You . . . you . . . oh, you low . . . you . . . no-good—"

But she never said the word. With two living servants, and one dead one, present, she managed, barely, to throttle it—though it had never been in her lexicon anyway. But she was fighting tears now. Finally Augusta and Phoebe led her away. Sampson was shaking.

43

THE TELEPHONE RANG. Roxanne, in the kitchen, stopped doing the dinner dishes long enough to go answer it. At once, then, before three words had been spoken, she recognized the shy, gravelly voice. She hesitated, momentarily, to call Haley—upstairs grading papers—but finally did so.

"Who is it?" he said, slowly descending. "Some student?"

"It's trouble," she said. "Pick up and see."

The ensuing telephone conversation was brief. And, hanging

up, Haley was left musing. "What do you make of that?" he said, entering the kitchen. "He's coming over."

Roxanne was scalding a platter. "It's been a long time," she said. "Something's up. That wasn't a courtesy call."

Haley was patting himself for his pipe but had left it upstairs. "He sounded strange," he said. "Maybe worried. It's old Dabney, I'll bet. That old woman's probably giving him so much hell he can't take it any longer. Well, it was all our own doing. Now we've got to face the music."

"He's probably been fired," Roxanne said.

"I hope it's nothing worse than that." Haley had never felt good about what he (they) had done. Sometimes, even from the best of motives, officiousness could be carried too far, he had often thought since. One had to be careful meddling in other people's lives. You could do more harm than good. It was probably more often than not better to keep hands off. Maybe in this case he would have done so had not Roxanne, always ribbing, taunting, him about his "prize protégé," been the one at the last minute to get into the act and come up with a possible "solution." Yet what alternative had he (they) had? None, they had both, often since rehashing the whole dreary familiar picture, agreed. Moreover, as for him, Haley, he was always brought to think of his baby sister Yolande, which then rendered things more or less conclusive. He knew, otherwise, the psychic punishment would have been too great. You never really recovered from a thing like that. It kept gnawing you all the time. He had therefore gone along with, indeed eagerly welcomed, Roxanne's "brilliant" idea, immediately calling the old doyenne, Mrs. Dabney, in town—yet almost certain she would give him a flat, cold no. Ah, but she had not. Her answer, strangely, had been all but passive and automatic—robotic—indeed even as if somehow she had been expecting the call.

When shortly before eight the knock came, Roxanne, none too subtly—having gotten him into this—flicked off the kitchen light and took off upstairs, as he gazed after her. Thanks for nothing, he thought.

Cager, highly agitated, entered already talking. "Prof, I wouldn't be bothering you like this if I wasn't in a bind. Can't seem to think my way out of it, although, Lord knows, I've tried—day and night. Old Caleb died last Tuesday and she wants me—I ain't kidding, Prof, *me!*—to be butler now. *I* don't want to take on anything like that. I'm only planning to be around here long enough to finish studying a few more of her war books, books I really need to know,

239

then get outa here—to my *main mission*. She's already got me hooked out there at Billups with those blind Negro kids where she's spending a lot of money to improve the place. Prof, I don't know what's come over this evil old woman."

Haley was motioning for him to sit down on the sofa. "I'm not so surprised," he said. "She's complicated. Otherwise I wouldn't have found the nerve to ask her to hire you—even if I wasn't sure at all she would."

"She's given me a good pay raise, too. I tell you, Prof, I don't understand that old woman. The only thing I know for sure is that she's the world's champion racist. Don't *ever* forget that!" Towering over Haley, he stared down at him with wildly glowing eyes. "Do you *hear* me, Prof?"

"Lord, I've been knowing that," said Haley. "But we can't be picky and choosy. Most white folks are racists. We've got to learn to take help wherever we can get it until we come out of this thing—emerge. Well, what are you going to do?"

Cager heaved a heavy sigh. "Prof, I really don't know. I don't wanta leave until I'm prepared, knowledgeable enough, to take on what I want to do. I want to go to Chicago."

Haley was already frowning. Then he started futilely patting himself for his pipe again. "What are you *talking* about?" he said irritably.

"Oh, Prof, they're doing *big* things up in Chicago. That's the place for me to start my movement. Have you ever read their newspaper from up there—*The Chicago Hawk*? Lord, it's a *man-killer*. Whew! . . . Have you seen it, Prof?"

"Of course. Who hasn't? Good God, is that what's put these latest brainstorms in your head? You've *really* gone off the deep end now. That sheet is one of the biggest frauds in the country. Practically none of that glaring red headline stuff is true. It's mostly tampered-with 'facts' or complete lies. Chicago Negroes are no better off than in many other places. All the sensational stuff in that loud rag is just to try to build circulation, but even that's having no success. Good Lord, wake up, Rollo."

Cager's countenance had fallen. He started to say something, but, harried, confused, he could not. Finally, then, a powerful bitterness came on his face. "Prof, don't *say* things like that. They're not true."

"You mean you don't *want* them to be true. You've finally got to face it, that there are no shortcuts, Rollo, and the sooner you realize this, the better off you'll be."

"But, Prof, when are we ever going to start getting rid of our negativism? Why're we always telling ourselves it can't be done— before we try the first little thing? Huh?" He had not even sat down yet. "Things are getting worse instead of better. A black GI on his way overseas can't buy a sandwich or a Coke right down here in the railroad station. But they'll serve German prisoners of war down there, all right. I saw it. We almost deserve what we're getting. What I want to know is, when are we gonna start doing something about it? I mean showing some *firepower*. Our problem is that too many of us are still alive. Did you ever hear about a slave named Ofield Smalls, who was one of the early—yes, right here during the Civil War—real freedom fighters? He and his cohorts died for it, of course, but he took a lot of the plantation enemy with him. Huh? But we're all alive yet, way, way, too many of us. We need to recruit some *men* and establish us some '*units.*' You hear me, Prof?"

Haley shouted at him: "Will you please sit down there and stop standing over me lecturing!" He scooted to the forward edge of his chair, again patting his pockets for his pipe. Now he yelled upstairs: "Rox, throw my pipe down here!" He returned to Cager. "You probably don't know it, but then again you may, that there are a lot of people who think you're off in the head—loco, nuts. I'm not necessarily one of them—*yet*—but there is a growing number."

Cager had finally sat down on the sofa. "Maybe they're the crazy ones," he said. "Where are our leaders? I'm no leader, and know it, although there was a time when I first came here that I sure thought I was, or could be. But *somebody's* got to start the movement, Prof!"

"Well, answer me this, will you?" said Haley heatedly. "While you're setting up your 'units,' as you call them, your black regiments, what do you think Uncle Sam—I'm talking about that J. Edgar Hoover in Washington, D.C. and his FBI—what are they going to be doing? Playing tiddlywinks? That's why people say you haven't got all your marbles."

"You see what the Confederates back there thought about your Uncle Sam in Washington," Cager said. "They came within a hair of whipping him into the ground. But they had real leaders."

"Yes, yes, there you go!—you and your idol *Lee!*" Haley was furiously loading his pipe. "Everybody remembers it—that disgraceful performance. The sorriest day of your life, if you live to be a hundred, was when you went downtown there and laid that big wreath at his statue and damn near got lynched for it. What you did was disgusting!" Haley's pipe angrily erupted in sparks. "But maybe I'm too hard on you. What you did seems more like the acts of a crazy man, especially when you add it to what you want to do now—raise a black army. Have you ever really thought how absolutely *impossible* that would be? Good God! First of all, what are you going to use for money? And even if you had it, how're you going to persuade able-bodied men, some with families to support, to drop everything and come join your nonexistent army? And, with an extralegal outfit, how're you going to enforce discipline? Where're you going to quarter your forces, too? You can't look me in the eye and tell me you've considered any of these things and still thought you could bring off such an absolutely *demented* scheme." Cager's face was long, troubled, as he averted his gaze. "Why don't you say something?" said Haley. "Tell me how it can be done. And how you're going to get black people as interested in it as you are. Some of the masses don't yet happen to be as educated as you but they're no fools. Look what happened when you and Shorty George tried to get something like this off the ground here. It was a fiasco—actually laughable. Listen, Rollo, I don't want to be ugly about this, don't want to scold you, but I *must* somehow make you see that all these dreams you've had of military power, and saving the Negro race by force of arms, or trying to be a black Robert E. Lee of some kind and wage war against the white folks, you *must* be made to see it's pitifully silly, if not plain unbalanced."

Sorrowfully, his face somber, Cager took a huge, deep breath and finally exhaled. He looked at Haley. "Why were we slaves, Prof?" he said.

Haley became exasperated again. "If you'd stayed around here in school long enough, instead of practically flunking out, you might have learned why. We were kidnapped off the shores of Africa, or often brought out to the shores by our own rival tribes, thrown on the stinking Middle Passage ships, and transported here against our will—then sold into slavery. Your great General Lee owned some of us. I even hear you at one time were saying around here you were one of his descendants."

"Why *were* we slaves, though, Prof? Why were we taken in Africa and thrown on those ships? There were more of us—thousands and thousands times more—than there were of them. Why didn't we board the ships, slaughter everybody aboard, then burn the ships to the waterline? Or else before we failed we could have

242

died. Right, Prof? Sure, some did die, but not enough. The question's not so much that we failed, but how many of us were left *after* we failed. Too many, Prof—far, far, too many."

In his angry frustration Haley had half stood up, his eyes fairly popping. "In all my life I've never known anybody so out of touch with reality," he said—"so ignorant of history, especially one who was a former student, and, I thought, an excellent student, of mine! We hadn't the *means* to resist, Rollo—adequate weapons! We hadn't yet developed gunpowder—we had no guns, no cannon!"

"*Why*, Prof? Why hadn't we developed them?"

"OH!. . . " Haley threw up both hands in confused, flustered outrage. "I say if you were better educated you'd know why. It's a long story . . . it's sad history, and—"

"Tell me about it, will you, Prof?" Cager's voice dripped irony.

"Lord God—tonight? It would take a week, a month. You'd also have to read a dozen or more books. It's an involved history . . . or proposition."

"What proposition? Would you spell it out a little?" Derision now.

Haley had become more nervous than angry. "Basically, it's that peoples in different, isolated parts of the world develop at different rates. This is primarily because of the radical variations in climate and topography and other natural environmental factors. Some environments are friendly, others are hostile, both, of course, in varying degrees. Millennia ago northern Europe, for instance, had bitter, frigid, glacial periods. Most of the inhabitants didn't survive it. But those who did, did so because they were cruel and rapacious, cunning too, and always utterly selfish—caring about no one's fortunes but their own. They were a race of pillagers and murderers. But they had to be to stay alive. They had only a single mission in life—to survive. At all costs."

"Hey, tell me this, Prof. Are you arguing with me or agreeing with me?"

"Don't interrupt me, please," said harried, frustrated Haley. "On the other hand, there were other parts of the world where, by comparison, the environment was far more hospitable—sub-Sahara Africa, for example, where life was much easier, the vicinage far more friendly. There it took little or no effort to survive. We didn't have to plot, plunder, and kill to do it. Rather, we could afford to be more easygoing and trusting, didn't have to be so wily and resourceful, and so cold-blooded—ah, and above all,

243

not so *inventive*—in order to survive. *That's* why we didn't have guns or gunpowder. We didn't need them. And that's why today the white man (*and* some Negroes who readily come to mind) say, or think, we're dumb as hell by nature and produce a thousand athletes and show-biz people for every physicist." Haley was trembling.

Cager shook his head, a sickly, bitter, manic smile on his face. "And, Prof, you call *me* crazy," he said. "Pardon my language, but do you really *believe* this shit? Lord, have mercy!" He was clearly struggling to contain himself.

"And that's not all!" shouted Haley, furious at the taunting. "Being top dog in the world, as the white man is right now—or certainly thinks he is, as I do too—is only a temporary thing! History goes on and on, sometimes swiftly, sometimes slowly, but it's never static. This myth of being 'superior' rotates, you know. In time it gets around to just about everybody. Ahead today, behind tomorrow, is the way it really works. Also, the so-called 'time' involved means little. Five or ten thousand years in the history of mankind and his forebears on this planet are nothing, absolutely nothing, a trifle, a mustard seed—it's like five or ten *seconds*, actually!"

Cager was scornful. "So what you're saying, Prof, if I understand you, is wait another ten thousand years, then *our* time will finally roll around, eh? Is that it?—pie in the sky. Well, *I* say we gotta strike now. Ten thousand years of what we already been through will wipe us out. We can't stand it, can't survive it! . . . Lord, have mercy!—We can't wait no longer, Prof!"

But excited Haley went on obliviously. "Besides, what's the white man got to show on the *good* side of the ledger? What's he accomplished during his term of 'superiority,' with all his scientific acumen and technical know-how?—things like generosity, compassion, altruism, the propagation of humane values, and so forth? At best it's a mixed bag, I'd say, although his development of anesthesia, as well as the science of bacteriology, is historic, a great boon to mankind, and there are others, not a few, in fact." Haley paused and reflected, then finally sighed. "But, alas, in other respects," he said, "his term, his 'reign,' has been a living hell for those he's bested. Oh, yes—*it's true!*"

"I repeat, what side of this debate are you on, Prof? You don't have to tell *me*, and other Negroes, about his 'hell'!"

But Haley plunged on. "Just think of the millions over the cen-

244

turies who've suffered from his depredations. His methods are very simple, very direct, not at all complicated—in fact, classic. He's just demanded of you whatever you happened to have and if you didn't give it to him he killed you, took it, and enslaved your family and people. Then he's sent over the Christian missionaries to 'convert' you and teach you all about Jesus and the Golden Rule. Your man Lee, for instance, may have been a great gentleman and Bible reader, but he was also one of these same predators. He loved the smell of blood. Didn't he say at Fredericksburg"— Haley curled his lip in scorn—"after that great battle—I'm sure you, as such a *devoted* student and partisan of the Confederacy, know all about this—didn't he say, that day after his bloody victory over inept Burnside, that 'It is well that war is so terrible, or we should grow too fond of it.' Didn't he say that? He's typical— rapacity and piety, the white man's twin creeds. Yet, Lee is your idol and you want to be just like him. Christ Almighty, are you mixed up, Rollo!" Cager could only gape at him now. "So where are we now, in your present personal crisis?" said Haley, out of breath. "We're *nowhere.* After my wife and I have tried to fix things so you might be able to return to Gladstone, what have you done? Why, you've instead decided, after reading some phony, inflamatory, Chicago newspaper, to run off up to Chicago, recruit a nigger army, and be a black Robert E. Lee! You're crazy as a bedbug—*and an ingrate besides!*" Haley was shouting and wildly jabbing his finger in the air, just as Cager jumped up and started for the door.

"*Haley!*" came a voice from on high. "Rollo, you wait a minute!" Roxanne was already halfway down the stairs. "I heard everything," she said. "There's nothing more to be accomplished tonight. You two are only cutting each other up—making no headway at all. Who knows the answers for you, Rollo? None of us. We need to think on it more and talk again. But you may not want to come back, Rollo. You don't have to if you don't want to, though— if you think Professor Barnes has insulted you, although I know he hasn't meant to. But if you do want to come back, you're welcome—after you've tried to think everything over again. That's what I really want you to do. *Think,* son!"

Cager, downcast, subdued, his cap in his hand, stood at the door now. "I been *trying* to think!" he said, his voice anguished. "But . . . but . . ." He bit his lip. Finally he opened the door and left.

44

HER HUSBAND WAS ALIVE at the time. He called what he said about her merely "joshing." She, though, had never appreciated it. Nor did it much improve things that their three teenage daughters, especially Augusta, also characterized his remarks as "only kidding." It was not merely unpalatable because gratuitous but, besides, she thought, sacrilegious. For the girls would sometimes giggle. This caused her to suspect that they enjoyed their father's sport at her—and God's—expense.

"It's true, girls," he, Nathan P. Dabney, would laugh at dinner. "She just won't. She somehow refuses to get down on her knees to God—as we were all taught to do. She talks to Him sitting erect in her Hepplewhite chair in the parlor, or, if she happens to be in the bedroom, her rocker—and talks conversationally, chats with Him, actually. Ha, ha! No looking up at Him from two humbly bent knees. No, no, but straight into His eyes, face-to-face. Almost as if someday she might stare Him down." The judge would then laugh again and the girls would titter, or feign amused embarrassment, all as Mary Eliza Fitzhugh Dabney sat listening and unsmiling. Yet she knew, even if it had been said in jest, that it was true. She indeed prayed sitting, or even standing, but never kneeling. She prayed, though, no less devoutly, or fervently. Yet now, at 10:30 at night, alone in her bedroom, the "joshing" judge nine years at rest out in the family's huge Mount Calvary mausoleum, she felt a new, a different, urgency—a crisis.

"Dear Lord," she prayed, "it's disquieting. I'm puzzled, at this late time in life, when I should be sure of everything. Why the present trials, doubts, all the unsettled questions, when my life should at last be tranquil, free of uncertainties and anxieties, as I wait for You to call me home to rejoin my husband and my father and mother? Sometimes I even presume to think it unfair, if You will allow me to be perfectly candid, when I think, for instance, of what I had to go through in connection with Caleb's recent death and burial. What happened to him was absolutely scandalous, it was ghastly, a typical nigra debacle that only they can create! How shameful that Augusta and I had to stand there and witness it all. I have yet to recover from it, Lord. As I say, rather than diminishing, my trials and dilemmas seem somehow to be mounting, converging on me, and I'm borne down by them, something I've never had to experience until now. Why is this happening to me, Lord? I so need Your infallible counsel tonight!

"I also beg of You not to tell me, as Augusta does, that I've changed. I can't accept that, for it's not true. She, poor thing, is not the most experienced and perceptive of my offspring, though *greatly* loved by me. I have not changed. I follow Your dictates as I have always tried to do, and they are of course immutable, so how could I have changed? Still even more farfetched is her inclination to link my recent efforts out at Billups school, for those blind nigra children, with this change in me she insists has taken place. But most outlandish of all, she thinks it's because of the influence that, of all people in the world, *Rollo* has had on me! How preposterous. Poor Gussie. She even reads something into the fact that I took him, this benighted nigra boy, into the house to do various domestic chores and thus gave him a chance to improve his life—she claims in this perfectly routine act to see *his* influence and *my* change. She doesn't realize I've done things like this all my adult life, certainly ever since I've been in a position of authority and responsibility—which is a long time.

"But now, Lord, I'm embarked on the greatest—and, I'm afraid, the last—significant project of my life. And although its purpose is to honor the memory of my late husband, it also I hope seeks in some small, final way to further Your own glorification and that of Your works. Augusta is greatly disturbed by this, my new undertaking, and points to it as added proof that I'm a very much altered person. Ah, my Gussie—it's the same old refrain. But I shall not, absent Your overruling me, be deterred in the least. Yet the strain, the weight, of it all bears heavily on me. I bespeak, as I have said, Your help and guidance, Lord.

"Most of all, however, I need Your reassurance that You accept these, my final undertakings, not as attempts to butter up to You, nor to placate You for some sin or error of mine that I might imagine, nor even to find some other favor in your sight, as if there were something in my past for which I now, at this late time, seek to atone. No, none of this. I have searched my heart, Lord. I withhold nothing from You—it would of course be futile anyway—and confess all. Please vouchsafe to me, then, Your balm, for I'm not without, yes, anxieties as I embark on this last endeavor, toward which You, in Your wisdom, must surely have pointed me after what, as an object lesson, I've been privileged to learn in my efforts at Billups. Yes, yes, I admit that Billups has made this new venture seem altogether logical, indeed highly desirable, once blessed with Your holy sanction. Grant me therefore this final success, Lord, that it may become the capstone of a lifetime of faithful service—even hard labor, if I may say so—in Your vineyard. Succor me, *I pray You!* Amen." For the first time since childhood, then, she rose from her knees.

Already, though, by only the following day, her spirits—as if indeed due to divine intercession—had lifted, so full was she of her exciting new project's planning. Accordingly, following lunch, she summoned Sampson and directed him to drive her over to Augusta's

"Revenge can be sweet," she said to her daughter on entering Augusta's cheerful bedroom. "I realize, though, it's not very nice to harbor such sentiments—even if they are at Renfroe's expense." Augusta, a pitcher of orange juice at her elbow, lay propped in bed, victim of a summer cold. She at first stared uncomprehendingly at her mother. Then she blew her nose, coughed once, and seemed suddenly eager to hear more as she wriggled into a still higher position on the stacked pillows. "Do you know why I say that?" asked Dabney.

"Poor Renfroe," Augusta said. "I'm sure he wonders, as do some of the rest of us, what on earth's going on here. How did he take it, Mother?"

"Oh, my heavens—you can imagine. He was shocked. He got sullen then and gave me the silent treatment, before his outrage would get the better of him when he could hardly contain himself, much less be civil. He's cooled down some now, though, I think. Yet he pouts and talks very sarcastically. Besides, he's probably smarting at the way I fooled him in the Billups orphanage matter and hasn't said *yet* he'll represent me in this new development. He will, though, all right—in a matter of this magnitude he'd never stand by and be disgraced by letting me bring in one of those big Memphis law firms. He'll come around."

"Is his reaction any wonder? I could have expected him to faint dead away, as I almost did." Augusta pinched her runny nose with a handkerchief. "What I wonder now, though, Mother, is how *Rollo* figures in this project."

"What are you talking about?" Dabney bristled. "He doesn't even know about it. Besides, he's been too busy getting broken into his new duties as butler."

"You don't see what I'm getting at. I'll bet he does figure in it in some way, even if only indirectly—even if neither of you realizes it. His influence, in one way or another, seems everywhere around your house—especially now that you've made him your butler."

Dabney shook her head. "Gussie, you can say such exasperating

248

things, and not very bright things, either. You and your pet theories. Once you get them in your head there's no getting them out. And they're not nearly as profound as you think, and certainly not funny."

"Mother, dear, I only wish the subject *were* funny." Augusta sighed and blew her nose again. "What kind of butler is Rollo making?"

"As good as could be expected at this time, I guess. He'll do better as he goes along. It's all been so sudden for him. The only real crisis so far was when the tailor came out to measure him for his new black tailcoat and striped gray trousers. Rollo balked. It took us fifteen minutes to get him to cooperate. Old Morehead, the tailor, a bona fide redneck at heart, was thoroughly disgusted —with me, though, more than Rollo. He thought I coddled him, which I didn't at all, but if I hadn't been patient, given Rollo time, he'd have walked out, he was that upset—and of course Morehead didn't help matters. But Rollo's finally settling into the routine now, I think, and for much of that we have Haley Barnes and his wife to thank. They've played a helpful role in getting him to stay put. They've got a stake in it, though, because they want him back out at Gladstone eventually. Ah, that Gladstone," Dabney sighed. "How it's troubled my thinking lately. And my prayers!" Her face suddenly flamed crimson with passion. "Even *God Himself* seems troubled and indecisive!" She lapsed into a distressed silence.

"Where on earth, though, Mother, did you come up with *this* idea for Gladstone? You used to hate the place. I can't get Rollo out of my mind on this. There's got to be some connection."

"You're wrong, Gussie. The connection is Billups."

"Well, through whom did you get interested in Billups? Tell me that."

Fearfully, Dabney rushed on. "I repeat, the connection is the school—those children, blind and groping, but no longer hungry. And Annie Baker, the matron. And . . . well, yes, of course, Rollo . . . to a certain extent."

"To a 'certain extent'! You've been saying he runs the place."

"I'm not denying that. But the real seeds of it all came to me about three weeks ago as Sampson was bringing me back from a visit out there."

"Oh, Mother, you talk about 'seeds.' Can't you see there's only *one* seed—Rollo!"

"Will you let me talk, Gussie! As Sampson and I were driving back in, I began to realize what an uplifting experience my visit had been that day. Annie Baker—and, yes, Rollo have worked wonders out there."

"So has your money, Mother—don't forget that."

"Tell me, Gussie, honey, why is it you've lately become so upset about my money matters? Your face gets real long whenever the subject comes up. Soon you and Renfroe will be trying to get old Judge Ramsey to appoint a conservator to manage my affairs. I'll bet you've thought about that more than a time or two. But let me hasten to reassure you that, even after this project, there will be plenty of proceeds left in my estate for you girls. You really don't need it, anyhow—you've all married well, thank God—yet I know you all worry. Oh, why couldn't I have had just one son along with you three?"

Augusta's twelve-year-old daughter, Hope, trailed by Callie, the maid, came in now with Augusta's medication—two aspirins. Augusta swallowed them quickly with orange juice, never taking her attention from her mother, whereupon Hope and Callie marched out again.

"That day out at Billups," Dabney said, "was truly an inspiring one, an experience, Gussie, I shall never forget, no matter what. The children simply adore Rollo, a fact, by the way, which seems to embarrass him no end, and what Annie Baker has taught them can only be called incredible—when you consider that they are all blind . . . and . . . and also possibly handicapped in other, quite natural, ways. I marvel at Annie's education, too, especially since learning she's a Gladstone graduate. How glad I am that someone of her caliber chose to stay here rather than run off up North where darkies think things are so much better for them—which of course they aren't. But she, as I say, has worked wonders with these children. She even had them recite for me. They've tried to memorize all manner of things, including Lincoln's Gettysburg Address (which your father used to say was pure humbug), Kipling's 'Recessional,' short parts of Booker T. Washington's great autobiography, *Up From Slavery*, as well as innumerable verses from the Bible. And, listen to this, even passages from *Shakespeare*. I'm telling you the truth, Gussie. I've never been more amazed in my life. It opened *my* eyes, believe me. Shakespeare!"

Augusta reached for a fresh handkerchief, all the while observing her mother, though evincing little of her ardor. "What else, Mother?"

"What else! Why, I'd think that was plenty. Annie had this little pickaninny girl, who couldn't have been more than ten—and fittingly named Ophelia—give a halting recitation of a part of Hamlet's soliloquy, followed then by some of Prospero's speech near the end of *The Tempest*: 'Our revels now are ended,' and so on. You remember. It was my dear father's favorite passage in all of Shakespeare. He loved it as much or more than anything in the Scriptures. I thought of him as I sat there and listened to this sightless black child mispronouncing all those polysyllabic words yet reciting them so bravely—poignantly, actually—as if she knew, as if she *really comprehended,* what Shakespeare was telling us, that our revels now must soon end and our little life be rounded with a sleep. Oh, my heart went out to her. It was a terribly moving experience for me. Think of it! I was almost reduced to tears thinking of my father also, a great, humane, and compassionate man, who sought only to do good. The experience was a revelation, no less, especially as I realized it was all Annie Baker's doing, an idea to uplift those children which she doubtless—oh, what an irony—got while still a student out at Gladstone." Dabney, almost as if alone in the pleasant bedroom, sat staring out the window now. "The tables have turned, haven't they?" she said. "Ah, on me . . . on me."

Augusta lay studying her, then shook her head, saying, "Poor Renfroe, I repeat. He's got his work cut out for him. You've been completely swept off your feet, Mother."

"Now, don't get on Renfroe, Gussie."

"*Me* get on him! It's you who's been on him, Mother, all along."

"Well, he's probably not all that bad. He's a product of his background, as we all are. Your father was right, though, he's a good lawyer. He's cooled down some by now, I'm sure, and is just waiting for me to call and insist he represent me. I couldn't possibly have passed him over. It would have been considered almost an insult to the community. On the whole, contrary to your impression, I think I was very discreet, restrained, when I talked to him. I told him at first only that I was considering an idea to memorialize my husband, which is certainly the truth, and reminded him of his own high regard for your father. Then, bracing myself, mustering all the courage at my command, I told him that for this tribute to my husband I had decided to erect a building. '. . . *Well,*' he said, anxious delight already in his voice. But then, as if he had betrayed his feelings prematurely—as indeed he had—he waited. But I imagined I could hear his amazed, expectant, heavy breathing. Then I told him. That it was to be a fine, new, grand edifice—to be located on the campus of Gladstone College. It was of course my imagination again but I thought I heard him grab for something, as if collapsing. What I really heard, though, was an unbelieving gasp."

"*Great heavens!*" said Augusta. "Were you surprised?"

"Of course not. I went on then, though, to describe the kind of grand structure I was talking about—in keeping, I said, with what we all thought of my husband. It would be exceptional in every way, I said, dwarfing all those other smaller grubby-looking buildings out there; in fact, more imposing even than most of the buildings on Vanderbilt's campus in Nashville. This brought from him what sounded over the phone like a sudden, astounded, seizure of pain, after which he then became briefly sullen. I fear, though, speaking of my revenge, that I then, rather cruelly perhaps, hastened on into greater detail. The completed edifice, I told him, would bear—high up over its entrance and cut into a broad frieze of Carrara marble—the noble inscription: NATHAN POOLE DABNEY MEMORIAL HALL FOR THE LIBERAL ARTS."

Augusta, though hearing it for the third or fourth time, still could not keep her hand from going to her face— "Oh, my heavens!"

"He seemed wilted by now," Dabney said. "Yet he finally found the voice to ask, 'Did you say for the liberal arts, ma'am?' 'Yes, Mr. Renfroe.' 'Then, I can only affirm, ma'am,' he said, 'that this is the most incredible development in my memory. It's also what you might call . . . yes, an irony. I think you may have forgotten how shabbily that board out there treated Judge Dabney, constantly overrode his views on curriculum and the whole question of liberal arts, especially whenever instead he stressed the need for solid, basic, vocational training with no frills for those students. You backed him to the hilt, too, ma'am, and after he passed you gave them what you said was your final financial contribution—in effect, really, the back of your hand. Now you're not only putting up a big brand-new building out there, which will cost a fortune, but dedicating it to the liberal arts—all in *his* name!' In trying to control himself now he began to stutter. 'Why, ma'am . . . why, ma'am, it's outrageous! Pardon me, maybe I should take that back—it's your money, even if it did all come from him—but just let me say it's something that's not easy to understand. Are you well, ma'am? *My goodness, ma'am!*' His voice was trembling. He was literally outraged. It was clear it was all he could do to keep from shouting at me."

"Oh, my heavens!—is there any wonder? What on earth did you say?"

"I said nothing, absolutely nothing. I didn't want to get him any more upset than he already was. Nor did I care to argue with him and send my own blood pressure sky-high. He wouldn't have understood anyway—all that you and I have been discussing all week that is involved in this situation. For, really, with his background, he's had to deal with so few matters partaking of high ethical and moral principles. Of course, he's not to be blamed for that. It's just the fact. So I did nothing to make the situation worse. I kept silent."

Augusta, lying there, could only gaze in wonder, awe, at her. "Strange, strange," she finally said, almost musing now. "Yes, so strange the way he entered your life. . . . And you've been under his spell ever since."

Dabney started. "*Renfroe's?*"

"No, Mother. Rollo's."

45

CAROL, MY CAROL. The process had broken down, the center would no longer hold, her cold disdain at one point, followed, almost as if in time-lapse photography, by her furtive compassion at another, was for me, your narrator, anything but therapeutic. Yet why did I do such things, as I had just done only the night before, if not in utter desperation?—taken a plane, a bumpy 727, in the violent white January storms—as mortally afraid as I am of flying—well-knowing from a profusion of weathercasts what it would be like, that the White Plains airport, already darkened and snowbound, was right and left waving flights off; yet only to have this twenty-nine-year-old pilot/captain insist to the tower that the wrong lights in his cockpit were berserkly flashing and that he must come in—which at once he did, barely. That, then, had been my dire situation, to have deliberately been aboard in this daring-do foray that only highlighted another of my periodic psychic emergencies. I *had* to see her, on "business," *my* business! I needed her strength and counsel. It was yet another (as when I had summoned her to my trial before Judge Jeffreys) of my psychotherapeutic SOS's.

I had called her—quaking from the landing, my ears still painfully popping—as soon as the plane was on the ground. She, though, was in one of her moods—cool, aloof, hesitant, parsimonious with her words—and, having early in the brief phone conversation skipped, or deleted, the amenity of asking me to come to her apartment for some hot food, had suggested rather that she see me at my hotel for lunch next day. There was even to that a chill proviso added: "No talk of past dark things," she admonished. That jolted me. We had never—*never*, I mean—discussed our mutual past. Quickly, though, reading my mind, she put me straight. She wanted, she said, to hear no more, absolutely nothing, about that foolish, that hapless, even tragic, case that still, after all these years, seemed *forever* on my mind . . . of Rollo Lee. It made her feel too miserable, she said—not just the case itself, but my reaction to it, my obsession with it. It was I, she said, who worried, who depressed, her. I knew then, all right, it was my daughter talking—for example, the telltale genetic high-misery quotient, the residual angst, the whining attention to self, especially when she added that it had all made of *me* something of a chronic crybaby and self-flagellant! All of which, however, alas, was true.

Nevertheless, it furiously angered me, almost as much as would have the other possibility, that is, of "past dark things"; and most certainly when she added (again truthfully) that, besides, I seemed all along to have acquired more and more of this gigantic chip on my shoulder. It all sprang, though, said she, from my obsession and confirmed her long-held view that I was . . . well, to put it euphemistically, not a very robust person—emotionally. That, as a result, I was less than always in possession of myself, or my saner faculties, was, in fact, in a perpetual frenzy, and so forth. In a word, that I was mad. What a seer! I scornfully thought, visibly curling my lip. Who did *not* know that I was unhealthy? I was seething now. She was talking down to me—shrinklike!

The following day at lunch in my hotel room there was more of the same, her repetition of the identical . . . I want to call them her calumnies, though, no, they were not. They were expressions of her genuine anxieties—her hang-ups—about me. Nonetheless, my hackles were up again—especially when she asked me why I had come all the way from home (Berlin, Kansas) in this horrible winter storm just to see *her*. She, of course, knew perfectly well why. I told her the obvious, that I so needed to talk to her, that my past, in all its various failures, sordidness, sham, and other misprisions had really caught up with me, and somehow in the process had raised Cager to yet new heights of virtue in my sight, almost as if he were some gigantic, remote, inscrutable Buddha knowing and doing only those things good and most beneficial to mankind; yes, definitely now, formally, elevating him to sainthood. So, I said, no matter how far away she lived, and irrespective of weather, I had to talk to her about these things that were virtually killing me, that there was no one else for the purpose. (Bahr was no more.) She said nothing, only sat munching a roll and observing me, although, according to what she had said, these were the very things she did *not* want to talk about. No matter, in her silence she seemed to savor this tacit admission that I was, yes—psychologically—wholly dependent on her. What utter callousness, though, I thought— and to link it, however remotely, to Cager! But to myself I conceded she was not far off the mark, though when calling her from Kansas to tell her I *must* come see her, I had of course not once mentioned him, though she well knew that the crux was my fascination with—no, addiction to—the moral question involved, that is, my saturated, exhaustive, organic necessity to compare my sad career with his glories. (The "rivalry.")

It made no difference that I had discussed everything (I do mean everything) concerning his life with her numerous times in the past—strange, uneasy times for both her and me—as I say, depicting for her, as it were, the patent and tragic nonparallels between our (his and my) lives, and that she had forgotten none of it was all too clear. Apparently, at last, though, trying to demonstrate some degree of rapport, even sympathy, with me and my lot, she tried her hand at a sort of recap of the situation, historically, as she implied she saw it. It was the phenomenon, she said, of my again juxtaposing (she used the more pointed word "contrasting") my own choice of life-style (and I challenge her word "choice") with that of the martyr-hero's; it was this she claimed so clearly to see and to which she attached much significance; insisting thereby that she had finally divined the reason why his life, totaling a mere twenty-two years, this, so to speak, existential series of time warps, this brief sojourn of a paragon, no, a paradigm, called Rollo Ezekiel Lee, this spurious hoaxman claiming affinity with, passing himself off as great grandson of, General Robert Edward Lee, no less, his, the boy's, inconceivable and outlandish hero, why all this had so desperately, so recklessly, appropriated *my*, your narrator's, total life and sensibility was the rub; but then she neglected to come clean, to *say* why; this after claiming, proclaiming, how clearly she perceived, fathomed, everything. *Bosh!* I thought. I was thoroughly exasperated with her—until, that is, I realized that what she had said, and the *way*, the grandiloquent fustian used, in which she had said it, again merely marked her as my own daughter who had heard, from childhood, far too many of my phony sermons. Then I felt sorry for her—and of course myself.

Soon then, a second time, she strayed from her point, failed to follow up, overlooked stating what the real reason was behind his, the hero's, life, his "sojourn" amongst us, a profound mystery, this oversight in her eagerness to go on into even more thickly mazed prolixities, all the while being quite solemn and opinionated about everything, further contending even that the mere "comparing" of the two lives was not really all that she had had in mind, not all even that was actually involved, that indeed it may have had little to do with what she now (to my utter impatience) referred to quaintly as "the nub of the matter." But my stare of pique (and incomprehension) diverted her not one whit. She explained—it turned out to be an expatiation—that, essentially, it only showed, on my vulnerable part, the death wish! I literally struck my forehead with the heel of my hand, then somehow grimly laughed. *Death wish!* That is what I did *not* wish—death! I was mortally afraid of it!—although I believe in no hell. It was rather the hero who fancied death—apparently so, if you look at the evidence. It was the evidence, with which she was vastly familiar, which, ironically, was so illustrative of *my* point here, and which, from tedious repetition, I am sure is clear to you, that had tripped her up. I told her so. She slowed down some then. She did not exactly mean, she said, that I was "that *type*," that is, to self-inflict . . . etc.—ah, no, not for me the bare bodkin, was what she claimed to be saying. It is not too clear. If that is what she meant, she was right, of course—had I not confessed as much that time to Bahr's departed spirit? Nevertheless, by the time we had finished our lunch and the busboy had cleared the dishes, she was restless, showing signs of readiness to depart. I was furious. "Carol," I said, "I'm going straight to the airport and back home to Berlin! To hell with you!" I was quivering. Whereupon, inexplicably, she began to cry—and soon was sobbing. It was, you see, I later came to feel, her own disaster, too.

That night in her apartment she somberly listened as I, under the lash of my own driven necessity, went over it all again with her, for the umpteenth time—his, and his victim's, ordeal and its whirlwind culmination. Once more I detailed, as if masochistic, or else purging myself of something abhorrent, the seeming earthquake, as it were, that in the end, as scruffy old Joshua, the Trojan horse vendor, had foretold, brought down the ancient courthouse, and the draft board with it, at Valhalla (Valhalla, Tennessee, that is), sending the town into even further bloody frenzy after the first, *main*, lynching. "But before all this," I said, "though on the eve of it, he couldn't seem to believe what he'd just heard from her (Dabney's) own lips." Carol, well knowing what was coming, began to tense, then acted as if she would have preferred to leave the room. The room was not comfortable, in any case. Outside the weather was subzero and even her small, but nice, apartment was cold now near midnight as she sat huddled in a wool skirt, sweater, and jacket. "But," I said, "although she was somehow pensive, subdued, even grave, she spoke cheerfully enough, saying the building would be even larger than the courthouse. Resplendent in his butler's new sugarspoon tailcoat and striped pants, he had just brought her a pot of tea into the library where she sat at her writing table with a profusion of notes, legal documents, and architect's blueprints strewn before her. He stood gaping at her as she talked. 'I still haven't got the complete hang of all this, Rollo. I don't read blueprints well at all, actually, but my imagination, I think, makes up for it. I can see the building even before it's built—just how it will look. Ah, so grand.' She pushed a large blueprint toward him— 'Can you make any of this out? Did they teach you how to read these things out at Gladstone?' 'No'm . . .' was all he could manage to say (though it was the truth) in his utter stupefaction and numbness—she had disclosed to him her grandiose plans for Gladstone only ten minutes before. 'Well,' she said, 'I think they *should* have taught things like this.' He gave her an incredulous look but remained silent. She pulled the pot of tea toward her, saying, 'Rollo, as I've said before, you sometimes mystify me. You now seem not in the least impressed by what this means for Gladstone. Don't you think you should be quite pleased? Your teacher and mentor, Professor Barnes, you know, expects you to be able to reenroll out there in the not-too-distant future. If you do, you yourself, before you graduate, may turn out to be one of the beneficiaries of this humble tribute I pay the memory of my late husband. This is so even if the building—with so many of the needed construction materials unavailable because of the war—takes two years to complete. But it *will* be completed. Even Attorney Renfroe says that now. Oh, it will be magnificent.

257

Are you listening, Rollo?' She was staring at him. 'Yessum,' he finally said.

"That evening, in a terrible mental state he himself could not have understood, he again went looking for Haley Barnes. What was happening to himself? he wondered in alarm. Why, conceding everything, was he so *frightened*? Also, what was happening, or had happened, to *her*? Lord, have mercy!—putting up a huge *liberal arts* building on, of all places on this earth, *Gladstone's* campus! After her years of furious condemnation! It taxed the senses, blew the mind. And all this in addition to what Haley, with the highest intentions, had done to him—talked, indeed bullied, him out of his great plans for Chicago, though Haley would have insisted he had rather 'reasoned' him out of them. No matter, to Cager his own reluctant, tortured yielding had been a devastating and irremediable development. As if this were not enough, then, Dabney, poring worshipfully over her blueprints, had in effect insisted he show happiness about *her* (ironic) plans! It was too much. He felt smothered, swamped, by the inundation of crises and wanted, sorely needed, to talk to Haley. Yet, through the screen door, Roxanne had told him Haley was up in Nashville attending a Fisk University meeting. As a final resort, then, he came looking for, of all people, *me*! I was of course flabbergasted when he walked in the campus library that evening where he had been told in the dorm I could be found and beckoned me out into the hall. Out there, the moment he turned and faced me I knew something was radically wrong. It was the look on his countenance —disaster. It was a sick look, too. He, moreover, seemed not only numbed by whatever it was troubling him but tongue-tied, unable even to talk about it, and soon then became shifty-eyed, his eyes balking at squarely meeting mine. What, however, had I known, would really have astounded me was that he himself had no idea whatever why he felt as he did. His confusion was total.

" 'What's up, Cage?' I said, in our customary lingo of greeting each other. His grin was sheepish, inept. 'You tell *me*,' he finally said and tried a weak laugh. I soon realized we were just standing there trying to deal with something I was entirely at sea with and that he was too petrified about to even begin to talk through rationally no matter how curious I was. 'Do you need money?' I asked. He looked shocked, before another painful grin came on his face, doubtless remembering the ample precedent for my question. 'No, do *you*?' he again tried to laugh. 'Are you in some kind of trouble, then, Cage?' I whispered it, actually. 'Naw, naw,' he said—

'I just wanted to come out here and bounce some ideas, some questions, maybe, off some of you-all's heads. But Haley's up in Nashville tonight. I shouldn't have come bothering you, though, with all that homework you got to do.' 'We can't talk standing here like this, anyway,' I said—'we've got to go some place else.' Why then this perfectly inexplicable brainstorm hit me, I'll never know. I said, 'Hey, why don't we go by Flo's? We can talk there as long as we want to.'

"A stricken look, almost of terror, at least grave alarm, or something just as strange or beyond fathoming, came on his face. I should have known, though, but apparently wasn't thinking. She brought bad, indeed devastating, memories to him. But at the time I was thinking of something else—what did he *know*? This was uppermost in my mind. About Flo and me. It was doubtless my ego, though, for Flo and I, in the context I had in mind, were probably the least of his thoughts. 'Oh, forget it,' I finally said to him—'how about going over to shorty George's?' But his mind seemed not to have moved. 'I haven't seen Flo in a month of Sundays,' he at last mused aloud, slowly gazing off in space. 'Neither have I,' I hastened to add. She had of course barred me. 'But,' I said, 'if you're hungry we could still go to Shorty's place.' He wouldn't go for it— 'Naw,' he said, 'it's too far. You'd have to come all the way back here afterward. Let's skip it—we can talk some other time; it'll wait.' And despite my protestations he soon left. He had other things in mind.

"But I was worried. I dropped everything, caught a bus into town, and went straight to Flo's—my heart beating wildly; how would she receive me—if at all? I found no one at home, though— the house was dark. She and little Annette, I would learn, were also up in Nashville, the state capital (but for a somewhat different reason than Haley had gone) where the legislature—including of course the Senate—was in session. But even had she been at home, and received me civilly, how could she have helped me with Cager? I found myself asking this question as I returned to campus. Then it occurred to me why I had really gone into town. I wanted Flo to see that, despite her charges of my perfidy toward him, I was capable of intense concern for Cager. Alas, though, she was never to know this."

"I'm sure you understand why she was in Nashville," said Carol, mockingly.

"Of course I understand," I said. "I've just intimated as much— the senator. So at last, utterly desolate, Cager that night had gone to Shorty George's little restaurant, where Shorty tried to get him to eat but he refused. He wanted only to talk, which he did, volubly, nonstop, as bewildered Shorty sat listening. This went on till very late, when Shorty, badly shaken, as well as still puzzled, by what he'd heard—all about Ofield Smalls, Dabney, the Chicago vision, blasted hopes, and now Gladstone's new Liberal Arts building-to-be—finally made him take some soup and crackers, then got him to go home."

Carol seemed unimpressed, her mind elsewhere. "I'm pretty certain he knew about you and Flo," she said. I started. I had forgotten that, in one of my many maudlin confessions to Carol, I had told her about Flo and me. She seemed, though, to have shivered when she said it, and I wondered whether it was the frigid temperature of her attractive little living room where we sat, or her sad, rebuking emotions.

"I don't know whether he knew it or not," I said. "How could he have, though?"

"As wacky as she was, Flo herself could have told him. She may even have told him about her white senator."

I bridled. "I don't believe that. She wouldn't have hurt Cager like that. Besides, he might have killed her."

"Oh, a woman, when she's really, *really*, in love, can do strange, even reckless, dangerous, things." She was staring at me—a burning stare. "Father, can you possibly understand me?" She was shivering again.

I sighed. "Yes," I finally said. For an instant I did wish I were dead. I hurried on. "We then see Cager a few evenings later," I continued, as if describing on behalf of the protagonist some newly developing, tense, pregnant—but somehow wholly unmotivated—cloak-and-dagger maneuver. "But, paradoxically, he's now, or so it seems, for some reason in possession of a much clearer mind and mood. He feels time is more on his side now, as if he's vaulted on its mossy back and subdued the critter, brought it to heel. He's wavered for a painful spell but at last that's over. He must, he will, reverse Haley. He vows it. Once more, ad infinitum, but this time, he thinks, with finality, he understands he must go North and carry out his former great decision—go, depart, quit this god-awful distressing scene, this town, this house, leave this strange, racist old woman behind forever with her bizarre, her ironical, even if perhaps now well-intentioned philanthropies, and reembark on his great mission; yes, despite poor Haley, his wife as well, for there must be no more faltering; his sudden break, yes, will be earlier than planned and at sacrifice of any further study of the great war books, yet it must be done in order that he may redeem *himself!* There was no self-redemption in what Haley preached. Cager was convinced he saw it all now so clearly. He must act, strike while the iron is hot, while time, all too briefly, is his ally. *He must go!* His obdurate, his unpacifiable, will would give him no rest. Yet, yet, neither will that little ninety-two page book he still keeps hidden away under his mattress (alongside the lone copy of *The Chicago Hawk*) give him any rest. It plagues, harasses, and haunts him—its great riddle still unsolved, intact. He's unable, he realizes, to tear himself away from it, from its evil mishmash of bigotry and illogic, its maddening, baffling acrostics, the brooding conundrums. He also sees it—where his vacillating Chicago plans have figured—as a diabolical thwarting agent, which, again he vows, must at all costs be stamped out, destroyed. There is no other way, he tells himself, if he is ever to attain the resolve to do what he must. He must, yes, rid himself of it, despite its mystery and challenge, and go. Just go!"

Carol sat listening. But her teeth were chattering. Abruptly now she got up and went and got her overcoat. "I also just turned the oven on," she said, having returned from the kitchen. "Maybe that will help some."

At once I was alarmed. "You use *gas*, don't you?" I said.

"Certainly," she smiled. "What's the matter, Father? Are you afraid of asphyxiation? Or, tell me, what *is* it you're afraid of? Oh, I still hear those beautiful, sonorous sermons of yours back in the days when you were so sure, so really bold, about everything. The congregation was spellbound—oh, so impressed—as you spoke so fluently, using string after string of those big jawbreaking words you loved to use but which I couldn't understand. All during the week before, though, in your second-floor study when we lived in Philadelphia, you really slaved over those sermons, and wrote them, it seemed, right out of that big old unabridged Webster's dictionary we had. You searched and searched and the longer the words were you could find in it, the happier you were. You took those words very seriously and didn't like to be interrupted. I recall sometimes I'd come in and crawl up in your lap and talk to you, sometimes softly in your ear, but you'd get very excited and up-set—angry, really—and make me get down and leave, especially if you heard Mother coming up the stairs. But even if she weren't around, you acted as if you didn't want to talk to me and God at the same time, or as if you thought we might be telling you

261

conflicting things. But my point is that when you stepped in that pulpit on Sunday morning, you were a different man—Mr. Self-Assurance himself. Now you're afraid of your shadow—of my little oven in the kitchen."

I am sure my face was pitifully long. "Oh, Carol," I said, almost pleading, "it's because I've been through so much! My life is an ordeal now!"

But she was bent on further torturing—terrorizing!—me. "I can still hear you preaching, Father. 'Face life with resolve and, above all, *courage!*' you would say, oh, so earnestly, so mellifluously. As a little girl I would sit there, sometimes with the other children in the first pews, and listen to you, and, most of all, watch you—such a handsome man, so distinguished-looking and all. You made me swell with pride, that you were *my* father and not the other kids'."

I was softly crying.

"Things have changed now, though, haven't they, Father? You were able to endure what must have been for you the perfect horror, panic, of flying here in a blinding snowstorm, the wildest of blizzards—for what? For the purpose of telling me, as if I were your mother instead of your daughter, that you're afraid. I repeat, afraid of *what*, Father?"

I was limp from her water torture, helpless in the face of her cruel taunts. I had neither the strength nor will, nor the inclination, to fight back. Sometimes, really, I think I secretly relished her assaults, as if, instead of myself habitually in the role of perpetrator, it was *she* now with the psychological whip, making *me* squirm, recoil, cry out, and suffer the "lashes." But again, drying my eyes, I hurried on with my pressing, necessitous narration. "The only thing that seemed to sustain him," I said, now all of a sudden trying to bounce back, be blasé, "was that inflammable newspaper out of Chicago. It was as though there had developed a struggle, symbolic of so very much, between those two inert objects he kept secreted under his matress—*The Hawk* and Cynthia Ambrose's vicious, impenetrable little book, *Bloody Treachery.* He was adamantly determined, though, that Ambrose would never prevail. He hated this book with a vengeance despite its unwitting portrayal of Ofield Smalls as hero and knew his anger, his spleen, was directed entirely against its author. But he must dispose, rid himself, of it, demolish the spell which its profound riddle, Ofield's 'higher point,' held over him. He found himself somehow furious. Yes, yes, he thought for the nth time, this evil little book must be destroyed! Suddenly he wanted to shout it from the rooftops—as in the Roman Senate Cato the Elder unceasingly inveighed against Carthage: '*Carthago delenda est!*'" I stopped, I was out of breath, and had noticed my right hand, high in the air, had been wildly gesticulating. I was "preaching." No wonder Carol was gaping at me. Now I was embarrassed.

"Shall we just leave things there, Father?" she finally said. "It's late. Why don't you let me call you a taxi?"

"No, no!" I said. "We—*I*—must go on! If for no other reason than out of respect for the martyr-hero!" I was suddenly very upset by her attempt to get rid of me at this crucial point in my unburdening recitation. "What you don't appreciate," I said, "is the critical nature of this history—it's *moral* significance, especially. If anyone in this world should be studying it, it's *us!*"

"Father, please stop preaching. And shouting. I know you're serious about this but it's late. I have neighbors." She glanced at her watch.

"You forget his born integrity, his selfless courage, and, above all, his terrible sacrifice! You refuse to recognize his *saintliness!* and . . . his bitter resolve to *rectify* things! Certainly I compare my foul life with his pure!—how can I do otherwise? Oh, how I wish, even at this late date, this could help change things for me. But it can't—actually, there never was a time when it could have. Don't you see that!"

"Oh, Father, please let's not again go into your pet theories of determinism. I've heard them so many times it makes me want to scream—or laugh. You're not as fatalistic as you think. Sometimes I suspect you use this as a crutch—you see it as your only excuse; otherwise where would you be left? There are definitely times, of course, when I feel sorry for you. I know you suffer. It shows, though, you have still retained some measure of moral sensibility. But I feel sorry for myself, too. You seem to forget that. I haven't been a child all my life—*I haven't, I haven't!* . . . Free will is a truth. It's really available to us if we'll seize it. But I haven't! And I can't blame it on *you!*—I *haven't* been a child all my life! That's why I— I, Father!—suffer too!" Oh, how sorry I felt for her. For a brief moment I wanted to go somewhere and shoot myself. After all, she was my daughter, whom I loved.

"Father, please go," she said now. She had stood up. "Please. I'll call a cab."

"Wait, wait," I said. I had not given up—I was driven by inner demons. "It was *he*, don't forget, who learned not from Sir William S. Gilbert but from Ofield Smalls—*then carried it out!*—that the

263

punishment must fit the crime! That it must somehow be made, devised . . . even, if necessary, *improvised,* so as, exactly, nicely, to fit the historic outrage! Remember it was he, Cager, to whom it was at last vouchsafed, in a blinding epiphanic flash of endowed insight, as it were, the answer to Cynthia Ambrose's little book's riddle, one she herself, assuming she was capable of awareness of its existence, had been unable to solve. Do you remember I told you that, Carol?" My skin felt ablaze.

"Yes, yes!" she cried in a keening, outraged exasperation. "Oh, how many times do I have to hear it? And now you've flown all the way here from some remote Kansas crossroads, and in a whirling, ferocious, winter storm, to tell it to me again, then cry on my shoulder. Okay, it all came to him so quickly—yes, instantaneously—in one searing, blinding flash. Right, Father?" She was taunting me again. "But that great revelation striking out of the heavens like that, as if a purple bolt of lightning, never quite rang true to me. The whole incident happened so suddenly, *too* suddenly—the manifestation of the riddle's solution—as if zooming down from out of the clouds, yes, suddenly falling on him from out of the sky! How could it have just popped into his head like that, with apparently nothing at all to prompt him—and so fast? It was entirely unmotivated and implausible. It didn't happen, Father!"

I jumped up—quivering, pointing my finger at her. "Have you no faith? . . . Are you made, one hundred percent, of iron and steel! Are you a robot, an automaton? Have you no heart and soul! Must you see—and *understand!*—everything before you will acknowledge that it might exist? Even the hero—and even after the riddle's answer was revealed, the meaning of what Ambrose unwittingly called Ofield's 'higher point'—Cager still had to go a lot on faith. He had to accept Ofield's version of things, his rationale, a great deal on faith—and I'm talking about *religious* faith. The so-called 'revelation,' which you have already repudiated, incidentally, merely pointed the way for the hero. He, in league, as he felt, with God, had to intuit the rest. That's why it was a miracle and he a hero. Can you accept nothing, no matter how holy, on pure faith, Carol? I tell you it was a *miracle!*"

"Father, you're loco. And stop screaming. It was just a miracle, was it? I guess like in one of your sermons, right? Jesus feeding the great multitude on those few loaves and fishes—is that what you mean?"

She had me there, she knew—oh, what effective sarcasm! "*Yes,*" I said. "Where Cager is concerned, I mean a *miracle.* Nothing less will do. For he himself was a visionary. Had he not been he could not have done what he did finally. It was a miracle—including what *he* did—and I believe it to this day!" (And I do.)

Shaking her head in incredulity and resignation, Carol at last came, put her arm around me, and kissed me on the cheek. Then she went and called a taxi, bundled me up in my overcoat, muffler, and hat (with earmuffs), and led me to the door. I was docile and went silently, hanging my head. "Good night, Father," she said— "I'll see you tomorrow." I was perfectly helpless.

As a consequence, in short, I ended up recounting the rest— performing, as it were, my psychoneurotic ablutions—to *myself.* I mean, in my room—having gotten back to the hotel just in the nick of time. The immediate problem was my chronic, knifing, stomach cramps, which finally my tensions always brought on, causing, of course—what else?—my bowels to act up again. In fact, right then, they were liquid. With not ten seconds to spare, I made it to the toilet in my room, just barely, and sitting there, my trousers down around my ankles as I moaned and groaned, I could not help observing myself in the full-length mirror on the inside of the bathroom door—just as a tidal wave of self-revulsion inundated me, making me shudder in loathing. Suddenly then, though, there came into my head the bold, high-key, coloratura strains of "Lo, Hear the Gentle Lark." Why it is that almost always when this perky aria-tune comes bouncing and tripping into my consciousness I seem to be moving my bowels, I cannot say. But now, having been sent packing from my daughter's cold flat, my driven, necessitous conversation with her, for which I had come fifteen hundred nightmare miles, by her own whim terminated, I was now—alone, abandoned, repudiated—in my hotel room's bathroom seated on the throne. Thus I had been expelled to man my own devices, to scrounge as best I could the therapy I needed and craved, but all of which consisted in my finishing, once again, this telling of the miracle. Yes, but now to myself.

Back, then, to first principles. "In the hero's mind the struggle continues—newspaper versus book, *Hawk* versus *Bloody Treachery.* Though not for long. Soon he finds himself taking all his clothes to the cleaners. In a pawnshop he also buys an additional suitcase, to hold the still-unread war books he might possibly have to take with him—purloin. For time was now severely shortened. Yet he feels the great decision is somehow being made, slowly but inexorably, for him. He was glad of this. For there was Mary Eliza Fitzhugh Dabney to make tactical allowance for—her many kindnesses to all those around her, for example, her deeply felt interest, even solicitude, the quietness and depth of her brooding thoughts, her prayerful appeals for guidance in uncharted waters, all these have puzzled him, but, strangely, also made him anxious, uneasy. Their 'conversations' have now become her own dedicated, visionary, even noble monologues, so intensely caught up is she in *her* great mission. He listens, observes, and is awed. Plans for the grand new edifice absorb her every waking moment as she prays, checks out God's daily, almost hourly, approbation apace. Augusta, silently, anxiously, monitoring it all, and, loving her mother, wishing her all happiness and self-fulfillment, yet despairs of ever deciding whether to applaud or deplore the, now-obvious-to-all, stupendous change in her mother. She can only look on and sigh. One thing to the hero, though, is clear. His change of heart, mind, and will has given him a measure of relief—not entirely from his naturally expected uneasiness and nervous tension, nor his frequent doubts over what his new life up North will be like, but certainly now relief from the internal, pent-up suffering and mortification at having, even if only briefly, abandoned his original objective, been, in a short aberration, talked out of his mission, and all it represents, by what he admitted to be Haley's 'logic.' He is convinced what he seeks to do has little, or no, connection with logic in this sense. His great goal simply involves truth—an object he now sees more clearly than he has ever in the past. It is in this that he is certain, beyond any doubt, his salvation lies forever. He would have died, he thinks, had he tried to act out Haley's well-intentioned and selfless 'solution.' Now he will live.

"We, I, finally, then, see, envision, that the hero—in his contrition trying to keep Haley out of his thoughts—is all but packed and ready to go. Soon he is feeling heady and excited—though still not a little anxious. Nonetheless, he is ready." Sitting there on the throne, I, your narrator, continued talking to myself, at times mimicking the mock-serious chortling of a TV comedian I had often heard: "SELF, ah, you see, don't you? You see your friend and sidekick, whom throughout you have dubbed 'Hero,' as, in the midst of his feverish departure preparations, he finds that, think or do what he will, he cannot rid himself of the specter of that little book whose ninety-two pages of hate, stupidity, retribution, death —but mystery still—has so gripped his life and sought to alter its course. Even the more he has hated it for what its author had meant for it to stand, the greater, nevertheless, has remained its hold on him—hating it because of Ambrose, loving it for Ofield.

He also, though, saw the disadvantage it posed, the obstacle to his purposes, the psychological hindrance embedded in it, as he sought to justify his grandiose plans to himself. There was also, of course, from this perspective, again the ever-present matter of the book's riddle, for which he had a passion—to know its secret—and could only with extreme difficulty bring himself to think of leaving with Ofield's mysterious 'statement,' his message, which he somehow already sensed to be earthmoving, still unrevealed. It was, then, yet another enemy of his plans, prolonging the day when he would, or could, feel free to leave. Increasingly now, he saw the book in its true light. It was a curse—which must be broken, yes, destroyed. '*Carthago delenda est!*'—as I earlier phrased it to Carol. But, the hero insisted, that was not all. It must be destroyed *ritualistically*. This meant according to the old slave traditional rites. He was determined. Nothing less than the ritual would do. Do you hear me, SELF?" I feverishly whispered from the throne, all the while—breathless, manic—staring into the long bathroom door mirror. "Do you *understand* me, SELF?

"On this particular Monday night, then," I continued, as if I were merely beginning to spin some old wives' tale, "he made ready to go down to the river. River? you say. Indeed. There to perform the old folks' ritual of immersion in the 'blood of the lamb' of any objects thought to have displeased, aroused, or angered the already evil spirits. This, though, was not the route to exorcism alone, it also accomplished the spiritual cleansing of the ritualist, purged him of all his 'hurts, diabolics, and frets'—*or*, in hopeless cases, warned him of dire things to come. (Are you following me, SELF? Do you get the picture—*and* its import?) Therefore, up in his little cubicle of a room in the Dabney household that evening, shortly after dark outside, he goes to his bed, lifts the hoary mattress, and takes out the book. Alongside it, however, lies the newspaper. He thinks for a moment. Does he need *The Hawk* anymore? he asks himself. Besides, it is dangerous! Has it not, too, already served its purpose?—is not his commitment to Chicago now, at last, despite good Haley, absolute, irrevocable, unshakable? Is he not now soon, very soon, to leave this environment of confusion, this house of fright, and its aged, obsessed owner, behind him forever? *The Hawk* too, then, is now a mere artifact of the struggle—his *Mein Kampf*, as it were—and as such should participate also, along with *Bloody Treachery*, in the finalistic rite to come by which he intends, if only symbolically, to strengthen his already steely resolve, fortify even further his regained initiative of the will. Thus he now takes *both* articles (artifacts) from beneath the mattress and departs the house. His destination is Jeff Davis Bridge on Summit Street. This, he tells himself, is where he will do the deed, commit the emblematic act—*himself* become avatar—then turn his back and walk away forever."

My hotel room, if not exactly cozy, was still warmer than Carol's frigid flat. Yet I could readily hear the wintry blasts rattling my windowpanes. Sitting there confronting that brutally candid mirror, I was soon able, nonetheless, briefly, to resume humming the strains of "Lo, Hear the Gentle Lark." But almost at once, then, as was so often my wont, I again began to envy the hero. "You, SELF," I said, "unlike our hero on that unforgettable evening, will experience no such sudden epiphany on a damn bridge. For you there will be no unmotivated solution-in-waiting, no last minute deus ex machina, no divine thunderclap, or blinding nonlight, no elucidating and extricating marvel. No miracle! *No salvation!*" Now I wanted to weep again.

"At long last, then, SELF, we see old Cage—hero, yes, saint, martyr, what have you—*The Hawk,* in a wrapper (meat-market paper bearing vestiges of dried lamb's gore), in one hand, *The Day of Bloody Treachery* in the other, as he now mounts Jeff Davis Bridge under which, sluggishly, moves the muddy little Dixie river called 'The Darling' (née Rubicon). Although the feeble streetlights are on, the scene is darkly murky and portentous, shrouded in a Delphic gloaming, as he walks to the middle of the bridge and its ancient stone parapet. Then, heart pounding, teeth grinding (also rattling), he acts swiftly, almost ruthlessly. Hugging *The Hawk* to his breast with his left hand, with his right he hurls *Bloody Treachery* over into the viscous Darling—for a brief instant glimpsing the pages of the little book as they spread in flight and soar down as if on eagles' wings before disappearing into the slimy drink.

"This was when it came. The great lightless flash, the soundless explosion, the imagined very heavens opening up, the precise subconscious concatenation, whose claimed implausibility Carol had so strenuously, so adamantly, rejected—'It didn't happen, Father!'—all jarring the earth. The miracle! Throwing up the now-empty right hand as though he would shield his eyes from the blinding glare, the hero recoils, reels, then staggers. (Literally, Carol!) What has hit him, actually almost even *before Bloody Treachery* reaches the water, is the instantaneous realization, the comprehension, of the marvel, the miracle—Ofield's 'higher point.' Again he staggers. It has happened as if the book, just before sinking into the Darling and oblivion, has sent back up to him its swift revelatory message, the final unraveling of its mystery, and the revealed assignment—his horrible mission and fate. There is also the severe, almost truculent, admonition, the dread message of warning, not to falter, a vesting of a charge to carry out, the clinching of Ofield's 'statement.' But the hero is still addled. Again he reels from the suddenness of the shock and its tidings. The right hand is now at his forehead, his brow, groping. He wonders if his wild nightmares have returned.

"'Oh, Lord!' he finally cries out, having realized all too clearly what is required of him. No, this is no nightmare, he is obliged, forced, to tell himself. It is worse. It is real. But then a strange new reaction sets in. He finds his panic momentarily—but only so— subsiding. Is this some odd resignation? he wonders. Knowing all, everything, now, has he become stoical? Can it be? How can it be? For he could not possibly have foreseen this extraordinary eventuality—which has sealed his fate along with his victim's-to-be. Could there, though, have really here been intuition at work, somehow preparing him for the crisis? But almost as if in answer he suddenly begins to quake. He cries out again, 'No, no! Lord Jesus, let this cup pass from me!' Then, as if from the depths of the muddy Darling, comes Ofield's sepulchral voice, delivering, repeating, the charge—even naming her, as well as the specific means, the dire instrument, of dispatch! The punishment which it is now his duty to mete out must be, as it were, yes, custom-made to fit the crime, wrought oh so exquisitely to conform to the all-time tragic uniqueness of the history—the 'good' Obediah Smalls and the 'good' Mary Eliza Fitzhugh Dabney, Siamese twins joined at the hip. It is their fate—that is, their 'goodness!'—and their end. The cruel Oglethorpes could never have qualified. It is somehow, though, for the twins an accolade, a royal investiture, if you will, a solemn affirmation of their most highly selective, their rarest, eligibility.

"But, SELF, again the hero wavers, falls back; he is young; the quite natural fear of death paralyzes him. Then comes Ofield's repetitious, outraged voice. It blasts. Our paragon knows there is no escaping it now, that it is, perforce, only by this foghorn command that four centuries of history are to be rectified—and by a single symbolic act. Yet he is once more suddenly seized by the horror of it—not only for himself but his victim. Again he cries

269

out, 'No, no, not *this!*' Rather, he thinks, why not his original plan? . . . the huge black armies, his treasured legions? Even they would be more merciful, humane. Not this. Only ominous silence, though, from the Darling below. He knows now the cup will not pass and trembles as if from an ague. At long last then—it has seemed to him an eternity—he somehow draws himself up to his fullest height, returns to the bridge's parapet, and, after one sad hesitation, lets fall toward the waters (toward 'dark mutinous Shannon waves') the *Chicago Hawk*. But unlike the book, *Bloody Treachery*, the thin newspaper neither floats nor flutters down. It drops like a rock. The preliminaries are over."

The immediate above is my, your narrator's, version. Of course, as I say, Carol, in this matter the cold literalist, insists it is a spurious dream, conjured up by all my wild demons of envy and despair, a nightmarish chaos fresh out of Ionesco; that there took place no such scene on Jeff Davis Bridge. But, under lifelong necessity, *I must have my own version!*—this in order that, as if in my calloused hands clutching some nervous rope on a pulley, I might perennially raise (praise) the hero to highest heaven by lowering myself into the blackest depths of Styx. Ah, I don't know . . . I don't know. . . . Prometheus-like, sentenced for life to my Iron Maiden vest, I do what I must.

"SELF," in conclusion I said at last, though from emotion barely able to speak at all, "please don't sit there any longer looking with disgust into that mirror. Isn't this enough? How can you for another moment behold, much less abide, yourself? So make use of the tissue now, then flush, after which rise from your fetid throne, rearrange your clothing, and wash your hands. Then weep. Weep for Lycidas, for he is dead."

EPILOGIC NOTES

NOTE NO. 1. So there you have it. At least as best I, your narrator, have been able to envision and communicate it. Despite this seriatim epilogue, or coda, if you will, what transpired immediately following what has just been related may be of doubtful interest, or even value—indeed (except maybe for one or two unpleasant details) anticlimactic—to the reader, especially since he/she already knows the hero's and his victim's fate.

To a few minor matters, then, which still dangle. First, did your narrator's frequent reference to the protagonist as "hero" offend? After all, you say, he was a heinous murderer. So under what conceivable pretext is he called "hero?"—or "paragon," "martyr," or, of all things, "*saint!*" Do remember, though, for example, that in the Greek the word "martyr" may be translated as "witness." In the highest, if uncommon, sense, he *was* a witness—and for a high order of things. He viewed his times—that is, in the context of their horrible past—with a flaming repugnance, plus perennial shock. A "witness," he then testified against them, paid the terrible price, and became a martyr. His visions were lurid if irrational. They were also grand. Was he demented?—even a little. Who can say? Was John Brown? *I,* though, can say—which is not too far removed—that he was messianic, a seer, who merely thought things could be made better. But in any case these judgments are mine and, considering, by way of contrast, my own sorry record (though I insist the gods dealt me an execrable hand and I had no choice but to play it out—I could not throw it in and get a new one, you know), these my judgments, then, are of course highly subjective. Allowances must be made.

My further response, however, to those not sharing my canonization of the "hero," is, rather, a tactful suggestion that you reread the book. Oh, heavens! you say—no! Or, then, failing that, read, or reread, history—*any* history. Even that mass of apologia by one (American scholar) Ulrich Bonnell Phillips, detailing what happened after the memorable year 1619, will do. Read history, then. But read it *creatively.* Einstein said that one makes great discoveries only by questioning axioms. This was the way the hero read—creating his own figments, his armed legends. Consider it— here we have a black sharecropper's son, reading grimy cast-off high-school history textbooks for his dreams and visions, who, by his twenty-second, and last, year, had achieved a vision of life that can only be called . . . *apocalyptic!*

NOTE NO. 2. Tableau. She was quiet, absorbed, serious, and quite motionless, that afternoon sitting in the parlor in the Hepplewhite chair. Her gangling young butler, hands strangely shaking, had just served her a china pot of fragrant orange tea as, still deeply engrossed, she studied with myopic zeal the new set of blueprints freshly arrived by messenger from the architects. It was confirmed. In design the grand building's facade of Carrara marble would be Georgian (English, circa 1714–1830) and the proliferous liberal arts library would occupy the entire expansive fourth floor. On her arthritic knees for fully twenty minutes in her

271

bedroom the night before, she had prayed with an intense, fierce passion—about many things, but most of all that she be right. By which of course she meant that in this new herculean undertaking her heart be clean. "Although I'm near the end of the journey, Lord," she said aloud, "—in my last years, or maybe months—I'm not pandering to you. You wouldn't expect it for you know I'm not that type. I merely believe it is right that I do this. It has weighed on my mind!" Though trying not to, she had become emotional. "Correct me if I'm wrong, Lord! . . . I mean not only about the present undertaking, the building, but about the nigra himself, the race of people. The *phenomenon*, Lord! It's all somehow intertwined and plagues me mightily—it always has. I'm talking about the *concept*. I've never understood it. Indeed, if I may be so bold, I've often thought, in unguarded moments, that You haven't been as explicit, or instructive, on it as You might have been. Oh, I know You have Your own reasons, Your priorities—to which I'm not privy—yet I've wondered at times if the concept hasn't often really been as baffling to You as it has to me. But then I realize this is nonsense. The nigra, though, is a great mystery, Lord. You must concede it. He's a great trial also. But a *test*, too—which, alas, finally devolves into a matter of conscience. Ah, *there's* the difficulty . . . conscience. I haven't taken up this subject with You before in this way. It's because I've never before been obliged to deal with the *titanic dimensions* of it . . . as I have in these last difficult weeks. Things have happened to me that I would never have thought possible—a strange transformation, it sometimes seemed like. As I've said, Gussie attributes it all to Rollo's presence in this house—that he's influenced me; unwittingly, of course. What an irony that would be . . . if it were true. Poor Gussie is so naive, though—she *is*. Nevertheless, I can't seem to cope with any of it. Succor me, yes, I beseech You, Lord! . . . I need Your guidance! I want to be—*I must be*—right!" Her voice, hollow, desperate, carried through the closed bedroom door. Yet, finally rising from her knees, she quite soon, miraculously, knew perfect peace and that night, her last, slept as a baby sleeps.

The following afternoon, then, leaving her after having brought her the orange tea (his hands still trembling), he well knew that once—within the coming half-hour—he returned, the action, of necessity, would be short-lived, swift. That much was owed. Ten seconds, no more—thus mercifully—to redress the centuries. But the ninety seconds immediately prior to the ten—what of them? His route of movement would of course have to begin in the

272

portrait gallery. And it did. Having just returned downstairs from his room, his throat dry, whole body aquiver, the breathing rapid and spasmodic, he was nonetheless resplendent in the gray-green Germanesque military tunic that Shorty George (it seemed now a millennium ago) had miraculously retrieved and brought to him (and that Hortense Bangs, from her whoring ill-gotten gains, had tried to pay for), its scarlet-and-gold garnish on the sleeves and lapels, on its first, last, yet most vivid display, his long legs, however, still ensconced in his employer's gray-striped butler's trousers.

In the portrait gallery now he tries to quell his panic by looking up at that most serene of countenances—that of his chance surnamesake—which he has studied so long and so often. It does little good, though, now, and he attempts as best he can to close down his mind and memory against it. Yet somehow it vexes him and he gives it a rare disrespectful glance. Lee's unruffled expression, he thinks, seems callous, uncaring—impervious to her plight! He wonders what has become of Old Dominion chivalry. Finally he realizes he is seizing on any trifling pretext to stay, impede, time, the moment—pursuant to Ofield's charge to him on Jeff Davis Bridge—when he must act. He fears, though, his panic will paralyze him, that his knees will collapse, his frantically laboring heart will stop. His tender youth surfaces now and he wants to whimper. He wants his mother. Instead he takes yet another deep fathomless breath and holds on. Then he moves into action.

Quickly—swift as a fleeting shadow—he steps and takes down from its wallhooks the hoary, interminable, Enfield musket, its forward appendage, wicked and gleaming, seeming almost as long. Slowly then he turns his back on Lee and, heaving a sigh, stands facing up the lengthy gallery corridor toward the parlor where she sits. His feet and legs, however, seem now to have utterly betrayed him—they will not move. His terror-stricken mind has lapsed, wandered, until he thinks of his mother again. Yet now he wishes for anything but to see her, to say good-bye, well knowing he would be unequal to the experience. He knows only total oblivion —until, over his shoulder, he looks up at Lee, then, at that same instant, hears Ofield's flaming, admonitory voice.

Suddenly then everything becomes the demanding present. The eternal interim is over. Yet he gasps for breath. But then it is in a quick spasm that he jerks into motion, starting his long rush, a furious, awkward gallop, up the buffed sheen of the gallery hallway's oak floor, the gleaming point (the "higher point") of death now riding long and low fully eight feet ahead of him. Though requiring a hard, a ninety-degree, left turn just prior to the parlor's entrance, he crazily fails to slacken his speed, not one harsh breath, leaving then his left shoulder in his clumsy onrush to lean far, far—now *too* far—leftward. Then they go—his feet. On the burnished slippery floor they go out from under him as he sprawls full-length and from his hurtling gait slides halfway inside the carpeted parlor door, where now, in all his lurid military accouterments, he lies plainly in her view.

Her mouth open, staring at him, she is literally frozen in the Hepplewhite chair with a blueprint still in her hand. Face blanched whiter than white, pince-nez falling to her lap, eyes popping horror at the sight of the gleaming steel, she lurches up from the chair and tries hoarsely to speak, as if enraged at a demeaning Halloween trick. Almost as if embarrassed, then, he scrambles, lunges, to his feet and, swiftly, silently, inexorably, resumes the onrush, the charge, the ten seconds' timetable already lost and now recounting—ten, nine, eight, seven . . . her hands raised, though not high, her mouth still agape, the pince-nez on the floor. She knows now. By the seeming count of five she screams in a manner to chill the blood as the gleaming ("higher") point passes through, clearly, cleanly, and on into and through, by at least a foot, the back of the Hepplewhite chair. The resultant second scream is bloodcurdling. The next, though, hard upon it, is a kind of half-uttered diminuendo, all but frail, yet somehow guttural, one final time as, arms dangling akimbo, she hangs there and, in the not-rushing-but-merely-percolating blood, remains there, fixed, impaled, head drooped, one eye half open, chin now on chest, lips in dying, prayerful spasms of whispers. It is, yes, a tableau, a crucifixion, as he, his lungs near to bursting now, lets fall, abandons, the heavy Enfield musket butt, which plummets to the carpet, but whose affixed cold steel bayonet still remains through the chair and its occupant just as it was. She tries again, feebly, almost dreamily, to speak, but fails. Then, terribly grimacing—as if at a traitorous God—she is gone.

NOTE NO. 3. Barney Renfroe, the duly appointed special prosecutor, is unable to finish his frenzied, apoplectic summation to the jury, due, as was somewhere hereinbefore foretold, to the intrusion—violent, tornadic—of stormier community forces. The governor's call-out of troops, after many delays (and after Flo Ransom's frantic, tearful, but futile, pleas to her influential senator-friend), is woefully, hopelessly, late.

274

NOTE NO. 4. There is no hero's funeral. This is for at least two reasons. First, in the midst of the insane, unleashed local fury no black undertaker (least of all Ferguson) has the courage, or foolhardiness, to go get the "body." Second, as implied, there is precious little of it to "undertake"—merely char. There remains the left femur, the right (or left—it cannot be determined) tibia, fragments of radius, or humerus, bone (to which, however, bits of the martial German tunic, still worn by the hero at the trial, now acrid-smoke-infested, yet adhere), plus something in the nature of an incinerated crisp cranial object—slim pickings indeed—to inter. Yet, rest, Cage! *Rest, chocolate soldier!* Thy name is writ on fame's immortal scroll!

During these thirty-odd intervening years I have often, daydreaming, fancied myself back there again but this time, uncharacteristically, in the daring role of deliverer of the funeral oration, though with no remains before me, and with only a dozen or so brave souls in attendance—certainly no grand setting worthy of a Mark Antony. What I would have said, though, might have been something on the order of a rather sad, subdued, pep talk, a peripatetic, cavalier presentation, but of no longer than four or five minutes' duration in order to keep most eyes dry. I would have tried to speak in riddles, anyway, and quite appropriately, for my brief subject would have consisted of the revelation of a great secret—the deceased's religiosity. Few who knew him, though, would have believed it. But in, say, the first minute of my remarks I would have spoken of life, probably, suggesting that, though it was all we had, it did not amount to very much, really, that it was a rather nebulous, frustrating, maybe even nugatory, business. As Joyce tells us, through Anna Livia, at the end of *Finnegans Wake,* "How small it's all." After a case study or two, by way of exemplification of the principle, I might then have recited (it is hoped as well as Billups school's little Ophelia, who wrought a sheer magic she'll never know—almost got Gladstone a huge, fine, new *liberal arts* building!) a line or two of "The Seven Ages of Man," from *As You Like It*—"sans everything," and so on, and so on. No, life doesn't stand for too much, would have been my penultimate thesis. But that religion is everything. Actually, though, the deceased never mentioned the subject and, during the time I knew him, would almost never (with one notable exception, when he really needed help, when he was searching for the answers) have been caught inside a church as a grown-up—ever

275

true to his Clausewitz tutelage that right didn't necessarily make might. Yet, unlike your reverend narrator, he believed in God. I mean a *personal* God. A bottom-line fundamentalist, he disliked many *things* (or groups), but seldom if ever any individuals, including his victim, whom he had grudgingly come to admire, maybe pity. But therein lay the unraveling of the whole skein of things and left bare the crucial "higher point." The only individual I ever knew him to dislike—no, hate, and a scalding, purblind hate it was—was (another preacher!) Bearcat Walker. But Cage seldom *spoke* of religion. It was his simple theory—this is a surmise—that man was perfectible, all right, but that might was required to accomplish it, that is, troops, firepower, gold epaulets, scarlet chevrons, close-order drill, and so on, and so on; that, though, things would *never* be better for weaklings or cowards. He thus saw God as a God of wrath, yet in Whom he ever believed. This for me is more than ample foundation from which to take the critical hierologic leap, namely, that he knew—yes, intuited—that there is a God (even Aquinas and Erasmus occasionally had their doubts) and that he was therefore steadfast in his belief that his horrible deed had meaning, that he, then, like Ofield, was now to enter the pantheon of heroes. Think of me, though, your narrator, in that context, if you will, and see if you can, possibly, withhold from me even the tiniest mite of your commiseration, especially when I tell you that I know—beyond peradventure or doubt—that I shall, rather, die one of Gregor Samsa's *insects!*

NOTE NO. 5. Shorty George and his quickly rerecruited, reassembled, former henchmen, still trained members all of the old defunct "drill unit," night-dynamited the ancient courthouse (on whose lawn the hero-deceased had laid the wreath at Lee's ineffably serene statue), the structure collapsing as if it were the original Valhalla after Brunhilde's and Grane's immolation, sinking into the Rhine like a torpedoed superdreadnought, or as if it were a great megaton hippo, victim of some random poacher's Sten gun, submerging, sounding, into the river Niger and oblivion, the old courthouse thus kaput, all as duly prophesied by the scruffy vendor and draft-board janitor Joshua. At first, though—an ironic paradox—the structure's northeast wing withstood, for all of twelve hours, the prior force of the detonation, still standing, a gaunt ghost, amidst the sprawling, smoking mass of detritus, sulfur dust, and rubble, its blasted-open cornerstone yielding up, inter alia, the hoary dedicatory oration of the year 1831 (the same

276

annum, mind you, of that other hero's, Nat Turner's, Virginia rebellion and martyr's death). "It is a great and dangerous error," went the century-entombed cornerstone consecratory address, "to suppose all people to be equally entitled to liberty," and so on—delivered, yes, as hereinbefore related, by then Vice-President John C. Calhoun. But the old brick and mortar skeleton was smoldering debris now, though in the ensuing, running, murderous rioting thirty-eight Valhalla, Tennessee, citizens died, nine whites, twenty-nine blacks, including Shorty George—the ratio numbers hardly a fitting tribute to the hero-deceased or his mentor, Prussian General Karl von Clausewitz. Yet, rest, Cage, I say, "and flights of angels," and so on, and so on. . . . *But, oh, Lord, didn't he ramble!*

NOTE NO. 6. Flo fled with little Annette back to New Orleans to live, but where, in the late autumn of 1963 (November 22nd! to be exact—misery in Dallas and everywhere), then-current medical advances to the contrary notwithstanding, she died in a TB sanitarium. Ah, my (and Cager's) Flo! Shall one ever see your like again?. . .

NOTE NO. 7. It of course goes without saying—it need even hardly be broached—that the grandiose Nathan Poole Dabney Memorial Hall for the Liberal Arts project at Gladstone was forever scrubbed.

NOTE NO. 8. Haley, literally wiped out by life-lasting (unjustified) guilt, his stubborn, officious, yet noble and sublime interference having brought the two chief actors in the drama into their bewildered yet foreordained meeting—indeed rendezvous—eventually, with Roxanne, came North, to Dayton, Ohio, where, in deeply morbid penitence, he lived past his eighty-first birthday.

FINAL EPILOGIC NOTE (9): I, your narrator (a natural survivor), never quite summoned the hardihood to spend the remainder of my days out in a tiny crossroads hamlet in Kansas (which, I am sure, surprises no one), yet where I vowed, to Carol, to live a hermit-poet's existence till the end. But she it was who soon would hear none of this, who became adamant that I abondon this quaint, romantic, phony notion—which, I confess, required on me but little suasion. Through her amazing intercessory efforts, then, which were not altogether out of phase with her unsublimated Electra complex, I now have a small, staid (Negro) church in White Plains, where Carol, who has never married and lives alone, teaches math in one of the city's high schools and where at the moment (to keep up appearances) I am "courting" a very nice widow lady, a Mrs. Ruse, near my own age, who is also the church organist. I survive. In fact, I triumph. I regret, too.

To Cage, then, farewell—*Leb' wohl!* Eliot (T. S.) also speaks of regrets—in "Burnt Norton" (*Four Quartets*):

Footfalls echo in the memory
Down the passage which we did not take
Towards the door we never opened
Into the rose-garden.

ABOUT THE AUTHOR

Cyrus Colter is the author of *The Beach Umbrella, The Rivers of Eros, Night Studies,* and *The Hippodrome.* He is a lawyer, a former Illinois State Official (Commerce Commissioner), and an emeritus professor at Northwestern University, where he chaired the Department of African American Studies and held the Chester D. Tripp professorship in the Humanities. He lives in Chicago, Illinois.